ROMANCE ON THE RUN

Made redundant and left for a much younger woman by her husband Sam, lovable girl-next-door Melanie Morris is at rock bottom. However, a job offer from her cousin, leisure centre owner Shelley — and an introduction to gorgeous personal trainer Robert — mark the start of a whole new life filled with thrilling, and occasionally terrifying, experiences. A mixture of running, intrigue and romance paves the way for excitement . . .

DEBBIE CHASE

ROMANCE ON THE RUN

Complete and Unabridged

LINFORD
Leicester

First published in Great Britain in 2017

First Linford Edition
published 2022

*A catalogue record for this book is available
from the British Library.*

ISBN 978–1–4448–4824–3

Published by
Ulverscroft Limited
Anstey, Leicestershire

Printed and bound in Great Britain by
TJ Books Ltd., Padstow, Cornwall

This book is printed on acid-free paper

1

'Look, it's there if you want it, Mel,' said Shelley, 'Just let me know as soon as you can . . . otherwise Scott will say we have to advertise and you know what that means . . .'

'Yes, I know,' I replied, 'A lot of competition . . . that I could do without . . .'

'You're a good receptionist and we could definitely do with somebody like you welcoming people into the gym . . . you're young, attractive . . .'

'Young?' I exclaimed, almost laughing out loud. 'You think thirty two is young?'

'Melanie! Thirty two is nothing; I'm nearer forty now, less than a year until the big day.'

'Oh yes Shelley, forty, oh my God!' We looked at each other and laughed remembering, I suppose, that we'd grown up together really even though Shelley was eight years older than me. I took a sip of coffee. 'I do appreciate you offering me this job, you know, but I wouldn't say I was a very good advert for a gym at the moment . . . look . . . ' I pulled up my top showing a rather fleshy waistline, 'I can definitely pinch more than an inch . . . do you think it would put people off?'

Shelley shook her head and rolled her eyes. 'God Melanie, any one would think you were as big as a Sumo wrestler! You've only put on a little bit of weight because you're sitting at home alone, no husband, no job, so you're comfort eating. Having a new job, a new focus, should help with that, plus when you finish your shift, you can work out.' She took a long drink from her mug.

'Oh yeah, thanks Shelley, I'm suddenly going to become an athlete?'

'You'll have a swimming pool and a gym right there when you finish work, and there's a running club . . . actually we've recently taken on a new running coach, Rob . . . um, I can't remember, Rob someone, and he's very nice . . . could be right up your street, Mel.' She took a

2

gulp of coffee from her mug.

I shook my head. 'I don't think so, Shelley, men are not on my list of priorities at the moment and this bloke won't be up my street, down my road, or even round my corner come to that! And anyway a fit man like him would take one look at me and recoil in horror.'

Shelley laughed uproariously at my great wit. 'Don't be daft, Mel, he wouldn't do that. Why would he? You're lovely, really pretty and curvy, men like curves. He's a really nice guy, quite attractive too if you go for the dark sort of hippy looking types.'

'Well, that rules him out then, I can't be doing with these new age types. I expect he'll be into tarot cards and runes, and angels and . . . things!'

Shelley shook her head. 'Really, Mel, what are you on about? He's into running and weights, he also takes swimming lessons and has clients for personal training . . . he's very sporty.'

'I'm not interested, Shelley, men are just not in my world at the moment.

3

Surely you can see that after what Sam did to me?'

Shelley nodded her head. 'Yes, of course, Mel . . . I know, but what do they say? A change is as good as a rest?'

Oh, hi, sorry I didn't notice you before . . . yes, you, with your nose stuck in this book, trying to follow the conversation but not really having much of a clue what Shelley and I are talking about. I suppose I'd better introduce us before I go any further . . .

My name's Melanie, Melanie Morris, and, unfortunately, you've started reading this story when everything in my life is at a really low ebb. For starters, Sam, my husband of eight years left me around four months ago, oh my God, I hate to say the next statement, but it's true, 'For Another Woman!' And then, following very closely on from that, I was made redundant from my job as a receptionist at the local doctor's surgery, Skelmanthorpe Surgery, our home town, or Skelly Surgy as the locals call it.

As you may have gathered, I'm with

Shelley at the moment (she's my cousin) in her beautiful detached house, sitting in her brightly painted kitchen (all green and white and all mod cons of course) at her beautiful square pine table drinking coffee, Nespresso I think it is, those little pods that George Clooney advertises, um, yummy coffee, with a delectable smell. I'm sniffing at it right now and it's heavenly. I would even go so far as to say that the smell is even better than the taste!

Shelley is beautiful, one of those tall willowy women that seem to bend and sway as they walk and, actually, with her long golden hair and baby blue eyes, she puts me in mind of a host of daffodils languidly moving to and fro in a spring breeze. She's been married to Scott for around twelve years and they have two adorable little girls, Mya who's ten and Bethany eight. Mya is dark like Scott with a swarthy skin and eyes that glisten and glitter like currants in a bun but Bethany is pale and blonde and will probably be willowy just like her mum.

Shelley and Scott own a string of leisure centres around the local area, hence being able to offer me a job in the local one. They've sprung up like flowers from a bulb in nearby places like Southport and Preston and even in seaside resorts like Blackpool and Morecambe and even Liverpool. The leisure centres, the brainchild of Melanie, are called 'Hale & Hearty' and have a very distinctive bright orange logo of a stick man and woman running together.

The logo always fascinated me when the first gym was launched almost fifteen years ago, I suppose because I was an impressionable teenager then and totally in awe of Shelley and Scott and what they were achieving, also running was unusual in those days, not like now when you can bump into a runner huffing and puffing on nearly every street corner.

I have a really clear memory of going with Shelley and Scott to view the building that is now our local 'Hale & Hearty' Skelmanthorpe. It was a hot summer's day and I remember squinting against the sun at this very imposing building, a former school set amongst beautiful gardens and a lake which at the time was inundated with geese that honked warnings at us in their forthright manner as we toured the building and the grounds. Ducks swam on the lake, their tiny skinny legs clearly visible as they paddled beneath the clear water.

'Can you imagine an extension just there,' said Shelley, pointing to the side of the imposing building. 'Housing a swimming pool, a steam room, a sauna, and a Jacuzzi. Imagine relaxing in the Jacuzzi and looking out of the window at this view.' She spread her arms wide to incorporate the gardens and the lake.

'This is the ideal place for our first 'Hale & Hearty',' agreed Scott.

'And with many more to come,' added Shelley.

You can tell how ambitious Shelley was just by that statement and that she didn't aim to stop at just one 'Hale & Hearty'. The leisure centres are really popular now and Shelley and Scott have dedicated people on their books who have been members since the opening of the first one in Skelmanthorpe all those years ago. Shelley has done really well for herself, unlike me, of course.

The job Shelley is offering is based in the 'Hale & Hearty' in our local town, Skelly, as we all call it. If I accept the job, I'll be the first thing the members see when they come into the reception area and, really, if you saw me at the moment, you so wouldn't think that was a good idea! I've been neglecting myself, I know that for sure, I've only got to look in a mirror and first of all I cringe and then I frown and think 'now who is that?' When I realise it's me I sort of fold into myself like an umbrella and try to hide in terror! My looks at the moment are definitely not for the faint hearted.

My long brown hair needs a good cut, well, even a proper style would help, my face where I've put on weight is as round as the moon and I've developed curves sort of . . . everywhere! I definitely don't

8

look like the orange stick woman on the 'Hale & Hearty' logo, but more like the plump cherub that you see in the shops on pictures and cards (an older version of course).

It's got that bad that I've had to start going to a different branch of Bloomers the Bakers every time I buy sausage rolls or pasties so that nobody knows how many I've bought or worse, how many I've eaten. Sometimes I go to the tiny shop on the precinct where the shop assistant calls me sweetheart, or the one with a café by the bus station, and then there's the massively busy one where you have to queue out of the door on the retail park, and if I'm feeling really desperate I go to Huddersfield and buy from the shop that plays loud seventies music like a disco so I'm able to jig up and down whilst waiting for my pastry fix. Yeah, it's true I'm as sad as that!

I circle my thumb and index finger around the roll of flab that has made its home around my waist. I'm desperate to get rid of it, to evict it, but on what grounds? That it hasn't paid the rent? Or that it's squatting and that's against the law? I know that Shelley is holding out a kind hand and doing her best by offering me this job, and I must admit it probably will help to lift me out of this massive hole that I've just happened to fall into or, as I like to think, been pushed into by my ex Sam!

What Shelley doesn't know though is that I went for an interview last week. Yes, I managed to rouse myself from my pit of depression, made myself look passably attractive and went for it. The job is in a doctor's surgery again but really that's all I know. I'd been in my job as Receptionist in Skelly Surgy since I left college at nineteen. I'd be well out of my comfort zone anywhere else, especially in a leisure centre.

I daren't tell Shelley because I know she'd say that being on a reception is the same anywhere, you greet people and you make appointments, end of story. That's not true . . . and anyway look at the difference between being a doctor's surgery receptionist and a leisure centre receptionist, look at the difference in the type of people for a start, doctor's surgery — ill people, leisure centre — fit people . . . do you see what I mean?

Anyway reader now that you know some of the background, I think I can safely leave you to your own devices and trust you to read on with no further help from me. So here goes. Shelley has brought me out of my reverie by suddenly jumping up and announcing that she has to go to collect the girls from school. She picks up our mugs and puts them tidily in the dishwasher then flings her arms around me and kisses me on the cheek no doubt leaving a pink glossy lipstick mark on my skin.

She doesn't look as though she's just on the school run wearing tailored black trousers and a lovely red top with some sort of netting around the neck area. She's wearing full make up and her hair flows long and loose around her shoulders, and she's putting on a black belted trench coat, pulled tight at the waist giving her a fabulous silhouette.

'You'll have to let me know by tomorrow, Mel, about the job, okay?'

I nodded. 'Yes, okay . . . '

'We need you, Mel, you'll be doing us a big favour, you're a trained receptionist and would be great as the face of 'Hale & Hearty' Skelmanthorpe. You're not fat, you're lovely. Never forget that okay?'

I nod again; then hang my head as tears start to prick right at the back of my eyelids; kindness always seems to do that to me. I need to go now before I make a real fool of myself. Cold air hits me as I go outside to the car making me hunch my shoulders and button up my coat to the neck. It's early November and autumn leaves skitter in the wind and lay in bright crimson huddles on the paths leaving the trees bare and forlorn. The sky is a washed out grey like white underwear put on the wrong cycle.

I wave at Shelley as she gets in her car and I see her hand flutter at me through the windscreen like a little white flag.

Then suddenly she's out of the car and running over to me so I wind down the window wondering what she's going to say.

'Bryce,' she says. 'I've just remembered, his name's Rob Bryce . . . well, I think he prefers to be called Robert.'

I shake my head. 'Shelley, I'm not interested in men at the moment . . . I've got a broken heart, remember?'

She grins and says, 'I bet he'd help to mend that broken heart.'

I watch her run back to her car, a beautiful silver Mondeo, courtesy of the success of 'Hale & Hearty'. She looks like a little girl from the back, the little girl who cradled me in her chubby arms when I was just a baby. My orange Fiat starts like an old man coughing and I slowly drive away, to go home, I suppose, to that cold lifeless house that I really don't want to go to any more.

★ ★ ★

I wasn't prepared for Sam's revelation that evening back in July. It had been a hot day, the sky so very blue with not a hint of cloud; they'd all dissolved to nothing in the heat like candy floss on your tongue. I'd worked a couple of hour's overtime so we'd arrived home at around the same time. We were both a bit cranky I suppose, red faced and sweating like a baby just woken from its nap. I remember that it was a Thursday.

With relief I peeled off my blouse and skirt that, because of the heat, were stuck to my skin like glue and, wearing only bra and knickers, stood in the bedroom thinking of a cool shower. I struck a pose, hand on hip, and fluttered my eye lashes a little, as Sam appeared in the doorway but, tight lipped, he gave a tiny shake of his head and flung himself onto the bed and just lay there staring at the ceiling.

I remember asking, 'What is it?'

'Nothing, tired, hot,' he said listlessly. He barely looked at me. A faint unease stole over my body as in the shower cool clear water pattered onto my skin and the intoxicating scent of vanilla slid into my nostrils as I shampooed my hair.

'He's been like this for a while,' I thought to myself, as I put my face up to the shower head and let the water run down my cheeks like tears, 'Disinterested, tired, miserable . . .' I hadn't been too bothered really. I knew he was busy at work and the years that we'd spent trying for a baby had worn us both down but tonight, the look on his face, the languid response when I questioned him, it suddenly occurred to me that something was wrong, something was badly wrong.

I won't say anything yet, though. Maybe it's just that he's hungry and stressed from work. I'll make something to eat and we'll have a drink and then when he's had a shower, he might feel better and perhaps everything will be okay again.

I went down to the kitchen, my flip flops slapping on the stairs, and then rummaged in the fridge for something to eat, something quick, I really didn't think I had the energy to cook anything complicated. I found chicken that I could chop into cubes, in the cupboard a jar of Rogan Josh curry mix and rice that could be heated in the microwave in two minutes. 'Mm yes, a quick curry.' I poured myself a glass of red wine and set to work.

I remember that the chicken was bubbling in the pan when Sam finally came downstairs. I offered him a glass of wine which he chugged down in one and then poured himself another. He wore blue tracksuit bottoms and a white tee shirt that clung to the muscles in his arms and chest. His blonde hair, lightened by the summer sun, had been washed and was stuck to his scalp, little bits around his ears and his neck already drying and sticking up.

We sat in front of the droning telly, the curry on trays on our laps. Coronation Street was on but I remember that Sam had aimed the remote and the next minute Eastenders came on the screen, a violent scene of a woman and a man grappling and shouting at one another. He changed channels again but a very bloody operation on a dog came into view. I remember I said, 'Oh my God, not while we're eating,' so he switched the telly off and the sudden silence was awful.

'Had a bad day?' I ventured.

'No worse than usual,' he replied shortly. He chewed at a piece of chicken, his jaw moving around and around, the scraping of knives and forks on plates and the slurping of wine being the only sounds. I felt that I would explode if he didn't speak to me, give me an explanation for his behavior, when Sam, putting his tray down on the floor beside the settee, said so quietly that at first I didn't quite hear, 'Mel, I've met somebody else.'

It suddenly occurred to me that, yes, that was the only explanation and shell shocked, yet speaking quite calmly, I asked him, 'Who?'

He took a deep breath and said, 'Alice Jackson.'

'Alice Jackson?' I exclaimed, struggling to stand up then remembered the tray on my lap which I laid on the floor next to Sam's. 'But she's a baby; she must be ten years younger than us!'

He looked straight at me, his blue eyes gazing into mine. 'Yeah, she's twenty two.'

'Why Sam?' I asked him, shaking my head in utter disbelief, 'Why?'

He wouldn't look at me; nor would he answer but just sat there, leaning forward his forearms on his thighs, staring at the floor.

'How long has it been going on?' I persisted. 'Tell me, Sam . . .'

He took a deep breath. 'A while, Mel . . . you weren't interested in me anymore. All you wanted was a baby . . .'

'Oh what a cliché,' I interrupted. 'What an excuse . . . you're nothing but an . . . an . . . adulterer . . .'

I saw red, a wall of deep blinding crimson red like blood, and told him that he'd better get out. 'Pack your things,' I told him, screamed at him, 'And get out. I don't want to see you ever again.'

He didn't argue, but stood up and walked from the room. I heard him go up the stairs, his feet dragging and heavy on each step, and then after a while he left, just the banging of the front door telling me that he'd gone. I peered from the sitting room window and watched, my heart thumping and my hands shaking, as he put his suitcase into the boot of the car, before slamming the lid down with force, then he got in the driver's seat and moved slowly away from the kerb.

I stood there for ages, unmoving, looking at the garden, at the neatly cut lawn and the weed free flower beds, at all the beautiful flowers that we'd planted together. I must have looked like a shop dummy in that window I stood there for so long. When I finally did move, I ached in my bones and was so unsteady on my feet that I felt as though I'd aged by at least twenty years.

* * *

The beep of a text message awoke me the next morning and I fumbled sleepily on the bedside cabinet until I felt the smooth roundness of my phone and saw a text from Shelley which I could just about see squinting through gummy eyes, 'So, wot's the verdict then? I need to know x'

I checked the time six forty five. 'Six forty five in the morning and she has to have a decision! Is she crazy?' I hunched back under the duvet thinking, 'No, far too early, she can wait'. I closed my eyes and tried to drift off again back into the land of dreams but, oh God, I was awake now and sleep was elusive and slippery and I just couldn't seem to get hold of it. The more I reached out to grab it, the more it edged away and lurked in the shadowy corners of the bedroom, tantalising me and teasing me.

I snaked my hand over to Sam's side of the bed, feeling the smooth sheet, which was cold now and empty and the severity of my situation which could be summed up in two words really flooded into my mind, husbandless and jobless. I hadn't got the job in the doctor's surgery. They'd sent me a rejection email yesterday tea time, so what choice did I have now? Well, I couldn't do anything about the lack of a husband but it seemed that now I could definitely do something about the lack of a job.

Pulling myself up in the bed and leaning against the headboard and soft comfy pillows, I texted her back, 'God, you're an early bird, cheep, cheep. Yes Shelley, I'll be your new receptionist. Thank you so much xxx'

She texted me back, 'Fantastic, report for duty Monday morning for the 7.30am shift. Full uniform provided. Btw I'll make sure that Robert Bryce is fully prepared for you! x'

I shook my head in exasperation. What was this thing with Robert Bryce? This matchmaking thing with Shelley could be a problem because this guy just didn't sound like my type at all, and even if he was I didn't want a relationship with anyone at the moment, the situation with

Sam was still far too raw.

Annoyed and irritated, I got out of bed and, shrugging on my dressing gown, stomped downstairs to make a coffee. 'What was he anyway, but some new age hippy with a pony tail!'

2

Sleek, that was the word I was looking for. All the 'Hale & Hearty' Leisure Centres were sleek, sleek reception and pool area and sleek members, (well, maybe not all of them I thought as a rather large man struggled to get through the entrance turnstile,) especially this one, the local one, the one in Skelly where I was now reporting for duty. Seven thirty in the morning, oh my God, I couldn't remember the last time I'd been up at this hour. Since July, since Sam left, I'd loitered between the sheets for as long as possible, jumping out with only minutes to spare to get ready for work. I'd been unwilling to face the day and face up to the fact that my husband had left me 'for another woman', and then after the redundancy, unwilling to face the fact that I wasn't wanted in my job any more either.

At least back in July it had been light

in the mornings, and when I'd woken the yellow glow of the sun had been edging its way around the thick bedroom curtains lighting my way to normality I suppose, but this morning there'd been no sun not even any light, just pitch black windows as I peered out into a pitch black street, pulling the cord of my dressing gown tighter around my waist. With a jolt of surprise I noticed a milkman, his white cap shining in the gloom, trudging along next door's path and clinking a bottle of milk down on the door step. I wasn't even aware that milkmen still existed and had just assumed that everybody, like me, bought their milk from the supermarket!

As I waited for Shelley, I gazed around the busy circular reception area where the receptionist, a young girl with long blonde hair tied back in a pony tail was showing how good she was at multi-tasking by greeting members, answering the phone, giving out towels, answering queries and doing complicated looking things on the computer all at the same time. Would I be capable of doing that and so efficiently? I peered through the window which faced onto the large gardens and lake surrounding the building and from where I could also see in a beautiful blue haze, the swimming pool. Shelley's dream vision of sitting in the Jacuzzi and looking at such a view had become a reality.

It's a massive pool with lanes for fast and medium swimming as well as a great playing area for young kids and babies. I noticed spongy water toys and floats on the tiled poolside, pool woggles or noodles in bright shades of pink or yellow that can be used for aqua classes, floating, and swimming lessons, although I would imagine, and I say this with a smile, are more popularly used for kids to beat the living daylights out of each other. Yeah, they find it fun! I can smell a warm chlorine scent wafting from the bright blue pool and echoey voices and splashing sounds can be heard quite distinctly.

Even though it's so early, the pool is

a hive of activity and people wearing brightly coloured rubber caps and dark costumes swim ferociously up and down, their arms and legs thrashing the water into a foaming frenzy, whilst others trying to achieve a sedate breast stroke are, it seems, forced to ride on the crests of their waves. I noticed a lady wearing glaring pink headphones that nestled in her hair like a turkey comb, eyes partially closed and lips moving, totally immersed in her music and seemingly oblivious to all the mayhem around her as she swam. 'Yeah, good for you lady,' I thought to myself.

'Mel . . .' I turned around to see Shelley tripping along towards me. She wore the uniform for the office staff, smart black trousers and jacket and a white fitted shirt, a faint silver stripe running through it, either tucked into the waistband of the trousers or hanging loose. In Shelley's case the shirt was tucked in showing that she had a nice flat stomach underneath the trousers, in my case the shirt would definitely be hanging loose!

Her hair usually long and flowing around her shoulders was tied back into a neat pony tail and the only jewellery she wore was tiny gold hoops in her ears and her slim wedding band.

'Hey, Shelley, I'm here . . . the earliest I've been up and about for months!'

She laughed then said, 'Let's get you kitted out with a uniform first, then I'll give you a bit of a tour round and introduce you before you start work properly.' She beckoned me with her head, 'Come on.'

We walked past the circular reception area where the receptionist was just coming off the phone. 'Jenny, this is Melanie, our new recruit . . . she'll be working with you in a bit so will be looking to you for help, this being her first day.'

'Oh no problem,' said Jenny, 'Hi Melanie.'

We shook hands and grinned. I noticed that Jenny was very young, probably early twenties, and very pretty with dusky freckles on her nose like hundreds and thousands sprinkled over the icing

27

on a cake.

I followed Shelley into the back offices where a couple of girls and a guy were sitting staring at computer screens with glazed eyes. The walls were covered in posters of fit people wearing lycra shorts and tee-shirts or muscle tops, and brightly coloured trainers, all good looking and tanned, with rivers of hard earned sweat pouring down their determined faces.

'Hi there,' said the girls and the guy in one sing song voice, as Shelley introduced me then led me through to another room where large brown boxes were piled haphazardly on top of one another and plastic bags containing black items and white items of clothing were stored on shelves. I assumed these were the uniforms.

'Hmm,' she said, looking at me, eyes narrowed and looking me up and down. 'What size are you Mel?

'Umm, size 16,' I replied.

She did a double take before saying, 'Don't be daft, you're not a size 16.'

I giggled and said, 'Okay, an 18 then . . .'

She looked at me from the tail of her eye and made a face and then started rummaging through the glossy packets before settling on one and pulling out the trousers which were clearly marked as a size 14.

'There you go,' she said, waving them at me. 'Try these on.' Pointing her thumb like a hitch hiker, she declared, 'The loo's are just in there.'

'Shelley,' I whined. 'They won't fit . . .'

'For God's sake, Mel, just try them on,' She said this quite nastily really, throwing a white shirt in as well, clearly marked M for medium and not L for large as I thought it should be.

Full of an irrational hatred against Shelley for making me try and squeeze into too small clothing as well as the fact that I'd been up since five thirty this morning, I grabbed the trousers from her extended hand and pulled them on expecting resistance as I eased them over my backside and my stomach but they zipped up easily and the shirt fitted fine as well, buttoning up over my chest with no problem whatsoever.

I sidled from the toilet cubicle, eyes downcast, not wanting to see Shelley's smug I told you so expression. 'Wow, great Mel,' she said as she handed me a jacket which I shrugged on and buttoned up then, looking in the mirror, head to one side, assessing, unbuttoned the jacket and then tied my hair back with a black scrunchie.

'Wow,' she crowed, 'Looking good Mel, we need to introduce you to Robert Bryce asap.'

'No, we don't Shelley,' I replied whilst tweaking at my hair with my fingers and pouting in the mirror. 'I'm not interested in hippy Robert Bryce, okay?'

Shelley, lounging against the wall, arms crossed, giggling to herself, had just opened her mouth to reply when a voice said, 'Well, I've never been called a hippy before . . . especially by somebody I don't even know.'

Shelley and I spun around and from

the look on Shelley's face, I guessed straight away that standing in front of us was Robert Bryce, his hands on his slim hips gazing at us from very dark brown eyes enhanced by really long black lashes. His glossy black hair is tied into a pony tail and he's wearing the gym uniform of black shorts and green tee-shirt, Welcome to 'Hale & Hearty' emblazoned across the front next to the familiar orange logo of the running stick man and woman.

His chest is fairly broad and he's got prominent muscles on his arms. I notice that he wears a small silver hoop earring in one ear and that his mouth above a sexy dimpled chin looks as ripe and juicy as a strawberry. Even the 'Hale & Hearty' baseball cap perched on his head does nothing to hide the fact that he's a good looking guy.

I cupped my hands around my mouth and nose and took a deep breath, desperately trying to think of something witty to say, when Shelley said, 'Only kidding, Rob . . . I think it's just the pony tail that makes you look a bit of a hippy.'

He smiled, showing teeth that were very white and very even. 'Oh, okay, no problem . . . ' He held out his hand. 'You must be Mel?'

Feeling a bit shaky and nervous but doing my best to hide it I retorted, 'Oh, don't say it, you've heard all about me!' I held out my hand and as our palms touched, a lovely warm feeling spread through my body and my stomach clenched; a not altogether unpleasant feeling. Quickly though, as if I'd been burnt, I pulled my hand away.

'No,' he replied. 'I've heard nothing much about you. All I know is that your name's Mel and you're starting on reception today.'

I felt as though I'd been doused in cold water so said a bit huffily I suppose, 'It's Melanie actually.'

He smiled causing really nice dimples to appear in his cheeks to match the one on his chin, then gave a shrug, 'Well, actually, if you're going to be picky, I prefer Robert, not Rob . . .'

When I didn't reply, he grinned at me and said, 'Well, it's great to meet you, Melanie, I'm in the pool area today if you're coming along for a swim later.' He put his fingers to his forehead in a salute then left the room. I heard him talking to the girls and guy in the other room asking if they wanted a coffee and was anyone going for a break.

Shelley gave me a wry look then said, 'Well, I think you're ready for work now, Mel, come on . . .'

★ ★ ★

'Me and your Aunts are going to a convention,' stated mum.

'A convention?' I asked, 'What sort of a convention?'

'A twin convention, it's being held in Blackpool in January and we thought we'd go along. Helps with research and stuff, you know.'

'Hmm,' I replied, 'Sounds interesting, I might like to go along with you.'

'Why? You haven't got a twin have

you?'

'Duh, no mum,' I replied. 'I'm sure you'd know about it if I did!'

I looked longingly at the bottle of red wine that I'd put on the coffee table earlier, a squat blue glass ready and waiting at its side. Checking my watch I see that it's far too early yet so zone back in to what mum's saying, she's still babbling on about twins, 'There's loads of stories about twins on the internet. Fascinating . . . so fascinating . . .'

'You're using the internet? I thought you said at fifty you were too old?'

'I never said that!' Mum exclaimed.

I was just about to say, 'But Mum you did . . . ' then I thought, no what's the point, so said instead, 'What sort of stories mum?'

'Well, I googled twins and read a story about a pair of twins separated at birth. They had so many similarities in their life, it was untrue. Both were called James by their adopted parents, both married women called Linda and had sons called James, both got divorced and married women called Betty and both had a dog named Toy! What do you think of that?'

'Wow! How strange. You'll probably hear loads more weird stories like that at the convention. Toy's a bit of an odd name for a dog though isn't it?'

'What's that got to do with it?' I could imagine mum frowning and shaking her head, then deciding to change the subject, 'Anyway, Melly love, how's your new job going?'

'Yeah, it's good.'

'I hope you're grateful to Shelley and Scott . . .'

'Of course I am mum . . . really grateful . . . this job is helping me so much . . .'

'Yes, it's best to be out and about and not moping at home and working in one of the Leisure Centre's must be so good . . . have you been swimming yet?'

'Um, no, not yet . . .'

'Why not, it's just there, that lovely pool.'

I didn't want to tell mum that I felt too fat in my swimming costume at the moment and wanted to lose at least a stone before I even thought of putting it on and parading in front of people at the pool side. She'd go mad if I said that and so would Dad. He thought women looked good with, in his words, 'a bit of weight on them!'

'Yeah, I know, I just haven't had time yet that's all . . . probably will do during the week.' I kept my fingers crossed as I said that, I didn't want to develop a Pinocchio nose any time soon.

'Oh I forgot to tell you . . . '

'Thank God,' I thought. 'She's changing the subject. Let's get her off swimming for the time being.'

'I saw that Alice the other day.'

'Alice Jackson?'

'Yes, I saw her in that lovely big furniture shop in Skelly . . . looking at settees she was, on her own, not with that Sam.'

I had to smile. Since our break up, Mum always referred to Sam and Alice as 'That Sam,' and 'That Alice.' Nevertheless, I bristled at the thought of Alice Jackson, the breaker up of marriages, looking at settees in a furniture shop in

Skelly. In fact, I felt so stressed about it that I reached for the wine bottle and poured myself a very healthy glass. 'What did she look like?'

'A bit like a skeleton,' replied Mum, 'Pale and thin.'

'Well,' I said. 'She was always thin . . .'

'Yeah, but not like this . . . Oh, I'll have to go, Mel, there's someone at the door . . . see you later love . . .'

I shook my head, always surprised at the way mum so abruptly ended a telephone conversation. Aunty Iris didn't do that, so even though they looked the same, they certainly didn't act the same. I clicked off my phone and put it beside me on the settee then took another big glug of wine.

'Hmm,' I thought. 'I shouldn't really be drinking this if I want to lose weight, but the name Alice Jackson always makes me feel really sort of weird! Yes, that's the word, weird! I often wonder how she feels about being 'the other woman' and whether or not she feels guilty about taking my husband away from me.'

I thought back to last week when Sam had rung and gone on and on about me putting the house up for sale. 'I'm strapped for cash, Mel,' he had said. 'I need my half from the house.' He sounded whiny as a spoiled child and it suddenly hit me that maybe I should be glad that I wasn't with him anymore but then sadness and loneliness enveloped me once again in a black haze and I missed him desperately.

I gaze around the sitting room that, although looking a bit shabby now, we decorated together, full of happiness and hope, when we first moved in eight years ago. Those eight years obviously meant nothing to Sam who had taken up with Alice Jackson knowing how much it would hurt me, knowing that I was Alice Jackson's babysitter years ago when I was around fourteen and Alice a little girl of just four years old.

I'd looked after her and her two little brothers every evening after school for the couple of hours in between their mum going to work and their dad arriving home. I'd loved looking after them, Alice especially, who had been a beautiful loving child, pretty too with long blonde hair and big blue eyes. I remembered the times that she used to sit on my lap while I read her stories from an old Enid Blyton book and when we'd danced around the kitchen to my new record 'Debora' by T Rex. Who could have guessed then what would happen in the future.

My thoughts turned then to Robert Bryce, the new age hippy that Shelley was so interested in getting me involved with. Yes, okay, I did find him attractive even with the pony tail. I suppose I'd had a picture in my mind of somebody a lot older, hair thinning at the front and the bulk of it tied back at the neck, but Robert was nothing like that.

Our first meeting could have been better though, I recalled the comment that he'd made when for something to say I'd asked if he knew all about me. I'd felt such a total fool at his reply. Talk about being dashed in cold water! I found myself hoping that Robert and I would meet again and under far better circumstances.

I took another sip of wine feeling the effect of it like fire through my veins, and then, looking around the sitting room once more, came to a sudden decision. Picking up my phone, I texted Sam, 'Okay, you win; I'll go to the Estate Agent tomorrow and see what I need to do to put the house up for sale!'

★ ★ ★

I'm at work sitting at the busy reception desk doing exactly what I was really worried about a few weeks ago . . . multi-tasking . . . exactly as I saw Jenny doing when I came in that day for my first shift. The phone seems to have never stopped ringing this afternoon and people never stop pouring through the door similar, I suppose, to the red wine that pours from a bottle into my waiting glass a couple of evenings a week.

I'm handing out towels (members aren't allowed to take their own towel

now because of naughty people taking two instead of the allotted one) and
dealing with queries such as, 'What
time does the body pump class start on
a Wednesday?' and, 'Do I have to book
yoga on a Thursday morning?' or 'Why
do you have to keep closing the pool
when a child is sick in it?' Oh my God
people go mad when that happens but
do they really want to swim in a sick
infested pool? What I think though is
that most people would prefer no kids
at all and for the leisure centres to be
strictly adults only.

The 'Hale & Hearty' leisure centre
in Blackpool only allows kids in perhaps a couple of times a week so it is
more adult orientated but apparently, a
group of naturists have asked to hire the
pool for a private party! Wow, can you
imagine a naturist's pool party? Anyway,
the manager there, Dale Duckworth,
(no relation to Jack or Vera I don't think)
said yes at first and confirmed that the
pool was available to be rented out by
members but when he heard it was for

a naturist's party, he suddenly changed his mind. Well, of course, the members are up in arms and threatening to go to the papers. Shelley, in a raving irritable mood, has had to go to Blackpool today to investigate.

So, with Shelley out of the way, Melanie can play, which is why, hidden in the bottom of my sports bag is a black one piece swimming costume. When I come off shift tonight I've made up my mind (after thinking long and hard) that I'm going to change into my costume and go and have a bit of a relax in the steam room and the sauna. As much as I love her, I know that if Shelley was here and found out that I had my costume with me (and she'd definitely find out), she'd persuade me to get rid of the one piece and buy a bikini from the extensive array in the leisure centre's little sports shop, and before I could say 'Tom Tit the Wit' I'd be wearing it and in the pool looking like a beached whale.

So, as I'm on my own and unsure about actually swimming yet, I'll be able to hold a towel around my enormous buttocks (if the towels are large enough, maybe I should have brought one of my bath sheets!) without Shelley laughing at me so at least I'll have the confidence to walk into the pool area. I must admit though that being able to fit my generous curves into a size 14 uniform and not a 16 or even an 18 which I dreaded, has done wonders for my self esteem.

I answer the phone for about the millionth time and I'm trying to answer a query from a man enquiring what sort of swimming apparel he should wear in the pool when a young man walks past the reception desk, raises his hand to me in a salute and then saunters into the back offices.

'Robert?' I think to myself, 'Was that really Robert Bryce?' He was wearing the usual pool side uniform of black shorts and green tee-shirt. He certainly had the same good looking face with dimpled chin and juicy strawberry looking lips, but, and this was a big shock, he'd dyed his hair. Instead of the glossy black pony tail that I'd seen so many times bobbing around at the pool side or almost laying across some lycra clad woman whilst in a session of personal training, he had a blonde one. Yes, definitely, Rob Bryce had a blonde pony tail. I was so taken aback by this that I'd lost track of my conversation with the swimming apparel man on the phone.

'Hello? Are you still there? I'm really sorry about that, such a busy day today.'

'Yes, I'm still here. What do you recommend then the trunks or the shorts?'

I took a deep breath and said, 'Well, it's up to you, but I recommend the shorts, I personally find the trunks quite offensive.' Oh my God, had I really said that to a member? He'd probably put in a complaint now and Shelley and Scott would have no alternative but to sack me.

'Thank you so much for you help, that's exactly what my wife said, but I wanted to check first.' He hung up, happy and content, and promising to visit the pool soon wearing discreet shorts.

My mind went back to the blonde pony tailed Rob Bryce, or should I say Robert Bryce, that I'd seen walking past the reception earlier. What on earth was going on? Had he really dyed his hair or was it a wig? Hmm, I think somehow I would have to find out.

3

I peered out of the window at the front garden, looking slightly shabbier since Sam had gone, and noted with satisfaction the for sale sign standing firmly in the earth between the curly wrought iron gate that Sam had insisted on buying only a couple of months before we split up and the lilac tree which looked all but dead at this time of the year. 'Hmm' I thought, 'I've a good mind to get Sam round here to tidy the garden. After all it's him that wants to sell so surely he should have some input into making sure the place is saleable.'

Did I want him round here though, that is the question, and the answer is, unfortunately, yes. I wish he was still here and that I didn't live alone. If it wasn't for my job, which I'm really growing to love, (thank God for Scott and Shelley), I think I would be a very depressed fat person. The word 'fat' brought to my mind once again the happenings in the steam room the other night. I kept going over and over it all in my mind and the thought of it still left me with a shiver running down my spine, even though I knew that I really didn't want to feel that way.

I shivered now though for a different reason and hunched my shoulders at the sight of the sky, low and gunmetal grey, livid with black clouds and as soon as fleshy rain drops pattered on the window pane, I pulled the curtains almost closed and padded downstairs. As I put the kettle on to make a coffee, I thought how glad I was that it was my day off and I didn't have to go anywhere if I didn't want to.

Sitting on the settee my cold hands wrapped around a steaming mug of hot coffee I remembered how I'd felt the other night when I finally plucked up the courage to come out of the modesty cubicle at the gym wearing my black one piece swimming costume.

The changing rooms were fairly quiet

probably because it was quite late, getting on for nine o'clock, and I was virtually alone apart from disembodied voices from the other end of the lockers. I noticed that most of the lockers were actually locked so those people had to be somewhere around in the leisure centre, either in the gym or in a class or in the pool, hopefully not too many of them in the pool. I could hear the swoosh of water from the showers and voices echoed hollow from the pool.

Before I went in search of the steam room I plucked up the courage to look in the mirror and to my horror all I could see staring back at me was a vast black shape with pink things hanging from each corner. On further scrutiny I realised that the pink things were my arms and legs and the black shape obviously the swimming costume stretched across my flabby body. That did put me off a bit but, before I could even think of getting changed and going home, I took a very quick shower before tying one of the leisure centre's white towels around my waist.

Moist air hit me with full force as, clutching a bottle of water; I gently pushed open the door and went tentatively into the steam room. It was so steamy I could barely see and, furtively peering into the deep soup like fog, I came to the satisfactory conclusion that I was alone. Relaxed and happy now I sat down, and taking one more cautious look around, took the towel from around my waist, putting it to one side and then, after a sip of water and a great sigh of contentment, laid myself down full length and closed my eyes.

The not unpleasant scent of eucalyptus was all around, I felt as though I was immersed in it. It seeped into my skin and my hair, the scent of it slid into my nostrils so that I felt warm and soft and sleepy. I drifted, dreaming that I was on a beach somewhere hot, my toes wiggling into soft powdery sand, and the gentle shushing of waves in my ear, when somebody said, 'Hi, it's Melanie isn't it?'

I sat up as if I'd been shot at. 'Who?

What?' I gabbled, panicking as I reached for the towel and laid it across my lap.

Whoever it was laughed and said, 'Sorry, I think I scared you then, didn't I? It's only me, Rob . . . Robert Bryce . . .'

My heart plummeted so hard I felt as though I'd been pushed over a cliff. How long had he been there? 'I didn't see you,' I squeaked. Oh no, he must have seen me taking off the towel.

'No,' he started waving his hands about to disperse the steam. I could just about see them like little white lights moving about in the gloom, 'But it is a bit soupy in here.' As the steam thinned out, I could gradually just about make out his legs, then his chest, then his face. He grinned at me and his teeth shone very white like he was starring in his very own toothpaste advert.

'You've been here all the time and you didn't say anything. Did you know it was me?'

'Yeah, sure I did.'

'You could have said something!' I pulled the towel closer around me and sniffed my disapproval.

'What's with the towel? You don't need to wear a towel in here . . . as long as you're wearing a swimming costume of course.' He laughed,

'I prefer to wear a towel,' I replied disdainfully. The steam had cleared quite a lot by this time which gave me a fairly good view of Robert Bryce. He was a slightly built guy but had a muscular hairy chest and strong looking arms. He was tanned and had a bit of yesterday's growth around his chin. I noticed that he was wearing some sort of Axel Rose type headband on his dark hair and . . . now this is where I stopped and peered closer . . .

'You've got dark hair!' I exclaimed.

'Um, yeah . . .'

'I saw you earlier when I was on reception, you waved at me, and you had blonde hair! Are you wearing a wig?'

This amused him greatly because he laughed really loud and shook his head, then sniffed a bit and seemed to be wiping tears from his eyes. 'Don't be daft; you'll have seen my twin brother, Richard . . . he works at the gym as well but he's been away travelling for a few months and has only just got back . . . '

Two girls came into the steam room giggling and chattering like a couple of chimps. Both wore very brief bikini's in luminous shades of yellow and orange. They sat down, crossing their legs and folding their arms across their chests, and I noticed that even when sitting their stomachs were still wash board flat. I hastily pulled the towel closer round my protruding lump.

'Ha, that's a good one,' I replied. 'Nobody mentioned you had a twin. And anyway whoever heard of twins with such different hair colour?'

Robert leant forward, his hands on his thighs, 'Well, in this case it's true, we're not identical twins but what's called fraternal twins, the egg we were conceived in split in two, that's why we look alike but have different hair colour. Some fraternal twins don't look anything alike.'

'Oh right,' I said, interested despite trying not to be. 'Well, you certainly look alike. I thought it was you that I saw earlier apart from the blonde hair of course. My mum and aunt are twins you know but they're identical. They shared the same egg.' I suddenly remembered my conversation with mum the other night and said, 'Oh, I've just remembered there's some sort of twin convention in Blackpool soon . . . January I think she said.'

The two girls looked at us in disbelief and made some sort of gagging noise and put their fingers to their open mouths. 'People growing in eggs . . . how gross,' they exclaimed as they stood up showing acres of smooth toned flesh. Rob grinned at me as they pulled the door closed and left us alone once again.

We chatted for ages and I told him about my mum and the fact that she had five sisters and with her the family consisted of three sets of twins and that when I was a little girl I'd always called them the flower aunts because they were all named after flowers. My mum, I told him, is called Lily and her twin is Iris (who incidentally is Shelley's mum), and the others are Primrose and Fleur (the two eldest twins), and Violet and Marigold (the two youngest twins).

He seemed fascinated by all the twin talk and kept saying how amazing it was that one family had three sets of twins and then told me what it was like for him growing up as a twin. I remember him saying, 'When you're a twin, regardless of whether you're identical or fraternal, you are always 'The Twins.' Sometimes my mum and dad would just group our names together and call us 'Robrick,' or Rickrob.

We were together all the time so really it was good that Rick decided to go travelling without me. To tell you the honest truth, we don't always see eye to eye . . . ' He looked at me with those very dark eyes framed by those long long lashes and I said, 'Well, that's just like any brothers or sisters, not that I have any, but Shelley's more like a sister to me than a cousin, and we argue some times.'

'Yeah that's right,' he nodded. 'Oh, I didn't realise that Shelley's your cousin . . . '

I nodded and told him about our other cousins, George, Jim, Lisa and Liz, and then, before we could talk any further, the door opened and a group of rather large men came piling into the steam room all talking loudly to one another and it got so crowded that, rather than be squashed together like sardines, we decided to leave.

Once outside, red faced and sweating, I took a deep breath and said, 'Actually, I'm really hot now so I'd better go.' I wafted my hand in front of my face. 'It was good to see you . . . ' I turned to walk away when Rob said, 'Hey, no, wait Melanie . . . what about a dip in the plunge pool or come and sit in the Jacuzzi . . . '

'Oh no, really, I . . . ' Then I thought to myself, 'Hmm, the Jacuzzi would be really relaxing,' then an awful thought whispered through my mind. 'You can't go in the Jacuzzi, you'll have to take the towel off.' The thought just wouldn't go away, 'You can't go in the jacuzzi, you'll have to take the towel off.'

'Come on,' He beckoned to me with his head. 'You can tell me more about the twin convention.'

A little green imp sat on my shoulder chattering into my ear, 'You can't go in the jacuzzi, you'll have to take the towel off.'

I hesitated then followed him to the bubbling pool of water set between tall pillars as if we were in some sort of roman bathing house. A couple of people sat in the writhing water, heads back, eyes closed, oblivious to everything. It certainly wouldn't bother them if I took the towel off but what about Robert?

Before I could do anything he lunged at me and said, 'You won't need this,' and made a brave attempt at pulling the towel from me, but luckily I managed to grab it and held on for dear life, my knuckles white and strained.

'What are you doing?' I asked through gritted teeth whilst furtively looking around to make sure that nobody was watching us.

Coming back to the present I remembered his laugh and that he had said, 'You don't need that silly towel, you've got a lovely figure, why not show it off.' Annoyed with him, I stormed off into the changing rooms not even stopping to say goodbye.

He was waiting for me in the reception area, looking I must say rather sheepish. 'I was afraid that you were annoyed with me earlier, and well . . . I'm sorry . . . I shouldn't have done that, if you want to wear a towel in the pool area then it's none of my business.'

'It's okay,' I said haughtily as I walked past him, my sports bag banging painfully against my side, and out to the car park. Looking from the corner of my eye I was pleased to see that he was following me.

It was cold now and dark, but I felt sort of warm and tingly all through my body and I'm not sure if it was just because of the steam room and the brisk shower. I looked up at the sky and saw that it was black and teeming with stars and the moon hung motionless like a great silver globe.

'I enjoyed tonight,' Rob said. 'Let's do it again, hmm?'

'Maybe,' I replied coldly.

'We could even go for a drink in the bar next time?'

'Um, maybe we could,' I said, 'Well, this is my car here . . . '

Her put his hand out and touched my arm. 'Hey, look, Melanie, I really am sorry.'

He caught my eye and smiled at me, a smile that deepened the dimples both in his cheeks and his chin. This softened me somewhat and made me smile too. He came closer and said, 'You know earlier when you asked why I didn't say anything to you when you came into the steam room?'

I looked at him, his face a pale oval in the dark. I nodded, puzzled, wondering what he was going to say.

'Well, do you know what; I kept schtum

because I just wanted to look at you, especially after you took the towel off.' Abruptly he walked away, then turned around and began to back away grinning at me all the time. Then he turned around again and the next minute, to my intense disappointment, he was gone.

★ ★ ★

'This is a ridiculous situation,' said Shelley, 'And I've gathered everybody together today so we can discuss it and, hopefully, make a decision on what we're going to do.'

All the staff of 'Hale & Hearty' in Skelly had been gathered together to discuss the request from a Naturist Group to hire the pool in the Blackpool Leisure Centre for a swimming party. As I mentioned before, Shelley had gone to Blackpool in a tearing hurry to try to resolve this issue and had come back still raging over it.

We were sitting in one of the upstairs conference rooms and even Scott had come along which showed how serious this problem was. I gazed around the bright airy room, its large windows showing a great expanse of sky, and although it was a dour November sky, the sun was breaking through the cloud and shone in long dazzling yellow shafts on the plain walls.

Looking around the table I could see that all the reception staff were present, as well as the pool staff including Robert and his brother Richard who, now that I saw them virtually side by side, didn't look as totally alike as I'd thought. Interestingly, sitting between them, was a very pretty young girl who I'd never seen before so I assumed she must be a new recruit.

She had very bright blonde hair tied up in a pony tail and had, unusually for work in the pool area, very heavily made up eyes and lips, which did nothing to disguise the fact that she was very young, no more than eighteen or nineteen, I would have thought. She was dressed in the pool uniform of black shorts and green tee-shirt; although I noticed that she'd turned her shorts up a touch at the bottom, to show more leg I suppose, and an extra button or two were open on her tee-shirt than was strictly necessary.

Robert gave me a little wave and a smile which I guessed the young girl had seen because of the gimlet eyed look that passed from his face to mine. I cringed and felt like getting down on my hands and knees and hiding under the table!

'Just to re-cap,' said Shelley. 'A group of naturists, all of whom are members of the leisure centre in Blackpool, made a request there to hire the pool for a party next month, December, obviously a Christmas party. Dale Duckworth, the Manager at Blackpool, said yes that the pool was available for members to hire.

He quoted the price, the length of time it could be hired for and gave all the relevant details. He was in the process of putting together a contract for the group when it was brought to his attention that the booking was for a Naturist Group. Dale Duckworth immediately reneged on the whole thing and promptly said that the pool wasn't available to hire that evening.

'Obviously the group is up in arms about this and has said that they've been discriminated against. They've threatened to go to the papers and are also encouraging local naturists groups to contact our other leisure centres to make the same request to see what happens. Well, following on from that a request has been made here for a Naturist pool party, a Christmas one as well.

Just to give you a further bit of information a baths in Scotland has a regular weekly Naturists session in their pool for people to go for a swim, steam and sauna and also a gym in Southampton has the same thing, so this sort of request isn't unusual.'

Scott intervened, 'This is serious guys. What do we do? Do we go along with Dale Duckworth's view and not allow Naturists Groups to hire the pool or do we allow them and ultimately, I suppose, make Dale look a fool in his capacity of manager? What do you all think?'

There was a babble of noise as everybody started talking at once. 'Hey,' Scott held up his hand. 'Talk to Shelley and I please, not just to each other.'

Surprisingly, Richard put up his hand, 'I don't think that Dale should have played God and said no to this group. He should have contacted either you or Shelley to get advice; after all you two are the owners of all the gyms and the Board of Directors.'

Scott and Shelley nodded. 'Yeah, that's a good point.'

Rob put up his hand, 'Surely, though if naked people are going to be in the pool, it will need a longer more thorough clean afterwards which could affect when members will be able to use the pool the following day. Don't forget that the filtration system can only cope with so much and, also, there's the question of cost.'

'And also,' I bravely pointed out, much to the surprise of Shelley I could tell, 'Will the lifeguards want to work in such unusual conditions? Supervising a bunch of people with no clothes on?'

Most people in the room nodded their heads at this then Scott said, 'The trouble is though, if we don't allow them this party, and you may think I'm exaggerating here,' He paused for effect and there was a silence, a great big heavy silence, 'this group of people could tarnish all the gyms with a bad reputation which in turn could bring about the downfall of 'Hale and Hearty' . . . '

'And that,' finished Shelley, slowly shaking her head, 'Really doesn't bear thinking about.'

I looked at Scott and Shelley standing there together totally united. The two of them had worked so hard at creating these fantastic leisure centres for people to enjoy and I was absolutely certain that they didn't want to see their years of hard work come to nothing, certainly not for a group of trouble making naturists.

Scott looked so cool as usual dressed in smart blue jeans and a checked shirt.

His dark eyes shone out in his handsome face that boasted attractive high cheek-bones and a touch of designer stubble on his chin. I remember that I'd had a bit of a thing for Scott when Shelley had first started seeing him all those years ago. Of course, he'd no way been interested in a little kid like me.

One of the receptionists raised her hand, Diane I think she was called, 'I can understand them being annoyed in a way though. It is discrimination against them . . . if they weren't going to be naked, then the pool would be hired out no problem.'

'Yeah,' agreed the young receptionist, Sally, 'And don't forget what Shelley said earlier about the other clubs that allow Naturist swim sessions, maybe we should be keeping up with the trends.'

'Yeah, okay, that's true,' Scott spoke up, 'I've taken all your comments on board . . . thanks for that . . . '

Suddenly the pretty girl sitting between Robert and Richard piped up, 'Can't you make them wear a thong or something?'

There was general tittering around the room and Shelley said, 'Jeannie . . . they're naturists . . . that's the whole point, they don't want to wear anything', to which there was a great bellow of laughter from everybody. Jeannie looked quite put out at the rumpus she'd caused and glowered, her pretty face looking quite mean, before leaning towards Robert and whispering in his ear. He shook his head and then sat back, his arms crossed over his muscular chest.

'Hmm,' so she's called Jeannie,' I thought, 'Because she was so young I would have thought her to have been a Sophie or an Emily, or maybe a Claire.'

'So,' said Shelley. 'Come on then, what do you think we should do guys?'

4

I've been on shift since very early this morning and Shelley has just told me to go and get my break so, in desperate need of food and drink, I'm in 'Hale & Hearty's' cafe munching a toasted currant tea cake and drinking a hot cup of coffee, both of which are going down nicely thank you very much. My appetite satisfied, I'm sipping at the coffee and gazing out of the window. It's light at long last and I can see it's going to be one of those bright white days, with a sky low enough to bump your head on and looking ready to scatter snowflakes at any second. Even as I sit there, a few lazy flakes start to fall, twirling in the air and then shriveling to nothing on the emerald green grass.

Taking my gaze back into the cafe, I notice a few early risers sitting around sipping warm drinks and eating a good breakfast of toast, or teacakes or croissants, all red cheeked and healthy, most with wet hair from the shower.

Four very skinny people are gathered in a little huddle all wearing luminous running gear and stretching and laughing, making jokes about how hard it's snowing outside now and how they'll have to be careful not to slip. I watch as they run outside, massed together as one, the snow falling faster now and coating their hats and neon jackets with a layer of white. It's not long before they're gone, only their rapidly disappearing footprints across the frosted grass showing that they were there at all.

I feel a tap on my shoulder and looking up see Robert Bryce standing in front of me holding a plate of buttered toast and a mug which by the tantalizing odour must be hot chocolate. 'Hey, Melanie, mind if I share?' He nodded towards the empty seat opposite me.

'No, be my guest,' I replied, making a sweeping motion with my arm.

He sat down and took a sip from his mug, 'Umm that tastes good, I've been longing for a drink all morning.'

'Yeah, me too.' I took another sip from my now cooling coffee and, pointing at the window, shook my head making a comment about the snow and what a nuisance it was, even though it's very pretty, I added.

'Yeah,' Robert replied. 'It's laying quite thick now. I just hope my car will be able to get through it tonight.'

He spread jam on his toast, took a bite then said, 'What do you think about the decision from the meeting yesterday then?'

'What, about the naturists?'

He nodded.

'Well, I think they had no choice but to let them go ahead with both parties, here and in Blackpool, after all it is discrimination really . . . '

'Yeah, I think they've made the right decision. I may have to be a lifeguard that night though . . . '

I smiled at him, 'Oh yeah, how do you feel about that?'

'Well, it's gonna make the job a lot different that's for sure . . . I don't know how I feel about it really. I'll let you know after the event.' He grinned and raised his eyebrows. His eyes sparkled bewitchingly in the white light reflected from the snow.

'You will be clothed though, won't you?' A very disconcerting image of Robert Bryce sitting in the steam room suddenly popped into my mind. I remembered his toned chest covered in thick dark hairs, the image coming to an abrupt halt, thank goodness, as my eyes moved down to his stomach.

'Of course, I will,' replied Robert, almost choking on his toast.

I laughed then said, 'Dale Duckworth must feel a bit of a fool though?'

'Well, apparently he threatened to leave but changed his mind.'

'Yeah, he's been with Scott and Shelley for a long time and is probably very well paid.' We smiled wryly at each other.

I noticed that he was dressed slightly differently and said, 'Are you dressed differently because of the weather? You know, track suit bottoms instead of shorts?'

'No, I've got some clients for personal training this morning. I usually wear shorts just around the pool area.'

'Ooh, anybody nice for the training this morning?'

He took another bite of toast and a sip of his drink then laughed, 'Yeah, a couple of women . . . but you know, Melanie, there's nothing sexual in it, it's just exercise . . .'

For some strange reason my heart started beating like a drum at Robert Bryce saying the word 'sexual.' I glanced at him, at his strawberry red lips that he touched briefly with his finger tip. 'I didn't mean to imply anything like that,' I said with a mock hurt expression.

'No, you didn't need to,' he replied wryly. 'It's there in your expression. It's amazing how many people make that reference when talking about personal training.' He sipped again from his mug then said, 'Anyway, when are you coming for a drink with me?'

I was surprised at that question and

felt a sort of clenching feeling in my stomach, it had been a couple of weeks since we'd talked in the steam room and he'd said nothing further about going for a drink. I looked at his face, at his lovely dark eyes and mouth ripe as a strawberry, that alluring dimple on his chin, and I knew that if I wanted it to, I was pretty sure that something could happen between us, but that wouldn't be fair on him, not the way I felt at the moment. Shelley had been right when she'd told me about Rob; he was a nice man, nothing like the new age hippy that I'd been expecting.

'Look Rob, it's not long since I split with my husband and I'm still feeling a touch fragile . . . going for a drink with you just wouldn't work at the moment.'

'Yeah, what happened there, why did you split?' He put his mug down on the table and wiped away a few crumbs with his hands.

'Well . . . ' I took a deep breath. 'He left me for another woman.'

'Really? Is he wrong in the head?'

I had to laugh at that but didn't know what to say in reply.

'We can go for a drink as friends surely?'

'I'd rather not at the moment,' I replied. 'I need to get my head together. I don't need any complications.'

'Are you still in the house where you lived with him?'

'Yes, but it's up for sale. Maybe things will be better for me when I get a place of my own. There's too many memories there.' I noticed that a long queue had formed at the reception desk and, glancing at my watch, saw that I'd had the allotted twenty minute break. 'Anyway, I'd better get back to reception . . . looks as if they're busy.'

I stood up and was just about to move away when Robert took hold of my arm. The touch of his hand on my skin made me feel extremely warm and I almost expected to see smoke curling lazily between us. 'Hope things get better for you, Melanie . . . I'll see you around at work? . . .'

I nodded and smiled wondering for a split second if I'd done the wrong thing. Perhaps I should have said yes to that drink but it was too late now. 'Yeah, see you around, Robert . . .'

★ ★ ★

I walked out of work that evening into a world white with snow, a beautiful winter wonderland glowing in the dusk, which I couldn't appreciate as much as I would have liked to because of the unexpected verbal abuse that I'd just suffered at the hands of that awful young girl, Jeannie. With great relief I got to my car and almost threw myself in the driver's seat, breathing heavily; hands shaking; thinking back to what had happened when I'd finished my shift.

I'd gone to the locker room straight away, I needed to get changed and collect my bag and, truthfully, after eight hours work, I was longing to get home and put my feet up with a relaxing glass of wine. Jeannie was rummaging around in her own locker as I came in so I smiled at her as I opened mine and got my bag, checking that I had my phone and my purse. Glancing around at her before going into the toilet cubicle to change, I said, 'Hi, I don't think we've met yet, I'm Melanie.'

I held out my hand which she totally ignored and said, 'Yeah, I saw you with Rob earlier, in the café?'

'Hmm' I thought, 'Doesn't she know that he prefers to be called Robert,' but then a dark sense of foreboding gripped me as I replied, 'Oh yes, just having a friendly cup of coffee.'

She came very close, her nose almost touching mine, so I pulled my head back a little, a bit like a tortoise retreating into its shell, talk about invading your personal space. 'Well, back off, Rob's mine,' she hissed like an irate goose.

My heart started beating really fast but I said quite calmly I hoped, 'Oh, you're going out with Robert are you? He never said. Anyway, there's nothing going on between us,' I assured her. 'We're friends.

I don't see anything wrong with that.'

'Oh you don't see anything wrong with that, huh?' she mimicked but in a sing song baby voice.

I put up my hand and shook my head, 'I'm not putting up with this,' I told her and went to walk away and that's when she grabbed me by the arm and pulled me back. I struggled to get away but she held on tight, her nails digging into my skin.

'I'm warning you okay,' she snarled, 'Keep away from him.' She let me go so suddenly that I stumbled and almost fell at which point, pony tailing swinging, she walked out of the locker room slamming the door behind her.

I think I was in shock and at that moment felt only capable of sitting in the car, rubbing my arm where it felt tender and sore to the touch. Had that really happened? Had I really been warned off a man by a girl almost young enough to be my daughter? Okay I would have had to be very young when I had her, but even so!

I switched on the ignition and the headlights and turned the heater on full, then used the wipers to dislodge the packed snow from the windscreen. The radio came to life, Steve Wright and his Big Show which cheered me up a bit as did a little robin that was perched on the hedge fluttering its wings, its breast very red against the white of the snow.

A little tap on the car window brought me out of my thoughts and I turned to see somebody who at first glance I thought was Robert but on closer inspection could see by the tell tale blonde hair that it was Richard. With great curiosity I wound down the window to see what he wanted. The cold air bit at my skin straight away.

'Hi Melanie, um, are you okay? It's just that I saw you coming out of the gym and you looked a little upset.' He was wearing a green parka with a hood the fur of which framed his handsome face beautifully. He looked like Robert and had the same timbre of voice and even some of his mannerisms were similar, and yet he wasn't Robert if you know what I mean.

'I'm okay thanks . . . ' I wasn't sure how much I could say, but if I did tell him what had just happened, maybe he could tell me the truth about whether or not Robert was seeing Jeannie. 'Well, to tell you the truth, Richard, I've just been warned off Robert.'

He nodded his head and gave a small snort of laughter, 'Jeannie?'

'Yes, to say she was angry was an understatement.'

'Yeah, she thinks she owns Rob because they're going out together. I don't know why he's interested; she's far too young for him.'

I couldn't understand it. Why had Robert asked me to go for a drink if he was going out with Jeannie? I didn't question that but said, 'Oh, how old is she?

'She's nineteen, but seems very naive, and Rob's twenty nine. I told him that there was too much of an age gap. He didn't take any notice, just went ahead with it, but that's typical of Rob.'

'Well it certainly shook me up a bit; I've never come across anything like that before.'

'Ah, take no notice. Rob's his own man; he can go out with you if he wants. It's nothing to do with her.'

I smiled shakily then said quickly, 'Oh I'm not seeing Robert!'

He just shrugged at that and said nothing.

'Can I drop you anywhere?' I asked him.

'No, it's okay thanks.' He looked behind him and indicated with his thumb. 'I've got my car and it's usually okay in the snow.' He looked up at the sky. I followed his gaze and saw a beautiful winter sky, the moon glowing and stars studding the navy blue like sparkling rings in a jewellery box. 'But it's stopped now anyway, and what's left is only slushy.'

I drove home very carefully on the slippery roads and, I had to admit it, feeling a bit down and I hadn't felt like that so much lately. I was enjoying my new job and didn't want it tarnished by Jeannie and her threats. Oh my God, how glad I was now that I'd said no to going for a drink with Robert, a pity really because he's a lovely guy but, and I was totally sure about this, no way worth the hassle. The whole situation still puzzled me though, I hadn't taken Robert for a two timer but there you go, you never really know anybody.

Trees and bushes shrouded in snow kept appearing quite creepily in the car headlights, and the moon, suspended like a burning lamp, seemed to be following me home, trailing me as I drove along the slushy roads. Steve Wright was playing the non-stop oldies, the choices of somebody called Dawn Pearson from the Midlands, when I noticed a couple walking along the path, very close together, both wearing similar outfits of slim fitting jeans and boots topped with a red coat, the woman's pulled in tightly with a belt showing off her tiny waist.

They were gazing at each other, seemingly unaware of the cold and looking very happy to be together. I smiled as I drove past, glad to see a couple looking so good together, when, with a jolt, I realised that they looked very familiar. I slowed down until I could see for definite, for absolute sure, that it was my estranged husband, Sam, holding tightly to Alice Jackson's hand as if it was a life line.

*　*　*

I had a phone call early this morning from the Estate Agents, Wellman & Wyatt, telling me that an offer has been put in on my house and that if I would like details of flats in the local area, they would email them to me. I remembered then that I had asked about flats for myself when I'd gone into the offices originally. What good timing. I would be able to look through details of accommodation this morning as today I was on a late shift. I accepted the offer immediately which was more than generous and asked them to get on with things as quickly as they could.

I went into the kitchen, lovingly fitted and decorated by Sam in the good old days, and flicked the kettle on. I thought about yesterday as I waited for it to boil, and went over the awful happenings with Jeannie in the locker room. I remembered her harsh words and the ugliness of her expression as she told me to 'keep away from Rob.' I then went on to think about what mum had said about Alice Jackson. I remembered her words clearly, that she (Alice) had looked pale and very thin and when I said, 'Well, she's always been thin,' she had said, 'Not like this.'

I'd had thoughts ever since then of Alice being ill, anorexic even, pale and unhappy, and, do you know what? and I hate to admit this, but I'd been glad, glad that Alice was looking miserable and ill. Maybe she was unhappy with Sam and regretted running off with him, maybe the relationship just wasn't working out and she would leave him and Sam would be free again. Free to return to me, because that's what I wanted, I wanted Sam to come back to me. Unfortunately, after seeing them together last night, it was perfectly obvious that they weren't unhappy together as I had hoped but ecstatic actually and very much in love. Sam would definitely not be coming back to me any time soon.

And yet even though I thought I wanted Sam back, I'd enjoyed the attention from Robert Bryce. I found him attractive and really did want to go for a drink with him. Whenever we spoke to each other, I found it difficult to take my eyes away from him and imagined kissing those strawberry lips and running my fingers over his day old stubble and the little hollow in the dimple on his chin. What was wrong with me? I was even more convinced now that I needed to be alone for a while. Once this house was sold and I had a place of my own, I wanted to concentrate on just being me for a while and doing my own thing.

Alice came into my mind, such a pretty and slim Alice holding on so tightly to my husband's hand. Oh, how I wished I was tiny and thin like Alice Jackson and could wear a coat just like hers belted tight at the waist. Ignoring the kettle which came suddenly to a bubbling crescendo, spitting water all over the work top, I dashed into the sitting room and looked in the large oval mirror hanging over the mantelpiece.

I still looked fat with far too much flesh around my waist and my hips, and my face come to that. The weeks had flown by and it still clung on stubbornly like barnacles to a boat. I had to do something about it and that something was right under my nose every day when I came off my shift, swimming, running, yoga, body pump. Determined now, I rushed to the computer and googled swimming costumes and fitness clothing. As each item came up on the screen, I clicked and clicked and clicked again as, avidly, I made my choices.

★ ★ ★

I had to ring Sam to tell him about the offer on the house. He was over the moon, I could tell by the tone of his voice. He did have the common sense to ask about my living accommodation though and I told him that I was going to have a look at a couple of flats on my next day off.

'We're not all as lucky as you,' I thought bitterly, 'To be able to move straight into a house all bought and paid for by your girlfriend.' I had heard on the grapevine (my mum) that Alice Jackson's parents had helped her out financially with the purchase of her own property. How else, at the age of twenty two, could she have afforded such a lovely big house in a very up market part of town.

God knows why Sam was in such a rush to get his share from the house. Maybe Alice was asking for a contribution from him? Who knows! Whatever, Alice's parent's fortune had certainly perked up from when I babysat all those years ago. After all Alice's mum had had to work then, I don't think she did now.

Anyway I was looking forward to

viewing the flats that the estate agent had picked out for me. With any luck I could be in my own place in the New Year and then I really would be ready for a fresh start.

5

I'm sitting with Shelley in the café at 'Hale & Hearty' discussing our work's Christmas party. She's suggested that we have it a few nights before the Naturist's Pool Party and for it to take place in the big conference room upstairs. She's also hoping that I'll arrive earlier to help her decorate the room with a tree and decorations and plenty of holly and mistletoe. 'Huh,' I thought thinking of the mistletoe, 'Shelley might be lucky enough to get a Christmas kiss but I doubt that I would.'

Maybe if I'd accepted the offer of a drink from Robert Bryce I could be looking forward to a smooch under the mistletoe but I'd barely seen him since the day in the café and he'd hardly spoken to me when he'd walked past the reception desk on his way either to the pool, personal training or the running club. I had been on the phone, but even so. Well, I suppose if he was seeing Jeannie, he was better keeping away from me anyway. I didn't want her anger vented on me again that's for sure.

The snow that had looked so beautiful only a week ago had melted away and soaked into the already wet earth, and since then a watery sun had shone from a blue sky speckled with filmy cloud and the air had been mild and green as spring. My morning prayers for a white Christmas were definitely being ignored.

The good news was though that I'd received all my new swimming and running gear and had actually braved the pool and swum around twenty lengths just the other night. I'd made sure that it was late and there were hardly any other swimmers and God, I'd enjoyed it so much. I'd ditched the plain black costume and bought myself some beautiful brightly coloured one pieces and even a tankini.

I was now getting myself psyched up to go for a run. I wanted to go alone first then maybe think about running with other people. Shelley had suggested that I join in with Robert and his group but after seeing them all set off, Jeannie right at the front with Robert, her long legs scissoring elegantly from a very short running skirt, I'd definitely ruled that one out.

'Mel, what do you think then?' asked Shelley, 'Mel . . . God, you're miles away!'

I looked at her. 'Sorry, Shelley, yes of course I'll help with decorating the room for the party. I'd love to.'

'Oh great, thanks Mel. What do you think of the tree in reception then?'

From where I was sitting I could see the tall stylish tree that stood in the entrance way. It was silver and decorated in red spiky tinsel and red baubles and beautiful coloured lights that flashed on and off all overlaid by a sort of white cobwebby effect which looked really good. I took a sip of hot chocolate, savouring the warm creaminess of the drink on my tongue.

'It's a fantastic tree, Shelley. Do you

remember the real trees that we always had when we were kids?'

'Ooh, yes, the smell of pine wafting all the way through the house.'

'Yeah, I'm sure our mums had a competition to see who had the biggest most beautifully decorated tree, don't you?'

Shelley laughed, 'Yes I agree there. The only trouble with a real tree is the pine needles that embed themselves in the carpet for months after Christmas, so hard to get rid of, and then, of course, having to carry it through the house to chuck it out in the garden once Christmas was over.'

'Mm, there's nothing worse than seeing a dead tree in the garden once Christmas is gone . . . 'We smiled at each other, two little girls still in love with the festive season.

Christmas songs were on all the time now and Wizzard's 'I Wish it could be Christmas Every Day' was playing for about the millionth time. I loved all the Christmas songs from the 70's but what had happened to Elvis and Bing Crosby?

Didn't they play them anymore?

'All the clubs have been decorated exactly the same. I got somebody in to do it this year to keep them all stream-lined and branded. It's like the logo, it identifies the 'Hale & Hearty' clubs, just the same as the way we decorate them at Christmas does too. Do you get it?'

'Yes of course I do. The paintwork, carpets, curtains, everything is the iden-tity, the branding of each individual business.'

'Well done, Mel, you're learning. Unfortunately, though, the company only decorates the reception area, that's why we'll have to do our party room.' She shrugged and, leaning closer towards me, said, 'Anyway, I haven't asked you, have you seen Rob lately?'

'No, he asked me to go for a drink but I'm not ready for a man at the moment . . .'

Shelley shook her head sadly, 'Honestly, Mel, even I would be tempted to go for a drink with Rob, married to Scott or not,' She grinned at me then said, 'You're wasting your time mooning over Sam and wanting him back. You've got to get it into your head that he's with Alice Jackson now.'

'Yeah, I know . . . I'm stupid . . . '

'You're not stupid, Mel. You were married to Sam for a long time, you're bound to miss him, but you've got to move on and make your own life. Going for a drink with Rob would have helped maybe?' Then as an afterthought she said, 'I've seen you talking to Rick quite a lot lately.'

'Yeah, I've talked to him quite a lot lately. I told him all about Sam, he listens, you know, doesn't pass comment. He's a nice guy and at least he hasn't tried to come on to me. No, going out for a drink with Rob would complicate things and I don't need that right now. Anyway . . . I meant to say, you didn't tell me Rob had a twin.'

'Yeah, I never thought to tell you at the time . . . even with our mums being twins. Did your mum mention the twin convention next month? . . . Ah, talk of the devil,' whispered Shelley, nudging me hard in the ribs. 'And he will appear.'

'Hey Shelley, Melanie, are you both alright?' Richard stood in front of us wearing the usual pool uniform, looking so much like Robert that my heart made little tripping motions in my chest. 'If you've got a minute Shelley, do you think I could have a word?'

'Yeah, sure, I'll be with you in five, Rick, I just want another quick word with Mel.'

'No probs,' he said as he gave me a little wiggle with his fingers and moved away back to the reception desk where I could see him talking to Jenny.

'How are you getting on with flat hunting?' she asked, turning back to me.

'Yeah, good, I think I'm going to put in an offer on the one on Alexandra Road. It's really nice; it has a little balcony and lovely views. I might see if I can look at it again tomorrow, it's my day off.'

'Brilliant Mel, getting away from the house that you shared with Sam will really do you good.'

I nodded and said, 'Yeah, I'm sure it will, Shelley. Oh, in answer to your question earlier, yeah, mum told me about the twin convention. I might go you know, how about you?'

'Yeah, I'm interested, I just need to know exactly when it is . . . anyway, I'd better go, Rick's waiting for me . . . '

I went back on the reception desk and soon became immersed in phone calls, enquiries, and giving out towels to the long queue of members who bustled into the club wearing trendy sports gear (well mostly) and carrying massive sports bags that kept getting stuck in the entrance turnstile. 'Fairytale of New York' was playing now which made me feel like dancing a jig on the reception desk to the delight (I don't think) of the members.

I suppose around ten or fifteen minutes had passed when all of a sudden Richard came flying out of the back offices, his face red and screwed up in temper like a spoilt child. He shot past the reception desk with no acknowledgement to me whatsoever which was unusual and, with a momentary hesitation at the main doors as if he was thinking of running away, went on through to the pool area.

Squinting I could just about make out the slight figure of Jeannie sitting on a green plastic chair at the side of the pool and Rick now towering over her, his hands on his hips, and his mouth going nineteen to the dozen, obviously, relating everything to her that had happened in the office. I could see no sign of Robert.

'Hmm,' I thought to myself. 'I wonder just what exactly had happened in the office. Well, no doubt Shelley will tell me at some point.' The harsh ringing of the telephone brought me back down to earth and picking up the receiver I said very sweetly, 'Good afternoon, 'Hale & Hearty', Skelmanthorpe, Melanie speaking, how may I help you?'

★　★　★

95

I've come to have a look around the flat on Alexandra Road again and I'm standing outside on the street waiting for the estate agent to arrive. I'm well wrapped up against the cold today wearing jeans and knee high boots and a short black padded jacket with a really warm fur lined hood. My hands are encased in furry mittens which I've also got pushed deep into my pockets because the weather today is freezing.

Gone away, maybe never to return for the next few months, is the gentle mild spring like air that everybody's been getting used to and back with a vengeance is that low white sky bearing down on glittery frosty paths and silvery tipped grass. I stamp my feet on the slippery pavement and hunch my shoulders until my head almost disappears into the neck of my jacket. The estate agent appears, a man in a smart black suit and dark overcoat, who comes rushing headlong along the pavement bearing a silver key.

'Thank you so much,' I say to him as he unlocks the door and lets me into the flat.

'No problem,' he replies. 'I'll hang around out here while you have another look around.'

'I need to take measurements as well,' I say, 'But I'll try not to be too long.'

'Take your time,' he says kindly as he takes up his stance by the front door, ungloved red hands thrust into his coat pocket and neck buried into the collar like a tortoise.

I stand at the sitting room window and peer out into the street which is wide and lined with blossom trees which, although bare of leaves and flowers now, will look fantastic in the spring. I measure the length and width of the room picturing my new settee and chairs grouped together on the pale cream carpet, the sideboard against the far wall and the television in the alcove by the fireplace. I wander into the fairly large kitchen, where once again I admire the trendy red cupboard doors and units complete with black laminate work surfaces.

I measure again in the bedrooms to

make sure my new bed will fit and then peek again into the white and lemon bathroom, shower room and toilet. Smiling to myself in happy anticipation, I wander around again looking into the cupboard space, there's even a surprise old fashioned type of airing cupboard in the hallway and fitted wardrobes in both bedrooms.

I go back into the sitting room and step out of the double doors and on to the balcony. Freezing cold air hits me straight away burning at my face and I hunch my shoulders and cross my arms over my chest. I notice that the balcony area is big enough for a table and a couple of chairs and I also notice the large plant pots and containers full of frost rimed dark earth with, amazingly, tiny green shoots already trying to thrust their way into the light. With any luck the plants and foliage will look fantastic out here in a few months' time.

After giving the key back to the estate agent, I'm walking briskly to the car when I feel my mobile juddering in my bag and picking it up, I see the name Shelley flashing on and off the screen.

'Hi Shelley, are you okay?'

'Yes, having a ten minute break so thought I'd give you a bell, so how's things?'

'Yeah, good, I've just had another look round the flat on Alexandra Road, and also took some measurements . . .'

'Are you going to put in an offer then?'

'Yeah, I'm pretty sure I will . . . it's really nice . . . I think I can make a good home there, even though it'll be a solitary one.'

'Oh God, Mel, don't you realise how much married couples with kids sometimes envy you single girls living in a place of their own?'

'Yeah . . . well . . . ' I'd arrived at the car and was fishing around in my bag for the keys, mobile phone clamped between my neck and my cheek. 'Nobody's ever truly happy with what they've got are they? And, anyway, I'm not single . . . I'm still married . . . to Sam.'

'If you think you're going to be so

lonely, Mel, why don't you get a dog or a cat to share your life with?'

'Yeah,' I replied, giggling a little, 'a dog or a cat would certainly be a lot less trouble than a man!'

'You're right there,' she giggled, 'And yeah, I know . . . you're still married to Sam . . . anyway Mel, I'd better go, there's quite a queue at reception . . . Mya and Bethany are swimming after school tonight if you're able to come down.'

'I'll see, Shelley. I've got a lot to do today; I'm going to start doing a bit of packing . . . when I've picked up some big boxes from the supermarket.'

We were just about to hang up when I remembered Richard storming out of the office, his face as red and tetchy as a child's. 'Oh, wait a minute, Shelley, what was up with Richard yesterday? He stormed out of your office . . . '

'Yeah,' Shelley interrupted and I noticed that she lowered her voice, so much so that I could barely hear her. 'He asked for more time off over Christmas, and not just a couple of days either, all

Christmas and New Year. He wants to go away travelling again apparently. Anyway, I said no, we're going to be short staffed because other people are having time off and, after all, he has just been away for three months.'

'He won't have enough holidays anyway, will he?'

'No, he won't, I reminded him of that and he said he'd take unpaid leave but I still refused it. It's not fair on other people, Mel. Anyway, he was really mad at me and said that he'd get even somehow. You haven't spoken to him since then, have you?'

'No, I haven't. What did he mean by that? Get even? How? He looked fit to explode when he stormed past reception and I noticed him talking to Jeannie in a really uptight way when he got back to the pool area.'

'Yeah, I don't think there's anything to worry about, when he's calmed down I'm sure he'll forget all about it . . . look, I've got to go, Diane's looking pretty stressed out and members are queuing out the door.'

We hung up so I got in the car rubbing my hands together in the furry mittens and turning the heater up high until hot dry air hit me full in the face. I flicked the indicator, pulled out to join the rainbow stream of traffic and headed for home.

★ ★ ★

I drove to the local supermarket first and armed myself with an enormous roll of black bin liners and plenty of cleaning fluids and cloths. They had so many large cardboard boxes to give me that a young man wearing a long white overall, his name 'Josh' clearly displayed, and a baseball cap bearing the tag line, 'Sparta Supermarkets, Just the Best Food Ever', helped me to carry them to the car and fit them all in carefully, making sure that I could still close the boot.

He was so cheerful and helpful and very obviously going that extra mile in his job that I was tempted to tip him like I would if I was in a restaurant or at the hairdresser, but I had to make do with shaking his hand and seeing a smile as bright as sunshine light up his face.

I set to work as soon as I got indoors, only pausing to put on the kettle and make myself a good hot cup of coffee. Sipping my drink, I wandered around the sitting room, picking up ornaments and taking pictures from the walls. I'd made up my mind to be ruthless so some items went in the cardboard boxes and others went straight into a black bin liner.

A pile of newspapers and magazines that had been loitering with intent on the coffee table for months went into the bin liner, silly little souvenir ornaments that Sam and I had amassed over the years like a Mexican man wearing a huge sombrero with the words 'Souvenir from Spain' curling around its base in thick black letters, went into the bin liner, as well as a big fat Buddha, its belly stuck out like a shelf. I could just imagine mum at this very moment, 'Oh my God, Mel, you can't throw away a Buddha, they're lucky!'

'Hmm,' I thought to myself, 'Well, they say that some people's luck goes out the window, well mine's gone into a black bin liner!'

I picked up our framed wedding day picture that I had slapped face down on the mantelpiece on the very night that Sam had left. I gazed at the photo for ages seeing a very young couple, their expressions full of happiness and hope, stepping out of the church doors into a shower of multi coloured confetti and sunshine. The couple held on to each other, laughing and squinting their eyes against the glare of the sun. It was a lovely natural photo. Tears pricked right at the back of my eyes, but before I could give in to such useless grief and with a sudden spurt of anger, threw the offending picture into the black bag.

I carried on all around the house, even packing plates, and bowls, knives and forks, only leaving out a few essential items in the kitchen. In the bedroom, I ransacked the wardrobe, throwing away clothes that I hadn't worn for years, even band tee-shirts of Sam's that he'd left behind, Bon Jovi, Deep Purple, Hawkwind, all mixed together in a coloured swirl and thrown into the bags.

I couldn't be bothered to contact him to ask if he wanted to keep them, it was best to get rid of it all. I very tentatively peered around the door of the spare room as if I expected somebody to be sitting on the spare bed or for a chubby faced child to be standing up in the cot, that we'd never had the courage to dispose of, holding onto the bars with clenched fists, yet I still clutched the roll of black bin liners and was still more than ever fully prepared to throw things away. Momentarily my courage deserted me as I walked into the room, as I gazed around at the nursery wallpaper featuring Humpty Dumpty sitting on a wall and Little Miss Muffet sitting on her Tuffet, even Rapunzel with her long silky hair cascading down the wall of her tower (reminding me with a pang of Alice), which we had so hoped would entertain this mysterious baby that was going to come along. The cot was still full of all sorts of varieties of soft toys; teddy bears, rag dolls and even the famous Bungle from Rainbow that one of the flower aunts had given me years ago.

A baby hadn't come along, despite finding out after tests that there was nothing wrong with either Sam or me, but just the awful blatant fact that a baby didn't seem to want to come and live with us. I remember Sam suggesting that we adopt, but in my naivety and grief had said, 'No, I want a baby that's just mine and yours, Sam, not somebody's cast off.' Oh my God, how stupid I'd been. Regrets, regrets, yet I suppose we all have regrets, but no wonder Sam had left me for another woman. More than ever I was convinced that I was meant to be on my own.

I bagged up all the soft toys, apart from the teddy, Bungle, who I put to one side as a little keepsake, a reminder of what could have been, and made up my mind that I would take the rest of them to a charity shop during the week, along with the dismantled cot and the beautiful lemon crocheted quilt and bumper.

Wearily, with a heavy heart, I carried on with my work, not stopping until late that evening when I sat, exhausted, on the settee, my feet up on Sam's old bedraggled pouffe, sipping at a glass of wine and looking around at my sadly depleted sitting room, realising that I'd put more items in the bin liners than in the cardboard boxes.

6

It's mid-morning on the day of our 'Hale & Hearty' Christmas party and I've made up my mind that I'm going out for a run, and once I've come to a decision, that's it, I've got to do it. I've worked out a route and it's fairly flat, the flattest route I could think of actually, and that still includes one unavoidable hill. Peering from the window I see that once again the weather has changed and the frost rimed paths and white tipped grass of only a few days ago is all gone and the sun is playing a glowing game of kiss chase with the clouds in a clear blue sky.

Taking off fleecy pyjama bottoms and a Mickey Mouse top, I put on black leggings, a pink sports bra and a long pink tee-shirt, making sure that my trainers are tied firmly as I definitely don't want to fall and put myself off running forever. Diane the receptionist fell only the other day and made such a mess of her face that, at the moment, she looks as though she's done ten rounds in a boxing ring!

Walking down the garden path, I put my Sony MP3 player over my head, push in the ear buds and let Donna Summer singing 'The Last Dance' entice me into actually moving, so there I go setting off at a slow walk, building into a steady jog, my trainers making resounding slapping sounds as my feet pound along the pavement. My music progresses into T Rex singing '20th Century Boy,' then Barry White making my heart soar with the yearning 'Loves Theme,' and then to get me really running, Godsmack and 'Generation Day.'

By the time I get back, I'm so out of breath, that rather than collapse on the ground like a big embarrassed ungainly heap, I bend at the waist, my head and arms hanging light and loose and swaying like apples on a tree. What a fantastic feeling. I can breathe now, slowly in tiny short gasps.

I've been told it's important to stretch after running so I reach my arms above my head and clutch each elbow and then bend at the waist from one side to the other, and then lean over my straight leg, first one side then the other. By the time I get back indoors, I'm on a terrific high. 'I've been running,' I think to myself, 'Oh my God, I've been running!'

Then I realised that I hadn't looked through the bin as I'd meant to while I was outside. Sleepless in bed last night, moving around and becoming wrapped in the sheets like somebody demented, I'd had thoughts about all sorts of things. The situation with Sam, the feelings that I was denying for Robert, even Richard had blown through my mind, and I'd had regrets then about throwing away mine and Sam's wedding picture and wanted to get it back, so that's why I was in the garden, my head deep inside the green bin and my, no doubt about it, enormous backside in tight black leggings high in the air, my fingers fumbling on the slippery black bags, when I hear a voice behind me, 'Hey, Melanie, what are you up to?'

I take my head out of the bin and look behind me to see Robert Bryce standing at the garden gate with several expectant looking faces surrounding him including that of Jeannie. They're all dressed in running gear and all look flushed and happy, apart from Jeannie who's her usual glowering self. 'Wow,' I thought, 'If they've run from the gym to here, they must have covered almost four miles already, and they haven't finished yet!'

Robert looked good wearing tight black leggings which I had to say didn't leave much to the imagination, and a green tee-shirt, his shiny black hair tied back in the usual pony tail and his lips looking extra red and strawberry like because of the exertions of running I suppose. My heart was beating so hard that I could barely speak and my legs felt quite soft and jelly like, whether it was because of Robert's presence or the fact that I'd just been running for the first time I really wasn't sure.

'Oh hi Robert . . . Um, yes, just looking for something that I threw out by mistake.' I grinned at him, 'And of course hunting for scraps for my dinner . . . '

Everybody but Robert looked at me blankly. He laughed uproariously then said, 'Hey, have you been running Melanie?'

'How did you know that?' I asked suspiciously.

'Well . . . you're wearing running gear. A dead giveaway don't you think?'

'Oh yes . . . ' I laughed, 'I'm only a beginner,' I assured him, 'I've only just done a couple of miles . . . three at the most.'

'That's brilliant for a beginner and on your own,' he said, 'Though you're welcome to come with us you know.' Jeannie butted in, staring hard at me all the time, 'Maybe Melanie prefers going alone.'

'Well,' I replied, 'I was thinking of getting a bit of practice first, you know, getting up a bit of speed, then I may join you . . . '

'Hey,' he replied. 'Sounds like a good

idea. Anyway, we'd better get going, we'll seize up if we don't. See you tonight at the party, Melanie.'

I waved as they all ran off, their heads bobbing up and down above the garden hedge, Jeannie loitering behind and giving me a thoroughly dirty look as she ran past. I put my head back into the green bin, frantically searching for the picture, which I found eventually after putting my hand into the remains of an Indian takeaway curry that I'd had the night before. 'Ugh,' I thought, as carrying the picture indoors, I went upstairs for a shower.

* * *

'Hale & Hearty' is busy when I arrive for my shift that afternoon and I'm pleased to see that Mya and Bethany have come for a swim again and are playing in the pool. It will give me a chance to see them as I'm aware that I probably don't spend enough time in their company. Maybe when I settle in my new flat, I'll ask

Shelley if they could stay for a weekend. It would give Shelley and Scott a chance to get away together and I'm sure they'd both like the idea of that.

I'm pleased to see that Robert is on pool duty with another one of the lifeguards, a very nice young girl called Laura whose mum and dad are members and also part of the Naturist group that put in the request for the Christmas party here after hearing all about the controversial group in Blackpool.

I shake my head at the thought of how Robert and the other lifeguards will feel at having to supervise a party of naked people, especially if Laura is one of the lifeguards on duty as well. Thinking about it, though, surely Laura wouldn't be able to work that evening if her parents were going to be in the pool. I'd have to ask Shelley about that.

I can see Robert quite clearly from where I'm sitting and I follow him with my eyes as he talks to Laura and as he moves around the pool watching the kids playing and hunkering down on the pool side to talk to somebody when they ask him a question. I like the way the light reflects off his dark hair, and I like the way he narrows his eyes when he's speaking to somebody, as though he's really properly listening to what they're saying.

I think about the time that we talked in the steam room and how much I enjoyed it and how much I'd like to speak to him again, just the two of us, alone together, and for a split heart rending second I really regret not having gone for a drink with him. Then all of a sudden I come to my senses and remember Jeannie and the fact that he asked me to go for a drink when all the time he was going out with her. I take a deep breath and think to myself, 'Get over it Melanie Morris, just get over it.'

I get the chance to see Mya and Bethany when they finish in the pool. It's getting near tea time and they come through to the café with Scott to have something to eat. I've arranged with Shelley that I take my break at the same time so I can sit with them. The café is busy as it always is at this time of day with children who have had swimming lessons or children like Mya and Bethany who have just come to play.

Many of the kids are admiring the Christmas tree as well as trying to unwrap the brightly wrapped empty boxes that they assume are presents. There's a mixture of deafening chatter and loud Christmas music which has turned the café from a tranquil oasis into bedlam.

'Hi Mya, Hi Bethany,' I say as I go over to their table with a cup of steaming hot coffee.

Hi Melanie,' they chorus and both jump up and fling their arms around my neck. Their damp hair smells slightly of chlorine and their cheeks against mine are soft and downy as rose petals.

'Hey girls,' Scott reprimands them, 'Once you've finishing kissing Mel, sit down and get on with your meal.' They both scuttle back to their seats and carry on eating their very tasty looking chicken burger and chips. Bethany has tomato sauce smeared all around her mouth. Discretely I wipe my face with my finger tips just in case some of it has been transferred to me.

'How's it going, Mel?' asks Scott, 'Enjoying the job?' He took a sip from his own coffee, then put it down and added more sugar whilst making a face and patting his stomach, 'I shouldn't really . . .'

'There's nothing on you Scott,' I exclaim, shaking my head. 'Oh, I love the job,' I tell him, 'I'm really happy working here.'

'Well, that's good news. Shelley told me that you're buying a flat on Alexandra Road?'

'Yeah, I should be able to move in in the New Year.'

'Great, Alexandra Road is in a really cool area. I'm glad things are looking up for you Mel.'

'I've got to say, Scott, that you and Shelley have helped me the most with giving me this job . . . I was in danger of becoming a big fat recluse.'

Scott smiled and patted me gently on the shoulder; 'It's more than a pleasure, Mel, really . . . and anyway you're a good worker,' He broke off here and shook his head whilst making a face at me, 'That's a terrible thing to say . . . you were never fat!'

'Mel?' asked Bethany in her sweet little voice. 'Can we come and visit you when you move to your flat?' I noticed that the girls were wearing matching outfits of jeans and boots and Disney tee-shirts, the only difference being that Mya's featured Minnie Mouse and Bethany's Donald Duck.

'Yes, of course you can . . . hey, I love your outfits.'

Mya speared a chip and tried to put it in her mouth lengthways whilst at the same time saying, 'I love this song, Melly . . . ' Just above the busy hubbub of noise I could hear Wizzard singing, 'I Wish it could be Christmas Every Day (again).'

I went on to tell them that perhaps they might like to come and stay with me for a whole weekend when I'd got settled in. I turned to Scott, 'Maybe you and Shelley might like a weekend away together?'

The wide grin on Scott's face told me all I needed to know.

* * *

I get a chance to speak to Shelley about Laura being a lifeguard at the Naturist pool party just after we've finished setting up our party room that evening.

'Oh,' she replied. 'I didn't realise that Laura's mum and dad are naturists. Oh well, I just won't have her on as a lifeguard that evening.'

'How does it work, Shelley, are the lifeguards clothed?'

'Melanie! Of course they are, the lifeguard has to be recognisable from the naturists! I've done my research as this is new to us, even after being in the business for so many years. A pool in Southampton hires out to Naturists and they have a fully clothed lifeguard.'

'Oh,' I laughed, 'I had visions of them having to be naked as well . . . '

'Ha,' replied Shelley, nudging me hard in the ribs. 'You mean you had visions of Rob being naked at the pool side!'

I was just about to explain that I was more concerned about Laura being naked in front of her parents and that this had nothing to do with Robert, when Shelley handed me a rather large glass of red wine and said, 'That's for helping me set up the room. It looks fantastic.'

We both gazed around whilst sipping our wine, and, yes, I had to agree, the party room looked great, cleverly transformed from a conference room into a fairy dell. The round tables looked good covered in snowy white cloths complete with red napkins, silver cutlery and, of course, crackers, at each place setting; and a beautiful centre piece of a thick white candle entwined with holly taking pride of place on each table.

Colourful balloons and large bunches of mistletoe hung from the ceiling and the Christmas tree, so enormous it's taken over a whole corner, is decorated with a sort of white cobwebby, misty stuff through which twinkling lights glow secretly, subdued, red, blue, green, and yellow. I felt a sudden tightening in my throat and my eyes pricked with tears as I thought back to last year, not realising in any way that it would be my last Christmas with Sam. Nostalgia for all the previous years overwhelmed me and to steady my erratically beating heart I took a big slug of red wine.

Thankfully Shelley didn't seem to notice and said gleefully, 'I'm so excited, while we're eating I've got a fantastic band to play, they're called Ruby Lounge, which I thought was a brilliant name, and they're an acoustic quartet that are going to play Christmas songs for us.'

'Wow, they sound great.'

'Yeah, then when we've eaten, it's disco time . . .' Shelley raised her arms in the air and began to run around the room like an excited child. Leaning against the side of the curved bar, the front of which is padded with a really 70's like red dimpled material; I could do nothing but laugh which I have to say is better than crying which I was so tempted to do earlier.

'Come on,' I say to Shelley, sniffing, and dabbing at my eyes with the pads of my fingers, 'Let's go and get changed. I've got a fantastic new dress that I just can't wait to change into.'

* * *

I wake up and it's still dark so I reach across the bedside cabinet and fumble for my phone. Sudden panic grips me as I can't feel it and think it's been lost the evening before, that it's been taken whilst I was in a drunken haze, but no, thank God, it's there and, squinting, I can just about make out the time, 'Five o'clock in the morning,' I think in despair, laying on my back staring at the gloomy ceiling, 'My God, I didn't get home until after two!'

Getting out of bed I pad to the bathroom and take a long long drink of water, leaning over the sink, my neck out-stretched like a giraffe at a water hole. I also force a couple of Paracetemol down my strangely swollen throat which, hopefully. will ward off any morning hangover. I lay there then my head sunk into soft pillows, my eyes closed, images of the night before running through my mind. I smile as I re-live Robert's kisses, the taste of his juicy strawberry lips on mine, the feel of his hands in my hair and his voice murmuring in my ear, 'Oh, Melanie, I really like you . . . '

I recall the smell of his skin and the softness too as I ran my hand around his chin and felt the tiny dark hairs on his chest. His words kept running through my mind, 'Oh, Melanie, I really like you . . . '

Then with a start I sit up, my hands to my mouth, and wonder how I could have been kissing Robert so passionately when Jeannie was there at the Christmas do. Where was she at that time? 'Jeannie is his girlfriend,' I think to myself, 'What-ever were we thinking?'

123

I'd been talking to a group of people sitting at our table and vaguely remember saying to them that I needed to go to the ladies and wouldn't be long. That must have been when I bumped into Robert. I don't think I went back to the table. I put my fingertips to my head willing myself to remember but nothing else will come, no more images, no more little scenes played out in my mind, no more pictures of me going back to the table or of me kissing Robert.

'I need more sleep,' I thought drowsily, 'Everything will become clearer in the morning.' Then I was on the edge, I was falling as if from a high building and when I closed my eyes I was spinning into a deep black dreamless pit of sleep, spiralling out of control, when something that Robert said to me last night came crashing back into my mind and I sat up in bed, my heart pounding and my hands clammy with sweat.

'There's lots of things you don't know about Rick, Melanie,' he had whispered in my ear. He was very close, his cheek against mine, I could smell the faint odour of whiskey on his breath. 'He wasn't really away travelling, that was the general story though; that's what he told everybody . . . except me.' He paused at this point and spoke so low that I had to strain towards him to hear what he was saying, 'Rick was incarcerated at her Majesty's Pleasure,' and when I looked at him questioningly, 'Melanie . . . he was in prison.'

7

My ringing phone awoke me the next morning. I thought it was in my dream at first and very languidly I turned over and huddled back under the duvet. I felt very soft and very sleepy and soon began to drift away from the bed and the bedroom as my eyelids drooped and I began to fade into sleep, but the ringing went on and on and on until I thought I would scream. Unfortunately, I was back in the real world and in the real world the phone was ringing. Blearily I reached for it, noting the time, ten past nine, before I put it to my ear and said, 'Hello?'

'Hi, Mel, it's Sam, how ya doin?'

'Sam? What do you want?'

'Oh thanks Mel, I do what I think is the right thing and give you a call . . . and you don't sound at all pleased to hear from me.' He gave a rather loud chuckle which reverberated through me nastily like a drill at the dentist.

'You woke me Sam . . . you know I don't like being woken by the phone... and it is quite early.'

'Actually it's quarter past nine,' he said, 'I've been up for ages . . . '

'Well, good for you, now what do you want?' I said this slowly and patiently as if speaking to a half wit. Surprisingly I felt fine with no banging headache and absolutely no nausea. After a few red wines sickness usually gripped me all day as if I'd been sailing the high seas the night before.

'I just wanted to know if you're going to buy that flat you were telling me about.'

'Oh,' I said sarcastically (I know they say that sarcasm is the lowest form of wit but I really can't help myself at the moment), 'So you need to know this vital piece of information at a quarter past nine on a Saturday morning?'

'Look Mel, me and Alice are worried about you that's all . . . '

'Worried about me?' I asked through clenched teeth.

'Yeah, you know, I've made you sell

the house, move to some little flat, I'm living in this beautiful big house with Alice . . . Alice has memories of being looked after by you as a child . . . nostalgia I suppose . . . '

'Forget about nostalgia, Sam, I don't let myself be bothered with things like that,' I said nastily, 'Regarding selling the house, you're doing me a favour; now get off my back . . . '

'What?'

'You heard me . . . get off my back and at the same time . . . get off the phone . . . '

'Mel?'

I hung up before I exploded and was distributed all around the bedroom in a million pieces. Getting out of bed, I shrugged into my dressing gown and went downstairs to put the kettle on. I needed caffeine and I needed it now. 'How stupid I was,' I thought to myself, 'To think that I wanted him back. Alice could have him with absolutely no charge! Worried about me indeed, maybe they should have worried about me a long time ago, when they were in the midst of their passionate love affair.'

I sat in the kitchen at my little square table, a cup of steaming hot coffee in front of me. I usually sat in the sitting room in the mornings but it wasn't a good place to be at the moment; I couldn't face the boxes piled up behind the settee and the black bin liners bulging with rubbish. I wanted to get out of this house now and settle into my new flat. I really couldn't wait.

My phone beeped, a message from Sam, 'I'm sorry, Mel, didn't mean any harm, will be in touch over Xmas S x'. I slammed the phone down and, restlessly, stood up and peered from the kitchen window, at the garden which at this time of year looked brown and quite boring really except for the vibrant splashes of pink and red from the still flowering geraniums and the fuchsia, their blooms like dangly earrings. I smiled at that and thought how brilliant it was that through rain, sun, and even snow, the geraniums and fuchsia still flourished.

My thoughts went back to last night and what Robert had told me about Richard. He'd been in prison, oh my God, it hadn't occurred to me at the time to ask what he'd done. He could be a mass murderer for all I knew. The whole evening played out in front of me now and I sat back down at the table, took a sip of coffee whilst letting the pungent aroma fill my head, and let it all run through my mind like a film that I'd once seen.

After going to the ladies I'd stepped outside for some fresh air, I'd drunk a lot of red wine and wanted a clear head, and there was Robert lounging casually against the wall, his legs crossed at the ankles, smoking a cigarette, the tiny red tip floating mystically in the air like a fire-fly. Brightly coloured lights flashed at the windows and disco music pounded from the party room, Sister Sledge singing, 'I want your love, I need your love . . . '

'Hmm,' I said, nodding towards his cigarette, 'Not a very good advertisement for a runner or a personal trainer, eh?' I gave a shake of my head, hoping that he'd notice my new trendy hair do as I'd finally plucked up the courage to get my hair re-styled.

He gave a dry laugh as he stubbed the cigarette out and flicked it into the nearby bin. Our eyes met and locked and moving towards me, he reached for my hand, pulling me into his arms and letting his beautiful strawberry lips claim mine. I recalled the look on his face when I'd tried to pull away from his embrace and his reply when I'd said, 'What are we doing, Rob? You're going out with Jeannie, if she should see us . . . '

I couldn't believe it earlier in the evening when I'd first set eyes on Robert, he looked so smart in his black suit and white shirt, and I had to say he looked even better now that he'd loosened his tie and I could see a tiny bit of his bare chest. It occurred to me that I'd only ever seen him wearing his pool or gym clothes and seeing him dressed up like this was very intoxicating and made fending off his embraces even more difficult, but the thought of Jeannie catching us in a clinch was enough to make me panic and scuttle away like a rabbit caught in headlights.

He pulled away slightly so he could see my face and said with a tiny smile on his face as if he thought I was joking, 'Going out with Jeannie? What are you talking about? I'm not going out with Jeannie.'

I stood there my bare arms wrapped around my body; cold now in my lovely sexy black dress which surprisingly was only a size 12. It seemed that all the running and swimming was paying off. Robert grabbed me by the shoulders and said, 'Who told you that, Melanie?'

Flustered I replied, 'Well . . . Richard did, he said that Jeannie thought she owned you because you were going out together and that he'd told you that the age difference was wrong, yet you took no notice.'

'But that's a lie,' he said, 'A total lie.'

'Jeannie warned me off you, you know, one evening in the locker room. She was quite nasty with me, scared me to death.'

'She warned you off me? Why didn't you tell me before? God Melanie, it's not true, I am not going out with her. Yeah, okay, she suggested we get together at one time but I said no . . . good God, Melanie, I'm ten years older than her.'

'Huh,' I said, 'What difference does that make, Sam is ten years older than Alice.'

'Well, that's not for me,' he replied.

'But why would Richard tell me that then? He's your brother, your twin, why would he tell lies about you?'

'I've no idea .... but, well, there are things you don't know about him, Melanie . . . '

'Well,' I replied, 'I do know that he's a nice guy . . . I've told him the situation with my ex, and do you know, he's never tried anything on with me, always been the perfect gentleman . . . ' I stopped here because I was shivering now and could barely speak I was so cold.

'Here,' said Rob. He took off his jacket and placed it carefully around my shoulders. Gratefully I hunched into its warmth, and said, 'And at least he's never tried to pull my towel off me in the pool area!'

Just as he had at the time, he looked shamefaced and said, 'Yeah, okay, but I have apologised for that, Melanie. But what you don't understand about all this is that Richard's gay . . . that's why you've never had to fend him off, that's why he's never come on to you. It's nothing to do with your female sensibilities.'

'Oh, I see, yes, now why didn't I see it?' I shook my head at my own stupidity.

'I've gotta say,' and here he grinned at me.'He doesn't come across as a gay guy does he?'

I shook my head and that's when he told me about Richard having been in prison and now I remembered why and it definitely wasn't for mass murder.

'He's been in for petty thieving, house breaking, you know, and taking cars . . . and arson . . . ' Robert told me.

'Wow, I take it that Shelley and Scott don't know about this?'

'No, of course not, I doubt whether he would have got the job.' He looked at me long and hard, I felt myself blushing, my face burning, 'You're not going to tell them are you?'

'I don't know . . . this is big Robert, really big, they should be aware of it.' I hugged his jacket even tighter around myself. It smelt so good, of Robert and a mixture of cigarettes, whiskey, and some sort of spicy aftershave, 'I'm freezing, I need to go inside . . .'

Robert took hold of my arm, his lovely brown eyes anxious, and said pleadingly, 'You can't tell them, he'll lose his job, please Melanie . . . this will break him . . .'

Coming back to the present, I'm still sitting in the kitchen, a cup of cold coffee on the table, a ring of scum coating the surface. Putting my head in my hands I wish to God that he'd never told me about Richard, this is such a big secret to keep from Shelley and Scott and I'm not sure if I can do it.

135

I've barely seen Robert since the evening of the party, only the occasional glimpse of him around the pool side and off running, Jeannie bobbing along at his side; I haven't sought him out and spoken to him because I just don't know what to say.

I don't know why he hasn't come looking for me; after all, we did spend a lot of time wrapped in each other's arms and kissing but, like me, he probably doesn't know what to say or it may be that he's worried that I've spilled the beans to Shelley and Scott and is waiting for himself and Richard to be called into the office. Well, I haven't said anything at all to Shelley or to Scott, for exactly the same reason as I haven't said anything to Robert; I really don't know what to say or what to do at the moment.

Richard came to talk whilst I was eating breakfast one morning in the cafe, munching my way through a toasted currant tea cake and enjoying a creamy hot chocolate. That was such a difficult meeting and I really hope that Richard didn't notice my discomfort, but I felt unnatural and wooden like one of those puppets that move around jerkily on strings. Every time I looked at him I imagined him sitting in a cell wearing a pair of trousers and a top decorated with little white arrows (or do convicts only wear those outfits in films?).

Then I had unwelcome visions of him stealing a car from outside in the car park (oh please not mine), or breaking into our lockers and taking personal possessions or even, God help us, setting fire to this building. I really wished that I could go back to the day before the Christmas party and not know what I know now. Sometimes I resent Robert for telling me all about Richard and I wish I didn't feel that way. Unwelcome thoughts flashed through my mind, was Robert lying about Richard? If Richard could lie about Robert, what's to stop it happening the other way around?

Shelley has given me this afternoon off

because she's asked me to work tomorrow evening on reception at the Naturist Pool Party, and to help her to prepare the buffet for after the swim, so I'm taking the time to do some Christmas shopping. Only presents that is, because I've had an invitation to spend Christmas day with mum and dad at their house, food and drink provided. I don't think they can bear the thought of me spending Christmas alone.

Mum's also asked the flower aunts and uncles and Shelley, Scott, Mya and Bethany for lunch so, hopefully, it will be a good day. It's no good stocking my place up with Christmas goodies and inviting people around, because, half bare as it is, it's a really miserable place to be at the moment.

Wandering around the brightly lit and tinsel decorated shops, Christmas music pumping out everywhere I go, even Bing singing 'White Christmas' I'm pleased to add, I can honestly say that I feel a bit out of it, a bit like I'm trapped behind a thick glass wall where I can see everything but, however far I reach out, I just can't get there, I can't get to the heart of it. I suppose that's how you'd feel if you snorted cocaine or took some other sort of drug, a bit weird and spaced out.

I trail disconsolately around in the Skelly indoor shopping centre, going into Boots to look at smellies and make up, I queue, a mountain of cards in my hand, in the discount shop, then search for long tunic like jumpers for mum in Peacocks (long enough to cover my big backside I remember her saying), my last stop being the wine shop called rather embarrassedly I always thought, 'Ye Old Wineo,' where I buy a few bottles of red and white as my contribution to the big day, oh and I also pick up a massive iced Christmas cake from Booths just because I like the look of it! So there!

I'm walking back through the indoor shopping centre, laden down with bags, my hands aching with the lack of blood flow, past the 3 mobile phone shop, past WH Smiths and the discount book shop, when I see Richard, his long blonde hair tied back in his usual pony tail, wearing black jeans and a really nice red 'Weird Fish' sweatshirt. I see him go into the book shop so, without asking myself why, I follow him in and, keeping a discreet distance, follow him around the shop like a private detective. Slade and 'Merry Christmas Everybody' is playing really loud.

Everything seems to catch his eye for he touches the paperback books and the children's dot to dot and colouring books, great heavy tomes on steam trains and murderers, the chunky five year diaries and the slim one year diaries. Indeed, he spends quite a bit of time turning one of these over and over in his hands, a nice shiny black one, whilst looking around rather furtively I thought from the tail of his eyes, before slipping it nonchalantly into the pocket of his jeans. 'Wham bam thank you mam,' as David Bowie used to say, 'No messing!'

I really don't want to see any more so, rushing away, carrier bags banging heavily against my shins and my hands curled around the handles probably never to be straightened out again, I eventually get to the car park, start up my car and make my way home.

★ ★ ★

The group of Naturists arrive promptly at seven thirty for the party to begin at eight. I don't suppose they need a lot of time to prepare, after all, they only have to go to the changing rooms, undress and, ta da, they're ready. How easy it is for them.

Robert came by the reception desk earlier and gave me a cheery wave so things seem to be looking up. He obviously thinks that he can trust me and that nothing is going to be said by me about Richard and that everything will carry on as it is. I'm not sure what I think about that, all I know is that I need to talk to him again at some point.

The group stream through the turnstile, their heavy sports bags getting stuck at regular intervals, although I have to ask myself, 'What do they have inside their bags?' They don't need a costume, the towels are courtesy of the leisure centre, I suppose they'll just carry shower gel and shampoo and conditioner, why then are the bags so heavy?' They pick up the 'Hale & Hearty' specially logo embroidered towels with jovial smiles and thank you's. I notice that Robert is at the poolside, kneeling down with a little glass capsule taking samples of the water. I assume that he's making sure that the pool water is properly balanced for the Naturist Christmas party to go ahead.

Shelley and I watch discreetly as all the Naturists who, to my delight, are wearing festive Santa hats, swarm into the pool area, some heading straight for a swim, while others opt to relax in the steam room or the sauna and the more adventurous take a hearty jump into the freezing cold plunge pool, being careful, of course, not to lose their hats in the process. Robert is the perfect lifeguard, acting totally naturally and without any embarrassment, as if everybody in the pool is wearing a swimming costume. Festive music is playing through the speakers and I have to say the whole party has a really good vibe.

Shelley goes to check the buffet that we laid out earlier in the cafe when I sense rather than hear a kafuffle coming from the pool area and see Robert hurrying towards the steam room. I put on some blue paper slip-on's, grab a couple of towels just in case and rush to the pool to see what's going on. Shelley and I almost collide as she comes running from the cafe, a look of panic on her face. 'Don't worry,' I assure her, 'I'll go and see what the problem is.'

Robert, an unclothed lady on each arm, comes staggering from the steam room, his face red and sweating. Quickly I drape the towels around both ladies and escort them to the changing rooms. Everything is taken care of so promptly and efficiently that I doubt many people noticed anything happening at all but I can hear Robert assuring everybody that there's nothing to worry about and please to carry on enjoying the Christmas party.

'Look,' said one of the ladies, they're sitting side by side on a bench by the lockers now and she pulls her towel up to show her thighs. At first I thought they were simply mottled red with the heat from the steam room, but on closer inspection I see they're covered in rather nasty red lumps as if she'd been bitten about a million times by a very angry mosquito.

8

'Peace, perfect peace,' I think to myself as I stand at the reception desk in 'Hale & Hearty', my first day back after having time off for the Christmas holidays. As much as I love the Christmas songs, it's so good to have a break from them. There's music playing right now but it's definitely not festive and its muted which is just right at the moment. Christmas and New Year has flown by as quickly as a flock of frightened birds and for all that time I've had mixed feelings of missing Sam and constantly thinking back to what we were doing last year, and wondering how things are with Robert after what happened at the Naturist Pool Party.

It was the main topic of conversation on Christmas day as we all sat around the festive table; paper hats perched on our heads and discarded silver and red shiny crackers, and the jokes and toys, strewn about. Shelley and Sam were distraught after finding out that somebody had put over the regular amount of chlorine in the pool which had caused the awful itchy skin condition for the two ladies who had caused such a rumpus in the steam room.

I remember one of the Flower Aunts saying, 'Why would they put in a formal complaint, they only had a few itchy spots, what's the problem?'

Shelley shook her head, 'That's not the point, aunt, nobody should get anything bad from a swimming pool, well, a verucca or athletes foot, perhaps, they're far more common complaints, although still horrible, but not an itchy skin condition, and one or two had difficulty breathing for a few days after the party. It's worrying for the reputation of the leisure centre.' Everybody nodded and agreed that they could see what Shelley meant.

'We're not going in the pool again,' said Mya stoutly, 'Are we Bethy?' Bethany shook her head whilst trawling once again through her Christmas pudding, a sticky mass of currants and cream, to see if she could find any more silver coins.

'Don't be daft, you two,' said Shelley, 'The pool is sorted now and it won't happen again.'

Both girls pouted and asked if they could please leave the table and play with their Christmas toys. Shelley nodded and they scampered off into the sitting room giggling and counting on their opened palms how much money they'd managed to find in their pudding.

'I gave both ladies an antihistamine tablet straight away,' I told Shelley, 'And it really seemed to ease the itching and the swelling. I think that they must have sensitive skin as nobody else came forward with similar skin complaints.'

'That was quick thinking,' said Scott, 'Thank God for Mel, she saved the day.'

I grinned and then before I realised what I was saying I was telling everyone that I'd seen Robert kneeling at the side of the pool with a glass capsule and had assumed that he was testing the water in preparation for the pool party.

'What time was that?' I remembered Scott asking me.

'It was when the Naturists started arriving,' I told him, 'Around seven thirty.'

He nodded his head, a serious look on his face. 'Oh my God,' I said, 'Surely you don't think Robert would do such a thing?'

'He was the person in charge of the pool that evening,' said Scott, 'It was his responsibility. I'm going to have a word with him and find out just what he was doing to the water at seven thirty that evening.'

'I wish I'd never told you now,' I blurted out.

'You had to tell us, Mel,' said Shelley.

I felt guilty then at the things that I hadn't told them. Not about Robert of course, but about Richard. All the things that I knew about Richard and hadn't told Shelley and Scott seemed to be hanging over my head like an axe at a beheading. If I didn't come clean, if I didn't tell Shelley and Scott everything, what would happen? Would the axe fall? Aah! I could almost feel my head rolling off my shoulders and landing with a giant splash right in the middle of 'Hale & Hearty's' beautiful swimming pool. I knew that if I did tell Shelley and Scott about Richard, I would lose Robert's trust and I really didn't want that to happen.

It turned out that the two ladies were the mum and grandma of Laura, the nice young girl who I'd often seen working as a lifeguard with Robert. I remembered then about her parents being Naturists and part of the group hiring the pool because I'd spoken to Shelley about Laura not being put on the rota for lifeguard duty that evening.

Both ladies were very upset at the time and it remained to be seen whether or not they would lodge a formal complaint against 'Hale & Hearty'. I think that Shelley and Scott are keeping their fingers crossed that, as Laura works for them, and has done for some time, that the two ladies will be pretty lenient in this case. Four people in all had been affected from that evening, the two ladies and another couple who had suffered from breathing difficulties for a short time afterwards.

'It could have been a lot worse,' I remember mum saying, 'A lot worse . . .'

* * *

'January, sick and tired, you've been hanging on me . . . ' I hum the Pilot song to myself as I peer from the window on this cold January morning, so icy cold that the paths and the roofs of houses are rimed with frost and yet, amazingly, in the garden shy white-faced snowdrops push their unwilling, torturous way through the frozen earth. The sky is grey and sunken as if the clouds are sleeping.

Whatever the weather, I can't be miserable today because at long last I'm moving. I'm finally going to leave this house where I've been so miserable for the past six months and move into my new smart flat, so that I can start my new smart life as a new smart girl! I carry on humming the Pilot song, 'You make me sad with your eyes, you're telling me lies . . . ' 'Hmm, yes, somebody certainly was telling lies. Richard was lying to me about Robert, but was Robert lying to me about Richard?

'Please God,' I find myself thinking as I stand by the window hunched into my new cosy green dressing gown, a Christmas present from mum, my hands clasped as if in prayer, 'If anybody has got to be lying to me, please don't let it be Robert.'

Sam had been in touch as he said he would over the Christmas time and, very surprisingly, he'd called round to mum and dads on Christmas day with a card and a present which I still couldn't make sense of. What on earth was he doing coming to see me on Christmas Day? Didn't he have anything better to do? Especially since the last time we'd spoken on the phone, I'd been extremely short with him.

I went into the hall where he was standing on the door step hidden behind a large bouquet of flowers. I looked around the flowers at him and said, 'Hi, oh my God, Sam, I haven't got you a present,' and when he just shrugged, asked, 'Where's Alice?'

'At her mum's,' he replied, more or less pushing the bouquet into my arms. 'She always goes on Christmas Day; her mum's lonely without her dad.' His breath came from his mouth in little frosty puffs like speech balloons.

'Why aren't you with her?' I asked him.

'What's this, twenty questions?' he joked, 'Mastermind?' He laughed really loud reminding me of what an unusual sense of humour he'd always had. I shook my head and smiled as I sniffed the scent of jasmine that seeped from the flowers. I could feel the woody stems digging into my fingers.

'I'm giving them a bit of time together and I wanted to make sure that you're okay.' He rubbed his hands together to keep them warm.

I shook my head and said, 'Don't you ever think of wearing gloves?' and when he didn't reply added, 'Well, don't worry, I'm okay.'

'Have you met anybody yet then, Mel?'

'There's somebody I like,' I told him, thinking of Robert, 'But it's complicated at the moment.'

He looked down at his smart black shoes, then back up at me again and said, 'It wasn't because I didn't love you, you know, Mel . . . '

'Oh go on with you,' I joked and nudged him in the ribs, 'Go on home . . . go to Alice . . . ' It was weird, but saying Alice's name didn't hurt me anymore but even so, tears threatened, I could feel them prickling right at the back of my eyes, even in my throat, and I really didn't want to cry. Not in front of Sam.

He put out his hand and squeezed my shoulder. I recognised the expression on his face, his upset face, as I always used to call it. He walked down the garden path pausing at the gate, 'Merry Christmas, Mel.'

'Thank you for the flowers . . . and the card,' I said to him. 'Oh, Sam, I'm sorry I was a bit off with you last time we spoke on the phone . . .'

He gave a little smile and raised his hand in a wave, and then turned around and walked away, his shoulders hunched to ward off the cold. I stood in the doorway for a few minutes, inhaling the beautiful wintry scent of the flowers.

'Life is so strange,' I thought, 'I still cared about Sam, still loved him even, but, I just didn't want to be with him as a couple anymore and I suppose soon, the word 'divorce' would have to be mentioned.' The thought scared me a little, made me catch my breath, but also made me realise how much I'd come to be just me over the past six months and what a great feeling that was.

★ ★ ★

'Why did you tell Shelley and Scott that I was at the pool side testing the water at

154

seven thirty on the evening of the Naturist pool party?'

I looked up disorientated from reading the paper and eating a really tasty
cheese and pickle baguette, to see Robert standing in front of me, his hands on
his hips and a truly hurt expression on
his face. He wore his usual pool uniform
and even though it was January, winter
time, he looked as tanned and as fit as
ever.

It's lunch time now and I'm sitting in
the cafe. I'd finished my shift but had
decided to have something to eat before
going home to my fantastic new flat.
It was so good for me to actually want
to go home now instead of dreading it.
'Why don't you sit down, Robert,' I said,
'Then we can talk about this properly.'

'Why should I want to sit with you,
Melanie? What are you trying to do?
Cause trouble for me? Get me sacked
or what? I really didn't take you for that
sort of person.'

'You're absolutely right, Robert,' I
said trying to speak calmly even though

I was panicking inside, 'I'm not that sort of person. Sit down . . . please . . .'

Reluctantly he sat down opposite me, right on the edge of his seat as though he didn't plan on staying long. 'Well?'

'I told Shelley and Scott that I saw you because I did see you by the pool at around seven thirty on the evening of the pool party. I didn't tell them that to make trouble; I just assumed that you were testing the water to make sure it was safe for the party to take place. I didn't for one minute think you were tampering with it in any way. I know you're not that kind of guy.'

'Well for your information, I didn't test the water at that time. It was earlier than that, around seven. After that I went to the locker room to get my cigarettes and at seven thirty I was outside, at the back of the building, where we were on the night of the Christmas party, do you remember? and I was smoking. I've told Shelley and Scott all of this.'

Robert mentioning us being outside at the Christmas party made my stomach

156

lurch and my heart thud painfully in my chest. Would he ever take me in his arms again and kiss me with those lovely strawberry lips? At the moment, the odds on that happening seemed very remote.

'You're absolutely sure then that it was seven thirty that you were outside?'

'Positive. I had a phone call at that time . . . I've showed them my phone which records the call and the time I took it, so there's no doubt whatsoever.'

'Well, I must be hallucinating then . . . but whoever it was looked exactly like you . . . ' My voice trailed away as I realised that there was somebody who did look very much like Robert.

Our eyes locked and cupping my hands over my mouth, I said, 'Oh my God, Robert, it must have been Richard. I assumed it was you because you were the lifeguard for the party, and I didn't know that Richard was anywhere around.'

'You didn't notice the blonde hair?'

'No,' I shook my head, 'He had a baseball cap on though and if you pull it right down, it can hide your hair pretty well.'

'Oh God,' groaned Robert, 'Surely he wouldn't stoop so low? He wasn't working that night, there was no reason for him to be anywhere near the pool.'

'Huh,' I said, 'He did say that he'd get even with Shelley didn't he?'

'Get even? What? You've lost me, Melanie.' He raised his hands in the air, palms up.

'Oh, didn't you know?' I told him what had happened when he'd asked Shelley for all of the Christmas period off because he wanted to go travelling but that Shelley had refused because he'd already used up his annual holiday. I also told him that Richard had said he'd take unpaid leave but Shelley still said no. Robert groaned again and massaged his forehead with his fingertips.

'I've got to tell them, Robert, you do see that don't you?'

'No, Mel, please; leave it with me. Considering the trouble that he's already in, and having been in prison as well, it's really best that I take the blame for this.'

'No, I can't let you do that,' I said

decisively.

'Yes, you can,' His eyes flashed with annoyance, 'I'm warning you, Mel, leave it, okay?'

I leaned closer to him, so close that I could smell the spicy aftershave that he wore and whispered, 'I've kept my mouth closed, Robert, when I should have opened it a long time ago, but this . . . this is really too much . . . and as well as that,' I glanced around to make sure that nobody was listening, 'I saw him steal a diary from the discount book shop in Skelly . . .'

He put his head in his hands and said, 'Oh no, I despair of him, I really do,' and then he glared at me and hissed, 'Leave it, Melanie, please . . . don't make things any more difficult for him than they already are . . .'

9

Moving day has been and gone and I'm finally in my flat surrounded by my lovely new furniture and also ornaments and pictures that I really didn't want to part with. What freedom there is for me to be able to choose where to put everything, what to put in each room, which pictures to put in the sitting room or the bedroom, will the spider plant look good in the bathroom and the rubber plant in the hallway? There's a lot of decisions to be made and all to be made by me, and only me!

I'd only been a little upset at leaving the old house and as I'd walked around the rooms checking that I hadn't left anything, my boots echoing hollowly on the thin carpets, I felt sad more than anything else. I thought back to the day that Sam and I had moved in and how excited we'd been as we arranged our new settee and chairs, our book case and coffee table and our telly, and that on the first night we'd huddled on our brand new rug in front of the sputtering flames of an old gas fire eating a Chinese takeaway before curling on the settee and cuddling and kissing until our lips were numb.

Standing out on the balcony I gaze at the view, at the impressive tree lined street, the wet pavements shining now in a weak sunlight, and the hills and valleys beyond, a misty green and purple above the glistening roof tops. I'm pretty sure that in the spring and summer I will spend many happy hours sitting out here enjoying the outlook and sipping at a glass of wine, but for now the irresistible urge to go for a run suddenly gripped me and, closing and locking the balcony doors, I hurried into the bedroom to get changed.

I set off at a slow trot feeling good in my black leggings and blue running skirt topped with a long sleeved black top zipped to the neck and the all important black gloves, there's nothing worse than freezing cold hands at the beginning of a run. Cold air spiked my face like little pin pricks and I shivered reminding myself that very soon I would warm up and probably be too hot. I plugged in my ear buds and as music flooded through my head, I increased my pace and, being careful on the slick paths, ran slightly faster.

A couple of miles into the run, my body warm now and loose, I saw a familiar figure just ahead of me, running steadily; the fluorescent strips on his top and leggings shining, dark pony tail flying in the air like a banner. Turning off my music I increased my pace and running along beside him, I smiled and said, 'Robert?'

He glanced at me from the tail of his eye, 'Hey, Melanie, how are you?'

'Yeah, good,' I replied, thinking how often I'd dreamed of this, of running along the streets beside a good looking guy, and, the best thing of all, being able to speak as I ran. 'Yeah,' I thought, 'Some dreams do come true.'

'How come you're on your own?' I

asked him, 'Where's Jeannie and the rest of the running club?'

'I'm not at work,' he replied, 'This is a private run so to speak, and Jeannie's gone anyway.'

'Gone?'

'Yeah, left 'Hale & Hearty' a couple of days ago; had to move away with her mum and stepdad, she wasn't very happy about it.' Robert indicated to the left and said, 'Do you fancy going through the woods?'

'Oh yeah, great,' I replied, and then said, 'Wow, do you miss working with her?'

He shook his head as we sprinted over the road and into the dark woods, through a creepy tunnel of skeleton trees, their branches interlocked overhead. Our trainers made a satisfying crunching sound on the uneven surface of tree roots and stones.

Robert told me to be careful as it was easy to trip in here in the gloom, so we slowed down a little and concentrated, our eyes, after a while, adjusting to the dimness. The river like a thin silver needle meandered nearby and I breathed in the scent of wet moss, mud, fish and chilly water.

'No, Melanie, I don't miss her particularly, she could be very difficult but I think a lot of that was because she's been having problems with her stepdad, they've never got on apparently. Reading between the lines, that's why she didn't want to move with them.'

'Where have they gone to?'

'I'm not sure,' he frowned as he thought, 'Down south somewhere, Essex I think.'

We ran for a while in silence, only the sound of our harsh breathing and the slap of our trainers on the hard ground, accompanying us. Piles of brightly coloured leaves shuffled around our ankles. I wondered if he would mention anything about Richard or Shelley and Scott and whether or not I'd said anything to them about the Naturist's pool party or, indeed, whether I was going to say anything at all, or if he would once again tell me that he'd never gone out with Jeannie and had never wanted to.

Surprisingly he didn't talk about any of that, but just asked if I was okay and I found myself telling him about Sam's unexpected visit on Christmas day and the bouquet of flowers and the card as well as the unlikely truce that we'd come to over Alice and our splitting up. I also told him all about having been Alice's babysitter when I was younger and how much I'd cared for her and that it had been a real kick in the teeth when I found out that she and Sam had been having an affair.

'She's ten years younger than me as well,' I pointed out.

'Hmm, not a good situation,' he replied, 'You did tell me a while ago that he'd left you for another woman. Do you feel better about it now?'

'Slightly,' I said, 'But coming to terms with it I suppose is the only answer I can give at the moment. I need time on my own though,' I carried on, giving him a sideways look, 'Just to enjoy my own space in my own home.'

We stopped for a few seconds on the river bank and had a quick stretch of our arms and legs, then ran onto the towpath and back along the busy main road to the tranquillity of Alexandra Road and my flat.

'So this is your new home,' he said, standing with his hands on his hips, breathing heavily and gazing up at the tall building.

'Yes, the second floor,' I told him, 'I've got a balcony, look.' I pointed up where we could clearly see a small red painted table and chairs and the plant pots where I knew that even now small green shoots were pushing their way through moist dank earth and into the open air. By spring time the balcony would be awash with brightly coloured flowers and foliage.

'It's been a great run, Melanie. Shall we do it again soon?'

'Yeah, that would be good.'

'Okay, I'll see you at work; we'll

arrange another time and place. I've got plenty of different routes we can run.' He smiled at me, his lovely brown eyes seeking mine. Then, unexpectedly, he put out a finger and traced my bottom lip, an action so erotic that a shiver ran down my spine and I almost succumbed to the feeling and threw myself into his arms. My lip felt swollen and warm from his touch and I had to use all my self control not to pull him towards me and demand a kiss from those strawberry lips.

'You're very pretty, Melanie,' he said tenderly, which made me blush so hard that I thought I might combust in a ball of fire and only my trainers be found in a smouldering heap on the pavement. 'If you're ever ready for me, then please just say so.'

Wordlessly, I nodded, and then stood, shivering, on the top step of the building, watching him as he slowly jogged away, his fluorescent clothing shining in the murky afternoon, as the sun had disappeared behind dense clouds and our little corner of the world had begun to turn dark.

* * *

I'd been thinking about it all night and had come to the decision that before I said anything to Shelley and Scott or about the situation with Richard, I would first of all speak to Richard himself. He couldn't possibly want Robert to take the blame for the Naturist's pool party fiasco and when I told him that I knew about him being in prison and that I'd seen him at the pool side on the party evening tampering with the water, I felt confident enough that I could persuade Richard to give himself up to Shelley and Scott himself.

I went into work the following day floundering now in my too big uniform like a clown in baggy trousers and knowing that I would have to call in at the office to ask Shelley for a smaller size. How brilliant I felt about that. Looking in the mirror this morning, I smiled at the difference in my reflection from only a few months ago, or even a few weeks ago. No more chubby cheeks, but actual sculpted cheekbones making my eyes look bigger than ever. Also I'd had my dark brown hair cut into a shorter fringe which looked good with my new svelte look.

I closed my eyes and smiled secretly to myself, remembering how shocked and happy I'd been when Robert had told me that I was pretty; nobody had told me that before, not even Sam. I'd felt like a super model that day, eat your heart out Kate Moss and you Naomi Campbell! I'd lost weight around my tummy area too which meant that I could wear my work shirt tucked into the trousers instead of hanging loose for the sole purpose of hiding my enormous backside; a big bum? 'No way,' I say breezily, 'A thing of the past!'

I called into the office to ask Shelley if I could have smaller uniform. She accompanied me to the store room where we'd gone on my very first day and, rummaging through the boxes, gave me a pair of size 12 trousers and a top with S for small proudly displayed on the packet. 'Well done, Mel,' Shelley said enthusiastically, 'You've done so well, I told you you'd get into exercise didn't I?'

'Yeah,' I replied, 'You did and you were right, thank you.'

She smiled at me as she handed me the new uniform, 'Go and put these on then. Will you be okay on your own? I've got to go; I've a meeting soon with the two ladies from the Naturist Pool Party.' She checked her watch. 'They should be here in around ten minutes.

'Oh my God, I'd almost forgotten about them. Will they give you the verdict today?'

'Hopefully, they'll tell me whether or not they're going to make a formal complaint, and yet we still haven't found out who actually did tamper with the pool water. We've questioned Robert and Richard but haven't been able to get any further forward. Obviously, one of them is lying and one of them is telling the truth.'

'Ah,' I thought, 'This is my chance to find Richard today and do my own questioning, then he might give himself up.'

'Surely, Shelley, you don't think Robert's lying?'

She looked at me, her eyes narrowed suspiciously, 'Why should I believe Robert over Richard, Mel? Do you know something that I don't know?'

'No,' I said hurriedly, yet under Shelley's scrutiny I felt really guilty. Hurriedly I said, indicating the packets in my hand, 'I really must put this new uniform on. I'm due on reception very soon.'

'Okay,' she patted me on the shoulder and gave me a quick hug, 'You look really good Mel, well done for coping so well with this Sam and Alice business.' Of course, her kind words made me feel even more upset and, as usual, tears pricked at my eyes. Kindness always does that to me.

'Oh, before I forget,' said Shelley, 'Do you still want to go to that twin convention in Blackpool?'

'Yes,' I replied, 'When is it? Did you

171

find out?'

'Next weekend, Scott said he'd drive us and our mums, he's due in Blackpool the same day at 'Hale & Hearty.' There's a meeting regarding the refurbishment of the building and the pool. Scott said he'll go to that if I want to go to the twin thing.'

'What about the Flower Aunts?'

Shelley shrugged, 'I suppose they'll make their own way, I'll check with mum though.'

'Yes, so will I,' I say, as, Shelley, glancing once more at her watch; rushed off to her meeting. I go into the loos to change into the new uniform which fits perfectly, the zip on the trousers gliding over my almost flat stomach and the shirt buttoning up easily over my much smaller chest, and whilst in there check my appearance in the full length mirror.

'Yes,' I think, nodding my head, 'I really am beginning to resemble the stick running woman on the 'Hale & Hearty' logo which suits me a lot better than the chubby cherub image that I had before.

Going into the locker room with my bag I see Richard straight away and expect him to turn around and acknowledge me because surely he must have heard my rustling carrier bag and heavy footsteps in my clumpy work shoes. I'm just about to say hello when I realise that he's not standing at his locker, but Diane's, the receptionist. He's standing sideways to me so that I can clearly see that he's holding what looks like a part of a wire coat hanger in his hand.

Curious, I keep still and, barely breathing, watch, as he pushes a piece of the coat hanger into the lock and twists, nothing happens at first so he tries again, then again and, unbelievably, at the third attempt, the locker opens.

Getting increasingly angry, I carry on watching him as he fumbles around inside, his greedy hands raking through Diane's personal belongings, pulling out a black leather purse from which he takes two or three notes and shoves them in his pocket. He wires the door closed and is just about to try another locker when, heart pounding and palms sweating, I eventually find my voice and say, 'Richard, what are you doing?'

He spins around so fast I'm afraid he might topple over. 'Hey, Melanie, I didn't hear you come in.'

'Obviously not,' I say icily, 'I think you should put that money back in Diane's purse, Richard . . . '

'What are you talking about?' he said nastily, 'What money?'

'The money you've just put in your pocket,' I tell him.

'Keep your nose out, Melanie,' he rasps, 'For God's sake, you're always interfering in other people's business.'

'No, I'm not Richard,' I said, 'I'm just trying to help you.' I feel so angry with him that everything comes pouring out, everything that I know about him, all the pent up worry and anger that I've been holding inside for so many weeks and he just stands there taking it, swallowing nervously, his hands balled into fists. I told him that I knew it was him that sabotaged the pool for the Naturist party and that he was trying to pin the blame on Robert. 'Why Richard?' I asked him, 'Why?'

He got angry then and flung the bent up wire coat hanger hard against the wall and then, surprisingly, he put his hands to his face, cupping his eyes and his nose, trailing his palms tightly against his skin and said tearfully, 'It was Shelley I was mad with, not Robert . . . '

I said to him, 'Oh, Richard, Robert's under suspicion for spiking the pool. You must tell Shelley and Scott everything, otherwise I'll have to tell them and I really don't want to.'

He took a step towards me, his dark eyes glittering menacingly and for a split second I was afraid, but then quite suddenly his face dissolved like an effervescent tablet in water and he burst into tears. 'Okay, you tell them, Melanie . . . tell Shelley and Scott everything, tell them what I've done, I don't care.'

'No,' I replied, 'It has to come from you, Richard,' Tentatively I reach out and pat his shoulder, 'For Robert's sake,

Richard, it has to come from you . . . '
He came close to me and pressed himself into my arms and, with his cheek against mine, sobbed until I thought his heart would break.

* * *

'Oh my God, what a day,' I thought, as I sat in my lovely new flat that evening sipping a glass of wine. I laid my head on the back of the settee, tears still streaming down my cheeks as I re-lived the episode with Richard in the locker room. The whole thing seemed unreal now, how I'd witnessed him stealing from Diane's purse and how seeing that had made all my pent up anger and frustration of the past weeks pour out of my mouth and into Richard's guilty waiting ears.

He deserved it, I was well aware of that, but it didn't make me feel any less easy about things. In a way I felt sorry for Richard, something had driven him to steal and to set fire to buildings. Instead of locking him away in prison, why wasn't there somebody for him to talk to, somebody who could get to the bottom of his anguish; somebody who could help him to stop. I remember Shelley saying to me after Richard's confession, 'We've been so lucky that he hasn't tried to burn down 'Hale & Hearty.' What a tragedy that would have been.'

Sniffing heavily, I leave my cosy nest on the settee and pad into the kitchen to get the wine bottle. I glance in my new big oval mirror that hangs in pride of place over the mantelpiece and recoil in horror at my reflection. Mascara in long snail like tracks coats my cheeks. Good God; I look like that glam rocker from the seventies, the singer that my mum likes . . . Alice Cooper. My eyelids and nose are red and sore as if I have a really heavy cold. I don't think that Robert would find me very pretty now. I pour myself another glass of wine and take a huge gulp, savouring the fruity taste on my tongue as I peer from the window at the street below.

It's dark now and rainy and the trees

that line the road sway back and forth like dancers in the wind. Rain drops slide slowly down the window pane and the pavements look slick and shiny under the orange glow of the street lights. A man walks past hunched into the collar of his overcoat, his wet trousers flattened to his legs, and a hat shielding his face. Cars, rain falling like silver rods in their headlights, drive slowly by, their wipers drawing an arc on the windscreen. I shiver and pull my lovely thick red curtains across the window to block out the inky night.

I remember holding on to Richard as we walked to Shelley's office, passing the two girls and the guy still mesmerised by their computer screens. When we got there I remembered that Shelley was in a meeting with the two ladies from the Naturist Group so we waited outside, sitting on a couple of wooden chairs, mostly in silence, Richard his head bowed and his arms folded across his chest.

Shelley and the two ladies eventually came out chattering to each other, then shaking hands, big smiles on their faces. 'Hmm,' I thought, 'Hopefully good news there then.' Shelley grinned at me and gave me a discreet thumbs up sign, then looked at us and frowned, so I told her that Richard would like to have a word with her. She said that I would need to be present as well so all three of us trooped into the office.

Richard cried again as he admitted all the things that he had done, that, yes, he had put too much chlorine in the pool, and, yes, he hoped that it would all backfire on Shelley because she wouldn't let him have time off over Christmas and, yes, he had been in prison for stealing and for arson. He said that he hadn't thought it through properly when planning to spike the pool, not realising the trouble it would cause for Robert because he hadn't wanted to get his brother into trouble.

He proudly admitted to being the person that had set the fire in a factory in Preston, and served my time, he pointed out, and had also been involved in the fires that were set in a national park in Sicily. I was really confused now because a prison sentence for arson would surely be for longer than a few months. Shelley took the words right out of my mouth by asking, 'When did you serve your sentence for arson?'

'Oh, a couple of years ago now, I got three years but was out in two and a half. When I said I was travelling recently, I was in for theft.'

'Why Richard?' asked Shelley, 'Why do you do these things?'

He'd stopped crying by this time and sat there like a little boy, his hands between his thighs, his shoulders hunched, an open look on his handsome face, 'I steal because . . . well . . . because I can and I set fires because I love watching things burn. It gives me a good feeling.'

'You know don't you, Richard,' said Shelley gently, 'That I'm going to have to tell the police?'

He nodded and said, 'Robert's gonna be really mad. He didn't want anyone to know about any of this . . . but then,' and here he turned and looked straight at me, his face contorted, 'He had to go and tell you . . . I don't know why he did that.'

Before I could try to stick up for myself and Robert, there was a tap on the door and Robert (talk of the devil) peered into the room. He looked really surprised to see us and I found out later that he'd only come to Shelley's office to talk to her about the new rota and that he'd had no idea that Richard and I were there or why we were there come to that.

'Come in, Rob,' said Shelley, she nodded towards the chair next to Richard and said, 'Sit down.'

'Thank you,' he murmured, and then looked around perplexed, 'What's going on?'

Richard turned towards him and said quite nastily I thought, 'I told you not to get involved with her didn't I? She's only gone and made me tell Shelley everything . . . '

'No,' I said, 'It wasn't like that.' I stared hard at Robert, trying to make him look at me, but his lovely brown eyes slid away as if on a patch of ice. I think he'd already made up his mind that I was the bad one, the trouble maker, the whistle blower. 'I found Richard breaking into a locker in the locker room and taking money from Diane's purse, I realised then that Shelley had to be told everything, but it was Richard that told her, not me.'

'Yeah, but only because you made me,' he said.

'That's not true, Richard.'

Shelley butted in here and said to Richard, 'As far as I'm aware, Richard, you told me of your own accord. Melanie hasn't said a word against you or Robert since you both came into this office.'

She then turned to Robert, 'You'll be pleased to know that Richard has confessed to sabotaging the pool on the night of the Naturist party so you won't be questioned again Robert, and I've got to say, I'm sorry you had to go through that. I will say though, that Richard did it to get at me, he didn't intend to cause trouble for you.' Then she leant forward, her hands clasped in front of her and addressed Robert again, 'I'm going to have to tell the police about Richard. You do realise that don't you?'

He nodded his head, his face troubled, then said, 'Yes, I understand, so as Richard will obviously be going, there's no alternative for me; I'm handing in my notice as of now.'

10

It's the day of the twin convention and I'm rummaging around in my wardrobe looking for something to wear. All the things that I used to wear are too big for me and I'm having problems trying to put even a simple outfit together. I'm so used to just wearing my uniform every day or my running gear or my swimming costume that I'd quite forgotten I had any other clothes.

Eventually I find a pair of jeans that are too big around the waist but cling bravely to my hips, holding on for dear life like somebody hanging from a mountain top. I've teamed them with a green fleecy top with cosy hood and finger holes that I think I'm going to need because it looks cold out today. When I'd peered from the window this morning, the sky arched overhead as grey and leaden as pewter, and the paths were sheets of ice masquerading as a beautiful glittering black.

A group of boys slipped and slid like skaters as they tried to play football on the black ice, and a little girl wearing a bright red coat and woolly hat, fell down hard and grizzled monotonously until her mum rushed over to pick her up. Idly I stared at her and wondered what it would be like to have a little girl like that.

Although I'm trying not to be, I feel a bit down, a bit depressed. I haven't felt this way since Sam left and the reason for it now is the whole situation with Richard and Robert. Robert's gone for the time being. He hasn't left 'Hale & Hearty' (Shelley persuaded him not to) but been transferred to the Preston branch for a while, to keep away from me I suspect, and of course from the gossip, but Richard has gone, sacked, for the theft of the money from Diane's purse and for sabotaging the pool on the night of the Naturist pool party.

Before I knew of the transfer to Preston, I texted Robert one sad lonely evening asking him to let me know if he'd like to go for another run. He replied eventually saying, no, it's probably better that we don't. He told me that Richard was more than ever his responsibility now and he, Robert, was going to the doctor with him to try to sort out his issues. Even so, he went on to say, he'd been transferred to Preston 'Hale & Hearty' now and thought that he would be there for quite some time.

I remember staring helplessly at my phone, tears in my eyes, willing the message to be different, knowing now that nothing further would happen between me and Robert and that he would never hold me in his arms again or kiss me with those lovely strawberry lips.

I still stood by my decision that Shelley and Scott had to know about Richard, surely Robert could understand that. Surely he could understand that I'd been in a very vulnerable position and that I couldn't carry on lying to my cousin. And yet I knew that he didn't understand and that he blamed me for everything. The thing that I'd been afraid of had happened; I'd lost Robert's trust.

To cheer us up though, welcome good news came from the meeting that Shelley had had with the two Naturist ladies. They'd decided that as a group they would not be putting in a formal complaint after what happened at the pool party. In fact, they'd asked if they could have a regular weekly Naturist session as it was such a great place and had the best outlook from a pool than anywhere else in the area. She also said that the friendliness and helpfulness of the staff was second to none and had helped them through the incident at the pool party and that they'd have no hesitation in recommending the leisure centre to all their friends.

Shelley assured them that the person who had mistakenly put too much chlorine in the water was gone now and it wouldn't happen again. In fact, she had told them, they could have the first session totally free as a way of trying to make up to them for the anxiety they'd suffered. I was so glad, for Shelley and Scott's sake, that everything had turned out okay in that respect. It was so important, after all their hard work over the years that the reputation of 'Hale & Hearty' should remain intact.

Rousing myself, I put on my new coat, beautiful scarlet wool just like Little Red Riding Hood and, on hearing the beep of a car horn, rushed downstairs and out onto the street where Shelley and Scott and my mum and Aunty Iris, sitting in the back seat like twin dolls, were waiting for me. I smiled as I raised my hand to them.

★ ★ ★

I'm cross eyed and seeing double and no, I'm not under the influence of alcohol. Everywhere I look there's two of everyone from tiny babies and toddlers, through to octogenarians, although some of the longest living twins have been well over a hundred years old. I look at mum and Aunty Iris and the other flower aunts all sitting together around a big round table talking animatedly, all of them seeming to know what the others are going to say next and all talking at the same time. Twinship is amazing. This, of course, makes me think of Robert and Richard and the fact that they might have been here now if things had turned out differently. Robert had said ages ago that he would be interested in coming to the convention.

Gazing from the floor to ceiling windows of this lovely room, I think what a fantastic hotel this is, The Grandoise right on the seafront in Blackpool. From here I can see a full view of the beach and the churning sea and although it's a dull day, the sun hidden somewhere behind greasy looking clouds, I'd still like to be out there running along the beach, inhaling the briny smell of the ocean and tasting tiny particles of salt on my lips. In a perfect world Robert would be with me, telling me that I was pretty as he jogged along by my side.

I sat down at the table next to Shelley. 'Are you okay, Mel?' she asked.

I nodded and then said, 'Well, I suppose I feel a bit down, Robert refuses to see me and won't run with me any-more, although I've only just found out that he's transferred to Preston 'Hale & Hearty.'

'Hopefully he'll see sense at some point,' Shelley replied, 'He must realise what an awful situation you were in, he shouldn't really have told you that Rich-ard had been in prison. It was too big a secret to keep from me and Scott.' She then added, 'I got him a transfer to Pres-ton because I didn't want him to leave our employment. He's too good a worker to lose and I'm sure he'll come back to Skelly at some point.'

'Yes, I think he expected me to keep quiet for his and Richard's sake, but you and Scott are family . . . I wanted to tell you ages ago but I was really torn. I was tempted to tell you at Christmas when I saw Richard steal the diary, but when he stole from Diane's purse, well, that really made me realise that you had to know.'

'Yes I understand the dilemma you were in. Just think, though, Mel, I bet there are loads of employed people out there with sordid pasts that their employer's know nothing about.'

I nodded and said, 'Yes, no doubt there is.'

There was a short silence between us, then I said, 'It's so strange, Shelley, not so long ago I was refusing to see Robert because I still wanted a chance with Sam and now I don't want Sam and want to see Robert but he doesn't want to see me. How mad is that?'

'As I've always said, Mel, you were with Sam for years; it took a long time for you to come to terms with him leaving you, especially as he went off with another woman! Robert should have been more patient and far more compassionate.'

'How long do you think he'll stay in Preston?'

Shelley shrugged. 'I'm not sure, I think he'll be back within around six months. By then he might want to come back. In the meantime, we've got another guy starting next week on a temporary contract, Tony Harris I think he's called.'

'Six months?' I exclaimed, 'That's a long time,' and then giving Shelley a sideways glance said, 'Don't bother introducing me to this Tony Harris, I'm definitely not interested.'

Shelley laughed just as mum and Aunty Iris called over to us asking what we were talking about. 'Man trouble,' mouthed Shelley.

'Hmm, what else,' said all the flower aunts who had been nosily listening in.

'My Mel shouldn't be having any man trouble,' said mum rather loudly I thought, 'At least she's got rid of that Sam.'

'Mum!' I said, as a man with a microphone appeared by my side. He was wearing smart black trousers and a white open necked shirt, the sleeves rolled up to show dark hairy arms and his chin sporting the longest most bushy beard I'd ever seen. Maybe he was here as a twin of one of the members of ZZ Top. 'Hello, there,' he said. 'I've got to say that you and your twin, (indicating Shelley) are the least look-a-like I've ever seen, you're obviously fraternal?'

I hid a grin and said, 'Oh no, we're not twins, she's my cousin, our mums and aunts are twins, though.' I indicated to the rest of the table. Shelley seemed to be in a state of hysterics, obviously at the thought of us two being twins, as the man turned his attention to the flower aunts and spent a long time chatting and taking pictures, assuring them that he would run a big feature on them in the local newspaper.

'Actually,' I said, 'talking of twins, you're definitely a dead ringer for one of the members of ZZ Top!'

'Hey, it's only the beard,' he said jokingly, before returning to his microphone and informing everyone that before the convention started proper, refreshments would be served.

The smell of hot strong coffee wafted through the air as a couple of young girls wearing black skirts and white blouses wheeled in a trolley trembling with cups and saucers, silver coffee pots and spoons and tea urns, milk jugs and sugar bowls, and then another trolley appeared crammed with creamy doughnuts, éclairs and sugary topped apple turnovers, the cloying scent of which hovered in the atmosphere like a sweet dust.

I'd just taken a sip of my coffee when my eye was caught by two men milling around in the crowd of twins at the door. One was dark haired and one was blonde and both had long pony tails and very dark eyes. The man with the microphone went straight over to talk to them and over the hubbub of conversation I could just about hear him commenting on the difference in hair colour, although, hey, you can tell you're twins.

As Robert looked around the room he saw me and our eyes locked. He leaned towards Richard and whispered something and then began to walk across the room towards me, elbowing his way through small knots of people as he moved nearer. As I watched him, time seemed to stand still and my heart hammered in my chest so hard that I could barely catch my breath. I felt Shelley stiffen next to me as she caught sight of him and I heard Robert say, 'Hi Melanie.'

I knew that I was being watched by mum and all the flower aunts and could feel my face burning a slow red like a hot poker. 'Hi Robert,' I squeaked like a little mouse. 'Oh God help me,' I thought, 'Why can't I act cool, calm and collected and not have a frenzied attack of the nerves?'

'Hey,' he smiled, 'You're looking well . . . doing much running?'

'Yeah . . . a lot of running,' Oh good, my normal voice had come back. 'Actually, I'm pretty well hooked on it.'

He nodded to Shelley and she nodded back, leant towards him and whispered, 'How come Richard's here?'

'He's out on bail at the moment and he's on medication from the doctor which is helping him a lot. Hey,' he glanced around, 'It's a great turn out for the convention. It's surprising how many sets of twins there are, even a lot that look less alike than me and Richard.'

I nodded in agreement then said, indicating the table full of ladies, their mouths gaping wide open, wondering who Robert was and wondering when I was going to tell them, 'This is my mum and my aunts. Do you remember that I told you about the flower aunts?'

Robert nodded, 'Well, here they are.' I introduced him and he walked around the table shaking hands and marvelling at how much they all looked alike. He didn't mention that he had a twin who was here as well. When he came back, he put his hand on my chair and hunkered down next to me. 'You told me about the flower aunts that time in the steam room, didn't you?'

I nodded and because I couldn't look at him for fear of crying, I kept my head down pretending to be inspecting my nails before saying, 'How's Preston 'Hale & Hearty?' I didn't hear his reply because the man with the microphone was now up on the stage telling everybody that the convention was open and did anybody have any good twin tales to tell.

Everything was pandemonium then and we didn't have time to talk any more. Robert tapped me on the arm and indicated with his head towards Richard. I caught sight of them later in the afternoon balancing coffee cups and plates like a couple of jugglers. I was too upset to go and speak to them. I didn't think I could stand looking at him again, at his dark eyes and strawberry lips and the lovely dimples that appeared when he smiled, if I couldn't have him. I don't think they stayed until the end of the convention because I didn't see them when we left to go home, and Robert didn't come over to say goodbye.

★ ★ ★

A couple of months have flown by and we're in April now. Everywhere there are daffodils, great yellow and cream seas of daffodils, bowing their heads like bashful ladies in the chilly breeze and all along Alexandra road, the trees, dancing and swaying, drip pink blossom on the grass verges and paths. Tiny pastel crocuses raise shy purple and white heads above the damp earth and in a silky blue sky fluffy clouds play kiss chase with the sun.

I spend a lot of time during the now lighter evenings sitting on the balcony, a glass of wine in my hand, nurturing the green shoots in the pots which have grown now into clematis, honeysuckle and vines. As much as I enjoy that, I'm truly hooked on exercise, especially running and swimming; and I've taken up yoga and pilates and use weights in a class called Body Pump. I've dropped another dress size and once again had to go to Shelley to ask for a size 10 uniform including an XS (extra small) blouse.

'You're a shadow of your former self,' moaned my dad, whenever he saw me.

'What's happened to your chest?' asked mum as she scrutinised my rapidly disappearing bust line.

Shelley, Scott, Mya and Bethany told me that I looked great and to keep up the good work. 'You look really pretty,

Melly,' Bethany whispered in my ear one day, as she sat on my lap in Shelley's immaculate kitchen. I had to smile because she was only the second person in the whole wide world that had ever told me that I was pretty, the first one, of course, being Robert.

'How did you get on with Tony on Saturday night then?' asked Shelley. Even though I'd said many times that I wouldn't go on a date with Tony Harris, the guy who had taken Robert's place, I'd eventually given in and gone for a drink.

'It was okay,' I told her, 'He's a nice enough bloke.'

Shelley narrowed her eyes, giving the impression that she knew what I was thinking, 'No spark?'

She knew exactly what I was thinking. I gave a small smile and said sadly, 'No spark.'

'I don't know why you don't text Robert just to see how he is. After all he is a friend . . .'

'Oh no,' I said, 'I couldn't, he has to

make the first move.'

'Oh for God's sake Mel, text him and ask if he'd like to come to Skelly and go for a run with you . . .'

I shook my head, my face, no doubt, mutinous. 'What would you do, Shelley? Say, for example, Scott went off and made it clear that he didn't want to see you again, would you go chasing after him?'

'That wouldn't happen, Scott wouldn't leave us.'

'Daddy wouldn't leave us, would he?' asked Mya with a tremor in her voice. Bethany just sat there, cuddling her big brown teddy bear, her blue eyes wide.

'No, of course, he wouldn't,' I told the two girls, 'It's just an example for your mum to answer, and then she might stop going on at me.' I took a sip of coffee from my mug.

Shelley grinned looking as cheeky as a naughty school girl and said, 'I think I'd chase him.'

'Chase Daddy, Chase Daddy,' intoned Mya and Bethany and began running around the kitchen like whirligigs, shouting and screaming, their pretty night dresses swirling in a white stream around their ankles, Bethany dragging Teddy by one arm.

Shelley and I went off into paroxysms of giggles when suddenly my phone starting ringing, making us all jump. Still laughing, I flicked it to take the call, put it to my ear and said, 'Hello?'

'Oh hi Sam, how's things with you?'

I strained to listen to what he was saying, but none of it seemed to make sense, and what was really strange was that he sounded as if he was crying, deep throbbing sobs wrenched from his heart. He began to gabble on and on and I really couldn't make head or tail of any of it. I tried to sound caring but impatience was getting the better of me so I asked him quite abruptly really, 'Sam, what are you saying? I can't hear you properly.'

I was very aware that Shelley, Mya and Bethany were staring at me, their mouths open, hanging on to my every word. I listened intently and then, my hand cupping my mouth of its own accord, said, 'Oh my God, Sam, I don't know what to say . . .'

'Oh my God,' I thought, 'It can't be true. Somebody up there must be laughing at me. I dreamed of this happening, begged it to happen, wanted it more than anything, and now that it has, I really don't think I want it anymore.'

I glanced at Shelley and mouthed, 'Alice has left him . . .'

11

'This place is a mess,' I thought, as I stood, hands on hips, surveying my once neat and tidy sitting room. Empty glasses and cans littered the coffee table and discarded wine bottles lolled on the floor by the settee, one corner of which looked as if it was in the midst of a World War! The once stone coloured leather looked grubby and there was a rather tell tale greasy black patch right in the place where Sam's head rested as he gawped leaden eyed at the television night after night after night. Dust motes danced in rays of blinding sunlight and with no windows open, the room smelt warm and stagnant as dirty water.

For the millionth time I asked myself the same question, 'Why on earth had I said that Sam could stay with me for a while after Alice left him?' To be fair to myself though, I had only agreed to one night, and that one night had lengthened into two nights, then three nights, and now it was almost three weeks, and he still didn't appear to be doing anything about getting a place of his own. 'For God's sake,' I thought as I looked around again, 'I haven't even lived here that long!'

I stalked around the room, arms folded; taking in what looked like chocolate cake crumbs embedded in the carpet and sticky finger prints (he was worse than a child) on the window pane which I noticed as I glanced outside at the glorious sunny May day. I opened the doors and stepped out onto the balcony breathing in the scent of pink flowering clematis and hardy woody geraniums. I could smell coffee wafting in from local cafes and I even got a whiff of hops from the pub on the corner which was more than welcome after the reek in my flat at the moment.

The kitchen wasn't in a much better state with dirty plates, cups and pans piled on the draining board. With a sinking heart I put everything in the dishwasher and flicked on the kettle to make some coffee. I'd been working a lot of shifts at 'Hale & Hearty' recently as well as doing all my usual running, swimming and exercise classes and I'd trusted Sam to keep the flat in good order. He'd left me with no alternative but to give him a good talking to when he arrived home from work and also a deadline for moving out. In the meantime, though, I decided that I would send him a text. I just needed time to think about what I wanted to say, to compose it in my mind.

I sat at the kitchen table, breathing in the pungent odour of the coffee as I took tiny tentative sips, my mind going back to that awful day when Sam had rung to tell me that Alice had left him. Well, not actually left him, because she was still there, living in that lovely big house like Rapunzel with her long golden hair (probably even hanging it out of a window somewhere), but she'd given him his marching orders I suppose and of course he'd been the one who had to leave. He'd arrived at my flat that same evening, suitcase in tow, which he'd pulled angrily from the boot of the car and dragged up the steps like an encumbrance. I remember that he'd dumped the case on the floor in the spare room where it still sits now, it's lid wide open like a gaping mouth.

'Bang goes Shelley and Scott's romantic weekend away together,' I thought as I watched Sam test the bed for comfort with a vaguely possessive flat palm and peer from the window at the street beyond. Curious I padded up the stairs and peeked into the spare room which, although not quite as bad as the sitting room and kitchen, was still unkempt and frowsy, the bed unmade and the curtains hanging crooked. My own room, fragrant and powdered as a Queen's boudoir was a welcome respite from the rest of the flat so I lingered for a while as I made the bed and tidied my clothes before showering and dressing for work in my 'Hale & Hearty' uniform.

I dashed off a text to him before I left. It read like this,

Hi Sam

Hope you're okay?

I'm off to work and will be home around eight thirty. It would be really good if the flat was in a much better state when I get back. I know you've been fighting your own private war, but it looks as if World War Three has been fought in here!

Also would be good to know if you've got any further with finding a place of your own. I'm patient, Sam, but not that patient!

X

I read it through a couple of times and, okay, even I know it sounds a bit off but I need to scare him doing something or I could find myself living with him forever and it isn't as though I owe him anything is it?

The heat hit me hard as I went outside so I fumbled in my bag for my sunglasses then checked that I had my purse and my phone. My car was like a furnace inside and the steering wheel hot to the touch so my fingers danced as I pulled away from the kerb and made my way to work.

$$\star \quad \star \quad \star$$

It was a busy morning on reception with members ringing to book classes or to make enquiries or even, although it very rarely happened, to make complaints. People streamed through the turn-stile with their massive sports bags for an early swim or class and of course a lovely breakfast in the cafe afterwards as a reward for work well done. I breathed in heavily the smell of frying bacon and the odour of toast and coffee hung in the air like a mist. My stomach gurgled and, furtively checking the clock, saw that my break time wasn't too far away.

A group of runners clad in shorts and vest tops drenched in perspiration stretched their limbs like elastic bands by the front doors. They chatted to one another, their chests still rising and fall-ing rhythmically from their exertion. I watched as they went into the cafe, how they put their hands to their lower backs as they waited to be served and how they sat down carefully, stretching their thighs and their legs. I felt that I belonged, that I knew how they felt, how their bodies felt after a run, because I was a runner too. They were all tall and skinny except for one woman who looked far too short and stocky to be a runner.

Thinking of running made me think of Robert as I often did. I thought of his black hair tied back in a sleek pony tail, of his dark eyes and dimpled chin and his kissable strawberry lips. I wondered what he was doing now. Was he at work at Preston 'Hale & Hearty'? Or was it his day off and he'd gone for a run? It was such a gorgeous day that I couldn't blame him if he had. I had another thought, a thought which made my heart sink. Had he met somebody else? Somebody like Jeannie who wore her pool uniform just a little on the raunchy side, there was bound to be somebody like her at Preston 'Hale & Hearty.'

Or, and here my heart sank deep into my clumpy work shoes, never mind somebody like Jeannie, had Jeannie herself come back from Essex or wherever she'd gone and tracked Robert down and claimed him as her own this time? Was she, at this very moment, in the locker room in Preston warning somebody off him and scaring the wits out of some other poor unsuspecting soul like me. The thought of her heavily made up eyes and mouth bearing down on mine and her long nails digging into my skin gave me the horrors and made me feel like a little girl being pursued by the child catcher in the Wizard of Oz.

'Mel!' Diane nudged me hard bringing me out of my reverie. 'Good God, Mel, where were you then?'

'Sorry . . .'

'It's time for your break.'

I went through to the cafe and ordered a plate of toast and a hot strong coffee. Sitting down and sipping the coffee, I glanced into the pool area wondering if Tony Harris was around today. Even though I'd given in and gone for a drink with him, I knew full well that I wouldn't be repeating the experience. He was a nice enough guy, though not really my type, fairly tall with a full round face, hazel eyes and a mouth that looked just a touch too wet. I couldn't see him so he must be on a later shift today.

I gazed around the cafe which was full now with a general friendly hubbub of people talking over the music which I think was the Chris Evans Show on Radio Two. Taking a bite of toast spread with orange marmalade I noticed that the runners I'd seen earlier were still sitting together poring over something on the table in front of them. One of the group, a blonde lady maybe in her forties, caught my eye and said, 'Hi there, I noticed you out running the other day. I said hello but I think you were immersed in your music.' She made little motions beside her ears to indicate ear buds.

I swallowed my toast then said, 'Oh, sorry, yes I've taken up running quite recently . . . must have been busy concentrating . . . and maybe I was listening to T Rex . . . '

'Oh yes,' she replied with a knowing

smile, 'Marc Bolan.' She changed the subject by saying, 'We're contemplating a walk here,' she pointed to whatever it was they were looking at on the table.

'A walk?' I enquired politely.

'Yes, long distance, around eighty miles I think.'

'Eighty miles?' I spluttered. I'd just taken a sip of coffee and in shock had spat some on the table. 'Oh God, sorry about that,' I wiped the surface surreptitiously with a napkin.

The blonde lady laughed and said, 'I know, it sounds a long way, but we should do it in around five to seven days.'

'That's fifteen to twenty miles a day,' I said in a sort of horrified disbelief.

The rest of the group turned around to look at me and one of the men, also mid forties I would have thought, balding with very blue eyes, said, 'You've obviously never done any long distance walking then?'

I shook my head, 'No, never . . . '

'The Dales Way is a fairly short one. We've completed the Coast to Coast, that's almost two hundred miles and we did it in a couple of weeks.' He looked around at the rest of the group who were nodding their heads in agreement.

'That's amazing,' I said.

Another of the guys, a younger one with a blonde crew cut and green eyes beckoned me over, 'Come and have a look . . .'

I glanced at the reception desk where members were milling about either waiting for tickets for classes or queuing at the turnstile to get in. The sweeping black hands of the clock showed that I had five more minutes of my break left.

'This is the route for the Dales Way; look . . . ' He traced a red wiggly line on a map with his finger, 'It goes from here, Ilkley in West Yorkshire all the way to here,' He placed his finger on a red dot, 'Bowness-on-Windermere in Cumbia.'

'Wow, that's a long way. I'd love to do that.' I looked at the five upturned faces in surprise. Had I really said that?

'Well, if you're interested in making up a six,' said the blonde woman,

'Why don't you give it a go? You'd be fit enough.'

'Do you think so?' I asked.

'Yeah,' said the other woman. She was the small stocky one and had thick dark hair piled on top of her head. 'You run don't you, and I've seen you swimming so you'll have the stamina for it.'

I glanced again at the reception desk and said, 'I have to get back to work now but, yeah, it sounds great, although I wouldn't want to be the slow one at the back holding you all up.'

'That wouldn't be a problem,' said the blonde woman, 'We all keep to around the same pace don't we?' Everybody nodded and agreed including the third man who hadn't spoken much yet. He was probably around the same age as the blonde woman and the older balding guy and was dark skinned with great liquid eyes and a full mouth.

'Here,' said the blonde crew cut guy, 'Keep this.' He thrust the little booklet with the route map at me. 'Have a read of it and then let us know, we're usually around in here most days.'

I picked up the booklet, 'Thanks. When are you thinking of doing it?'

'Next month,' said the older balding man, who I took to be the partner of the blonde woman, 'June . . . so we'll need to get booked up soon.'

'Booked up?' I asked.

'Yeah, we need to book the B&B's on the route, unless you want to camp, but don't forget you'd have to carry a tent with you, and maybe we'll need to book the baggage carriers; or we may carry everything ourselves. These are things that we all need to decide.'

I must have looked suitably mystified because the blonde woman said, 'Look, give me your mobile number and I'll let you know when we have our next meeting then we can explain everything to you. What do you say?'

'Okay, that's good,' I gave her my number then excused myself with a little wiggly wave of my fingers and went back to deal with the onslaught of members at the reception desk.

215

★ ★ ★

I drove home slowly after my shift at 'Hale & Hearty' through the quiet streets of Skelly, past the imposing facade of the George Pub on the corner of the High Street, past Pizza World and Mogli's the Indian restaurant and the Red Lion near the roundabout. The new modern indoor shopping centre nestled like a canker amongst the dusty old buildings. I cruised past the somewhat down at heel row of local shops, the butcher, the baker, the candlestick maker (only kidding), there was a chemist and a 'Ye Old Winoe' and a shoe repair shop.

This is all I know really, Skelly, my little corner of the world. Okay I'd been abroad a couple of times with Sam but I'd never travelled anywhere else in England and to go to this place called Ilkley in West Yorkshire and walk all the way to Cumbria, to . . . where had the runners said? Bowness-on-Windermere? would be a real challenge.

Maybe it would help take my mind off

Robert, for whatever I told people, my mum, my dad, even Shelley and Scott, I still missed him and wanted him to come back to Skelly. I had an awful feeling that I'd lost a golden opportunity of happiness. Maybe I was wrong, maybe a real lasting romance might not have flourished for us as a couple but I knew that I would do anything to find out.

I pulled up outside my flat and, leaning forward, glanced up through the windscreen at the balcony where I could see my red painted table and chairs as well as all the plants cascading from the pots like a green waterfall. I noticed that the balcony doors were open. Was Sam actually letting fresh air into the place? Amazing! Oh well, at least my text seemed to have done the job.

It was almost eight thirty yet still light, although the moon and stars were etched faintly in the sky waiting for their time to glow. A group of young people strolled by, some in couples arm in arm, all dressed up and on their way to the pub. A bearded man sucked deeply on a cigarette and, as I locked the car with a beep, tobacco smoke bit harshly at the back of my throat. I glanced at my phone as I hurried up the front steps and saw a text from Sam which must have arrived unnoticed earlier, just two words, 'Sorry, Mel.'

He was sitting in his usual place on the settee bathed in lurid light from the television and the sound of a raucous sing song crowd told me he was watching football. He had his arms crossed over his chest and looked childish and innocent just like the man in the Febreeze advert. I sniffed the air, lavender polish, lemon cleaning fluid, a sudsy smell like washing powder or washing up liquid. The flat shone.

He jumped up straight away and fetched me a glass of wine from the kitchen. 'Thanks Sam, wow, the flat looks amazing.' He put the rest of the bottle on the coffee table. I took a sip of the wine. It was lovely and fruity and was just what I needed.

'Yeah, well, it was a mess, sorry

Mel . . . '

I put my bag down on the floor and eased myself into the arm chair. Sam immediately lowered the volume on the television.

'Have you found anywhere yet then, Sam?'

He gave a tiny shake of his head and, as he moved forward to get his can from the coffee table, I saw that the black greasy mark behind him had totally disappeared and been replaced with a very bright white mark that stood out like a sore thumb from the rest of the settee. 'I'm going to get in touch with Alice tomorrow. Her dad might have a flat that I could rent.'

I frowned at him. 'Do you really want to do that, Sam? Can't you find a flat on your own?' I took a big glug of wine this time.

'Yeah, but, oh I don't know Mel, I can't rouse myself at the moment, Alice's dad is loaded and has places for rent. He might even let me have it on a cheaper basis anyway.'

219

'What happened between you two Sam?' I'd wanted to ask him this before but he'd been in such a state three weeks ago when he'd rung me and asked if I could put him up for a while, and so angry when he moved in, that I hadn't dared to yet.

He lowered his head like a mutinous bull and said, 'I'm not sure really, I think she got fed up because I wasn't earning masses of money. She's used to having lots of things and going to expensive restaurants and bars. I couldn't always afford that.'

'But Alice works doesn't she?'

He looked at me in surprise, 'No, of course she doesn't . . . she's never worked.'

I kicked off my shoes leaving them like a couple of dead black birds on the floor and curled my feet under me on the chair. I was getting a very different picture of Alice from the child that I remembered and loved and also getting a different vibe from Sam than that I'd got from the happy couple walking along hand in hand wearing matching skinny jeans, coats and boots. I told him about seeing them together that evening and how happy they'd looked and how devastated I'd been then.

He shook his head sadly, 'I don't remember that, Mel. Yeah, it was great at the beginning, probably even better when we were just having an affair to tell the truth.'

'Hmm,' I said, 'Yes, more exciting I suppose, after all you were lying to me and getting away with murder.'

He leant forward then, his hands on his thighs and said quietly, yet not meeting my eyes, 'Would you ever consider us getting back together, Mel?'

'Oh Sam, no, it's impossible now. '

'Why, Mel.'

'Sam, I have feelings for somebody else . . . I wanted you back when you first left, but then I met Robert and everything changed.'

'Oh yeah, well, where's this Robert now then?'

'Things have been complicated, Sam,

I'll tell you all about it at some point, but for now I really think the top priority is that you get a place of your own.' There was a long heavy silence, only broken by the faint droning from the crowd at the football match on the television. I poured myself another glass of wine then said, 'Anyway, what about Alice, don't you want her back?'

I noticed that it was getting dark now so stood up and flicked on the lamp, the orange glow highlighting even further the cleanliness and neatness of the sitting room. I stepped out briefly onto the balcony inhaling the scent of jasmine and geraniums that hung in the humid air. The moon was visible now, a silver oval that looked to be cut out of dark paper surrounded by pin pricks of stars. Sam's voice brought me back inside.

'You know it's weird, Mel, but I'm not sure if I do.' He drank from his can of lager then wiped his mouth with the back of his hand. 'I do miss her but sometimes she was hard work. I can't talk to her about my favourite music or the charts in the eighties and nineties or even reminisce about the past, those are things that I can only do with you. She doesn't know what I'm talking about. I suppose it's the age difference.'

'Yes,' I agreed, 'It could be that, but . . . it's the same for Alice. She can't talk to you about the music in the 2000's, it would go right over your head. You're bound to face problems like that with a ten year age difference.'

'Oh, sticking up for Alice now are we?'

'No,' I replied seriously, 'but it takes two to tango, Sam.'

For some strange reason that expression made Sam laugh and he said, 'You always did come out with some weird sayings, Mel.'

We giggled and looked at each other, our eyes meeting and holding, and for a split second I remembered how it used to be, right at the beginning, when we first met, when we first fell in love and sadness overwhelmed me, and I looked away and so did Sam, and the moment was gone.

'What about a baby, Sam?' I asked him, 'Didn't you want a baby with Alice?'

His eyes were deep black pools in the gloom. 'I don't know if I love her enough for that, Mel.'

I shook my head in despair. 'Why did you leave me for her then?'

'I must have thought I loved her,' he replied, then turned his face back to the television and the football match as if he didn't want to talk about it anymore. He then said tonelessly, 'Don't worry Mel, I'll sort things tomorrow and be out from under your feet within a week.'

It wasn't until I was in bed later, my eyes closed and my head spinning from too much wine and not enough food, that I realised I hadn't told Sam about my impending adventure, my eighty mile walk along The Dales Way. A sudden thought occurred to me and my eyes snapped open, 'I haven't even got any walking boots . . . '

12

We set off on the Dales Way in mid June. It was one of those beautiful summer mornings where bees hummed amongst the flowers in scented walled gardens and the sun reached down its golden tendrils to touch your face as if with soft fingers. Countryside, lush and green as a painting, surrounded us on all sides and the sky blue and speckled with hazy cloud arched overhead. I felt as if I really was walking into a picture.

We'd arrived in Ilkley by train to meet the baggage carrier and now thankfully we were waving goodbye to our suitcases as they sped off in the courier's van to this evening's B&B and we now sported light rucksacks on our backs containing only essentials such as waterproofs, water, phones and our lunch of sandwiches, chocolate or energy bars and, in my bag, much to the delight of the men, a small make up mirror, eye liner and lipstick. My motto; 'Always look your best!'

I felt good wearing my new honed in walking boots with a blue skort and black vest top, a cosy blue fleece at the ready in case the weather turned cold. We'd lingered for a while snapping pictures at the beginning of the walk, at the huge plaque setting out the route and the history of the Dales Way, then off we went at a fairly brisk pace along the river bank, the imprints of our boots on the dry dusty earth following us as we went.

I felt great, fit and up for the walk. Life would be good if it wasn't for the ever present ache in my heart over Robert and his image in my mind's eye that never seemed to go away, but now I had a new somewhat uneasy thought in my mind that I'm sure would follow me along this walk and all because of a telephone call that Shelley had received just before I was due to go away, from none other than that old trouble maker herself, Jeannie.

Yes, the delectable Jeannie had reappeared as I'd dreaded she would, asking for her old job back. Shelley, not really wanting her back at all and also because 'Hale & Hearty' is fully staffed at the moment, refused her request. Not at all brusquely she told me but regrettably alas. Even so she'd still received a lot of abuse over the phone from her which really didn't surprise me at all.

For some reason I had a bad feeling about this, about the fact that Jeannie had returned and no doubt would get in touch with Robert, if she hadn't already done so and also the thought of her perhaps becoming involved with Richard. The last time I'd spoken to Robert at the Twin Convention in Blackpool, he'd said that Richard was doing well on medication. Obviously, this medication was suppressing his need to steal and set fires. What would happen if Jeannie decided to influence Richard to get back at Shelley?

I shook my head to try and clear these morbid thoughts. What on earth was I thinking? That Jeannie could influence Richard not to take his medication so that his need to set fires returned; I had an awful vision of 'Hale & Hearty' going up in smoke. I rang Shelley this morning and told her to be careful, that I didn't trust Jeannie.

'Oh, Mel,' said Shelley, airily, 'Forget about Jeannie for now. She's only a young girl and I think she's all talk. Just enjoy your holiday, although how you're going to enjoy walking almost eighty miles is beyond me!' She giggled then which seemed to lighten the atmosphere and I giggled too and said that I would send her regular text updates on the mileage.

The blonde woman, Kate, came to walk beside me, followed closely by the short stocky Sue. Kate's partner, the balding man, Roger, was avidly looking at his phone informing us that the weather report for the next five days was excellent. 'Sunny day after day after day,' he crowed, 'Seemingly not a drop of rain forecast.'

'Huh,' replied crew cut man, Nick,

'Don't speak too soon.' He pointed upwards with his index finger, 'Look, what's that, a black cloud?' We all gazed up in horror but only to see messy tendrils of white floating in the atmosphere.

'Hey, don't do that to me, man' said the dark skinned guy, Jaz, 'Scared the bejesus out of me. There's nothing worse than walking in pouring rain with your waterproofs rasping against your skin. Do you remember that one rainy day on the Coast to Coast?'

'Yeah,' agreed Sue, 'I felt as though I was encased in a big noisy wet bubble.'

I thought of the big bouncy colourful bubbles that we used to blow as kids and I remembered how I would blow them into the air and watch as they burst with a wet pop. Thinking of Jaz's words I imagined all five of them walking the Coast to Coast in the rain clad in their waterproofs, battling against the wind, rain drops trickling down their faces. I really hoped that didn't happen on this walk.

Coming back down to earth, I saw

that it wasn't wet at all but still hot and sunny, and all six of us were walking purposefully to our first night's destination, the quaint market town of Grassington. I hitched my rucksack higher on my back and, still carrying my heart heavily burdened with thoughts of Robert, matched my steps to that of the others and walked on.

★ ★ ★

I arrived home five days later footsore, weary, yet exhilarated and totally on a high. All six of us shared a taxi from the station, quiet now, tired, yet happy. My new friends dropped me off at my flat, waving goodbye from the open windows, as I trundled my little suitcase up the steps, each footfall jarring my aching limbs. I looked up at the balcony where I could see that my plants still flourished and that buds had opened since I'd been gone and now flowered brightly, red, orange and yellow, in the gloom. I felt as if I'd been away for years.

Sam had texted me while I was away to say that Alice's dad had agreed to rent him a flat that he owned on Viking Terrace in Skelly and that he, Sam, would be gone by the time I returned from holiday. He also told me that he and Alice had talked and were going to try again at their relationship. I texted him back wishing him luck and almost saying, 'if it doesn't work out, then please don't ask to stay with me again.' My urge for Sam to return to me with open arms had faded away.

I smiled to myself when I saw how immaculate he'd left the flat. I even suspected him of having brought professional cleaners in it was so pristine. Carefully prising off my now well worn boots, I hobbled into the bedroom, leaving my case on the floor then went into the kitchen and flicked on the kettle to make coffee. I eased myself slowly onto the settee and, sipping my drink, thought about the holiday and the great company the others had been, whether just on the daily walking or the evenings in the pub enjoying a much deserved meal and drinks.

The sensation of reaching Bowness-on-Windermere after five days of constant walking was exhilarating to say the least although in some ways a bit of an anti-climax. It just suddenly happened, one minute we were walking and the next minute an ordinary wooden bench bearing a plaque marking the end of the Dales Way appeared right in front of us, so, what did we do? We sat on it of course and Roger took photos while I inspected the insect bites on my arms and legs that I'd, unfortunately, collected along the way.

I wanted more drama, more action, I wanted all six of us to stand together holding hands and shout, 'We've just walked from Ilkley!' so that everybody would turn around and stare and say, 'Look at them,' or at the very least we could have cracked open a bottle of champagne and drunk a fizzing glass each, but, of course, not one of us would have offered to carry the rather heavy bottle in our rucksack on that final leg of the journey. Every ounce counts on your back whilst walking miles every day.

As it was we hugged and congratulated each other, exclaiming how glad we were that we'd made it and then made our way with once again purposeful steps after our short rest, to the Royal Oak, the official finishing pub for the Dales Way which offers Dales Way walkers the chance to rest their weary legs; enjoy their fine ales and indulge in their home cooked food. We did all three of those surprisingly good things that very evening.

Later, contentedly drinking a glass of red wine, I really couldn't believe that I'd walked from Ilkley in West Yorkshire to Bowness-on-Windermere in Cumbria but just by going to the lakeside and gazing out over the beautiful blue vista of Lake Windermere I could see that it was true.

With trembling eyelids and a weariness that had sunk deep into my bones, I went to bed; the soles of my feet feeling really sore as I padded into the bathroom to languidly brush my teeth and wash my face. The beep of a text message seeped into my consciousness as I drifted into a deep black dreamless pit of sleep, but I was far too tired to pick up my phone to see who it was from.

★ ★ ★

I've read the text message from Robert so many times it's imprinted on my brain. It goes like this, 'Hi Melanie, I'm coming back to work in Skelly 'Hale & Hearty' in a couple of weeks and would really like to go for a run with you. Please let me know if you think it's a good idea and when you'd be available. Hopefully see you soon. R x

My heart beat rapidly at the thought of a run with Robert and also at the thought of his silky hair, his stubbly chin and dark eyes that danced and glistened when he laughed. 'It's a good job,' I thought to myself, 'That he doesn't want to run for a couple of weeks. I don't think

I could put foot in front of the other at the moment to save my life!'

Slowly getting out of bed, my muscles screaming in horror at being moved, I hobbled into the kitchen and once again flicked on the kettle to make a cup of life saving coffee. Smiling I read the text again, composing in my mind my reply, which really could be one word or maybe two, 'Yes,' or 'Yes Robert.' I grinned and hugged the thought of seeing Robert again to my body, hunching my shoulders and wrapping my arms around my waist, once again making my muscles and bones shout at me to stop. I think I needed a good long soak in a hot Radox bath.

Instead I sat on the settee and composed a text to him, 'Hi Robert, good to hear from you. Yes good idea to run in 2 weeks also great to have you back working in Skelly. Just back from 'holiday' walking the Dales Way, almost 80 miles over 5 days, muscles screaming in agony at mo. Let me know when yr back in Skelly.' M x'. I pressed the send key and the message whizzed away never to return. Even now Robert could be reading it, his dark eyes scanning the words, knowing that I still wanted him, knowing that I still cared.

Did he still care though or was he contacting me as a friend, a friend that liked to go for a run sometimes or was he contacting me for romance? I thought about the last time we'd gone for a run when he'd touched my lip so erotically and told me that I was pretty and also said that I should tell him when I was ready for him. Well, I had been ready, I'd texted him and asked him to run with me, but he'd rebuffed me because of the situation with Richard.

Had he had second thoughts now that Richard was well and was prepared to try again? Hmm, maybe things would become clearer in a couple of weeks time. Singing to myself, 'And they called it puppy love . . . ' I ran a hot bath and poured in liberal amounts of sweet smelling Radox. Sinking into the deep water my muscles relaxing and almost creaking like the sound of a ship at anchor,

I laid my head back on the rim of the tub and closed my eyes as the words to Puppy Love filtered through my mind, 'Oh I guess they'll never know, how a young heart really feels, and why I love him so . . . ' Oh, what a silly sentimental mood I was in and all because of one single text message from a fit, handsome man.

* * *

'I just can't believe that you completed all that walking, Mel, you're super fit now.'

I gaze at Shelley's animated face thinking how attractive she is and so lucky to have flawless skin with barely any lines apart from a few creases around her big baby blue eyes and all of this framed by long honey blonde hair. That must be where the expression 'pretty as a picture' came from. No wonder Scott loved her so much.

'Yeah, it was really good, hard walking in some places but a great sense of achievement. My feet are still a bit sore though, but no blisters surprisingly.'

I was back at work on reception which was fairly quiet at the moment giving me a chance to have a quick word with Shelley about the holiday.

'Hey, do you remember when we took off our boots and thick socks and had a paddle in the river? Remember how good it felt?' asked a voice. I looked around to see Kate and Sue coming through the turnstile with their big heavy sports bags in tow.

'Ooh, yeah,' I replied, 'The feeling of that cold water on my hot pasties bucked me up no end.'

'Hot pasties?' Sue went off into infectious giggles and soon all of us, including Shelley, were laughing until almost crying.

'Shelley, this is Kate and Sue, two of the group I did the walk with.'

They nodded to each other and Kate said, 'We're having a meeting in the cafe about our next walk after we've been swimming, Mel. Can you have your break at the same time?'

I looked at Shelley for approval and she said, 'Of course, Jenny will be in soon so Mel can have her break whenever she wants.'

'We're looking at the Pennine Way,' Sue informed me.

'The Pennine Way?' I said slowly. I'd heard of it and had a feeling it was a long one so I said for confirmation, 'Isn't that a really long one?'

'Yeah,' agreed Kate, grinning from ear to ear, 'It's a three week job, around 250 odd miles.' They both breezed off in the direction of the changing rooms.

My heart sank into my clumpy work shoes and I noticed that Shelley, her hand over her mouth, stifled rising giggles, as she looked at the horrified expression on my face. Trying to hide mounting hysteria I said, 'Nothing from Jeannie then?'

'No,' said Shelley, 'We won't hear any more from her, Mel, you mark my words.'

'Hmm,' I replied, 'I'm not so sure, Shelley, I can't see somebody like her letting this lie. She's too mean and nasty.'

A fleeting worried look passed over Shelley's face and I felt guilty then at upsetting her. 'Sorry, I don't mean to be a harbinger of doom.'

She patted my shoulder and said, 'It's okay Mel, but forget about Jeannie, just look forward to your next text from Robert.'

13

It's been a whole week since the text message from Robert and I'm hoping upon hope to hear from him soon. I find myself constantly looking at my phone, pulling it out of my pocket and having a sneaky glance whilst at work on reception or carrying it around with me all the time at home. Quite frankly, it's driving me round the bend but I just can't help myself. That comforting little buzz and flash as the screen lights up and the little envelope icon appearing as if by some sort of sleight of hand, would go a very long way to easing my aching heart.

I'm on a late shift today so I've got time for a run this morning, the first one since completing the Dales Way. I feel ready for it now as the aching in my limbs has disappeared and my feet are no longer sore and verging on blisters, although, talking of feet, mine are in a really bad condition since I started running. I've lost count of the amount of times my toe nails have fallen off and the tops of my feet are sort of webbed like a duck's. It must be because I'm tensing my toes as I run making the tendons stand out more. I must remember to ask Kate and Sue what their feet are like when I next see them.

Great opener to a conversation eh? 'Oh hi Kate, Sue, what are your feet like since you've been running? Are they webbed like a duck's and how often do your toe nails fall off?' Maybe I could ask Robert about the state of his . . . um, maybe not!

I set off at a steady pace, Abba's Dancing Queen reverberating through my ears, on the flattest route I could possibly think of. I run all the way to the bottom of Alexandra Road, past the leafy trees, the pink blossom all gone now, dissolved like a magic trick into the earth and then turn left into Skelly town centre. The Bee Gees start singing about Too Much Heaven as I jog past the George pub and the little row of shops, where an old hobo, a quilt tucked around his shoulders, and a beard to his knees, sits outside 'Ye Old Wineo' strumming on a guitar and his dog sniffs at a old battered bin black with circling flies.

I run through Maylands Park where children play on primary coloured chunky swings and slides and screams echo in the air as an older child swirls the little ones around and around on the roundabout. A group of boys shout to each other in high pitched voices as they kick a bright orange football from one to the other. Rod Stewart asks Do You think I'm Sexy? as I leave the park and take the only hill on the route, the muscles in my legs straining as I take it in a slow steady trot all the way to the top. By the time I arrive back at my flat, I'm as high as a kite, high as a beautiful bright red kite flying in the sunshine, and I'm gasping and so out of breath, my heart chugs along like a steam train.

★ ★ ★

Arriving at work I'm pleased to see from the appointments book that we have another Naturist session that evening. Tony Harris is on shift as the lifeguard for the evening and I feel a sudden pang at the thought of the first naturist party and that Robert had been on duty then. Thinking of Robert compelled me to look at my phone but there was no comforting little envelope icon in the corner of the screen so no text message as yet.

I busied myself at the reception desk, making sure I had all the relevant slips of paper to give members when they came in asking for a ticket for the body pump class or the yoga class, or cycle. I was checking that I had plenty of fluffy white towels at hand when, glancing up, I saw Jaz coming through the door. He gave me a cheery wave and smiled, his very white teeth shining in his black face. He looked toned and fit wearing bright green shorts and a black vest top which emphasised his muscular arms and chest. If it wasn't for the constant thought of Robert and my attraction to him, I was pretty sure I could find Jaz a very alluring man.

'Hey, Mel, how ya doin?'

'Good,' I replied, 'You?'

'Yeah, cool. Made up your mind yet about the Pennine Way?' He lounged against the reception desk, a towel clutched in his enormous hand. After the meeting about our next walk the other five had given me a few days to think about whether or not I was up for such a big challenge.

'I'm 99% sure I'm going to do it,' I replied.

'Is that all,' he joked, '99%?' He laughed loudly, a lovely happy sound, and a few people looked around, smiling, to see where it was coming from. I noticed that his nose wrinkled when he smiled making him look most attractive.

I grinned. 'I don't think I can pass up such a great opportunity,' I told him.

'No, you really can't miss out on it; it'll be a great thing to do.'

'What have you come in for today then Jaz?' I asked him.

'Cycle class,' I gave him a ticket as he mimicked riding a bike, his arms bent at the elbow and his legs bent at the knees. 'You should try it, Mel, it's hard work but fun . . . makes you sweat though.' He carried on pedalling his imaginary bike, shaking his body and giggling.

I laughed at him as he went to walk away then stopped and said, 'Oh by the way, a few of us are doing the three peaks walk in a couple of months, September I think, if you fancy having a go at that. It's twenty six miles. If you complete it within twelve hours you're awarded with a certificate.'

'Oh wow, sounds good. I've heard of that, um, Pen-y-Ghent, Whernside and Ingleborough?'

'Yeah, I'm impressed Mel, well . . . have a think about it. See you soon.' He sauntered away, confident in his rangy, muscular body, his bright green shorts glowing like a light as he went off to do his cycle class.

The rest of the shift passed without incident. Tony Harris came in on time and went to the pool area to welcome the naturist group. I saw him at the pool side testing the water with a glass tube and immediately my heart began an unsteady erratic beating thinking back, I suppose, to the evening I'd seen Richard tampering with the water and thought it was Robert.

I hadn't known Tony Harris that long but got the impression that he was loyal and trustworthy and wouldn't dream of doing anything which would jeopardise his job in any way. I also had a feeling that he was dreading Robert coming back to Skelly because it would make his employment here at 'Hale & Hearty' very precarious. Shelly liked him though and he was a good worker so maybe his future here was secure. We definitely need people like Robert and Tony Harris whereas in turn we could definitely do without people like Jeannie who were nothing but trouble.

I had a quick check of my phone when I went to the locker room after my shift to collect my bag but still no text message.

Surely Robert would contact me soon, but then again he would be coming back to Skelly within a week so maybe he was waiting for that and wasn't even planning on sending me a message. All the days I'd waited and hoped could well be a waste of time.

Tony Harris and I were the last to leave that evening so walked to the car park together, both of us tired now after such a long shift. Tony yawned several times, not bothering to cover his mouth and I noticed that his lips looked even more sort of moist and gaping than usual. I shuddered and hunched my shoulders, hurrying along just in case Tony plucked up the courage to ask me to go out again and if he did I'd feel really bad at having to let him down.

The group of naturists had left already, fully clothed I hasten to add, and had all driven away so the car park, apart from two cars, mine and Tony's, was virtually empty. I thought how sad and abandoned our vehicles looked as Tony and I parted and he climbed into the driver's seat of his little blue Cortina and gave a honk of his horn and a wave as he drove by.

I raised my hand to him as I got in my car and was just about to turn on the ignition when I had a sudden overwhelming urge to check my phone again. I reached into the usual pocket but my phone wasn't there, my hand met empty silky smooth lining so, heart thumping heavily at the thought of losing it, I pulled my bag over onto my lap, turned on the car's interior light, and began searching through the contents.

I could see clearly my purse and make up, several old envelopes and packets of chewing gums and mints, even biscuit crumbs in the corners, but no phone. Oh my God, where was my phone? What if Robert had sent me a text? Oh my God!

I thought back to the last time I'd looked at it and realised I'd been in the locker room. I must have left it in the locker. I had no choice but to go back inside 'Hale & Hearty' on my own to get it. I couldn't wait until tomorrow, a whole evening without my phone and worrying about where it was, was unthinkable. Even now I felt as though one of my limbs had been severed.

I got out of the car and retraced my footsteps back across the car park and to the main entrance where, brandishing the large silver key, I unlocked the door. Just for a split second I wished that Tony Harris was still with me. I hated going into dark empty buildings on my own. Taking a deep breath, I went through the unlocked door and into the building immediately silencing the alarm as it beeped at me like one of the angry geese that live out on the lake.

With a shaking hand I turned on the lights then made my way across the wide, seemingly endless, reception area. I hurried down the long corridor to the locker room, peering to left and right as I went, feeling as if I was on the Ghost Train at the fairground and on the lookout for Dracula climbing stealthily from a coffin or screaming skeletons rattling their bones. Pushing the door to the locker room open, at first I couldn't find the lights, my hand met smooth wall but no heartening little switch rasped against my palm.

The lockers, lined up in rows, looked like people standing in the dark and I almost expected one of them to suddenly step forward and say, 'Melanie, what are you doing in here?' in a deep gruff voice. I stepped further into the room and hey presto the lights came on in a sudden blinding glare. In my panic I'd forgotten that the lights came on automatically in the locker room.

Rushing to my little compartment, I wrenched the door open and there it was . . . my phone, lying there, innocent as a new born babe, its screen shining in the darkness of the locker. I grabbed it, too afraid even to loiter and check for messages, and ran from the room as if the headless biker that a farmer had told us about on the Dales Way was pursuing me in all his shining glory.

I literally ran at great speed, my clumpy work shoes clattering on the tiled floor.

I stopped momentarily to set the alarm and then pushed my way through the main doors and out into the humid night air. My hands shaking badly now, it took a while to lock the door, my hands slipping and sliding on the silky key. I stood then, clutching my phone to my chest, breathing as heavy as if I'd been on a ten mile run. I began to walk briskly back to the car park, my heart beginning to slow down a little, when I heard a sound over by the swimming pool area.

I turned around and peered into the gloom. The lake was spread out in front of me, a glimmering mirror surrounded by the dark shapes of looming trees and squat bushes. Geese shining white as beacons honked greetings to each other across the water and the rustle of ducks settling down for the night unnerved me and my heart started beating hard again. A dark shape slunk slowly across the grass which I sincerely hoped was a cat and a flock of birds took off in a flutter and flew like flat dark shapes against the navy sky.

Another noise, not animal noises I was pretty sure of that, but human, definitely human. A giggle then rustling, then a voice, 'No, I don't want to, I need my tablets . . . please, you've got to give me my tablets, I do bad things . . . '

'Ssh, just do it okay . . . come on,' then another giggle. I peered even closer, narrowing my eyes to try to get a better view. I saw a flash of blonde hair, the swish of a pony tail, the flutter of a short skirt around milky thighs. 'Oh my God,' I thought, 'It's Jeannie.' And without any doubt at all, I knew that the other person was Richard. Poor Richard saying no and asking for his medication, 'I need my tablets . . . I do bad things . . . '

There was a scraping sound as if something was being dragged across the gravelled path surrounding the swimming pool extension and then a splashing and the glint of a metal container and more splashing and it suddenly hit me what they were doing. They were setting a fire. I couldn't let them see me but I had to alert the Fire Brigade. I backed away across the grass holding tightly to my phone, my hands trembling badly now. I dialled 999 and when the operator asked which service I said in a wobbly voice, 'Fire Brigade, please.' There was a momentary lapse, a buzzing silence, and then a ringing and a voice said, 'Hello, Fire Service, can I help?'

'Yes, please you must help; I need you to come to 'Hale & Hearty' in Skelly I mean Skelmanthorpe. They're setting a fire, oh my God . . .'

'Hang on a minute love, 'Hale & Hearty' Skelmanthorpe, that's the leisure centre isn't it?'

'Yes, please you've got to come quickly; they're pouring petrol all over the pool extension. I know who they are, but they haven't seen me, they don't know I'm here.'

'Okay love we're on our way.' My phone went lifeless and dead in my hand, just a faint purring like a contented cat in my ear. Then, taking me unaware, the phone sprang to life and lit up and beeped, the little envelope icon appearing on the screen. I jumped violently, my whole body jarring in shock. Close to tears now I saw it was the long awaited text from Robert, such magnificent timing. 'Hi Melanie, I'm back, I'm in Skelly. I no it's late but are you busy tnite? R x'

'Busy tonight,' I thought, quite hysterically, 'Busy tonight?' I didn't know whether to laugh or cry. I tried to press the button to reply to his text but my hands quivered so much I gave up, scrolled through my contacts and pressed Robert's name to call him.

I could see two dark shapes running around the pool extension, both with glimmering blonde hair, both holding silver cans that shone in the gloom, both pouring petrol all over the massive windows and the wooden structure. The phone rang and rang really shrilly, like somebody nagging, and then, oh thanks to God, Robert's voice, 'Hello?'

'Robert, it's Melanie . . .'

'Melanie, I've . . .'

'Yes, I've got your text, but Robert please listen, come to 'Hale & Hearty' like now,' my voice was breaking and I was close to sobbing and my whole body quivered like a jelly, 'They're setting a fire Robert . . . oh no, they've lit it . . . ' I could smell acrid smoke and saw the first glimmer of fire like a giant's tongue licking at the wood.

'Jesus Christ . . . '

'On the way, Robert, please call at Shelley and Scott's . . . I've rung for the Fire Brigade,' and then I added, 'Those two don't know I'm here . . . '

'Those two? Jeannie's with Richard?'

'Yes,' I said breathlessly, 'Yes . . . hurry Robert.'

'On my way . . . ' The phone went dead again and the contented cat purred in my ear and then an awful thought crept into my mind. 'The fire engine will alert them when it comes . . . oh no . . . '

And that's when it happened, I heard the sound of the siren, faint and far away as yet, and saw Jeannie stiffen, alert, her ears cocked like a dog rounding sheep. I heard her voice, 'Come on Richard, we've got to go now.'

'No, I'm watching the fire,' he whined.

I could see Richard now hunkered down, staring at the roaring fire. He was clearly visible in the glow of the blaze which was travelling as fast as a flame on touch paper, when all of a sudden there was a sharp shattering as one of the windows exploded and glass soared everywhere. Jeannie screamed and ran but Richard still sat there seemingly unconcerned, shards of glass sticking into his arms below his rolled up shirt sleeves and his face. Blood from a cut on his forehead ran sluggishly into his eyes.

The fire engine screeched through the open gates and pulled up short by the main doors, firemen clad in thick black uniforms and helmets swarmed out of the vehicle like busy ants. The fire was raging now and thick black smoke gusted into the air in flat plumes. Literally wringing my hands I called to Richard telling him that it was Melanie and would he please come over and sit with me, that I was hurt and needed him. Unrolling the massive fleshly hoses the firemen began to pump water at the inferno. I could feel the heat from where I stood and wished fervently that I was at an enjoyable bonfire party, crispy jacket potatoes baking in the fire, and not witnessing the annihilation of my cousin Shelley's first and foremost dream.

A loud crack rent the air and another window exploded causing Richard to come at long last to his senses as I saw him stagger to his feet, his hands in front of his face, and back away from the heat and the tiny pinpricks of glass that flew through the air like missiles. I held out my arms and he ran into the curve of them, dripping blood on my hands, saying over and over again, 'Melanie, I didn't mean to do it; she told me to, I said I needed my tablets.'

He went quiet then and looked away gazing at the crackling inferno and then sent a chill down my spine by saying in a dreamy voice, 'But hey, Melanie; isn't it beautiful, isn't the fire just so beautiful . . . '

'No, Richard, it isn't,' I told him, angry then and troubled, 'It's devastating and

destructive and can kill people and . . . '
I thought of Shelley and said, '. . . ruin
people's hopes and dreams.'

Richard seemed to revert back to
babyhood again then and whined fit-
fully, 'I want Robert, Melanie, I want
Robert . . . '

'He's coming,' I said tonelessly, 'He's
coming Richard . . . '

And then Robert was there, and Shelly
and we all joined together, our arms
around each other's necks as if in a rugby
scrum. All I could do was say sorry over
and over again, the same word, sorry,
over and over again. And then my legs
buckled beneath me, soft and loose like
skinny little pipe cleaners, and I began
to fall, the earth hard as nails beneath
my knees. Unable to help myself I closed
my eyes until the pandemonium faded
and then there was nothing.

14

I awoke, the smell of smoke still heavy in my nostrils, and glancing at my hands saw that, for some strange reason, they were black and sooty on the palms; the finger tips ghostly white, as if I wore fingerless gloves. Snatches of light and sound came into my mind, Jeannie's blonde pony tail shining in the gloom and her short skirt swinging to reveal creamy thighs, the silver glint of the petrol canister raised high in the air, and the first tongues of orange flame crackling on the wood whilst shards of glass exploded like cracked ice through the air. I don't think I want to know how bad the devastation is to the pool area at 'Hale & Hearty.' Not just yet anyway.

Glancing around, I saw that I was in a hospital bed in a room that contained one other bed which was empty. The sheets, pristine white as new snow were tucked securely around my body like a straitjacket and a sudden panic gripped me because I couldn't remember what had happened to Shelley and was Scott even there? and Robert and Richard. Putting my grimy hands to my face I thought, 'Oh my God, what would happen to Richard now? And Jeannie? Because, really, if anyone was to blame for this catastrophe, then it was definitely her. Yes, okay, Richard had set the fire too, but he wouldn't have done it without Jeannie's encouragement.

With a slow creak the door opened and, to my great relief, Shelley peeked in and seeing me laying there obviously wide awake, ran over to the bed and almost threw herself across my body. 'Oh Mel, are you feeling better now?'

Just for once Shelley looked awful, her hair usually so beautifully soft and fragrant, hung twisted as a corkscrew and grey with smoke, (Morticia Addams eat your heart out), and her lovely blue eyes red rimmed now and staring from her grubby face like those of a lunatic.

'Yes, I think so.' I had a really weird

sensation of falling and felt my knees throbbing, sore and maybe even cut and asked with a frown, 'Did I faint? Why am I in hospital?'

Shelley sat down on the chair beside the bed and said, 'You did . . . went down boom like a felled tree.' She made a falling motion with an upright hand. 'You're here because you fainted and because of the damage to your knees, oh, and smoke inhalation . . . oh Mel, you were so brave.'

'Brave?' I exclaimed, gazing at her in wonderment. 'No way, Shelley, I should have let Richard and Jeannie know that I was there. I should have got the petrol from them and stopped them somehow . . .'

'No, you couldn't have done that.' She shook her head vehemently, her ratty hair swirling around her face. 'Those two could have hurt you, especially Jeannie. They're dangerous, Mel, look what they've done to the pool extension . . .'

'Is it really bad, Shelley?'

'Yeah, really bad . . . there's not a lot

left of the extension, most of its in the pool. God knows what people will think today when they want to come in for a swim!'

'It can be put right though?'

'Of course, you know me, Mel, never one to give up. It will be restored to its former glory asap.'

'Where's Scott, and Robert . . . and Richard come to that?'

'Scott wasn't there, Mel, he stayed at home with the girls, we couldn't leave them last night could we? Robert went with Richard in the police car and the police have gone to look for Jeannie.'

'Yeah, she ran off didn't she? I knew she would when she heard the fire engine coming. If only they didn't have to make such a racket, she would have still been at the scene and they'd have locked her away by now.'

'Yeah that's true. She just ran off and left Richard to take the blame, not a good person.'

I shook my head sadly and told her that I'd had a feeling that a fire might happen and had thought about it fleetingly while walking the Dales Way. I told her that I'd thought that Jeannie had enough influence over Richard to put the whole thing into practice. 'The truth will come out though, Shelley.'

'Yes, you did mention that feeling to me,' said Shelley. I wish I'd listened to you. I suppose me not giving Jeannie her job back triggered it all off.' We gazed at each other nodding our heads. 'What were you doing there anyway?' asked Shelley, 'Your shift finished at ten o'clock and it all kicked off ages later.'

I related the tale about my phone and having to go back inside the building to get it. I was so afraid I'd miss a text from Robert, I explained. I grinned at her then said, 'I was terrified in there and thought all sorts of ghosties and ghoulies were coming after me.'

'Well, it's a good job you were there otherwise the whole place would have gone up in smoke and not just the pool area.' Shelley cupped my hand in her own small soft one and squeezed it gently.

'Come back to mine tonight, Mel.'

'Thanks Shelley but really I want to be at home in my little flat, I need to be in my own bed.'

She smiled and squeezed my hand again, 'Yeah, okay, Robert might get in touch anyway.'

'I really hope so,' I said, 'He texted me last night telling me he was back in Skelly and asking if I was busy, just at the very moment they were setting the fire, fantastic timing eh?'

'You two have definitely got a future together,' said Shelley, 'You mark my words. Oh, by the way, I've been in touch with our mums so expect a visit when you get home.'

'Yeah, I'll give her a ring when I get back,' I sighed heavily and then said, 'First and foremost though; I think we need to know what's going to happen to Richard don't you?'

★ ★ ★

'Good morning 'Hale & Hearty' Skelmanthorpe, Melanie speaking, how may I help you?'

Yes, I'm back at work where the phone hasn't stopped ringing with desperate enquiries from members about the pool and the fire. When will the pool be open again? What's happened to it? How did the fire start? Questions, questions and more questions. I had to say the same things over and over again, 'It will take a few months for the pool to be refurbished.' 'You must bear with us'. Irate members asking, 'How will I be able to do my aqua class?' 'How will little Sammy have his swimming lessons?' 'I'm in training; this is going to really mess it up.' Oh my God, some people can be so selfish!

All of the receptionists bonded together and dealt with the enquiries and complaints as best we could but it couldn't be ignored that a sense of mourning thick and black as a heavy rain cloud hung in the air over 'Hale & Hearty' not helped one little bit by the sight of the pool extension shrouded now in great swathes of thick plastic through which we could see timbers like the blackened stumps of rotting teeth and the deep hole of the pool, although drained of water, was full of buckled sheets and shards of glass.

The remains of the once beautiful roof, shrivelled plastic toys and floaters, together with the bright orange running man and woman logo, lay in a sooty mess, twisted and warped on the blue tiled bottom of the pool like the wreck of a ship on a sea bed.

I noticed that the clock, its glass face marred by a single wavering line, still, amazingly, ticked and tocked on one smutty wall, its long black hands sweeping around and around as if forever, and the Jacuzzi, its writhing water, quiet and still now, was littered with shrivelled leaves and burnt misshapen branches from overhanging trees. Even the plunge pool and the sauna hadn't escaped the devastation for they too were scorched beyond recognition, and yet the steam room looked passably intact, and showed clearly where I'd lain with my towel firmly around my waist the very first time I'd talked to Robert.

Tony Harris came by the reception desk to have a word expressing regret at the fact that he hadn't been there at my side when the fire started. 'It would have happened anyway, Tony,' I said to him. 'They were already there starting the fire before I came out of the building.'

I felt a twinge of irritation at Tony for assuming that events would have happened differently if only he'd been there. I was beating myself up for not making myself known to Jeannie and Richard and trying to stop them from starting the fire and I certainly didn't want it confirmed by him that I'd been wrong. Everybody that I'd spoken to including Shelley, Scott and Robert (the most important people in this case really) had agreed with how I'd handled it. Every time I looked at the now devastated pool area, I felt angry and annoyed with myself, and if Tony hadn't been called away at just that moment to help out in the gym, I swear I would have given him a piece of my mind.

'What time's your break, Mel?' Looking up I saw Robert standing at the reception desk. My breath caught in my throat as I gazed at him and for some reason his presence made me feel very close to tears. He smiled which caused his cheeks and chin to dimple most attractively and I felt a sudden great surge of affection and wanted to hold him in my arms and kiss him as we'd kissed outside 'Hale & Hearty' at our Christmas party when I'd thought that he was going out with Jeannie.

Jenny busily giving out gym passes to a group of new members and their families, glanced over her shoulder, her hair swishing as she moved which reminded me most unhappily again of Jeannie, and said, 'You go now, Mel, if you like.'

Robert, walking slowly and carefully, two mugs of steaming coffee clutched in his hands, came over to the table in the cafe and sat opposite me. Unfortunately, from where we were sitting, we could see clearly the remains of the pool extension, the sheets of plastic fluttering a little in the warm summer wind.

Giving me a small grain of comfort though was the sight of workmen wearing industrial hard hats and trousers, the side pockets of which bulged with tools, busily moving around inside, clearing the pool of the sooty debris and sweeping the blackened aqua blue tiles. I could hear Ken Bruce and his Pop Master Show on the radio which was turned up to a very high volume.

I sniffed appreciatively at the coffee and said, 'Thanks, Robert.'

'Hey, you're welcome. Richard's got to stand trial in a couple of months.' He told me tentatively.

'Jeannie?' I enquired.

'Yeah, her too.'

'I hope she gets suitably punished,' I said, quite viciously I thought and Robert must have thought so too for he looked at me in alarm. I couldn't help my feelings though. I blamed her for everything.

'How's your knees now?' He took a sip of coffee and I could see his Adams apple jerking up and down as he swallowed.

'Painful . . . I must have gone down with a bang.' I fingered the bandages on my knees through my trousers. 'They're just scabby and bruised now though.'

'As soon as you feel better, maybe we could go for a run?'

I nodded and drank from my mug leaving a pink lipstick mark on the rim that I quickly wiped away with the pad of my thumb. 'That's a good idea. You did say you had a lot of different routes to show me.

We smiled at each other and our eyes met and locked. Robert's dark as night and mine lighter, hazel green as a new leaf. I knew that I had to say something about the situation with Richard so suddenly blurted out, 'Robert, I'm sorry about asking Richard to come clean with Shelley and Scott, but after I saw him stealing from Diane's locker I knew something had to give. Actually I didn't think you'd want to run with me any more after all this . . . '

'Of course I want to run with you. I was totally wrong in expecting you to keep such a big secret from Shelley and Scott. You did the right thing, Melanie.'

He snaked his hand across the table, clasping my fingers, his skin so warm and dry against mine, 'Melanie . . . I . . . '

Whatever Robert was going to say to me was abruptly cut short with the arrival of Kate and Sue; closely followed by Roger, Jaz and Nick, all asking questions about the pool and the fire and was I okay? and good God what had happened that night? They didn't seem to notice our hands entwined like vines amidst the coffee cups.

From the radio, the volume even louder now, I could hear The Elgins singing so sweetly, 'Heaven must have sent you . . . into my arms.' Smiling wryly Robert let go of my hand leaving it exposed on the table, cold and forlorn, but, from the look in his eyes as they met mine once again, I knew that there would be a time for us very soon.

15

It's my day off, the first one really since I'd gone back to work after the fire. It seemed that lately everything that had ever happened was marked as 'after the fire.' We should call it AF, After Fire, as in BC, Before Christ. I was still plagued by dreams, weird panicky dreams where I found myself running swiftly through burning woods pursued by headless bikers and howling ghosts and choking on stinging smoke, my throat feeling raw and bruised, searching for my phone which I would always find eventually hidden amongst bushes or buried within the roots of a tree. My knees still felt sore but the bruises were gone now and on removing the bandages I'd seen that the scabs were falling away nicely revealing the pink shiny skin underneath.

'Don't you pick those scabs,' Mum had warned me. 'You'll be scarred for life if you do.' I remember as a child lying in bed picking with my sharp finger nails at the thick scabs that always seemed to cover my knees, bloody bits of which then became stuck to the slippery nylon sheets for mum to find the next day.

'Disgusting habit,' she would shout at me, even roar at me, her seventies afro hair-do resembling a lion's mane around her pretty face.

Shelley and Scott invited me around to theirs for tea and, over a truly delicious plate of fish and chips with minted mushy peas, told me all the missing bits from the night of the fire, the most important part of it being what had happened to Jeannie after she'd run away, after she helped to wreck havoc to the pool extension and then leave Richard to face the music alone. Mya and Bethany sat with us around the table spooning peas into their little mouths and listening wide eyed to the goings on of the night of the fire while they were both safely asleep in their beds and wandering aimlessly far far away in the land of dreams.

Apparently she hadn't got very far and

the police had picked her up in Skelly town centre, whimpering and cowering like a loon behind the big green bins at the back of 'Bloomers' the Bakers, a tiny building squashed between 'Ye Old Wineo' and 'Huntsman' the Butchers. She smelt of petrol and smoke and the reek of strong lager oozed like slime from her pores thanks to the copious amount of cans that she'd drunk earlier.

The story went that she'd hissed and scratched and kicked at the police like a crazy woman until they almost had to resort to a massive fishing line and net to reel her in. Anyone would imagine on hearing that, that she was a fish or perhaps a mermaid and not a young woman in the prime of her life, albeit a young woman that has maybe ruined the prime of her life by her stupid actions and could possibly face a couple of years in prison for arson.

Peering from the bedroom window, I noticed that it was a lovely August day, the great yellow ball of the sun glowing in a silky blue sky, dotted here and there with flaky cloud. I fancied a swim so thought that later I would maybe drive to the nearest 'Hale & Hearty' in Preston which many members were doing while the pool in Skelly was undergoing refurbishment. The good news though was that work on the pool was going along nicely and a tentative October date had been given for the grand re-opening.

'We're going to have a very grand 'grand re-opening' said Shelley proudly, 'A massive party for all staff and members.'

'You never give up do you Shelley?' I said, 'Even the devastation of a fire can't dampen your spirits.'

'No,' she agreed brightly. 'Nothing dampens my spirits.' Scott laughed and pulled her close to him, brushing a light kiss over her hair which looked beautiful again now, just as soft and flowing as it always had. 'The pool area will be restored to its former glory,' said Shelley, 'There's never been any doubt about that. Skelly 'Hale & Hearty' was my first born of all the leisure centres and I'll do anything to keep it in tip top condition. The place is going to shine brighter than ever before.'

I thought about all this as I sat on my little balcony on my red painted chair at my red painted table. I'm surrounded by foliage, beautiful deep green foliage, interspersed here and there with magnificent purple blooms from the clematis that rambles among the curly wrought iron and miniature rose bushes all yellow and creamy white their sweet smelling scent filling the air. I have visions of Skelly 'Hale & Hearty' shining brighter than ever before, a star glowing above the pool extension, just like the star that Jesus followed to Bethlehem, keeping it safe from harm and definitely safe from arsonists and fire.

Making a sudden decision, I close the balcony doors and, picking up my sports bag which is just as big and unwieldy as any member's, thank you very much, I clatter down the stairs and out to my car and, once behind the wheel, drive to Preston 'Hale & Hearty' to stretch my limbs in a relaxing swim.

There's banging and clattering coming from the pool area and workmen are visible through the new massive shiny windows, I can see them like little black bugs running around inside the still empty pool and the cloying smell of paint and turpentine floats through into reception. Gone is the thick plastic that shrouded the area like a murder scene and a brand new roof stands proudly in place, glittering and sparkling in the sunshine.

Chris Evans gamely competes with the din that the workmen are making and I can vaguely hear him introducing the eight o'clock news. My phone beeps in my trouser pocket and springs into life whilst the comforting little envelope icon appears on the screen. My heart jolts at the thought of a text message especially as I suspect it may be from Robert. Furtively, holding my phone low under the reception desk, I read it, 'Hey Melanie, what you doing this afternoon?

Fancy that run that we've talked about for ages? R x'

A woman comes to the reception desk demanding to know when the pool will be open. 'What are they doing in there?' she asks almost tearfully, 'I haven't been to an Aqua class for ages.'

I explained to her that the refurbishment was almost complete but that the workmen were in there making sure that the area was safe for members to use. 'Don't forget,' I told her, 'There was a really bad fire in there, and in the meantime,' I suggested, 'Maybe she'd like to try Preston 'Hale & Hearty' or one of our other branches?' She went away still disgruntled but, hey, you can't please all of the people all of the time (that's a famous quote isn't it? I think).

I spent some time then giving out towels and tickets for classes and when I got a moment's respite I texted back still as craftily as ever bending low behind the reception area. 'Yeah, a run later this afternoon would be good. I get home at around one. M x'

An immediate beep, 'Okay, we'll meet on route, c u in Maylands Park at around two. R x'

I texted back, 'Ok,' then laughed to myself at the disappointment that would probably be on Robert's face right now. Receiving a text just saying 'Ok' could put anybody on a real downer. Shelley did it to me all the time.

I checked the clock, its slim black hands flitting around its white face showing almost nine o'clock. Oh my God, it occurred to me that I had five long hours to wait until I could see Robert. Until I could be with him, until I would be able to breathe in the scent of his skin, an intoxicating mix of sunshine and vanilla, and glance at his strawberry lips and his sexy day old stubble as we ran. It was a wonder that I hadn't come a cropper whilst out running with him as I spent more time staring from the corner of my eye than watching where I was putting my feet.

Shelley comes to the desk and asks if she can have a word. Diane has just that minute come on shift so she suggests I take a break and have a cuppa with her in the cafe. We order mugs of foaming hot chocolate and sit at a table by the window so that we can see clearly the workmen busily scurrying around the pool and it's looking good.

Shelley smiles happily as we watch the men painting the walls in a soft white and preparing the inside of the pool, priming it, until it's ready to be filled with water. It's just a matter of time but, soon, very soon in fact, I don't think that anybody would ever guess that there'd been a fire.

'I've just had some news, Mel,' said Shelley. She took a sip of hot chocolate and winced as the hot brew burnt her tongue.

'Oh yeah,' I said, 'What news?' I gave my hot chocolate a cooling blow.

'Robert and Jeannie have been sentenced.'

'Oh my God . . . tell me, Shelley . . . ' A rather large group of members streamed into the cafe talking and laughing hilariously at some inside joke, their bags banging against each other, so I had to strain to hear what Shelley was saying.

'Jeannie has got a fine and a probation sentence of two years because it's her first offence and she pleaded not guilty, and also because it was significant damage to property, not minor or moderate but significant.'

'Wow,' I said. 'What's the fine?'

Shelley shrugged her shoulders and said, 'I don't know about that, Mel.'

'And Richard?'

'Richard's got four years.'

'Even though Jeannie wouldn't let him have his medication and drove him to it, really?'

Shelley delicately put her fingers to the corners of her mouth, being careful not to touch her lipstick, wiping away imaginary chocolate I supposed, and said, 'Yep, that's the sentencing.'

'Does Robert know?' I asked, 'It's just that I'm going for a run with him this afternoon and . . .'

'Yeah, he knows.'

We sat in silence for a minute or two

looking at the newly resurrected pool area and watching the men working so industriously inside.

'What did Scott say?' I asked her.

'Just what you said; that Jeannie should have a stronger sentence because she instigated it.'

I nodded my head pleased and in total agreement and then said, 'Don't forget Shelley that Mya and Bethany can come and stay with me for a weekend soon, so you and Scott can have some time on your own. I think you deserve it. Maybe for your fortieth?'

She smiled and said, 'Thanks Mel that would be wonderful.'

I eventually went back to reception feeling as sad for Richard as if he'd passed away and was standing at the pearly gates rapping hard with his knuckles and asking in his little boy way would they please let him in. What did I feel for Jeannie? Um, nothing much!

★ ★ ★

I've just arrived home and I'm in a tearing hurry to get changed into my running gear and meet Robert in Maylands Park at two o'clock. Should I mention Richard and Jeannie's sentences or should I keep quiet about it and pretend I don't know. I suppose he must guess though that Shelley will have told me. I flounder about in my bedroom looking for my little blue skort and my black short sleeved top and where's my blue sports bra?

I'm so excited about seeing Robert it's untrue and I feel all sort of warm and squidgy inside, I suppose it must be similar to what mushy peas feel like all squashed together in a tin! I scramble into my clothes and then dash into the bathroom to check my face. 'Yikes, what a horror,' I think, as I pat around my eyes with a makeup remover pad wiping away any stray black pencil lines and blobby bits of mascara. I apply a tiny bit of lip gloss to my pouting lips and tie my hair up with a black scrunchie and reach for my headphones so that I can listen to music before I meet up with Robert.

Slightly colder air hits me as I step outside and I shiver, the hairs rising on my arms and legs like I've been given an electric shock. I glance up at the still azure blue sky which is festooned now with dirty black clouds that look heavy and swollen as udders waiting to be milked. The wind has increased a little and, even though I'm no weather girl, I have a feeling that it's going to rain. I plug in my ear buds and let myself be lifted up by the music as I walk at first, warming up my legs and hoping that my knees aren't going to give me any pain once I get going.

I set off at a steady jog on my usual route to the bottom of Alexandra road, then turn left and head down into Skelly town centre, running past the George pub and then the little row of shops where I glance at Bloomers the bakers sandwiched between 'Ye Old Wineo' and 'Huntsman,' the butchers. Just out of curiosity, I run around to the back of Bloomers and glance at the big green bins where Jeannie hid on the night of the fire. It all looks pretty tasteless and squalid to me as I take in the overflowing bins around which empty crisp packets and sweet wrappers scuttle in the strengthening breeze and empty lager and cider cans rattle and roll along the concrete paths.

The old hobo, this time actually inside a scratty looking sleeping bag, sits outside the shoe repair shop, his large black dog, head on its paws, asleep at his feet. I see that his guitar is propped uselessly by his side and as I run past, he shakes a tin at me but I point at my ear buds and shrug my shoulders, making out that I no speak English, increasing my pace as I fly past him in a blur.

My stomach is churning with excitement and anticipation as I get nearer to Maylands Park. Knots of teenagers stand talking and smoking at the ornate entrance gates and the harsh smoke bites deep into my throat reminding me of the fire and Richard and Jeannie, my heart sinking at the thought of Richard spending four years in prison and how upset

Robert must feel about that. The first spots of rain splash onto my arms and in the distance I see the primary coloured swings and slides, the whirring roundabout and that funny little springy horse ride that children seem to love so much.

Looking around I can't see Robert anywhere. Where is he? He's a far faster runner than I am and should have been here ages ago. The churning in my stomach intensifies, becomes more violent, and I feel vaguely headachy and sick. Just to make things worse I'm getting wet now as raindrops, large and fleshy, splatter onto the top of my head and slide down my face like tears. I start to jog up and down, up and down, trying to keep warm as the wind picks up and blows my little skort into a frenzy, exposing the tiny shorts underneath and causing the aforesaid group of teenagers to whistle and snort derisively.

Then all at once I see him, he's running towards me, his black hair shining in a sudden ray of sunlight that peeks from the rain swollen clouds. He sees me and raises his hand, a smile, as bright as a summer's day, lighting up his face.

'Good God, Melanie, I ran as fast as I could and you're still here before me, what are you on, energy bars?' He comes so close that I can see the rain running down his face in tiny rivers and little drops fall from the ends of his hair onto his tee-shirt soaking through the material to the skin beneath.

'I'm so sorry Robert . . . about Richard . . . ' I begin to say.

'No, Melanie, be quiet . . . please . . . we've got years to talk about Richard. All I want to do is kiss you. After all I have been waiting since Christmas . . . '

Gathering me closely into his arms, the driving rain sealing us together like glue, he cups his hand around the back of my head, pulling my face towards his so that all I can see are his beautiful strawberry lips as they finally meet mine.

We do hope that you have enjoyed
reading this large print book.

Did you know that all of our titles
are available for purchase?

We publish a wide range of high
quality large print books including:
Romances, Mysteries, Classics
General Fiction
Non Fiction and Westerns

Special interest titles available in
large print are:
The Little Oxford Dictionary
Music Book, Song Book
Hymn Book, Service Book

Also available from us courtesy of
Oxford University Press:
Young Readers' Dictionary
(large print edition)
Young Readers' Thesaurus
(large print edition)

For further information or a free
brochure, please contact us at:
Ulverscroft Large Print Books Ltd.,
The Green, Bradgate Road, Anstey,
Leicester, LE7 7FU, England.
Tel: (00 44) **0116 236 4325**
Fax: (00 44) **0116 234 0205**

Other titles in the
Linford Romance Library:

CHRISTMAS ON THE ISLE OF SKYE

Kirsty Ferry

The Isle of Skye is a magical place, especially at Christmas, and there's nowhere Zac Fallon would rather be. But whilst Zac has everything he needs on Skye, there's still something missing — and that something is a somebody called Ivy McFarlane. Ivy used to work with Zac, but then spread her wings and moved to Glastonbury. He's missed her ever since. Now it's almost Christmas, and Zac realises that the Ivy-shaped hole in his life is too big to bear . . .

X - W I N G

BOOK FOUR

THE BACTA WAR

Michael A. Stackpole

BANTAM BOOKS
TORONTO · NEW YORK · LONDON · SYDNEY · AUCKLAND

THE BACTA WAR
A BANTAM BOOK : 0 553 40924 7

First publication in Great Britain

PRINTING HISTORY
Bantam edition published 1997

Bantam Books are published by Transworld Publishers Ltd,
61–63 Uxbridge Road, London W5 5SA,
in Australia by Transworld Publishers (Australia) Pty Ltd,
15–25 Helles Avenue, Moorebank, NSW 2170,
and in New Zealand by Transworld Publishers (NZ) Ltd,
3 William Pickering Drive, Albany, Auckland.

Printed and bound in Great Britain by
Cox & Wyman Ltd, Reading, Berkshire.

ACKNOWLEDGMENTS

The author would like to thank the following people for their various contributions to this book:

Janna Silverstein, Tom Dupree, and Ricia Mainhardt for getting me into this mess.

Sue Rostoni and Lucy Autrey Wilson for letting me get away with all they have in this universe.

Kevin J. Anderson, Kathy Tyers, Bill Smith, Bill Slavicsek, Peter Schweighofer, Michael Kogge, and Dave Wolverton for the material they created and the advice they offered.

Timothy Zahn for being a wonderful co-conspirator and vetting chapters so quickly.

Paul Youll for the stunning covers on the books.

Lawrence Holland and Edward Kilham for the *X-wing* and *TIE Fighter* computer games.

Chris Taylor for pointing out to me which ship Tycho was flying in *Star Wars VI: Return of the Jedi* and Gail Mihara for pointing out controversies I might want to avoid.

My parents; my sister, Kerin; my brother, Patrick; and his wife, Joy, for their encouragement (and endless efforts to face my other books out on bookstore shelves).

Dennis L. McKiernan, Jennifer Roberson, and especially Elizabeth T. Danforth for listening to bits of this story as it was being written and enduring such abuse with smiles and a supportive manner.

DRAMATIS PERSONAE

THE ROGUES

COMMANDER WEDGE ANTILLES *(human male from Corellia)*
CAPTAIN TYCHO CELCHU *(human male from Alderaan)*
CAPTAIN ARIL NUNB *(Sullustan female from Sullust)*
LIEUTENANT CORRAN HORN *(human male from Corellia)*

OORYL QRYGG *(Gand male from Gand)*
NAWARA VEN *(Twi'lek male from Ryloth)*
RHYSATI YNR *(human female from Bespin)*
GAVIN DARKLIGHTER *(human male from Tatooine)*
RIV SHIEL *(Shistavanen male from Uvena III)*
ASYR SEI'LAR *(Bothan female from Bothawui)*
INYRI FORGE *(human female from Kessel)*
IELLA WESSIRI *(human female from Corellia)*
WINTER *(human female from Alderaan)*
ELSCOL LORO *(human female from Cilpar)*

ZRAII *(Verpine male from Roche G42)*
M-3PO *(Emtrey; protocol and regulations droid)*
WHISTLER *(Corran's R2 astromech)*
MYNOCK *(Wedge's R5 astromech)*

ALLIANCE MILITARY

ADMIRAL ACKBAR *(Mon Calamari male from Mon Calamari)*
CAPTAIN PASH CRACKEN *(human male from Contruum)*

ALLIANCE INTELLIGENCE

GENERAL AIREN CRACKEN *(human male from Contruum)*

CREW OF THE *PULSAR SKATE*

MIRAX TERRIK *(human female from Corellia)*
LIAT TSAYV *(Sullustan male from Sullust)*

THYFERRAN FORCES

YSANNE ISARD, DIRECTOR OF IMPERIAL INTELLIGENCE *(human female from Coruscant)*
FLIRY VORRU *(human male from Corellia)*
ERISI DLARIT *(human female from Thyferra)*

1

Somehow the dead of night amplified the lightsaber's hiss, allowing it to fill the room. The blade's silvery light frosted the furniture and gave birth to impenetrable shadows. The blade drifted back and forth, prompting the shadows to waver and shift as if fleeing from the light.

Much as criminals would flee from the light.

Corran Horn stared at the blade, finding the argent energy shaft neither harsh nor painful to his eyes. He lazily wove the blade through joined infinity loops, then, with the flick of his right wrist, snapped it up into a guard that protected him from forehead to waist. *Relic of a bygone era, it still can conjure up images and feelings.*

He hit the black button under his thumb twice, and the blade died, again plunging the room into darkness. The lightsaber did conjure up images and feelings in him, but Corran doubted they were at all the images and feelings commonly felt by most others on Coruscant. To everyone, including Corran, Luke Skywalker was a hero and was welcomed as heir to the Jedi tradition. His efforts at rebuilding the Jedi order were roundly applauded, and no one, save those who dreaded the return of law and order to the galaxy, wished Luke anything but the greatest success in his heroic quest.

As do I. Corran frowned. *Still, my decision has been made.*

He'd felt it the greatest of honors to be asked by Luke Skywalker to leave Rogue Squadron and train to become a Jedi. Skywalker had told him that his grandfather Nejaa Halcyon had been a Jedi Master who had been slain in the Clone Wars. The lightsaber Corran had discovered in the Galactic Museum had belonged to Nejaa and had been presented to Corran as his rightful inheritance. *Mine is the heritage of a Jedi Knight.*

But that was a heritage he had only heard of from Skywalker. He did not doubt the Jedi was telling the truth, but it was not the whole truth. *At least not the whole of the truth with which I grew up.*

Throughout his life Corran Horn had come to believe his grandfather was Rostek Horn, a valued and highly placed member of the Corellian Security Force. His father, Hal Horn, likewise was with CorSec. When it came time for Corran to choose a career, there was really no choice at all. He continued the Horn tradition of serving CorSec. His grandfather had always admitted to having known a Jedi who died in the Clone Wars, but that acquaintance had been given no more weight than having once met Imperial Moff Fliry Vorru or having visited Imperial Center, as Coruscant had been known under the Empire's rule.

Corran found it no great surprise that Rostek Horn and his father had downplayed their ties to Nejaa Halcyon. Halcyon had died in the Clone Wars; and Rostek had comforted, grown close with, and married Halcyon's widow. He also adopted Halcyon's son, Valin, who grew up as Hal Horn. When the Emperor began his extermination of the Jedi order, Rostek had used his position at CorSec to destroy all traces of the Halcyon family, insulating his wife and adopted son from investigation by Imperial authorities.

Since exhibiting any interest in the Jedi Knights could invite scrutiny and my family would be very vulnerable if its secret were discovered, I probably heard less about the Jedi Knights than most other kids my age. If not for various holodramas that painted the Jedi Knights as villains and later reminiscences by his grandfather about the Clone Wars, Corran would have known little or nothing about the Jedi. Like most other children, he found them vaguely romantic and all too much sinister, but they were distant and remote while what his father and grandfather did was immediate and exciting.

He raised a hand and pressed it to the golden Jedi medallion he wore around his neck. It had been a keepsake his father had carried and Corran inherited after his father's death. Corran had taken it as a lucky charm of sorts, never realizing his father had kept it because it bore the image of his own father, Nejaa Halcyon. *Wearing it had been my father's way of honoring his father and defying the Empire. Likewise, I wore it to honor him, not realizing I was doing more through that act.*

Skywalker's explanation to him of what his relationship to Nejaa Halcyon was opened new vistas and opportunities for him. In joining CorSec he had chosen to dedicate his life to a mission that paralleled the Jedi mission: making the galaxy safe for others. As Luke had explained, by becoming a Jedi, Corran could do what he had always done but on a larger scale. That idea, that opportunity, was seductive, and clearly all of his squadron-mates had expected him to jump at it.

Corran smiled. *I thought Councilor Borsk Fey'lya was going to die when I turned down the offer. In many ways I wish he had.*

He shook his head, realizing that thought was unworthy of himself and really wasted on Borsk Fey'lya. Corran was certain that, on some level, the Bothan Councilor believed he—not Corran—was right and his actions were vital to sustain the New Republic. Re-creating the Jedi order would help provide a cohesive force to bind the Republic together and to drape it in the nostalgic mantle of the Old Republic. Just as having various members of nation-states placed in Rogue Squadron had helped pull the Republic together, having a Corellian become a new Jedi might influence the Diktat into treating the New Republic in a more hospitable manner.

Skywalker had asked him to, and Fey'lya had assumed he

would, join the Jedi order, but that was because neither of them knew of or realized that his personal obligations and promises exerted more influence with him than any galactic cause. While Corran realized that doing the greatest good for the greatest number was probably better for everyone in the long run, he had short-term debts he wanted to repay, and time was of the essence in doing so.

The remnants of the Empire had captured, tortured, and imprisoned him at Lusankya, which he later came to realize was really a Super Star Destroyer buried beneath the surface of Coruscant. He had escaped from there—a feat never before successfully accomplished—but had gotten away only with the aid of other prisoners. He had vowed to them that he would return and liberate them, and he fully intended to keep his promise. The fact that they were imprisoned in the belly of the SSD that now orbited Thyferra made that task more difficult, but long odds against success had never stopped him before. *I'm a Corellian. What use have I for odds?*

His desire to save them had increased with a chance discovery that embarrassed him mightily when he made it. In Lusankya the Rebel prisoners had been led by an older man who simply called himself Jan. Since his escape, Corran had caught a holovision broadcast of a documentary on the heroes of the Rebel Alliance. First and foremost among them had been the general who led the defense of Yavin 4 and planned the destruction of the first Death Star, Jan Dodonna. The documentary said he'd been slain during the evacuation of Yavin 4, but Corran had no doubt Dodonna had been a prisoner on Lusankya. *If I hadn't thought him dead, I might have recognized him, too. How stupid of me.*

Dodonna's celebrity had nothing to do with Corran's desire to save him. Jan, like Urlor Sette and others, had helped him escape. They had risked their lives to give him a chance to get away. Leaving such brave people captives of someone like Ysanne Isard not only failed to reward their courage but repaid them by leaving them in severe jeopardy of death or worse—conversion into a covert Imperial agent under Isard's direction.

"Couldn't sleep?"

Corran started, then turned and smiled at the black-haired, dark-eyed woman standing in the bedroom doorway. "I guess not, Mirax. I'm sorry I woke you."

"You didn't wake me. Your *absence* awakened me." She wore a dark blue robe, belted at the waist with a pale yellow sash. Mirax raised a hand to hide a yawn then pointed at the silver cylinder in his right hand. "Regretting your decision?"

"Which one? Refusing to join the Jedi Knights or"—he smiled—"or hooking up with you?"

She raised an eyebrow. "I was thinking of the Jedi decision. If you have reservations about the other decision, I can relearn how to sleep alone."

He laughed, and she joined him. "I regret neither. Your father and my father may have been mortal enemies, but I can't imagine having a better friend than you."

"Or lover."

"Especially lover."

Mirax shrugged. "All you men who've just gotten out of prison say that."

Corran frowned for a moment. "I imagine you're right, but how you came by that information, I don't want to know."

Mirax blinked her eyes. "You know, I don't think I want to know that, either."

Corran laughed, then crossed the room and enfolded her in a warm hug. "After my escape, Tycho expressed his regrets concerning your death to me. He told me how Warlord Zsinj had ambushed a convoy at Alderaan and destroyed it, including your *Pulsar Skate*. Everything inside of me just collapsed. Losing you just ripped the emotional skeleton out of me."

"Now you know how I felt when I thought you'd been slain here on Coruscant." She kissed his left ear, then settled her chin on his shoulder. "I hadn't realized how much you had become part of my life until you were gone. The hole the *Lusankya* created blasting her way out of Coruscant was nothing compared to the void I had inside. It wasn't a question of wanting to die, but of knowing my insides were dead and wondering when the rest of me would catch up."

"I had it luckier than you. When he got the chance, General Cracken pulled me aside and told me how you'd gone on a covert mission to Borleias to deliver ryll kor, bacta, and a Vratix *verachen.* Zsinj's ambush conveniently covered your disappearance so the Thyferrans didn't know what you were setting up on Borleias with their bacta."

"Yeah, they would not have liked it if it were known we were using the Alderaan Biotics facility there to make rylca and, eventually, enough bacta to dent their monopoly." Mirax shivered. "I would have preferred the original plan working, because as much as I didn't look forward to being reviled and hunted down for stealing bacta from the convoy, I would have rather endured that than having all those other people killed."

"Nothing you could do about that."

"Nor was there anything you could do about your fellow prisoners being whisked away by Isard when she escaped in the *Lusankya.*" Mirax backed up a half-step and held Corran at arm's-length. "You do realize that, don't you?"

"Realize, yes. Accept, no. Tolerate, no way." Corran narrowed his green eyes, but the hint of a smile tugged at the corners of his mouth. "You know, if you keep hanging around with me, you're going to get into a lot of trouble."

"Trouble?" Mirax batted her brown eyes. "Whatever do you mean, Lieutenant Horn?"

"Well, I precipitated the mass resignation of the New Republic's most celebrated fighter squadron and vowed that we'd liberate Thyferra from Ysanne Isard's clutches. So far, toward that end, we have a squadron's worth of pilots, *my* X-wing, and if you're really in this with us, your freighter."

Mirax smiled. "Versus three Imperial Star Destroyers and a Super Star Destroyer, not to mention any sort of Thyferran military forces that might oppose us."

Corran nodded. "Right."

Mirax's grin broadened. "Okay, so get to the trouble part."

"Mirax, be serious."

"I am. You forget, dear heart, that it was an X-wing and a freighter that lit up the first Death Star."

"This is a little bit different."

"Not really." She reached out and tapped his forehead with a finger. "You and I, Wedge and Tycho, and everyone else knows what it takes to defeat the Empire. It's not a matter of equipment, but of having the heart to use that equipment. The Empire was broken because, for the good of the galaxy, it *had to be broken*. The Rebels were given no choice, and because of that, they pushed themselves further than the Imperials did. We know we *can* win and that we *must* win, and Isard's people know nothing of the kind."

"That's all well and good, Mirax, and I agree, but this is a massive undertaking. The sheer amount of equipment we'll need to pull this off is staggering."

"Agreed. I don't think this will be easy, but it *can* be done."

"I know." Corran massaged his eyes with his left hand. "Too many variables and not enough data available to begin to assign them values."

"And three hours before dawn isn't the time you should be wrestling with such things. As bright as you might be, Corran Horn, this is not an hour when you do your best work."

Corran raised an eyebrow. "I seem to recall you singing a different tune last evening about this time."

"At that time you weren't concerned with Ysanne Isard, you were concerned with me."

"Ah, and that makes the difference?"

"From my perspective, you bet." She took the lightsaber from his hand and set it atop his dresser. "And I think, if you're willing to work with me, I can share that perspective with you."

He kissed her on the tip of the nose. "It would be my pleasure."

"That, Lieutenant Horn, is just half the objective here."

"Forgive me." Following her toward the bed, he stepped over the silken puddle her robe made on the floor. "You know, I just got out of prison."

"For that I won't forgive you but perhaps"—she smiled up at him—"I will make some allowance for good behavior."

2

Wedge Antilles felt decidedly uncomfortable out of uniform. *Actually, I feel uncomfortable out of the service.* During the covert mission to Coruscant, he'd not been in hailing distance of an Alliance uniform, and he'd even worn Imperial uniforms a couple of times, but that had not bothered him. He'd spent most of his adult life as part of the Rebel Alliance and now he had chosen to leave it.

There was no doubt in his mind that the decision to leave was the right one to make. He fully understood why the New Republic couldn't attack Thyferra and bring Ysanne Isard to justice. Since she was installed as the Chief of State through an internal revolution—as opposed to an invasion—her holding office was not a case of Imperial aggression, but of self-determination. If the New Republic rejected that idea in this one case, plenty of other nation-states would think long and hard before joining the New Republic or would consider leaving.

Wedge forced himself to smile and looked up at the light-brown-haired man with bright blue eyes sitting across the table from him. "Have we bitten off more than we can chew?"

Tycho Celchu shrugged. "It's a mouthful, but with some more teeth, we might be able to choke it down. There is some good news on this whole front you know. We have the ten million credits that Ysanne Isard placed in accounts to frame me. That money is mine, which means it's *ours*. We have the five Z-95 Headhunters that were used to help liberate Coruscant."

"But they're not hyperspace capable."

"True, but that's not going to be their value for us." Tycho began to smile. "The Z-95s are part of history. They're *collectable*. I've already had offers from museums and amusement parks to buy them. We can probably get one point five million for each of them—the Bothan Military Academy wants the one Asyr flew so badly they're not even trying to hide their desire for it."

Wedge's jaw dropped. "That would give us quite a war chest."

"It should take care of many of our needs."

"Provided we can find places where we can buy weapons that are restricted or illegal on most civilized planets."

Tycho nodded. "Winter and Mirax are working on that problem. Winter, from her work locating Imperial supply depots for us to raid, knows where there are bits and pieces of things that we can buy, borrow, or steal. Mirax is fairly certain she can locate sources for pretty much anything else we need. And we are getting donations of material."

Wedge smiled and looked around the small office in which he and Tycho sat. After their resignation, they had been forced out of Rogue Squadron's headquarters facility. Various citizens had turned around and offered the ex-Rogues apartments and offices. They'd been feted and celebrated and praised as if they were the only people in the galaxy who still had in them the rebel spirit that defeated the Empire.

"Do you think the Provisional Council ordered the grounding of all skyhooks just to spite us?"

Tycho shook his head. "That's a popular rumor after we were offered the SoroSuub skyhook, but we know the safety concerns over the things are well founded. The *Lusankya* blasted most of one out of the sky, and the falling debris obliterated a couple of square kilometers. Grounding the skyhooks in that area and where the *Lusankya* blasted out of Coruscant provides housing for the survivors of those disasters *and* allows the resources used to keep the skyhooks airborne to be diverted to other projects."

"Too bad for us, because a skyhook would have been perfect. It would have enough storage to let us house our equipment when we get it."

Tycho raised an eyebrow. "I think you're more concerned that it would provide Isard with a single target to hit when she comes after us, which she will. It minimizes collateral damage."

"Unless you're living beneath us."

"True."

"As was your speculation." Wedge frowned. "The fact is that we've declared war on Isard, but we're not going to be indiscriminate in waging that war. She knows no such restriction on her actions. In reality, we shouldn't be looking at any headquarters anywhere near Coruscant. There are a bunch of old Rebel bases we could convert."

"Even if we *could* get it, I'm not going back to Hoth." Tycho shivered. "I saw enough snow there to last me a dozen lifetimes."

"Which is about what it takes to burn that Hoth cold from your bones." Wedge shook his head. "No, I was thinking about Yavin 4 or Talasea. Endor would be nice, but the Ewoks would be targets for her."

A chime sounded from the door. Wedge looked up and said, "Open."

The door slid open to reveal a flame-haired man of above-average height wearing the uniform of a Captain in the New Republic Armed Forces. He started to salute, then hesitated, then completed the gesture in a crisp and respectful manner.

Wedge smiled and stood behind the table. He returned the salute, then waved the man into the office and toward a chair. "Good to see you again, Pash. I see you've got your rank back. You're rejoining your flight group?"

Pash Cracken nodded, then shook hands with both

Tycho and Wedge before seating himself. "Good to see both of you as well." His green-eyed gaze flicked down at the floor for a moment. "I really wish I were going to be with the rest of you. Just say the word, Wedge, and I'm a civilian."

The pain in Pash's voice started a sympathetic aching in Wedge's chest. "We'd love to have you with us, but there's no way you can resign and join us. Your father's the head of Alliance Security. If you came with us there would be no way anyone would believe we're operating independently. I know you'd not be reporting to your father, but the appearance would cause trouble for the New Republic."

"I know." Pash took a deep breath and let it out slowly. "I'm back as part of Commander Varth's wing. While the bulk of the fleet is off chasing Warlord Zsinj, we're being pulled Core-ward to cover some of the sectors where Zsinj used to run around. It's going to be something of an adventure for our people, because we'll be staging from Folor, that moon base orbiting Commenor."

"I remember it well." Wedge smiled. "Not a lot of creature comforts there."

"It'll beat what we've got out on Generis. It's backward enough that most folks there don't even realize the Old Republic has fallen."

Tycho smiled. "And they're wondering why nothing new is being shipped from Alderaan."

"That's pretty much it." Pash leaned forward, resting his elbows on his knees. "Our patrol area includes Yag'Dhul, the system that is home to the Givin. One of our initial exercises involves going in and rendering the space station there uninhabitable so Warlord Zsinj won't have it as a place to which he can retreat."

Wedge frowned. "Correct me if I'm wrong, but Zsinj hasn't been anywhere near that station since we hit it and stole his bacta."

"So it seems." Pash shrugged. "Anyway, my flight group has the job of denying this station to Zsinj. I was thinking that perhaps you might like to stage your operations out of that station. It would deny it to Zsinj and would provide you a decent fighting platform from which to work. It's conve-

nient to Coruscant and Thyferra as well as to a number of
other worlds."

Wedge's brown eyes narrowed. "And would allow you to
wander by and help out if we got into trouble."

Pash sat back and feigned surprise. "Why you didn't
think that was what I had in mind, did you? Not at all. I
mean, yes, my people might avail themselves of the station if
we needed to stop—no way I'm going to set down on
Yag'Dhul. The weather is too unpredictable to allow us to use
it as a viable staging area."

"Point taken."

Tycho nodded. "The station would make for a good staging area. If Pash were to report that it had been rendered
uninhabitable, then Isard might be led to believe it's junk.
There's no doubt in my mind that at some point she'll find
out where we are and come after us, but an operational space
platform has to be a bit more daunting than a skyhook or a
warehouse here on Coruscant."

"Definitely seems like this is our best choice." Wedge
nodded, then smiled at Pash. "Thanks a lot. You've solved
one of our major problems. We now have a home."

"I hoped you'd say that." Pash smiled broadly. "I ship
out at the end of the week. I'll be back in an A-wing, but
that's not so bad. We'll keep the station safe for you until you
can come out and take possession, and we'll transmit reports
about its destruction just to keep folks guessing."

"I appreciate it." Wedge frowned for a moment. "Pash,
when you joined Rogue Squadron, you said you wanted to
join to get a perspective on how well you fly and fight. You
wanted to be part of the best unit going to find out if you
really were as good as you have been told you are. Did
you get that perspective? Are you comfortable going back to
your own unit?"

Pash sat back, his brows knitted with concentration. "I
think I did get that perspective, Wedge. Granted, I've only
been with the Rogues for a short time, but we did some fairly
nasty flying. I don't think any fight I've been part of before or
since flying a Headhunter through a blacked-out city in the
middle of the mother of all thunderstorms will match that

experience. That was flying by instinct, by skill, and by luck. I made shots and pulled maneuvers I never would have thought possible. After that performance I almost wish there was another Death Star up there for me to take a shot at."

"I'd not go that far, Pash." Wedge shared a grin with Tycho. "You are good, *very* good. The Imps have every right to fear you."

"Thanks, Wedge. It means a lot coming from you." The pilot brushed fingers back through his red hair. "As for my being comfortable returning to my unit, yeah, I'm okay there, too. One thing being with Rogue Squadron taught me is that to be a unit, everyone has to pull their own weight. I've been afraid that my people wouldn't think for themselves and would follow me into disaster if I make a mistake. What I'd missed is exactly what you do. You give your people responsibilities and make them rely on each other. If we'd *just* followed your lead while on Coruscant, the Imps would still own this world. I need to do just that with my people. If I give them responsibility, they'll learn that I trust them. Once they realize that, they'll also trust in themselves and won't follow me blindly when I do something stupid."

Wedge stood and offered Pash his hand. "You'll be sorely missed, Captain Cracken, but our loss is your unit's gain. We'll see you soon at the Yag'Dhul station."

"Thanks, Wedge, Tycho. I look forward to seeing you there."

The door closed behind Pash, prompting Wedge and Tycho to exchange glances again. "Well, Tycho, it seems our housing problem is solved. Now all we need is a dozen or more X-wings, munitions for same, droids, techs, foodstuffs, and other supplies, not to mention all the equipment necessary to repair any damage to our new base."

Tycho winced. "That's quite the tall order. Dare I say it?"

"What?"

"I wish we had Emtrey to help us put this whole package together."

Wedge smiled as he thought of the black 3PO droid with a spaceport controller droid's clamshell head. Installed as the unit's Quartermaster, the droid had really been meant to keep an eye on Tycho in case he was a spy in the Empire's control. Despite his espionage duties, he had been a wonder at procuring supplies in a timely manner. Even so, he could be annoyingly voluble, which is why Wedge spent as much time as possible away from him.

Wedge sighed. "Yeah, I guess I miss him, too." He shrugged. "In his absence, I guess we'll just have to do the best we can."

"True, and hope that's going to be good enough."

3

His move to Thyferra left Fliry Vorru in a perpetual state of simmering anger. After years spent in the spice mines of Kessel, with its thin, arid atmosphere, and then his short stay on Coruscant—similarly dry but decidedly more metropolitan and to his tastes—Thyferra was all but unendurable. Green predominated, from the deep and dark tones of the tropical planet's rain forests to the lighter shades used in decorating, fashion, and even cosmetics. After Kessel's barren mines and the gray canyons of Coruscant, Vorru found the omnipresence of verdant life oppressive.

The world's humidity dragged on him as he walked the halls of the Xucphra corporate headquarters. *One does not breathe the air here, one drinks it.* The heavy humidity meant most of the fabric used on the world was light and thin, in many cases quite sheer, while the fashions themselves tended to be abbreviated. Although this did offer some distractions— for the women of Thyferra tended strongly toward tall, lean, and beautiful—many of the people he had to deal with were short, hairy, lumpen creatures who should have been swathed in bolts of the most opaque cloth available. Their positions as the scions of the various families that ran the Xucphra corporation and, now, the civil government, required him to be polite and even deferential.

This requirement to courteously entertain the most stupid of ideas ground on him most of all. Under the Empire's rule, the Xucphra and Zaltin corporations had been given a monopoly on the production of bacta. Thyferra served as the heart of the operation, with alazhi harvesting and kavam synthesis taking place primarily on Thyferra, but also at a few colony worlds elsewhere. The monopoly had resulted in both corporations becoming slothful and greedy—with their profits guaranteed, there was no need for expansion or diversification. As a result, people rose to positions of importance with no eye toward merit, just seniority.

Vorru's installation as Minister of Trade had given him oversight over the production and sale of bacta. His initial review of the whole production and distribution process had revealed to him hundreds of places where potential profit was being ignored. For example, bacta produced at a satellite facility would be shipped back to Thyferra before being transshipped to a world a dozen light-years away from the facility where it was produced. The only reason for such an activity was so the shipping firm, which was owned by Xucphra, could earn a profit, which ended up back in the pockets of the owners of Xucphra anyway—though it had been pared down by the cost of ship maintenance, crew, bookkeepers, and others.

This hardly surprised Vorru because of the way the Zaltin and Xucphra corporations had been set up. Ten thousand humans formed the management cadre for the corporations, and they oversaw the operations carried out by approximately 2.8 million native Vratix laborers. The Vratix were very efficient, requiring little or no supervision, so the galaxy-wide operations hardly required the legion of administrative personnel in place. Each corporation discouraged mixing and mingling with individuals from the other corporation, hence they became insular and fierce rivals. While their isolation had not caused problems with genetic inbreeding—though Vorru thought *that* was only a generation or two away— there certainly was philosophical inbreeding that led to sinecures being created for incompetent members of the corporate family.

I assume my last order to eliminate some of these fiefdoms is the reason Iceheart wants to see me. Xucphra had displaced Zaltin in the recent coup and installed Ysanne Isard as the world's leader. Most of the Zaltin folks had fled or been killed, making the Xucphra family the sole masters of a world they had long shared. As such they had no desire to listen to or comply with the orders of an offworlder like him. Even so, they were so thoroughly socialized to accept a hierarchy of command, that they would complain about him to Isard, another offworlder. It made no sense to Vorru, and in this lack of comprehension he felt fortunate. *The day I start thinking like my charges is the day I choose to die.*

Rounding a corner, Vorru strode past the desk of Isard's secretary, refusing to allow himself to be distracted by her spare costume. *That is a pleasure I will save myself for solace after Iceheart is through with me.* The secretary, a woman whose long black hair covered more than her clothes, smiled at him, but made no attempt to stop him or even announce him.

The Imperial Royal Guards flanking the doorway to Isard's office did not react to him at all, which reinforced the pity Vorru felt for them. Unlike everyone else on the planet, they still wore the uniforms they brought with them from Imperial Center. A thick scarlet cloak covered the red armor and though no puddles formed at their feet, Vorru knew they had to be roasting inside it. Even more burdensome to them, though, had to have been the orders to relent and not treat everyone like a potential assassin. *The Thyferrans reacted badly to the strict security Isard's Royal Guard imposed initially, so she has orderd her bodyguard to relax—something that will probably require gene therapy before they feel at ease doing it.*

As he entered Isard's office, he immediately felt a bit more comfortable. The only greenery in sight was located outside the building and ensconced safely behind large, amorphous transparisteel viewports. The room itself had been paneled with very blond wood, giving it a Tatooinish cast. As had been the case with her office on Coruscant, it remained largely empty and free of clutter. *Furnishings would be of use only if one wanted to linger here, and with* her *being present, this is not likely, even if she has gone* native.

On Coruscant the black-haired woman with white temple locks had been given to wearing a uniform similar in cut to that of Imperial Grand Admirals, though hers was colored blood red, not white. On Thyferra she had chosen to wear clothing that was more loose and flowing. The fabric she chose was still blood red—in keeping with the uniforms worn by the Imperial Royal Guard—but she eschewed the nearly transparent cloth others wore happily. *Pity, she is striking enough to wear it well.* Vorru had long since heard the rumor that Isard had been one of Palpatine's lovers and could not deny she was attractive.

Her eyes, and all that lies behind them, is undoubtedly what drew the Emperor to her. The Hothlike icy blue orb of her right eye contrasted sharply with the fiery molten red of her left. They seemed windows into the duality of her nature. She could be cold and calculating in the extreme, but also given over to towering incendiary angers. Vorru had, to date, avoided being immolated in one of them, but he *had* been scorched a time or two.

He bowed his white-maned head toward her. "You sent for me?"

"I have had information from Imperial Center that I thought you might find of interest." She kept her voice light, but that did not mean it lacked force. "You had been wondering after Kirtan Loor."

Vorru nodded. The Intelligence agent and leader of the Palpatine Counter-insurgency Front had disappeared just hours before Isard had fled from Coruscant, bearing Vorru away with her. "My assumption was that he had been taken and broken in interrogation. That was the only explanation for why so many of your operatives still on Coruscant were swept up in the aftermath of your departure."

"He was certainly the cause of the sweep, though it appears he gave the information up voluntarily." Isard's eyes narrowed. "He attempted to use an operation of his own to deal with the bacta convoy headed for Coruscant through the Alderaan system."

"The convoy that Warlord Zsinj hit." Vorru nodded slowly. "Loor had told me he had a squadron of X-wings painted up to represent Rogue Squadron. He wanted to use them to strafe the squadron's headquarters, but I stopped him. So the Rogues that Zsinj destroyed there really belonged to Loor. Amazing."

"Indeed." Her eyes flashed pitilessly. "Loor realized, after the disaster, that I had leaked word of the convoy to Zsinj so he'd strike at it. I assumed his need for revenge upon Rogue Squadron would make him hit it and destroy them. It would have, too, had the real squadron not been delayed. Loor apparently assumed I would realize he had attempted to deceive me, since his transmission of the report about the convoy and his plans to deal with it came too late for me to countermand them. He chose to run over to the Rebels and seek sanctuary with them."

Vorru nodded. "There are ways to deal with him. Boba Fett could find and kill him, I have no doubt."

"His skills will not be necessary." Isard smiled in a way that managed to mix glee with cruelty. "I had learned from another agent of mine about a secret witness to be brought forward in the Celchu treason trial. I thought it was General Evir Derricote and set traps to prevent him from reaching the Imperial Court. You'll recall I asked you to post a dozen people at various places in Imperial Center."

"Yes." *And I only sent three to each location, since I needed the rest to evacuate my bacta storage facility.* "None of them found Derricote."

"No, he probably was not there after all. Loor was their witness. I had thought Derricote had escaped from Lusankya, but he apparently died at the hands of Corran Horn, during his escape. Horn killed your men in the Galactic Museum, in fact." Isard pressed her hands together, fingertip to fingertip. "The agent I set as my failsafe to stop Derricote instead shot and killed Loor and, in turn, was killed by his own wife. She was one of Loor's escorts—she had known him from Corellia."

"Iella Wessiri." Vorru felt a moment's pang of sympathy for her. She had been an influential and intelligent member of the cabal that succeeded in stripping away Coruscant's planetary shields and opening it to the Rebel invasion. Though her background with the Corellian Security Force made him view her as an enemy, he did admire her skill and dedication. *If she had to shoot her husband, it will tear her up inside. She does not deserve that sort of pain.*

Isard smiled. "I find it rather delicious that she was forced to shoot Diric. He was useful, but really just a pawn. His love for her was enough, apparently, to get him to reinterpret some of my orders to him, though, ultimately, he belonged to *me,* not to her. I hope *that* hurts her more than killing him did."

Vorru frowned. "If Loor was killed, how did Alliance Security sweep up your agents?"

"Loor apparently encoded a datacard as a safeguard against them just killing him. It seems the key, which he believed known only to himself, was also known to Corran Horn."

"Ah, and Loor believed Horn dead." Vorru chuckled lightly. "I find the irony something that would have tortured Loor."

"Yes, but now his stupidity tortures me. The information coming to me from Imperial Center is severely limited. The official information service tells me more than my spies. This Horn has much to answer for."

"I could have told you he would be trouble, but even *I* believed you'd killed him. Horn's father and even his grandfather were very driven men. Of course, you have ample evidence of his drive, and now it's focused on us, here."

The color in Isard's red eye seemed to flare for a second. "You refer to the mass resignations from the squadron and their vow to liberate Thyferra?" Her laughter, which sounded quite genuine and unforced to Vorru, nonetheless had few of the pleasing tones usually associated with laughter.

"I appreciate the contempt you might feel for their effort, but it cannot be discounted. Yes, we have three destroyers, two of the Imperial, one of the *Victory*-class, and a Super Star

Destroyer to defend us, but your confidence in them is as misplaced as the Emperor's misjudgment of the Rebel Alliance."

Isard's face became a frozen mask. "Oh, you think so, do you? You think I am repeating the mistakes the Emperor made?"

Vorru met her stare openly. "You undoubtedly don't see it that way, but it is my place to remind you of the errors others have made so you don't repeat them. You are correct, Horn, Antilles, and the others have nothing right now, and it does seem apparent that the New Republic does not support their effort, but that could change. And, yes, we control the bacta output for the galaxy, but we must be careful. If we make it too dear, forces will join to oppose us, and the former Rogues are in an excellent position to make the most of that opposition."

Isard stared at him for a moment or two more, then abruptly broke her stare off. "Your caution is noted."

"I will also point out that we still have the Ashern to deal with here. They may be a minority among the Vratix, but they have struck in the past at key production facilities. Their strikes over the past year or so have become more precise and effective. I think they will become even more so because of the rumors that some Zaltin personnel have joined them."

"Yes, the Black-claw Rebels are a bother, but that's why I have deployed stormtroopers to defend our facilities."

Vorru smiled. "That was a good move, as was restricting them to play a defensive role. Establishing a Thyferran Home Defense Corps that will allow Xucphra volunteers to fight the Ashern themselves was also brilliant."

"Thank you. Xucphra's people will come to see themselves in an alliance with my stormtroopers in no time. Once a THDC force gets in over its head and my people rescue them, the humans here will see my stormtroopers as the stalwart white line that separates them from death. Those who are dubious about us will be won over." Isard spread her hands apart. "Erisi Dlarit is heading up the fighter wing I have given to the THDC. She is a hero among her people, and having her so elevated proves to the Thyferrans that I understand how superior they are."

Vorru nodded slowly. *There is no denying it, she is excellent at analyzing and utilizing the psychology of a subject people against themselves. Still, when there is someone she can't break down, like Horn or Antilles, she has no way to defend against what they might do.* He looked up at her. "And what are your thoughts on this rylca Mon Mothma pronounced a cure for your Krytos virus?"

"Propaganda, clearly, meant to calm the masses. The fact is that its existence and efficacy against the virus are immaterial. *If* Derricote had been successful in creating the virus I asked him to create or if Loor had delayed the conquest of Imperial Center, the New Republic would have been broken beyond repair. As it is now, they are hard put to deal with the demands their populace is making on them. As we restrict bacta flow to the New Republic and its worlds, we will alienate member states."

"You mean we will be playing the same game we did on Imperial Center but on a larger scale here?"

"Exactly." Isard glanced up, looking well above his head. "My goal has always been to destroy the Rebellion, then move to rebuild the Empire. In effect, by letting them take Imperial Center, we *have* destroyed the Rebellion. They are no longer an elusive force that can strike at will. They now have to take responsibility and deliver on the promises they have made. When they fail to do that, the people will look for the sort of stability they had before. If we play things carefully, we will not have to reconquer Imperial Center, we will be *invited* back to resume our rightful place at the head of the Empire."

"Interesting analysis, and accurate, I think, except in one thing."

"And that is?"

Vorru's dark eyes shrank to bare slits. "Antilles, Horn, and the others. They have the freedom the Rebels once had. They are a problem we will have to deal with and deal with swiftly."

"Or else?"

"I was in a position to see them render Imperial Center defenseless." Vorru's voice hardened. "If we don't deal with them I fear they will become a problem with which we cannot deal."

4

It didn't surprise Corran Horn to find Iella Wessiri in the Corellian Sanctuary, but the expression on her face threatened to crush his heart in his chest. Her light brown hair had been pulled back into a single braid and her broad shoulders were hunched forward. She sat on the front bench in the small chamber, leaning over and balanced precariously enough that he expected her to fall at any second. The way her grief pulled at her face, arching the corners of her mouth downward, made it seem as if gravity would, in fact, tug her to the floor.

Corran hesitated in the doorway of the small domed building. Because of the hostile relationship between the New Republic and the Corellian Diktat, repatriating Corellians who died away from the planet of their birth had become impossible. The Sanctuary had been created by exiled Corellians to give their dead a resting place. Unlike Alderaanians, who often sealed their dead in capsules and shot them into orbit within the Graveyard, allowing them to float forever amid the debris that marked where their planet had once been; Corellians cremated their dead exiles and used industrial-grade gravity generators to compress the carbon residue into raw synthetic diamonds. This imparted a physical immortality to the dead. The diamonds were then brought to the Sanctuary and imbedded in the black walls and ceiling to create a glittering series of constellations as seen from Corellia.

The sheer number of diamonds glinting in the ceiling sent a shiver through Corran. *We've given a lot to the Rebellion, though other worlds have given as much or more. As beautiful as this display is, it is also horrible. The Imperials who wished to make the galaxy over in their own image have, in fact, created here a small galaxy that is entirely given over to mourning.*

Corran walked forward and slid onto the bench next to Iella. She didn't look over at him, but melted against his shoulder and chest as he put an arm around her. "It's going to be okay, Iella, really."

"He never hurt anyone, Corran, never."

"I don't imagine Kirtan Loor would agree, but I'll concede the point."

He felt her chest convulse once, then she looked up at him with red-rimmed brown eyes. "No, you're right." Her mouth made a weak attempt at twisting itself into a smile. "As much as he admired your drive, Corran, Diric really appreciated your sense of humor. He said it marked your resiliency. He thought that as long as you could laugh, especially at yourself, you'd always heal from any trauma."

"He was a wise man." He tightened his embrace a bit. "You know he'd hate to see you like this, to think he was causing you this much pain."

"I know. That hasn't made it any easier, though." She dabbed at tears with a handkerchief. "I keep thinking that if I'd seen something there, I could have prevented what happened. He wouldn't have been a traitor."

"Whoa, wait, Iella, that is *not* your fault. There was nothing, absolutely nothing, you could have detected or done to help him." Corran shivered and felt his flesh pucker. "I know what Isard did to those she wanted to warp and convert into her puppets. I resisted, I don't know how. It could have been personality or genetics or training or anything.

Tycho and I both proved unsuitable for her—as did a few others, but I think she would have had an easy time of breaking Diric down."

"What?" Iella's hissed question carried with it undercurrents of betrayal. She tried to pull away from him, but he held on.

"That's not a strike against Diric, honestly it isn't. Diric was a victim, and you have to know that he resisted her mightily because even after his capture Imperial Intelligence didn't find you. I think he built a mental reserve around you and was willing to sacrifice everything to protect you. Even altering her orders at the end was designed to protect you, and in his mind, sacrificing himself to do so was not too much to pay."

Corran frowned. "The one thing about Diric that characterized him was his curiosity. We both saw it in the way he'd ask us about cases and push us to look at other explanations. He was thoughtful and thorough—espionage was a natural place for him. You said yourself that Isard first placed him in Derricote's lab to spy on the General. She probably suggested to him that his success in that role determined whether or not she'd let you live. She undoubtedly told him that lie concerning *any* actions he took after he rejoined you."

Iella's defiance melted into despair. "Great, now you're telling me that he'd not have been in that position except for me."

"No! You had nothing to do with where he ended up—that was entirely due to Isard and no one else." Corran sighed. "Look, think about the good Diric did. Aril Nunb pointed out that he was the only person in Derricote's lab that was kind to her and who helped her through her recovery from the Krytos virus. And after he came back, he was a great comfort to Tycho through the trial. He even pushed you to look for evidence to break the frame Isard had settled around Tycho. And, like it or not, he did kill Loor, and I can't fault him for that."

"He thought he was shooting Derricote but knew it wasn't him. He was happy he'd gotten Loor."

"Well, I *did* kill Derricote and I'd have been more happy

to kill Loor myself." Corran brushed a hand along her cheek and wiped tears away with his thumb. "Diric wasn't happy existing the way he did, but he regained himself in defying Isard and doing all the little things that sabotaged her plans. In the end he won. He'd often complained his life had no meaning . . ."

"But it did."

"Agreed, and at the very last he finally got to see how much it meant. He'd saved you, he saved Aril, he saved Tycho. He's at peace, and he'd want you to be at peace with his death, too."

"I know, but it's just not going to be that easy, Corran. I was there, I held him as he died from wounds *I'd* inflicted." Iella sniffed, then swallowed with difficulty. "Your father died in your arms. How did you get through it?"

Corran felt his own throat thicken. "I won't kid you, it wasn't, *isn't*, easy. There are things you expect, like seeing him again in the morning or at night or being able to call him to tell him about your day or to ask a question, and then he's not there. You know you feel hollow inside, but you don't know just how hollow until things like that help you define the edges of the void."

She nodded slowly. "There are things I see or hear and I think, 'Diric would like that or would be intrigued by that,' then his death comes crashing back in on me. It seems to me that such things will never stop happening."

"They won't. They go on forever."

A tremor shook Iella. "Great."

"The thing of it is, Iella, they become transformed. Now you feel the loss and the grief, and part of that will always be there. In addition to it, though, shining through it will be the triumph of having known Diric. When I hear that stupid Lomin-ale ditty or eat part of a ryshcate, I remember my father. I remember his booming laugh and that secret smile of contentment he could flash you when things were good."

"And the way that smile would carry on up into his eyes and how, with a slight shift, it would harden into something that would make the most fearless of Black Sunners begin to tremble in interrogation." Iella gave out a little sigh. "I can see it with your father, but not Diric."

"Not yet."

"No, not yet."

"But you will." Corran kissed her forehead. "It won't be easy, but the only way I got through it was because of you and Gil and my other friends."

"You didn't have any other friends."

"Yeah, well, that may be, but you *do*. Mirax and Wedge and Winter and all of us, we're here to help you. You're not alone. We can't feel the same depth of pain you do, but we can help you bear it."

Iella nodded. "I appreciate that, I really do." Her brows arrowed in toward each other as she concentrated. "I have decided I can't remain here on Coruscant. The memories are mostly bad and overpowering. I have to get away—even if it means leaving all my friends."

"I understand. I wanted to run after my father's death, too." Corran smiled. "The trick of it is, for you, that your running doesn't mean you lose your friends."

Iella's eyes sharpened. "What do you mean?"

Corran looked around the Sanctuary, then lowered his voice into a whisper. "We're leaving Coruscant, and we want you to come with us. You're part of our family, part of the squadron. We're going after the monster who warped Diric. We're going to make sure she doesn't do that to anyone else. We need you to come along and help us get her."

Iella pulled back and sat up straight. "The odds against success are astronomical."

"About the same as taking Coruscant from the Empire."

Iella nodded coolly. "Odds are for those who want to minimize their own risks. I want to maximize Isard's risks. Count me in."

5

Brushing brown hair out of his eyes, Wedge looked up at the people seated in the small, amphitheater-style room and smiled. "I want to thank you all for showing up for this meeting. This is our first organizational meeting, but some decisions have already been made. They will stand unless they meet with overwhelming protest. No one should hesitate to voice a question or make a comment—this is going to be a bit more democratic than the squadron was, primarily because plans and orders are originating with us, not being passed down from above."

Everyone nodded in assent with his remarks, so Wedge continued. "Corran Horn began this whole thing by resigning from Rogue Squadron first, but he's agreed to let me lead this group. I've appointed Tycho Celchu as my second in command. Lady Winter is our Intelligence Officer as well as handling part of the Quartermaster duties. Mirax Terrik is handling the other half of those duties. Tycho will let you know what we've got in the way of supplies."

Tycho turned around in his seat. "We have a fair number of credits—approximately seventeen million, give or take."

Gavin laughed. "Seventeen million, I'll take."

"So would a lot of other folks, which is precisely what they want to do." Tycho frowned. "Rumors of what happened at the reception, despite the spin the New Republic Information Ministry tried to put on it, have spread quickly. While we are getting a lot of support, the folks who deal in the things we need to accomplish our mission know how desperate we are. Right now we have one X-wing—Corran's ship—and the services of Mirax's *Pulsar Skate*. Other ships are fairly dear. I would imagine, to get the fighters we need, we'll probably end up hiring mercenaries who come with their own equipment. This shouldn't surprise anyone, though the prices might. All the little Warlords out there are looking for fighters, so its a seller's market."

Standing at the front of the room, Wedge nodded. "That's getting a bit ahead of ourselves, but it's worth keeping in mind. We've got some basic data to mull over first, concerning our objectives. Winter has put them together." Wedge pointed to the holoprojector toward the front of the room. "Winter, if you please."

Winter stood and walked to the front of the room with a stately grace that left no question in Wedge's mind why people on Alderaan had frequently mistaken her for Princess Leia Organa. Though Winter wore her white hair long and, today, in a thick braid, she carried herself with a nobility that matched her exquisite features. Slender and stunning, she seemed somehow incongruous with the dangerous missions she'd been on during her career as a covert agent for the Rebellion.

Which is exactly why she was never suspected.

Winter picked up the datapad that was connected by a cable to the holoprojector. She hit one button, dimming the glow panels in the room and bringing up a holographic projection of a planet. "This is our objective: Thyferra. It is a fairly normal terrestrial planet with a breathable atmosphere and two moons, neither of which has atmosphere or is inhabited. Thyferra is covered with rain forests and enjoys a day that is roughly twenty-one point three standard hours long. The axial tilt is negligible so there are really no seasons. Because of its proximity to the system's star, a yellow star, and the mildly elevated levels of carbon dioxide in the atmosphere, it maintains a tropical climate year round. The way Coruscant felt after the storms that took down the power grid is pretty much what this planet experiences all the time."

Wedge frowned. To take the power grid down and eliminate the defense shields on Coruscant, Rogue Squadron had caused a lot of water to boil off into the atmosphere, creating a huge thunderstorm. For a week and a half following that storm the air had been thick and heavy. *No wonder the plant that goes into bacta thrives there.*

"Thyferra has three stellar-class spaceports—one at what is now being called Xucphra City. The other two are located on separate continents and are primarily used for the loading and unloading of bacta. Inbound ships stop at Xucphra City first for Customs and Immigration inspections, then are sent on to the spaceports to do business. They leave from those spaceports and head directly out to the destinations."

Nawara Ven raised a hand. "I presume the metropolis's name change came about when the Xucphra corporation took over. What was it called before that?"

"Zalxuc City, which really is not much better." Winter directed the computer to zoom in and supply an aerial view of the city. "As you can see, it's not really a metropolis at all. The human population of Thyferra was only ten thousand before Isard took over. Many Zaltin families fled, and their housing is being used for Imperial Army and Navy officers and enlisted folk on leave from their ships. The *Lusankya* alone carries twenty-five times the human population of the planet, so there is no question about the possibility of occupation when or if Isard orders it. So far she has refrained and is using Imperial personnel and equipment to train and supply the Thyferran Home Defense Corps."

Winter nodded to the six-limbed, insectoid alien standing in the back of the room. "The native population of Thyferra refers to themselves as the Vratix. The production of bacta— literally the brewing together of alazhi and kavam—appears to produce an almost mystical amount of satisfaction for the Vratix. Qlaern Hirf here is a *verachen*—a master blender— who commands subordinates and creates bacta. A *verachen* is very much equivalent to a brewmaster at any Lomin-ale brewery, though a *verachen* also has highly defined rights and responsibilities within the Vratix society.

"I should also note that the Vratix are neither male nor female—those roles are played at different times in the life cycle, so referring to Qlaern as 'he' or 'she' is inappropriate. Moreover, since the Vratix do constitute something of a low-grade hive mind, they are more comfortable with a plural pronoun, so *they* and *them* will have to suffice."

The Vratix in the back clicked its curved mandibles. "Your dissertation honors us, Lady Winter."

"Thank you. Because of their desire—even *need*—to produce bacta, the Vratix welcomed the influx of humans who were willing to set up and run businesses that created a demand for more bacta, allowing and even compelling the Vratix to do more of what they enjoyed doing. While individual Vratix are part of the corporate ownership for both Zaltin and Xucphra, Imperial laws made it necessary to remove them from active leadership and decision-making roles in the companies. Zaltin and Xucphra were given Imperial monopolies on the production of bacta, presumably in return for bribes paid to the local Moff and the Emperor. This has made Thyferra a very rich planet and the humans who live there very wealthy. The Vratix, on the other hand, live very modest lives in tribal groups within the rain forests."

She typed a data request into the datapad, which switched the image of the city for a trio of individuals. "Ysanne Isard was installed as Chief Operating Officer and Head of State for Thyferra in a coup d'etat approximately two weeks ago. Preparations had been made well before that, since the revolution was completed prior to her Super Star Destroyer, *Lusankya*, arriving in orbit. Not much is known about her for certain—rumors abound about her having been one of the Emperor's lovers, for example; but there is no confirmation of that. We do know her father was the Director of Imperial Intelligence before her, but she turned over to the Emperor evidence that her father was going to join the Rebellion, causing his downfall and her elevation to replace him."

Nawara Ven raised a hand. "Was her father going to come over to the Rebellion?"

Winter shrugged. "If he was, I have no knowledge of his planned defection. There is no doubt his daughter was ambitious enough to have manufactured evidence against him, so she is very dangerous. Dislodging her will be difficult and probably require a ground assault. She is not, as nearly as we know, a pilot, so the chances of any of you getting to vape her in a dogfight are nil."

Winter pointed to the next figure. "Fliry Vorru, on the other hand, might well be able to fight you in a ship. He was a former Imperial Moff from Corellia, which this squadron liberated from Kessel. Vorru fled with Isard to Thyferra and is now the Minister of Trade. It is unclear when Vorru began to work with Isard, but the possibility that he struck a deal with her upon planetfall on Coruscant cannot be ruled out. While we put much of our misfortune concerning the operations to take Coruscant down to having Zekka Thyne and other Imperial spies in our midst, it is entirely possible Vorru was working directly for Isard at that point. He certainly was in her employ by the time he was appointed a Colonel in the Coruscant Constabulary."

She waved a hand at the third individual, a tall, slender woman with black hair worn short. "Erisi Dlarit should be familiar to all of us. She is from a Xucphra family and was the Imperial mole inside Rogue Squadron. Her actual value to the Empire was minimal. At best she was responsible for Corran's capture, Bror Jace's death, and the betrayal of the bacta convoy at Alderaan to Warlord Zsinj. While she did provide information on our operations on Coruscant to the Empire, the fact that Wedge allowed no outside contact prior to the final attempt to destroy the planetary shields meant she could not warn Isard of our plans. Short of crashing her Z-95 Headhunter into the construction droid we used, she could do nothing to stop the plan from unfolding. What she did do was transmit the codes that allowed Isard to take control of Corran's ship and bring him down."

As Winter dispassionately outlined Erisi's involvement with the Empire, Wedge watched the faces of his people. Erisi had been one of them, fighting alongside of them in numerous engagements. She'd been shot out of her X-wing, and Tycho had risked his life to rescue her. Even though her aid to the Empire was, as Winter had indicated, really insignificant, it had been enough to kill people who didn't deserve to die.

In himself, Wedge found anger mixed with chagrin and a little admiration. Erisi Dlarit had successfully played through some very difficult situations without revealing her role. Until she was fleeing Coruscant, Wedge hadn't known she was a spy. *Some signs were there, but not all of them.*

Wedge caught Corran looking in his direction and half-smiled. "She played the game well."

"True, but she's going to have to play much better when we come to visit." Corran's only concession to the emotions he was feeling came in the edge to his voice and the thin-lipped smile he offered. "As a spy she was good, but the next contest is one of pilots, and in that one she'll lose."

Winter changed the holographic image again. "If she loses it's not going to be because she's lacking the equipment she needs to win. Defending Thyferra are four Imperial warships: a Super Star Destroyer, two Imperial Star Destroyers, and one *Victory*-class Star Destroyer. *Lusankya, Avarice, Virulence,* and *Corrupter,* respectively. *Lusankya* is the ship that blasted its way out of Coruscant. It was previously unaccounted for, causing us to raise our estimates of how many ships the Kuat Drive Yards and the Fondor Yards produced. Oddly enough, both places claim to have produced Vader's flagship, *Executor.* It appears two ships were manufactured under that name, with one having been turned into *Lusankya* and buried on Coruscant—probably to serve as the Emperor's get-away ship. The other *Executor,* the one from Fondor, was destroyed at Endor."

She circled a finger through the hologram, encompassing the trio of smaller ships. "*Avarice, Virulence,* and *Corrupter* have hardly had sterling careers, but the crews are competent. I'm in the process of assembling files on all the staff officers, but the most dangerous of them, Captain Ait Convarion, commands the smallest ship. *Corrupter* has done very well in the Outer Rim hunting down pirate groups which, for better or worse, we resemble."

Wedge stood as Winter shut the holoprojector down. "As you can all see, we're dealing with a fairly formidable foe that is well armed. One of the things we have to face is that we may be unable to accomplish our goals in this operation. Unseating Isard may, in fact, turn out to be impossible."

Seated behind Gavin, Corran reached out and tapped the younger man on the head. "Gavin, this is where you're supposed to tell us that unseating her isn't tough and relate the whole thing to varminting on Tatooine."

Gavin blanched. "I didn't hear anyone mention a trench or canyon or womp rats. Taking a planet is beyond me."

Wedge smiled. "It's beyond most of us. I've sent communications out to some individuals who might be able to help. The problem is enormous. First we have to eliminate the ships, then take the world. The key to nailing the ships is to get them spread out so they can't support each other. We can do that by forcing Isard to use them to cover bacta convoys, but to kill the ships we need weapons, and a lot of them."

Riv Shiel, the Shistavanen wolfman, curled his lips up in a snarl. "It sounds as if we need the Katana fleet."

"That would be nice." The legendary ghost fleet of warships was supposed to be skipping through hyperspace, just waiting for someone to come and claim it. Wedge frowned. "We could also hope that the Outbound Flight Project finally produces results, with a host of nonhuman Jedi Knights coming from outside the galaxy to help us, but I don't think it's likely."

Gavin raised a hand. "What about that ship that Alderaan loaded all of its weapons on when it demilitarized? I can't remember the name, but I thought it was supposed to go through space and return if needed. Maybe Princess Leia has a way to summon it or something."

Winter shook her head. "You are thinking of *Another Chance.* While it is not as much of a legend as the Katana fleet, or Jorus C'baoth's mission outside the galaxy—the ship *did* exist—it is not the solution to our problem. The *Another Chance* was actually recovered by Rebel sympathizers prior to the debacles at Derra IV and Hoth. The weapons recovered were all of Clone Wars vintage and suited for use by infantry. They were useful in filling the gap caused by the loss of the convoy at Derra IV."

Gavin's shoulders slumped. "Oh, I never knew all that."

"Not that you should have, Gavin." Winter smiled. "Aside from the individuals who found the ship, a few smugglers who helped transport the merchandise, and higher-ups in the Rebellion, no one does. The Empire devoted resources to trying to find and take it, diverting them from pursuing us."

"Finding a miracle ship is not our only hope, people." Wedge held a hand up. "One of the things Winter has done for the Rebellion is locate old Imperial supply dumps. Most of them have been thoroughly stripped, but not everything is accounted for. We're going to go back over some of those sites and see what we can find. In fact, we have one mission that will be heading off tomorrow. Mirax will be taking Corran and you, Gavin, to Tatooine. One of the arms caches we found a couple of years ago had been plundered by Biggs Darklighter's father."

Gavin raised an eyebrow. "Uncle Huff?"

"The same. He said at the time he used some of the cache to arm his own security force then sold the rest off. But I don't buy it for a moment. There is no way he would have gotten rid of *everything*." Wedge smiled. "So, you're going to go home, Gavin, and talk your uncle into sharing the wealth with us."

"I don't know if he'll listen to me."

"That's why we're sending Corran, too. Your uncle has secrets to hide, and I expect Corran can ferret them out. That will help."

Gavin's face froze for a moment, then he began to smile. "I can get behind this. Serves him right for always seating me at the children's table at family gatherings."

"Gavin, he did that because you were a kid. Big, but a kid." Corran scruffed up Gavin's blond hair, then looked at Wedge. "While we're on the world that water abandoned, what are the rest of you going to be doing?"

"We're moving to our new home." Wedge held his hands up to calm the sudden buzz of voices. "This move is a covert op, so we'll be taking a lot of precautions to get there. There's no chance we can keep the location secret from our enemies forever, but as much time as we can get up to that point is what we want. Pack your things and get ready to move. The Bacta War is about to begin."

6

Corran Horn sneezed violently, initiating a wave of dust rippling across the cantina table toward Mirax. "How can anyone live on this infernal world? Even the dust has dust."

Mirax stretched languidly. "It's really not that bad, Corran, as worlds go. On Talasea things would mildew from plate to mouth."

"Sure, but there you had ovens to bake things, not a whole world to do it." Corran swiped a hand across his forehead, then shook the perspiration from it in a spray that spattered a pair of hooded Jawas, who themselves stank of ronto sweat. "I hate this."

She looked at him over the lip of her Corellian whisky glass. "At least it's a *dry* heat."

"So's a blast furnace, but that doesn't make it any less hot." Corran arched an eyebrow and tapped the stained and patch-welded top of the round table where they sat. "And why are we here? This table has seen more combat than most of the squadron's X-wings. The patrons here make this place look like a maximum security compound at Akrit'tar."

"Keeping up appearances, dear heart." Mirax shifted to the left to give her a full view of the t'bac-smoke-choked bar.

"Chalmun's cantina is known as *the* place that hotshot pilots hang out. I certainly qualify on that count, as do you. Right now I don't need work, but it could be that some of these folks need cargoes hauled, and those cargoes might be the kind of thing we want. Can't hurt to be here. Besides, Gavin recommended it as our rendezvous."

"Right. That's because he's never been in here before and didn't want to come in alone." Corran allowed disgust to pour through his words, but he mitigated it with a smile. "If I'd been asked to raid a place like this, my plan would have begun with the phrase, 'After the strafing runs are completed . . .'"

Shock rode freely on Mirax's face, but was exaggerated enough that Corran figured she was really only mildly horrified at his suggestion. "This might not be the most savory bunch of characters ever gathered together in the galaxy, but they're not that bad. My father used to bring me in here all the time when I was a kid. Some of these hard cases may be crusty on the outside, but they were very kind to me. Wuher, the bartender over there, used to synth up a sweet fizzy drink for me, and more than one of these guys would bring me little trinkets from the worlds they'd visited."

Corran shook his head. "I'd have loved to see those Immigrations forms. 'Purpose of the visit to our world?' 'Murder, mayhem, glitterstim smuggling, and purchase of a gift suitable for a small Corellian girl.'"

Mirax giggled. "Yeah, I imagine there are a couple like that in databanks somewhere."

The sound of her laughter managed to cut through the dulled buzz of conversation in the cantina. Corran sat up in his chair as he noticed two individuals turn from the bar and look in their direction. One was a Rodian and the other was a Devaronian, yet they both shared a lean, hungry look that made Corran feel antsy. They started toward the table, and Corran took it as significant that they abandoned full drinks at the bar, primarily because that left their hands empty.

The Devaronian nodded curtly. "You are sitting at our table."

Seated with his back to the alcove's wall, Corran had

protected himself against ambush from behind, but it also allowed the two ruffians full view of the blaster he wore. *No way I can draw it and shoot them before they get me.* It seemed obvious to him that the simple way out of the situation was to graciously offer them the table and buy a round for them. "We were unaware of the situation here . . ."

"And we couldn't care less." Mirax jutted her chin forward and poked her left index finger into the Rodian's middle. "If a pair of gravel-maggots like you are sandsick enough to think we're moving just because you mistake us for Jundland dew-pickers, you better get used to careers as Sarlacc bait."

Corran's jaw dropped. "Mirax?"

The Devaronian thumbed his own breastbone. "Do you have any idea who I am?"

"Do you have any idea how little we care?" Mirax jerked her head to the left. "Tell it to the Jawas so they get your name right when they bag your body."

The Rodian began buzz-squawking, but the loud *thwap* of a street club being pounded on the bar stopped him.

The human bartender pointed a finger toward the alcove. "Hey!"

His horns gleaming in the half-light, the Devaronian waved his protest off. "We know, 'No blasters.' "

Wuher's face scrunched up in a sour expression. "Not that, sand-for-brains. Do you know who you're talking to? That's Mirax, Mirax Terrik."

The Devaronian's grayish skin lightened appreciably, and the Rodian paled to a new-shoot green. "Terrik? As in Booster Terrik?"

Mirax smiled.

The bartender nodded as he pulled their drinks from the bar. "Now you're thinking. She's his daughter. Now's the part where you apologize to her or the Jawas continue measuring you for luggage for your final jump." He glared at the little knot of Jawas jabbering to each other. "Dibs on the Rodian."

The Devaronian bowed deeply to Mirax. "I, ah, we, beg your pardon for disturbing you. I am, well, that's not important, but if I can be of service to you, please, don't hesitate to ask." His apology came accompanied by Rodian buzz-squeak, which Corran took to be a simultaneous translation.

Mirax raised her chin and gave them a chillingly Imperial stare. "You're blocking our light."

The two of them backed away bowing profusely. Laughter ran through the cantina, bold in some spots and hushed in others, but amusement at their predicament united the cantina for a moment or two.

Corran licked his lips and realized his throat was absolutely parched. "Ah, Mirax, what possessed you to do that?"

"As I said before, keeping up appearances." She smiled broadly at him. "You've really only seen the kind, sensitive side of me."

"I seem to recall you burning down a stormtrooper on a speeder bike on Coruscant."

"Oh, yes, I guess there was that, wasn't there?"

"Yeah, there was, but even so there's no reason for provoking a fight like that."

She shrugged. "I wasn't worried. You could have taken them."

I could have taken them? Corran stared at her for a moment. "Thanks for the vote of confidence, but . . ."

Mirax reached across the table with her left hand and gave his right hand a squeeze. "I knew Wuher would intervene—this is an old game we've played from time to time." Her right hand, the one that had been hidden from the open edge of the table, came up and she deposited a small hold-out blaster on the table. "I had things covered; but the moment Wuher mentioned who I was, I knew we'd not have any more trouble."

Corran frowned. "Does everyone but me have relatives here? We land at Docking Bay Eighty-Six because some cousin or something of Gavin's owns it, then he takes off to set up a meet with his uncle Huff. Your father's got enough pull here so that two guys who'd suck the eyes out of a dead bantha's head run like droids being pursued by Jawas."

Mirax shrugged. "Tatooine is really a fairly small community. The Darklighters are a well-known and powerful family here. That estate we flew over on our way in here was Huff's place. And as for my father, well, he had quite the reputation before your father tossed him into the mines on Kessel, and his surviving his time there didn't hurt his rep at all. I'm sure that in some CorSec bar back on Corellia your name would be taken as being just as impressive."

"Maybe, but let's not test the reaction to it right now, okay?"

"I don't think even invoking my father's name would save you if you ran into an old enemy here."

"And invoking my name would doom me if we ran into your father here." Corran shot Mirax a sidelong glance. "Have you sent your father a message letting him know that you've developed an affection for the son of his nemesis."

" 'Developed an affection,' have I?" Mirax toyed with the hold-out blaster. "I thought we were a bit beyond that stage."

"True, we are, but no fair dodging the question."

She frowned. "No, I haven't told him. While you were dead, there was no sense mentioning it—I didn't want to be dealing with his anger while my heart still felt ripped out of me. And in the time since you came back from the dead, well, I've been busy; and ever since he retired, I'm never really sure where he is."

"Most folks, when they retire, settle in one spot and re-lax."

"Most folks aren't my father." Mirax smiled slightly. "For Booster, retirement means he still does deals, but he does them for friends, not for profit. Folks use him as a nego-tiator—he works out terms and the like. It keeps him getting the best of the business without the risk. He's happy, which is better than the alternative."

Which is why you've not mentioned us to him. Corran nodded. *I fully understand. My father wouldn't have, so not having to explain it to him is about the only good thing I can think of concerning his being dead.*

Gavin came in through the doorway and paused in the foyer near the droid detection unit. He twisted left and right, shaking a cloud of Tatooine's fine dust from his tan cloak.

Beneath it he wore what was once a white shirt, a black vest, dark brown pants, and knee-high boots. Around his middle he had strapped on a blaster and had tied the lower end of the holster around his right thigh.

"Looks the fair pirate, our friend." Mirax raised a hand. "Gavin, over here."

Corran agreed with Mirax's assessment, though Gavin's sloppy grin kind of marred the image. "Everything set?"

Gavin nodded. "I have a landspeeder waiting out front. It's not much, but it was the best I could do. I tried to borrow one off Uncle Huff, but he said the last time he loaned a landspeeder to someone from Rogue Squadron it wasn't returned in the best of conditions."

"We might as well head out, then." Mirax stood and clipped the hold-out blaster to her belt. She dug around in a pouch for some credits as she headed toward the bar. "How much?"

Wuher shook his head. "Your friends got it." He glanced toward the Rodian and Devaronian.

She smiled. "And they took care of you, too, yes?"

"The spirit of generosity, they were."

"Good."

Mirax followed Gavin from the cantina and Corran brought up the rear. He poked his head through the middle of his desert tabard and settled it down around his shoulders. The side flaps allowed for quick access to his blaster or the lightsaber, but he hoped he would not have need to resort to either.

He felt kind of awkward wearing the lightsaber. It had always seemed to him to be something of a genteel weapon of limited use. In his line of work, a Stokhli spray stick and a blaster were usually considered more than enough to handle any situation. Lightsabers had been all but unknown while the Empire considered them a sign of being a Jedi, but now that Luke Skywalker was a great hero, some folks had developed an affectation for them. It seemed to be the sort of weapon one carried if one was afraid to carry a blaster.

That characterization of it made Corran uneasy to wear the weapon, but flipping the bit the other way, he felt proud to be heir to one. He felt as if he had the *right* to wear it. At first he thought doing so might show disrespect for his grandfather, but then he realized Rostek Horn had risked his own career and life to protect Nejaa Halcyon's wife and child from Imperial Jedi hunters. Not only had he valued them for who they were, but he had valued them in memory of his fallen friend. *I think grandfather would be happy to see me wearing this lightsaber and* that's *all the reason I need to wear it.*

Corran hooded his eyes with his hand as he emerged into the harsh twin-sun noon. Gavin waved him over to the landspeeder. To Corran it looked a lot like the old SoroSuub XP-38, but the normally compact, dart-shaped craft had been heavily modified. The passenger compartment had been boosted forward by the addition of more seating and cargo space between it and the engines. More disturbing than how the addition had destroyed the fine lines of the vehicle was the fact that beneath the dust Corran saw a pink and puce paint job.

Corran hooked an arm over Gavin's shoulders. "You know, the womp rats you bull's-eye in a thing like this might be color-blind, so they don't care what your speeder looks like, but, really, look at this thing."

Gavin smiled wryly and spun out from beneath Corran's arm. "It beats walking, which was the other alternative given our operational budget. Get in. This baby will still hit three hundred klicks per, despite the modifications, and the krayt dragons don't see the color scheme as edible. We'll be there in no time."

The trip actually took half a standard hour, which wasn't "no time," and speeding through trackless wastes actually seemed close to forever. If it weren't for the cloud of dust billowing out from behind them, Corran would have been hard pressed to cite evidence that they were going anywhere at all. The Jundland Wastes mountains became a heat-warped stain on the horizon, and nothing else came even close to serving as a landmark.

Despite the lack of signposts or other waymarkers, Gavin got them to his uncle's estate without incident. The brief glimpse of it Corran had gotten from the *Pulsar Skate* as they came in had not prepared him for what it really looked like. From above it looked fairly normal—a compound surrounding a number of buildings including a tall tower. From the ground what became apparent was that, aside from the entryway and the tower itself, the buildings he'd seen were all constructed below the planet's surface. Gavin slid the landspeeder to a stop near the entryway beside several other landspeeders and then led Mirax and Corran down through the stairs to the compound's main courtyard. The stark white color of everything aided the suns in producing glare, but Corran realized that white absorbed far less solar energy— too much of which already made Tatooine unbearable as far as he was concerned.

A slender, gray-haired woman emerged through one of the arched doorways and immediately smiled. "Gavin Darklighter, how you have grown!" Boiling out around from behind her came a number of small children, ranging from toddlers to curious preadolescents.

"Aunt Lanal!" Gavin trapped the woman in a hug, then freed her and performed introductions that included her and the half-dozen cousins. Corran shook hands all around, but immediately lost track of names.

Lanal explained that she was Huff Darklighter's third wife and all of the children were hers. "Biggs's death shook Huff. He decided he wanted more heirs. His second wife decided she wasn't interested in having any more than the one she'd already borne. She left, and Huff married me."

"Biggs's mother died before I was born. Aunt Lanal is actually my mother's sister, so she's my aunt on both sides." Gavin gave her a kiss on the forehead. "Is Uncle Huff available?"

Lanal nodded. "He asked me to put you in the library. He's meeting with someone else right now, but he should be free shortly."

"Great."

The Darklighter estate struck Corran as an expensive compromise between the practicalities demanded by Tatooine and the essence of elegance as defined in other places within the galaxy. Fountains and pools would have been a foolish waste, but Huff succeeded in providing water features by encasing them entirely in transparisteel. Whereas a simple decorative column in any other home might have been painted brightly, Huff filled it with water and bubbled air up through it. Tiles on the thick walls were decorated and colored in such a way that they created optical illusions meant to diminish the blockiness of the house's design. Liberal use of transparisteel gave the dwelling an openness that it would not have otherwise had, yet elsewhere in the house more traditional design and decoration made Corran feel as if he'd never left Coruscant.

The library into which Lanal guided them was just one such room. Floor-to-ceiling shelves lined all the walls except where the doorways split them in two places. They entered through the south wall, and a closed double doorway bifurcated the east wall. The shelves and the doors were probably of duraplast, but Corran couldn't rule out actual wood having been used. *If that's true, it had to be imported from many light-years away and probably cost as much as a squadron of X-wings.*

Corran felt a chill run through him as he entered the library. Box after box of datacards filled the shelves, though trinkets and other odds and ends spaced them out a bit. What made Corran feel odd about the room was that it reminded him very much of the library in the *Lusankya* annex facility through which he had escaped from Isard. Though no trace of it was found after the *Lusankya* blasted its way free of Coruscant, the setup had been almost identical to the Imperial library in the private floor of Imperial Palace. At least it seemed so to Corran when he viewed a broadcast hologram about the palace.

I suppose a businessman like Huff Darklighter would want a decor that made Imperial officials feel at home. The briefing files Winter had given Corran about Huff Darklighter left no doubt that Huff had worked out an accommodation with the local Imperial officials that had given him free rein to operate on Tatooine. Those same arrangements also got his son Biggs his appointment to the Imperial Military Academy and, in the end, led to Biggs's death. *Since Darklighter isn't prone to accepting blame for anything himself, the favor Imps had done for him was seen as the cause of his son's death. Conversely, because Biggs is a hero of the Rebellion, Darklighter is willing to deal with the New Republic.*

Gavin looked around at the shelves, then smiled. "Huff's working office is up in the tower. His *negotiating* office is next door. Once he ushers out whoever is in there, we'll get to go in. Once he learns you're from Corellia I bet he finds you some Whyren's Reserve whisky."

Mirax smiled. "I'll take that and maybe make a side deal for any extra he has stashed away."

"Sure, but remember our main mission." Corran held up a finger. "We're looking for weapons, munitions, and spare parts. Anything else we get is extra."

The two of them nodded, then turned toward the eastern doors. One-half of them slid into the wall and Huff Darklighter entered the library. His belly preceded him by a second or two, but therein the resemblance to a Hutt ended. A coronet of white hair surrounded a pate the color of tanned leather. Darklighter's arms and shoulders looked powerful and were somehow complemented by the luxuriously full moustache he wore. His dark eyes glittered coldly as he instantly assessed his visitors, but then the corners of his mouth rose.

"Gavin, it is a pleasure." The tone of voice didn't seem to quite match the smile as far as Corran was concerned, but the elder Darklighter pulled Gavin into a polite hug, so he assumed there was no problem between them. Huff fingered his moustache. "Darken your hair and grow one of these, and you'd be the spitting image of my Biggs."

Mirax shot Corran a hooded glance. Corran didn't think Gavin and Biggs looked anything alike, but he realized Huff Darklighter wasn't viewing Gavin through the same frame of reference. *Huff made Biggs into a hero long before the Rebellion ever did.*

Huff drew back from his nephew and smiled toward Mirax and Corran. "I just stepped in here to let you know I'd be a bit yet. Negotiations are delicate."

"I understand, sir." Corran started forward and extended his hand toward Huff, but the larger man made no move to match his gesture. "I'm Corran . . ."

Huff held his hands up. "Time for introductions later, I'm sure. Really, I hate to be rude, but . . ."

Corran's emerald eyes shrank into crescents. "Just as I would hate to report to the New Republic that one in ten of the freighters bearing Darklighter products from here burns seven percent more fuel than is necessary—*if* they're actually carrying the cargo on the manifest. Suspicious minds might think that means they're carrying seven percent of their weight in illegal or exotic items, and the trouble you'd have to go to to straighten that mess out would be more than rude."

What little was left of Huff's smile melted clean away. "Nasty friends you've got here, Gavin."

"Corran used to be with CorSec, Uncle."

"Out of your jurisdiction, Corran."

"True, but I can still be trouble." Corran turned toward Mirax. "This is Mirax Terrik."

"Terrik?" Huff's smile struggled to return to his face. "Related to Booster Terrik?"

"He's my father."

"I see."

"I'm sure you do, sir. Something else you should see is that we're here to negotiate with you for weapons, munitions, and spare parts you have left over from the looting of an Imperial weapons cache several years ago."

The smile blossomed in full on Huff's face. "Imagine that. My current visitor was inquiring about the very same things. This could be amusing."

Corran saw Huff's eyes glaze over just imagining the profit potential. "Hey, no one is going to make you a better deal for that stuff than we are. No one."

"Oh, how interesting." Huff walked back toward the doorway and rested his left hand on the door that remained closed. "I have some people here who want what you want. They say no one can make me a better deal. Fascinating, no?"

Corran heard a bellow from the other room. Huff shoved

the other door open to reveal a huge, powerful man freeing himself from the clutches of a spindly chair. The man, whose hair was a short bristle of white and gray, dwarfed Gavin and even made Huff look small. Where his left eye had been, burned a red replacement, though his right eye was a normal brown. "Come to deal, have you?"

Corran gave him a hard stare. "Listen pal, you can leave right now because your dealing days are over." Thinking back to the cantina, he let a smile slowly spread across his face and jerked a thumb over his shoulder back at Mirax. "That's Mirax Terrik, Booster Terrik's daughter. If you know what's good for you, you'll go."

The large man stopped, his jaw hanging open, then he reared his head back and laughed.

Corran turned and looked at Mirax. "How come that scared people at the bar, and this guy laughs?"

"It worked on the people at the bar because they're afraid of my father." Mirax smiled sheepishly at him.

"And what's wrong with this clown?"

"Well, Corran," she winced, "he *is* my father."

7

"Oh," said Corran, without missing a beat, "I guess you take after your mother."

Though he saw mirth and astonishment mix on Mirax's face, and saw a smile begin to blossom on Gavin's face, Corran wished for nothing so much as a chance to inhale and suck those words out of everyone's ears. *Could there have been a more stupid remark you could have made?* A dozen different candidates flashed through his mind, including several that could have reminded Booster of his stint on Kessel. *Okay, it could have been worse, but not by much.*

Booster Terrik's laughter died. "Mirax, who is he, and why shouldn't I show him why others fear me?"

A smile fitted itself on her face, but her eyes tightened. "This is Corran Horn."

"Horn?" Booster's voice descended into bass tones. "This is Hal Horn's boy?"

Corran turned to face Mirax's father. "I am."

Booster's hand's balled into fists the size of Corran's head. "So, then, there's no reason I shouldn't give him the beating I owed his father. If you don't mind, Huff."

The rotund Darklighter shook his head. "I'd prefer it to happen outside, otherwise, beat away."

Mirax stepped up beside Corran. "There *is* a reason, Father."

Booster's face slackened for a moment, then he frowned. "I've heard that tone of voice before. You don't want me to take a round out of him. You even want me to *like* him, but there's no reason in the galaxy why I'd like him."

"Yes, there is."

"Why am I going to like the son of the man who sent me to Kessel?"

"Because I do."

"What?!"

Mirax slipped her hand into Corran's. "You heard me. Corran's saved my life, I've saved his, and we like each other. A lot." She gave his hand a squeeze. "You can jump in any time, Corran."

"Me? You're doing fine."

Her father's face went through all sorts of contortions. "No, no, not a daughter of mine. If your mother weren't dead, this would kill her, you know that." Booster snarled, then spitted Corran with a stare. "And *you!* Your father would be mortified. Your grandfather would tear his hair out. A Horn keeping company with *my* daughter! It's unthinkable."

Mirax's face twisted down into an angry mask the equal of the one her father wore. "It's not unthinkable at all, at least not for someone who is willing to use more than one synapse on it. Wake up, Father. The Emperor is dead. It's a new galaxy."

Booster shook his head, then looked toward Huff. "The Emperor dies, and the natural order gets its double helix all twisted the other way. Next thing you know it will start raining here on Tatooine, and you'll have tourist trade for seaside resorts."

Huff smiled. "Actually, I have some sites picked out to cover that eventuality."

"I bet you do." Booster frowned at his daughter again. "A Horn! Hal Horn's son! I wouldn't have wanted this for you for all the glitterstim in the galaxy."

"What you want for me, and what *I* want for me have

long been different, Father." Mirax let Corran's hand fall away, then walked to her father and gave him a big hug and kiss. "That doesn't diminish my pleasure at seeing you again."

Booster returned the hug and swung his daughter off her feet so his broadly muscled back hid her from Corran's sight. Corran couldn't hear what father said to daughter, but the smiles on their faces as they again turned around told him their exchange had not been acrimonious.

Booster kept his left arm draped over Mirax's shoulders and posted his right fist on his right hip. "I was sorry to hear about your father's death. No love lost between us, but I respected his tenacity."

"And my father respected your ingenuity." Corran gave Booster a thin-lipped smile and got the same one in return. He lifted his chin. "Huff indicated that you're here to negotiate for the remains of an Imperial arms cache. I'd gotten the impression from Mirax that you were retired and only dealt in collectibles."

"You'd be surprised what prefall Imperial artifacts are going for today."

"Lots of weapons collectors out there?"

Booster shrugged. "You Rebels made going to war against the government so popular that everyone is taking it up these days."

"So you'll supply them?"

Booster smiled. "I'm merely a broker."

Huff rubbed his hands together. "So, we can have an auction here. Opening bids."

Corran shook his head. "No bids. We need what you have. We get it."

Booster blinked his eyes in surprise. "You need? *You* need? You're not on Corellia, Horn. You have no authority here. Your needs are immaterial."

Mirax twisted out from beneath her father's arm. "It's not Corran who needs this stuff. Wedge needs it."

The elder Darklighter's smile broadened. "Good, get Wedge Antilles here, and then we'll have our auction."

"Wedge, eh?" Booster frowned at Mirax, then glanced over at Huff. "Give it to them."

"Fine, if you don't want in, that's all right by me." Huff's smile shrank as he turned toward Corran. "What I have will cost you two million credits—four if you expect me to trust the New Republic for it."

Booster reached out and slapped Huff on the shoulder. "I told you to give it to them."

"I am."

"No, you're *negotiating* when I said you should be *giving*."

Huff looked confused for a moment, and Corran could sympathize. "You want me to give it to them for *free*?"

Booster nodded. "If not, I think you'll find that records of certain transactions that could be considered Palpatinistic could come to light."

"That's extortion."

"No, that's deal making. I have something you want— my silence—and you have something I want—the weapons to go to Wedge. We exchange wants and everyone is satisfied."

Mirax interposed herself between Huff Darklighter and her father. "Extortion or deal making, it doesn't make a difference. We're not doing it that way, period. If we take things away without compensation, we're as bad as the Imps. If we let ourselves pay inflated prices, we'll be as stupid as the Imps. That isn't what's going to happen. We're going to be fair about this."

She pointed a finger at Huff. "You will get me a complete inventory of the material we're looking at *and* will let us inspect the merchandise, choosing random bits to examine ourselves. My father will prepare a list of the prices for all these things in the prevailing market. We'll pay something below the going price because everyone knows the father of Biggs Darklighter wouldn't try to make a profit off his son's comrades, but you will be capitalizing assets for which you have little use here on Tatooine. We'll pay half now and half when we take possession of the items."

Huff's jowls quivered as he shook his head. "You'll pay fifteen percent over the current—"

Mirax held a hand up. "Stop. I said we'd be *fair*, I never said we were negotiating. If you want to negotiate, we'll start from my father's position and work down to the details of your paying the freight to move the goods we're taking off your hands."

Huff Darklighter stared at Mirax, his jaws agape. "Do you know what you're asking?"

Mirax smiled sweetly. "Only what's fair."

Gavin laughed. "Admit it, Uncle Huff, you'll accept her terms, because you're not going to get anything better."

"True, I accept." Huff nodded his head slowly. "Listen to me, young lady. If you ever find yourself in need of a steady job, please come see me. You have talents I could use."

Huff Darklighter invited them to remain as his guests for the duration of their visit to Tatooine. They accepted—not only were the accommodations he offered far nicer than those they had booked in Mos Eisley but Gavin's family traveled from their farm to see him. With Booster's presence and the extended Darklighter clan getting together, the visit began to feel like a big family vacation.

Corran enjoyed meeting Gavin's parents. His father, Jula, looked similar to Huff Darklighter in the face, but the lack of a moustache on Jula made telling them apart rather simple. Likewise, the fact that Jula's hard work on a moisture farm had left him harder and more weathered than his prosperous brother helped differentiate them. There definitely seemed to be affection between the brothers, though Huff tended to keep Jula in his place by referring to the cost of this item or that and feigning astonishment when Jula said he didn't own one.

Jula, for his part, showed incredible restraint and even resignation over his brother's lack of manners. Corran shook his head. *If I had a brother and got that treatment from him, my sister-in-law would be a widow.* Jula's responses were polite, and in some ways his forbearance seemed to bother Huff more than any direct confrontation would have.

Gavin's mother, Silya, could have been Lanal Darklighter's twin. Her concern for Gavin rolled through every question and comment, though she managed to avoid tears all but once or twice. In the way she looked at Gavin, Corran recognized the same expression his mother wore when he graduated from the Corellian Security Force Academy. *Pride and fear—a mother's dreams and her nightmares—fight for supremacy.*

The focus of the gathering quickly became Gavin. He thrilled his cousins and younger siblings with stories of what he'd seen and done, though Corran noted that he down-played nearly getting killed on Talasea. That didn't surprise him, but it was also clear to Corran that Jula had not missed what had gone unsaid. The specter of Biggs's death formed the foundation for every question and comment.

And the comparison of Gavin with Biggs fuels the analysis of stories he's telling. There was no doubt that Biggs had been a hero and had acted heroically. His death at Yavin had allowed Luke Skywalker to blow up the Death Star. His death marked the extreme danger of the situation and was not unexpected, given the circumstances. Even so, the situations in which Gavin found himself were no less perilous, yet he had survived them. To Corran's mind, Gavin's parents had to be thinking that made him better than Biggs in some unde-finable away, and for Huff it planted the seeds of doubt about how great his son truly was.

Because he had been an only child born of only children, the Darklighter family gathering gave Corran a window into a whole different family dynamic. Because there were so many children among whom things were shared, personal boundaries and the ideas of ownership were weakened. Younger kids seemed to see every adult as part of the family, fearlessly climbing into laps or asking permission or asking for help.

At first this threatened Corran—in part because of the utter chaos of the situation but mostly because the children thrust responsibility into his hands. The fact that none of the Darklighters seemed to mind their children paying him atten-tion—as long as the kids didn't seem to be bothering him or to be ill-mannered—meant he had to accept that responsibility and act on it. The openness of the families drew him in and they accepted him, but Corran was uncertain if he was ready to be accepted.

Mirax and her father, by way of contrast, formed a little insulated party within the grander goings-on. The hushed tones of their conversation, their quiet laughter and their general ease with each other reminded Corran very sharply of the relationship he'd had with his own father. Hal Horn had been friend and confidant as well as parent and work associate. Corran had always thought of family as a place where he could open himself up and get advice without fearing censure or ridicule. *Shared blood meant a bottom-line alliance that no disagreement could shatter.* He and his father had disagreed on plenty of things, but that which united them was far stronger than anything that could divide them.

Despite the efforts of everyone to include him in what was going on, Corran began to retreat a bit as melancholy over his father's death slowly seeped into his heart. It was all too easy for him to imagine his father at the gathering, again hearing his laughter and watching the others react to the stories Hal used to tell. *They would have loved him here. And he would have loved being here, too.*

A chill ran down Corran's spine. The openness of the families twisted like a vibroblade into his guts. His father, Hal Horn, had known his own father, the Jedi Master Nejaa Halcyon. Hal had never told Corran anything about Nejaa. *I know he did that to protect me, but I know he had to have been proud of his father. When I told my father that I had "hunches" and he told me to go with them, he knew they were manifestations of my—our—Jedi heritage. That was his quiet way of telling me of his pride, but it must have torn him up to have to remain silent. Perhaps he anticipated telling me about that stuff later, after the Rebels had destroyed the Empire, but he never lived that long.*

Corran absented himself from the gathering, walking up the steps to the surface of the planet. The twin suns had set, letting the day's heat begin to bleed off into space. The chill creeping into the desert likewise began to gnaw at him. It found a willing ally in the sorrow sloshing around in Corran's guts.

"Excuse me, Lieutenant Horn, I don't want to intrude."

Corran looked back and saw Jula Darklighter silhouetted against the glow from the pit mansion. "No intrusion, sir. I came from a small family, so this is rather overwhelming."

"I came from a big family, and it's overwhelming." Jula glanced down at the ground and toed an alkali crust into dust. "I wanted to say thank you for taking care of my son out there."

Corran smiled, but shook his head. "Gavin takes care of himself out there."

"He said you had confidence in him and that you got another pilot to stop picking on him. He didn't say it that way, mind you, but he's not hard to read."

Corran laughed lightly. "No, your boy—young man—does tend to digitize and broadcast his emotions. The situation he refers to, though, was one where another pilot, Bror Jace, and I were having a bit of a conflict, and Gavin just happened to find himself in the middle. I'm glad he took heart in my having confidence in him, because I did and do believe in him and his skills, but he needs no protection. You raised a man of whom you can be proud."

Jula smiled and nodded, then looked Corran straight in the eyes. "He's almost ended up like Biggs, hasn't he?"

"We've *all* almost ended up like Biggs, sir. The Empire may be in retreat, but there are plenty of folks still willing to fight for them." Corran raised a hand to his breastbone and unconsciously stroked the Jedi medallion he wore. "Gavin has been wounded and did almost die, but the fact is that he was too tough to die. As a pilot, he's getting better and better and has vaped his share of the enemy we've faced. He's brave without being stupid. He's the sort of person who is the Rebellion's backbone and the reason it has succeeded as well as it has."

"What you're saying, Lieutenant Horn, makes me very proud indeed." Jula sighed. "It also fortifies me against anticipating the worst. I imagine your parents are equally worried about you and proud of you."

Corran frowned. "My parents are dead, sir."

"I'm sorry."

"Thank you."

Jula jerked a thumb back toward the sounds of the gathering. "This isn't very easy on you, is it?"

Corran shrugged. "Compared to an Imperial prison, it's actually very nice. The trick of it is that there I had a focus for my negative thoughts—the people who had me imprisoned. Here there is no such focus."

"Perhaps that means that you should just let your negative thoughts go." Jula patted him on the shoulder. "Nothing wrong with feeling and acknowledging sorrow and pain, Lieutenant Horn. The crime is letting them hold you prisoner. Come on back, and we'll do all we can to set you free."

He's right. Mourning is appropriate, but not here and not now. Corran smiled. "Thanks. I think I *will* rejoin the group. In fighting the Imps I've been in so many places where I've been reviled, it's great, just for once, to be welcomed so openly and graciously."

"I'm glad you feel that way." Jula threw an arm over Corran's shoulder and steered him back toward the light. "Darklighters believe in treating friends like family and family like friends, and we're always glad to add yet one more to the family."

8

This has to be a dream. A nightmare even. Wedge cracked his left eye open and let it slowly attempt to focus. At first he noticed nothing unusual in the unlit room, but then he caught sight of little motes of light streaking like shooting stars across night sky. The possible presence of something in his quarters did convince his sleep-besotted brain that he should continue his trek toward consciousness, but until he heard the voice a second time, he wasn't wholly certain he wasn't enmeshed in a nightmare.

"Good morning, sir. It is very good to see you again."

Wedge rolled over and reluctantly opened both eyes. "Emtrey?"

"How kind of you to remember me, Comm—I mean, *Master* Wedge." The black 3PO droid with the clamshell head stood beside the bed with its hands splayed out. "I realize you may not have fully recovered from your journey here, and were it up to me I'd have allowed you to sleep longer, but this is the time at which you requested awakening."

Wedge groaned. Shortly after Corran, Mirax, and Gavin had left for Tatooine, Winter located a possible store of X-wings and parts on Rishi. Using some of the unit's money,

Wedge rented a modified Corellian YT-1300 light freighter named *Eclipse Rider* and headed out with Ooryl Qrygg to check out the report. The trip out from Coruscant went well, but once they arrived in-system they ran into trouble. The freighter lost a repulsor-lift coil upon landing. Ooryl worked on replacing that while Wedge wound his way through a labyrinth of H'kig religious laws that seemed, to him, to prohibit or limit anything that could make life easier.

He did locate the cache of X-wing parts and managed to purchase it. He estimated two fighters could be cobbled together from the parts, which was something, but far short of what he'd hoped when he set out at first. Regulations on the use of repulsor-lift vehicles complicated the loading timetable and, ultimately, delayed their departure from the world by twelve hours.

When he and Ooryl finally did make it to Yag'Dhul, Wedge was four days behind schedule and exhausted. He docked the freighter, then had someone show him to his quarters. *I thought twelve hours of sleep would be enough, but apparently not, because I'm hallucinating the presence of a droid that should be on Coruscant.*

He rubbed his eyes, then opened them again. Emtrey was still there. "What's going on here? Did General Cracken send you to keep an eye on us?"

"Since I do not have eyes per se, sir, I would have to say no." The droid's head canted to the right. "I do not recall any orders being given to me by my former owner."

"Former owner?" Wedge realized he was becoming more awake all the time, but nothing seemed to be getting much clearer to him, and that caused him some concern. *Someone has to be having fun with this.* "Get Tycho for me."

Tycho cleared his voice and Wedge turned to see him leaning against the doorjamb of the bedroom. "Thought you'd like to wake up to a familiar face, since you're in unfamiliar surroundings."

"Right." Wedge narrowed his eyes. "As I recall, I've not gotten you back for the other trick you pulled—that postmortem message from Corran at Borleias. You better watch your step."

"Or what? You think you can cause me more trouble than a treason trial and a stay in an Imperial prison?" Tycho thrust his chin out defiantly, but softened the gesture with a smile. "You're welcome to try any time you want, Antilles."

Wedge shook his head. "One hopeless battle at a time. Got any caf out there?"

Tycho nodded. "Brewed hot and strong enough to dissolve transparisteel."

"Great." Wedge rolled out of bed and slipped into the thick robe Emtrey held out for him. Knotting the belt around his middle, he followed Tycho into the small parlor attached to his bedroom. The furnishings were a mixture of styles and colors, but all of them were fashioned from hollow metal tubes and light but strong cloth. *Less mass means less cost in transport and energy to maintain the gravity generation for the station.*

Wedge dropped into a chair across a low table from Tycho and wrapped both hands around the barrel of a steaming mug of caf. The steam caressed his face and could have been melting his eyebrows for all he cared because the caf tasted wonderful. He felt the warmth spread out from his belly and a layer of fog in his brain began to dissipate.

"So, Tycho, how is Emtrey here?"

Tycho's smile broadened considerably. "Politics."

Wedge sipped more caf. "Okay, give me the exploded view because I'm not seeing it."

"It gets weird, but I'm not complaining." Tycho leaned forward. "Before his capture at Yavin 4, Jan Dodonna designed the A-wing fighter. The Alliance got it into production and introduced the A-wing late on in the Rebellion. Most of them were made in locations that weren't so much factories as they were private shops. They all worked from the same design, but were constructed on an individual basis. The one I flew at Endor, for example, had Fijisi wood panels in it—I'm guessing it was built on Cardooine."

"I recall how reinforcements of those ships used to dribble in."

"Right, well Incom and Koensayer are afraid their X-wing and Y-wing fighter designs are going to be supplanted by the A-wing and B-wing designs, so they've been trying to get the Provisional Council and the Armed Forces to open bidding on new contracts. Incom thinks it has an edge on winning a contract for new X-wings, when all of us up and resign. Koensayer starts the rumor that part of our disaffection is because we don't trust the X-wing anymore.

"Incom turns around and says that it's working on some new designs and would be happy to bring Rogue Squadron's ships up to the state of the art. What they offer are A-wings manufactured by them that have been modified so the laser cannons can swivel and cover the rear arc."

Wedge nodded. "Nice adaptation, but it doesn't explain how we ended up with Emtrey."

"I'm getting there, and you'll appreciate the flight, trust me." Tycho pressed his hands together. "Someone in the military—probably General Cracken, but maybe even Admiral Ackbar—decided accepting Incom's gift was appropriate, so all the equipment in Rogue Squadron was inspected, listed as missing parts, and surplussed out. Winter found out about it before anyone else, and we scooped up the lot, including Emtrey and our astromech droids."

Wedge blinked. "Surplussed out? Our stuff was sold as surplus?"

"Broken surplus. It was missing parts."

"Such as?"

"PL-1s"

Wedge frowned. "PL-1s? I've never heard of them."

Tycho shook his head. "That's the designation for pilot."

Wedge immediately began laughing. *Someone back on Coruscant favors what we're doing or perhaps just wants to give us the tools to destroy ourselves. I'm trusting it's the former.* "Emtrey was just thrown in on the deal?"

"He cost a little bit extra, but I thought he was worth it." Tycho coughed lightly into his hand. "Zraii and his technical staff resigned and followed our ships over. We've got a full squadron, and the parts you brought in should keep them operational for a long time."

"Good. How does the base look?"

"Not bad." Tycho pointed back toward the bedroom.

"I'll give you a half an hour to get cleaned up, then I'll give you a tour of the place. It's not exactly a Death Star, but I think it will work fine for our purposes."

Clad in a tan jumpsuit, Wedge followed Tycho through the space station. The small suite he'd been given turned out to be one of the more luxurious ones on the station. Because of construction costs space was at a premium. Refresher stations were communal, as were dining facilities. While there were private rooms for dinner meetings, all food was prepared in a central galley and delivered to the half-dozen dining facilities on the base. Those same rooms also served as lounges and recreation facilities.

Tycho led him to the core of the station and punched a button on the wall. "Here at the core we have nine turbolifts: six are for personnel and three are for freight."

Wedge reached up and tapped a knuckle against the gray duraplast ceiling. "Everything seems shrunk down a bit. I feel like a giant."

"It *is* very compact. I think it was built this way to cause stormtroopers problems if they ever invaded." As the turbolift door slid open, Tycho passed through the opening. "There are twenty-five living levels above the docking facility and twenty-five below it. We're starting at sub-twenty-five. I've got Emtrey working on the moves that will be necessary to clear the last ten sublevels for our personnel."

"Moving everyone *but* our people off would make me feel better, since we know Isard will eventually figure out where we are."

"Agreed, Wedge, but if we send people away she'll find out about things all that much sooner. Because we hit this station not too long ago, and because Warlord Zsinj evacuated his folks, what's left behind is pretty much of a skeleton crew. If we do get rid of them, we're going to have to use our people to perform a lot of nonmission-specific duties." Tycho winced. "I seem to recall the meal you tried to make out of tauntaun meat on Hoth and . . ."

"I get the hologram, Tycho." Wedge frowned. "Do they know there's danger here?"

"They seem to think that after Zsinj, Isard might be taken as a change for the positive. I've spoken with the key employers here, and they know there could be trouble. They seem to think that with us here it's actually going to be safer because the scum of the galaxy isn't going to be drifting in every time they have liberty."

"True, but their revenues are going to be down, and that could make for trouble."

The turbolift stopped and opened onto the docking facility. Tall transparisteel walls gave Wedge a spectacular view of Yag'Dhul. Though small and dense, the world took on a curious appearance because of the three moons orbiting it and the tidal forces they generated as they orbited in the opposite direction to the planet's rotation. The atmosphere boiled and swirled, with storms sowing lightning through the gray clouds and flashes of red stone visible even from the station.

"Hard to believe life could have arisen in that maelstrom." Wedge folded his arms across his chest and shivered. "No wonder the Givin have an exoskeleton and can exist in a vacuum."

"It's a good thing they can. Our attack here apparently opened some of the station up to the vacuum, so they used Givin to make the repairs. Everything is fine now, though, with one exception: the old Station Master died while on an inspection tour of the repair work."

Wedge frowned, recalling an old Twi'lek with a pock-marked face who had been as oily as Darth Vader had been evil. "His name was Valsil Torr, right?"

"I guess so. Apparently he tried to force a Givin task leader to pay him a bribe. They agreed to discuss it in Torr's office, and there was a catastrophic loss of atmosphere." Tycho winced. "The Twi'lek was sucked out of his office through a hole the size of, say, a blaster bolt. The Givin lived and patched the hole."

"So now no one is running the station."

"The merchants here have formed an Economic Council and seem to be running things fairly well as far as they are concerned. We'll need to put someone in to control them, but I don't have a candidate in mind yet." Tycho opened his arms. "This is the main docking area, which contains ten levels all its own. The middle six deal with cargo transfer and storage. The outer two on each side contain crew housing, some small shops and two tapcafs—home away from home for freight haulers. The tapcafs serve exactly what the rest of us eat, but they lower the lights and hike the price."

"You know, with the right ambiance, that tauntaun would have tasted fine."

"Sure, Wedge, believe that if you want." Tycho pointed to the triangular landing extending out into space. "Ships land here, unload, pick up or exchange cargo, and head out again. If the crew wants to stop over, its ship is parked in orbit and the station shuttle service brings them to and from the station. Hangar space is rare, and what this station has is being reserved for us right now, though there is some space for repairs if a ship needs it."

"Fair enough." Wedge watched a small yacht make an approach on the station. Its sleek lines and down-curving wings reminded him of a native Corellian fish. "Looks like the *Pulsar Skate* is coming in. Have you had any word from them?"

"No, but there was a funds transfer to the account of Huff Darklighter, so I assume things went well."

"Good." Wedge pointed back at the lift. "Let's go down, greet them, and see exactly what our money bought us."

9

Wedge wondered if he weren't really still trapped in a dream as the turbolift door opened and he stepped into the squadron hangar. A dozen X-wings occupied the deck, and techs swarmed over them. That wasn't what had struck him as unrealistic, however, since the hustle and bustle of a hangar was something he'd witnessed countless times before.

He glanced over at Tycho. "What's going on here?"

Tycho gave him a grin. "Well, since we're no longer part of the New Republic's Armed Forces, we can't have ships bearing its insignia or colors, can we? Now, Corran's ship has always been green with that black and white trim, like his droid, so I thought we might just go ahead and repaint our X-wings to look like whatever we want them to be."

He pointed very specifically at an X-wing that was bloodred except for where white had been splashed at a diagonal down across the nose and the tips of the S-foils. A broad black stripe parted the white from the red. "That one's mine. I did some checking, and before Alderaan disarmed, that was the color scheme the Alderaan Guard unit near my home used to sport. I've also had Zraii switch my Identify Friend/Foe beacon over to an old Alderaanian code—the one from the

Another Chance, in fact. Individualizing the paint and switching our IFF codes to those of our home planets provides further evidence that we're not a New Republic unit."

Wedge chewed his lower lip for a moment. *Makes sense, all of it. And the fighters do look a bit more, ah, ferocious with the new paint jobs.* "I like it, Tycho, but I don't know what to do with mine. Corran's got the CorSec green, but he's earned it."

"How about a dark blue, with red stripes up the sides?"

"Corellian Bloodstripes?" Wedge chuckled. "I never was in the Corellian Military, so I never earned Bloodstripes. Han Solo wears them on his trousers because he went to the Imperial Academy and won them through his bravery."

"Oh, and you've not been equally brave?"

"That's open to debate, but the fact is I've never been sufficiently *military* to earn them." He smiled slowly. "Make everything from the cockpit back black, including the S-foils, and give me a green-and-gold check pattern on the front fuselage."

Tycho's eyes narrowed. "I don't recognize the color scheme."

"No reason you should." Wedge hesitated for a second. "Back when my parents operated a fueling station at Gus Treta, my father was saving up to buy the station and start his own chain. The green, gold, and black were going to be the colors he used for the logo and the uniforms. Your colors tie you back to your home, Corran's do the same thing for him, and I imagine the same is true for everyone else. Mine will tie me to the home I should have had."

"I'll put the order in immediately." Tycho started walking over toward where the *Pulsar Skate* had come through the hangar's magnetic containment bubble and was setting down. Following it in came a boxy station shuttle, but it landed further back. "Your ship and Gavin's will be the last ones finished."

Wedge glanced at Ooryl's white fighter. "You need to include Ooryl's ship on that list."

"No, it's done."

"But, it's so . . . *plain.*"

"Apparently not, *if* you can see in the ultraviolet range." Tycho shrugged. "Zraii says it's a masterpiece."

"That explains why I'm a warrior, not an artist." Wedge waved as he saw Corran, Mirax, and Gavin walk down the gangway from the *Pulsar Skate*. *Wait a minute, who's that?* The fourth individual proved taller than Gavin and much bulkier, yet wasn't slovenly or Huttlike. Then, when his head cleared the interior of the ship and Wedge saw the bristle of white hair, he recognized him.

"So that's why Corran is looking a bit subdued."

"What?" Tycho frowned at Wedge. "Who's the last guy?"

"Mirax's father."

"Oh. *Oh.*"

Wedge trotted the remaining distance and thrust his hand at Booster Terrik. "It's been far too long, Booster."

The larger man's hand engulfed Wedge's. "You grew up quite a bit during my five years on Kessel. After I got out, well, about that time you were freezing on Hoth, then you were on the go. I assumed I'd run into you sometime, and now seems as good as any."

"Indeed it is." Wedge glanced over at Mirax. "Your daughter's been a lifesaver, you know, and for more than just me."

"So I gather from what I heard during the trip." Booster Terrik threw an arm over Wedge's shoulders, then tightened it against his neck. "I would have hoped, though, you would have found a way to protect her from the likes of Horn there."

Wedge gently dug an elbow in the man's ribs. "First, if *you* can't control your daughter, how can *I* be expected to control her? Second, just as I told her, Corran isn't his father. He's one of the best men I know."

"You need to get out more, Wedge." Booster opened his arms and released Wedge. "Interesting place you have here. Not enough to stop a Super Star Destroyer, but you know that. Still, if you have to die in a box in space, this looks as good as any in which to do it."

"Tycho's taking me on a tour. You're welcome to join us."

"I'd be happy to."

Wedge nodded, then looked over at Gavin. "How was Tatooine?"

"Good, sir. We got a fair amount of personal armor and weapons, as well as some TIE parts and assorted other things Mirax thinks we can trade. Uncle Huff said that was all that was left from the *Eidolon* material."

"It all looked pretty good, Wedge." Corran leaned against a pilot-mover. "We've got enough in the way of small arms to supply a decent insurgent force. The armor is stormtrooper grade."

Corran's voice trailed off as the sound of footsteps drew closer. Wedge turned and saw a pair of individuals coming around *Pulsar Skate*'s stern. The hulking brute of a man, with a shaved head and a big bushy beard, dwarfed his petite female companion. Wedge hitched for a moment, then started to laugh. "How is it possible that you're here so soon?"

The auburn-haired woman smiled sweetly. "And I'm happy to see you, too, Wedge. You've not changed much, Tycho, or you, Mirax." She nodded to the others in the group, then offered her hand to Corran. "Elscol Loro and Sixtus Quin."

"Elscol joined the squadron just after Bakura and flew a few missions with us." Wedge jerked a thumb toward her taciturn, dark-skinned companion. "Sixtus Quin was a Special Intelligence Operative who was betrayed by his Imperial commander, so he helped us out in a mission on Tatooine."

Corran nodded. "We can always use more pilots."

"But that's not why we're here, kid." She shot Wedge a sidelong glance. "The reason we got here so soon was because we were inbound before your summons reached us. We'd heard of the coup on Thyferra and figured we'd ply our trade there."

Corran stiffened. "And what would that trade be?"

A lopsided grin contorted the left side of her face. "I do what I was doing at the time Wedge recruited me—I find worlds with Imperial tyrants, and I liberate them. Sixtus, what's left of his squad, and a group of other ne'er-do-wells come with me. We organize local resistance movements; provide them with expertise, weapons, and support; and help them get rid of their local Imperial officials."

Wedge smiled. "I think you'll recall that no one at our first meeting had any good idea about how to go about overthrowing a planetary government. Elscol has had more practice at it than anyone I know. She's never been much of a joiner, so she's been working outside the New Republic."

She shrugged. "Haven't formed an opinion about the New Republic yet, though during Tycho's trial my thoughts were none-too-positive. The Empire, on the other hand, left me without my family, so I'm doing what I can to strip them of theirs."

"Have you had a chance to review the material I sent you?"

Elscol nodded. "If the ratio of loyal humans to Vratix is at all accurate, the actual conquest of the world should be simple. The big problem there is the presence of those Imp ships. Anything we do can be undone by a planetary bombardment. If those ships can be scattered or neutralized—preferably both—we can stage an uprising that should topple Ysanne Isard. I'm confident we can do it, but I'll have a better idea of exactly what we're going to do after I get in there and take a look."

Mirax raised an eyebrow. "You're talking about going to Thyferra?"

"Yes, the sooner the better." Elscol held up a hand and started ticking points off on her fingers. "We have to liaise with the Ashern, or we'll fight them as much as we'll fight the Imps and their Xucphra allies. We have to determine the nature of the targets we'll hit, so we can be properly supplied for the strikes. We need to gauge the reaction of the populace to a countercoup, and we have to find a local leader who can handle being put in charge. If this were just some backwater world that no one cared about, we could be a bit more hasty. Thyferra, however, is of vital importance, so we have to be careful and surgical in what we're doing."

"Agreed." Wedge folded his arms across his chest. "We

don't have enough in the way of personnel or equipment to allow us to be sloppy."

Sixtus rested his fists on his narrow hips. "How long do you anticipate being able to keep the location of this station a secret from Isard?"

Wedge shrugged. "I have no way of judging that. We'll take all precautions possible, but we're as vulnerable here as the Alliance was on Hoth or Yavin 4. If Isard finds us, we're in for a difficult time."

"Then the sooner we're on Thyferra, the sooner she'll have to think about leaving at least part of her fleet at home."

Gavin frowned. "But I thought the fleet needed to be scattered."

"True enough, but scattered in a way that you can nibble it to death. I know you Rogues are hot hands on a stick, but a dozen snubfighters can't take four capital ships all by themselves. Isard has to be induced to send the ships out so you can eliminate them, but she also needs a reason to leave some of them at home so you don't get overwhelmed."

Corran raised an eyebrow. "Sounds like you're suggesting the only way we win this thing is if Iceheart starts getting stupid."

"Not at all, flyboy. What we need to do is to give Isard too many things to think about. She likes to be in control—that's clear—and she'll do outrageous things to remain in control." Sixtus smiled in a way that made it seem as if smiling were an effort for him. "We have to present her with enough problems that she's reacting to what we do, not acting by herself. We set the pace and determine what she does."

Tycho's eyes narrowed. "And if she doesn't dance to the tune we call?"

Elscol opened her hands. "Then we dance around her. Make no mistake about it, defeating her is going to be neither pretty nor swift, but it can be done. People are going to die, but if she remains in charge of the bacta supply in the galaxy, that's a given anyway."

Wedge nodded and felt his shoulders begin to ache as if someone had settled a lead-lined cloak across them. While none of the Rogues had ever attempted to minimize the difficulty of what they had set out to do, neither had they taken a close look at the realities of it. *It is almost as if we began to believe in the legend of Rogue Squadron—that impossible missions are for us just run of the mill. We know death and dying are part of any operation, but since we're the ones putting our lives on the line, we're accepting responsibility for our own lives. Elscol's pointing out, quite correctly, that a lot of other people can and will be hurt in all this.*

He nodded slowly. "Okay, we've got to start planning this all in earnest. We're gathering weapons and the ships we need already, but now we're going to have to designate mission goals, outline parameters, set rules of engagement, and establish just how far we're willing to go to accomplish the end we desire: the liberation of Thyferra. I take it that the fact that you're here means you're willing to help us do this, Elscol?"

She winked at Wedge. "Actually I was coming here to give you folks the joy of flying cover for me while my people handled the problem, but I think throwing in with you is the only way to get this done. We're in."

"Great." Wedge clapped her on the shoulders. "So, where do you suggest we begin?"

Elscol's smile blossomed. "I think the first thing we want to do is to make Isard very mad."

10

Corran made one last check on his instruments, but everything seemed fine. His screen showed him to be fifteen seconds from reversion to realspace. "Hang on, Whistler, this could be very strange."

He knew it shouldn't be at all out of the ordinary, but he couldn't escape the feeling that something odd would happen. He felt it was not because of any unknown factors attached to the mission, because there really were none. Their intelligence about the bacta convoy had been very good and double-checked. The squadron should be able to hit it and get away well before Iceheart could mount any sort of rescue operation.

Corran's uneasiness came from the fact that in this mission he was being asked to do something against which he had fought all his life. His father and grandfather had fought against it all their lives. Even Nejaa Halcyon had ventured out against pirates who preyed on interstellar convoys. Corran, who had once been an officer in the Corellian Security Force's antismuggling division, had become a pirate.

Rationalizing and justifying what he was about to do was simple in the extreme. Elscol Loro had said from the start that getting Isard angry was important, and stealing a convoy of bacta certainly would do that. It would also force her to devote some of her resources to safeguarding future convoys. Even if Rogue Squadron never engaged any of Isard's troops, the sheer volume of runs the destroyers would have to make would tax the crew and the equipment, forcing her to obtain more supplies from the black market at inflated prices.

All the while wearing her down for us.

The counter in the upper corner of his screen spun down to zero, then the white tunnel outside his cockpit shattered into pinpoints of light that resolved themselves into stars. Out ahead of him, the yellow sun at the heart of the Chorax system took up a quarter of the sky, while the single large planet in the system stood silhouetted against it like the pupil in some huge yellow eye.

Streaming away from the planet like tears, the ships of the bacta convoy headed out, their exit vector identical to Rogue Squadron's entry vector. Though closing fast with them, Corran could not make out any visual detail on the Thyferran ships, yet Whistler flashed a schematic of them on his screen in short order. Three hundred meters in length, from prow bridge to hyperdrives, the bacta tankers had an almost insectoid feel about them. The ship's central section had two parts, each of which held six cargo cylinders. In the various systems where the convoy stopped, smaller ships would fly up to the convoy, tease one of the cylinders free from the tanker's belly, then slip a return cylinder into its place. The returned cylinder might be empty, but most of them contained the world's native goods, to be sent back to Thyferra or traded yet further along the line.

Corran keyed his comm unit. "Nine here, Rogue Leader. The convoy is right where it is supposed to be. No hostiles yet."

"I copy, Nine. Stand by." Wedge's voice broke for a moment, then flooded through the helmet speakers. "Bacta convoy, this is Wedge Antilles. Prepare to alter course to coordinates I will supply you."

A new voice came back on the comm unit. "Antilles, this

is Thyferran Convoy Delta-Two-Niner. We do not recognize your authority to give us orders."

"You will. Two flight, make a run."

"I copy, Rogue Leader." Confidence bubbled through Tycho's voice. "Eight, Nine, and Ten on me. Lock S-foils into attack position."

"As ordered, sir." Corran nudged his stick to the left and pushed the throttle forward to bring his X-wing up on Tycho's left. Nawara Ven, in Eight, dropped in back and starboard of Tycho while Ooryl pulled his X-wing into the formation to the port and in back of Corran. As a unit they sped on in at the long string of tankers and tending vessels. *The tenders will be the ones that are armed.*

The boxy tenders, which really were just freighters hauling food and other supplies for the convoy, quickly outstripped the tankers and positioned themselves to make the fighters shy off their targets. The strategy of forming a wall in front of the freighters might well have worked had the battle been taking place on a planet with the Rogues in landspeeders, but in space the tight grouping of the freighters just made eluding them all that much more easy.

Corran hit a key on his console. "Seven, I show six freighters in that block in front of us, but there were eight originally. They're screening something."

"I copy, Nine. The two missing ones are the largest of them. Keep your eyes open for something tricky."

Suddenly the freighter formation opened up like a flower blossoming and eight snubfighters burst up through the opening at full attack speed. Led by four Z-95 Headhunters with blasters blazing, the Thyferran fighters zeroed in on the Rogue formation. Corran threw all shield power to the forward shields, dropped his crosshairs on one of the speeding Headhunters and hit his trigger.

The quad burst of laser fire pierced the Headhunter's shields. The red beams sliced into the joint where the port wing joined the fuselage, sheering it off. The engine on that wing exploded and the ship itself whirled off in a flat spin. Corran sideslipped to starboard to cut beneath its flight path, then hauled back on his stick to loop up and onto the trail of the Thyferran fighters.

Evening his shields out, he inverted the X-wing and dove onto the tail of the second set of Thyferran fighters. It was a mixed group consisting of two TIE fighters and two "Uglies"—hybrid ships consisting of a TIE's ball cockpit married to Y-wing engine nacelles.

"Ten, do you want the Die-wings, or shall I take them?"

"Ooryl would be pleased to take them."

"Ten, I have your wing." Corran smiled as Ooryl cruised up and broke to starboard as the pair of Uglies veered away to shake them. While affordable and effective for most convoy security duty, the Uglies were not well suited to engagements against military-grade snubfighters. The Die-wing variant—often referred to as TIE-wing among those who flew them—suffered from the deficits of their component parts. They had a Y-wing's sloth mated with a TIE fighter's lack of shields. Corran would have preferred to be handed a blaster and allowed to float his way into a fight than pilot one of those things.

He kept an eye on the location of the TIE fighters as Ooryl went in after the Uglies. Though the Gand's exoskeleton made him look blocky and clumsy on the ground, his handling of an X-wing was nothing short of fluid and even delicate. Whereas Corran's passing shot on the Headhunter had been lucky, Ooryl had a facility for doing exactly that sort of damage on purpose. *He shoots as if laser bolts were being rationed.*

Ooryl triggered a double burst of laser fire, sending two scarlet bolts lancing through the lead Die-wing's ball cockpit. Nothing exploded, though leaking atmosphere did combust and flare for a moment. The Die-wing hurtled on through space, but began to level out from the looping climb in which it had been engaged. That move invited a second shot, but the first had clearly killed the pilot, leaving the ship to fly on with no intelligence at the controls.

Unfortunately for him, the Die-wing's wingman failed to realize his partner had died. Flying in perfect formation, he began to level out, too. Ooryl's sideslip dropped him square on that fighter's aft. Before the pilot could begin to maneuver, Ooryl fired two laser bursts at him. The first shredded the port nacelle, lacing it with fire before ripping it apart. The second shot weakened the link between the remaining nacelle and the cockpit. The engine ripped free, rocketing off toward Chorax's sun, while the ball flew on out of control.

A small explosion wreathed the top of the cockpit with fire. A round plug shot upward; then the pilot followed, riding a command couch backed by a rocket booster. It carried the pilot clear of the doomed ship and out into space. The command couch gave the pilot marginal control over his fate—he was no longer bound for deep space in a runaway fighter—but without a pickup in a ship within a half hour, he'd suffocate or freeze to death.

Corran keyed his comm unit. "We have one bad guy EV."

Whistler's urgent hooting overrode any reply. "Got it, Whistler—TIEs inbound. Ten, you're my wing again."

"Ten complying with your order."

Corran shook his head as he brought the X-wing up on its port stabilizer and pulled back on the stick. Any other pilot in the unit who had picked off the Die-wings would have been ecstatic, or at least would have had his excitement show up in his voice, but not Ooryl. The only way to tell if he was excited or ashamed about something was to listen to how he referred to himself. Gands felt it the height of arrogance to refer to themselves with a personal pronoun unless it was felt by Gand leadership that the Gand in question had done something so great that every Gand would be aware of who was being referred to. As a result, when Ooryl was happy he referred to himself as Ooryl, when he was chagrined as Qrygg, and when he was really mortified as Gand, allowing himself to sink in anonymity as his shame grew greater.

His ego is just as strong as any of the rest of us—he just has a better grip on it.

Corran inverted his X-wing and leveled out for a head-to-head pass with the TIEs. The lead TIE broke off, but the following one began a corkscrew maneuver that jumped him around enough to make him hard to target. Corran snapped a shot at him, then climbed up and off after the fleeing TIE. *He's the lesser of two evils.*

The TIE jinked high and low, but did very little side to side maneuvering. *He's a rookie and has been training in atmosphere.* The TIE's octagonal solar panels caused a lot of problems with maneuvering in atmosphere because of the resistance they offered, though climbing and diving were no problem at all in a TIE. In space there was no atmosphere to limit the TIE's maneuverability, but the pilot he was chasing had not yet had a chance to learn that lesson.

And the lesson he's going to learn here is one of an entirely different nature. Corran snap-rolled the X-wing up on the port S-foil. Whereas the up and down juking had made the TIE difficult to hit before, Corran's roll left it trapped between the X-wing's lasers. Corran's finger tightened up on the trigger, spitting laser fire at his quarry.

The quad burst evaporated the port solar cell wing, letting the TIE trail threadlike tendrils of congealing metal on its left side. Corran pushed his stick forward to correct his aim, but before he could shoot again, the hiss of laser fire hitting his aft shield filled his cockpit. Jamming the stick to the left and shoving it forward, Corran kicked his fighter into a corkscrew dive that took him well away from the wounded TIE.

A glance at his aft sensor readout showed the remaining TIE was staying with him. *This guy is really good.* "Ten, I have one on my tail."

"Ten is shaking a lock."

"I copy, Ten." Corran frowned. "Whistler, find out what has a lock on Ten." He knew it had to be one of the freighters that had a concussion missile battery or proton torpedo launcher on board. Most freighters did not carry such weapons systems just because of the space needed for storing the missles and the sensor equipment, but those that did could be very effective against pirates, because they could engage them at the missiles' longer range.

Whistler shrilled at him.

"Yes, I know I have a fighter on my, er, *our*, trail." Corran pulled up into a climb, then rolled and shot off at right angles to the line of his climb. "I'll take care of him, you just tell me what I want to know."

The TIE stuck with him. *This guy is very good. His fighter can match mine in speed and maneuvering. He's not going to let me go head to head with him because my shields give me an advantage in doing that. He has to stay in my aft arc and keep nibbling away at my shields to get me, so that's what I'll let him do.*

Corran switched his fire controls from lasers to proton torpedoes and prepped the fighter to shoot them one at a time. He kept a loose hand on the stick and jinked a bit, but allowed his pursuit to take a couple of shots at him. They sizzled in on the aft shield, but didn't penetrate it.

This better work. Corran chopped his throttle back to zero, then yanked his stick back to his breastbone. The X-wing's nose came up and over, pointing straight back at the TIE. The TIE immediately shied to port, so Corran hit his left etheric rudder pedal and tracked the X-wing's nose along the TIE's flight path. The aiming reticle went from yellow to red, and Whistler screeched out a solid tone indicating target lock.

Corran fired a missile.

The proton torpedo rode a jet of blue flame as it streaked out after the TIE. It actually overshot its target when the TIE pilot rolled the fighter and pulled the starboard solar panel out of the torpedo's range. The proximity sensors on the proton torpedo caused it to detonate, filling the area around it with a rapidly expanding cloud of shrapnel. Before the TIE pilot could react, tiny bits of metal pierced the transparisteel cockpit canopy, shattering it into a million razor-edged fragments, that proceeded to reduce everything in the cockpit to debris.

Corran watched the TIE fighter begin to spin off lazily through space. *When I go, I hope it's that fast. No lingering for me.*

Whistler's mournful tone seemed to echo that sentiment. "Nine here, I'm clear."

"Seven here, Nine. We're all clear."

Corran brought his ship around and saw two of the

freighters hanging in space with fires raging internally. "Order, sir?"

Tycho replied quickly. "Wedge has convinced the convoy that once it makes delivery runs for us, it can go free. Form up with Ooryl, and take two tankers for your run. They'll slave their navicomps to yours. Once the cargo has been delivered, let them go and get back to base."

"As ordered, sir." Corran let a little chuckle roll from his throat. "Well, Whistler, this isn't much of a blow to strike against Iceheart, but it's something. I'll take it as a down payment on what she's going to get later."

11

A cloud of steam rolled toward Corran as the inner door of the thermal lock opened. He and Ooryl stepped through quickly, anxious to be well away from frigid conditions that existed back in the hangar. Corran pulled off his gloves, blew some warmth into his hands, then smiled as a small, balding man approached them. "You must be Farl Cort."

The smaller man nodded and extended a hand to Corran. "I am. I want to thank you for your mission here. When we put the word out, I had no reason to expect, you know, such a generous response so quickly."

"Pleased to meet you, sir." Corran shook his hand, then jerked his head toward Ooryl. "This is Ooryl Qrygg of Gand, I'm Corran Horn of Corellia."

Farl shook Ooryl's hand, then waved the both of them deeper into the rough-hewn stone tunnel. "You'll forgive the lack of decoration and refinement, but Halanit is a fairly small community that is still building to self-sufficiency, so we have little time to devote to anything that is not utilitarian."

"Ooryl can understand this. You have chosen a difficult world to make your home."

Corran shook his head at the Gand's understatement.

Halanit was a moon orbiting a gas giant. A thick coat of ice covered the planet, but beneath the frozen crust, the hot heart of the world heated water and rock enough to make life sustainable. The colonists began creating their community during the final days of the Old Republic. They had weathered the Empire and Rebellion all but unnoticed since the planet produced nothing of use and the inhabitants numbered just over ten thousand. It was just one more curiosity in a galaxy full of them, and it would have escaped Corran's notice except for an urgent message sent to Coruscant to request shipments of bacta.

Farl led them from the tunnel to the edge of a huge chasm that reminded Corran of Coruscant's artificial canyons. A hundred meters or so above them a double-walled transparisteel shield capped the chasm and spread over the area the diffuse light glowing down through the glacier. On both sides of the chasm lights shone through viewports carved in the stone and silhouetted the various bridges across the gulf. In several places, water streamed down between and over rocks to splash rather beautifully into the chasm's depths.

Corran raised an eyebrow. "This is a little more than simply utilitarian, I think."

Farl smiled. "This grand vista is the one concession we make to beauty. Standing here it is easy to see how our forefathers envisioned what Halanit would become. In two generations we have accomplished much, but we are far from our dream of making this world into a utopia. And, as pretty as this is, it does have utilitarian concessions. The double-walled transparisteel cap keeps warmth in and ice out. The waterfalls are wonderful to look at, but they fill our reservoir down below and feed our ichthyoculture farms."

"I concede the point." Corran smiled. "Tell me more about the disease that's causing you problems."

"It's a virus that mutates quickly and sweeps through the colony." Farl shrugged. "Left untreated the symptoms come and go inside two weeks, though there is lingering weakness for another month after that. The symptoms are congestion, coughing, fatigue, body aches, and a fairly ravenous appetite.

Bathing in the mineral springs here seems to help, but a bacta bath will be far more helpful."

Ooryl's mouth parts clicked open and shut. "Your virus sounds similar to the Cardooine Chills."

"True, though that illness can only afflict a person once before he or she develops immunity." Farl led them on through another atmosphere lock and into a darkened corridor. "This virus mutates so quickly that we can't create a vaccine. It spreads through the population such that someone just recovering from one strain catches the next. On a larger world there would be more of a lag time between epidemics, and a bigger world would have more resources to be able to deal with the illness. Right now, though, a sick person eats enough food for a family of four, and this threatens the whole colony.

"The most recent strains have been nastier, increasing the appetite and debilitating the victims, which is why we sent out our call for bacta." Farl sighed. "When we got word from Thyferra about how much it would cost to fill our order, well, we fairly well despaired. Then you showed up in-system with a tanker ship carrying enough to go a long way toward wiping the epidemic out."

The small man led them into an office and invited them to sit in rickety, rusty chairs. He walked around a makeshift desk and sat on a stool. "So, I need to ask, what do we owe you for this bacta? The market value for it is something in excess of a billion Imperial credits."

Corran glanced over at Ooryl, then shook his head. "You don't owe us anything."

"But this amount of bacta, it is valuable. You must have paid a great deal for it."

The Gand leaned forward. "Ooryl believes Corran would tell you that the bacta was collected as part of a bad debt. It cost Corran and Ooryl nothing; therefore it's offered freely."

The puzzled look of amazement on Farl's face slackened into an expressionless mask. "I see."

Corran smiled. "You needn't think of it as stolen, since

the government that would have demanded payment from you is not legitimate."

A wry grin twisted the lower half of Farl's face. "Dealing with pirates and smugglers holds no difficulty for us. The transparisteel and other modern conveniences you see here were not made here, so we have traded with outsiders before."

"If that's not the problem, what is?"

Farl frowned. "We've always given something in exchange for what we took. In some cases we have hidden people from their enemies. The fish we raise here are considered delicacies on some worlds and are extinct on others, so some collectors favor them. The problem is that a billion credits would buy all of them, and most of this colony, too. We will not take charity, but we cannot offer you value for what you have given us."

"I'm sure we can come to some sort of arrangement. You mentioned mineral springs as part of your treatment for the chills before, right?"

"Yes, but I don't see—"

Corran held a hand up and looked at Ooryl. "Flying in here didn't I tell you I'd give half a billion credits for a hot bath and a good fish dinner?"

The Gand hesitated, then nodded extravagantly. "Indeed, Qrygg remembers your using those very words. And Qrygg concurred."

"There you have it, Farl Cort." Corran opened his hands. "A hot bath and a hot fish for each of us and we're even."

The colonial administrator smiled. "I'll see to it that you get your money's worth."

"Liberating the bacta from Iceheart has already done that." Corran laughed aloud. "Getting to sit in a hot bath and think about how furious she'll be will make the experience just that much more perfect."

The moment Tycho Celchu's X-wing reverted to realspace, a chill ran through him. He had been to Alderaan—to its

Graveyard—before. He had seen and flown through the stony disk that was all that remained of the world on which he had been born and had grown up. His last vision of the world as a whole, cohesive ball had come when he shipped out to the Imperial Military Academy and the pride that marked that memory now mocked him.

He had returned to Alderaan before, but he had not yet *Returned*. Among the survivors of Alderaan, Returning had taken on a reverence and importance unlike any other tradition he could recall. It seemed as if all the mental and emotional energy that had been funneled into the planet's pacificistic philosophy had been shifted and focused on a person's Return. Some people even described their Return as a watershed experience, one that changed their lives completely and profoundly, opening them to the greater truth of the universe.

Those claims had been made by people wearing beatific expressions. They talked about what should be done on a Return. They specified what should be said, what should be offered, and what should be expected in return. They ritualized what Tycho felt should be a distinctly individualized experience, then encouraged each other to share their experiences so they could mutually reinforce their beliefs in the healing nature of the Return.

The Return had become something of an industry to service the Alderaanian community, and Tycho had not found himself immune to its lures. After guiding several bacta tankers to Coruscant, Tycho had set down on the planet and spent some time with a few Alderaanian friends. As a result of their conversations, he had decided to make his own Return, and then went out and proceeded to buy all the things he would need to do it correctly.

Following the dictates of others rankled him, but he could not deny that inside he felt a need to do some of the things bound up in a Return. He purchased a Memorial Capsule, then bought little gifts for all of his dead. He picked out things he knew they would have enjoyed—romantic holodramas for his grandmother and sisters, wine for his father, flower bulbs for his mother, and a datacard of the latest recipes for his mother's father—the gourmet. For his brother, he picked up a holobio of Luke Skywalker, knowing Skoloc would have thrilled at being able to meet Luke and learning the Jedi would be returning to the galaxy. While part of him rebelled at the idea of buying these things and jettisoning them to orbit amid the Graveyard, the symbology of it satisfied a need inside of himself to place amid the shards of the world items that would mark the lives of people of whom there was no longer a trace.

Choosing something to memorialize Nyiestra had been all but impossible. He had known her all his life, and before he hit puberty, he knew he loved her and would marry her. He had been as certain of that as he had been that the sun would rise and set on Alderaan for the rest of their lives. She had agreed to wait for him throughout his time at the Academy and then even through his first year of duty. If he survived a year as a TIE pilot, then he'd get moved up in the chain of fleet command, making it possible for him to marry and start a family. Never had he doubted, never had *she* doubted he would survive that first year, so to both of them their future had been assured.

Then the Death Star exploded that future.

Another chill sank through Tycho, puckering his flesh. Because his father was the CEO of Novacom, the largest HoloNet provider on Alderaan, Tycho had been able to make a realtime HoloNet call to his home on the occasion of his birthday. Everyone had been there, all smiles and laughter. They had presents for him and toasted him with wine. Though thousands of light-years distant from the celebration, he felt every bit a part of it; then the transmission went down, the holographic images dissolving in a gray-black blizzard of static.

Tycho had just smiled. Such interruptions had happened before and in each instance he had given his father a hard time about it. Throughout the next week he mulled over what he would say to his father. He had looked forward to the exchange, since matching wits with his father was a true joy in his life.

Then word filtered down through the fleet that Alderaan

had been destroyed. Blame had been placed on the Rebels, but he'd known instantly that they were innocent. While his Imperial indoctrination had left him no doubts that the Rebels *would* destroy a planet to gain their ends, he knew it would not be Alderaan. They drew support from Alderaan, according to the rumors, so destroying it would only make sense for the Empire. The fact that the Emperor dissolved the Imperial Senate *before* Alderaan died, instead of in reaction to its death, firmly focused blame as far as Tycho was concerned.

So he defected. At the next planet, Commenor, he went on leave and never came back. He joined the Rebellion and for well over seven years had fought to guarantee no other world would face the fate of Alderaan. *And guarantee no other man would have to decide how to memorialize the woman he had intended to share the rest of his life with.*

Part of what made the choice so difficult were the changes he had undergone since Alderaan's death. Had he made his Return immediately after leaving the Imperial Navy, he would have encoded a poem on a datacard and set it adrift in a device that would have broadcast it over and over again. The comfrequency traffic that his R2 unit scrolled across his main screen showed thousands of others had thought of the very same thing.

It hurt deep down knowing that the man he had become would not have been a suitable match for Nyiestra. The life they had planned together would have been possible in a bygone age, but only if they refused to look at what the Empire was doing within the galaxy. Wrapped up in its cocoon of pacifism, Alderaan had seemed insulated from things going on in the galaxy. *It was as if when we disarmed we set ourselves above and beyond the petty concerns of the galaxy, and we thought doing so would keep us safe.*

Bail Organa and his daughter, Leia, had seen the folly of that idea, but Alderaan had been slow to awaken to their call. Many people clung to their pacifism as if it would save them from anything the Empire could do. They had felt that the only way the Empire would win was if it could force them to abandon pacifism. Being sacrificed to preserve their beliefs was not too great a price to pay—an attitude especially easy to hold when no one believed the Empire could or *would* destroy a planet.

Tycho had long since seen the error of that philosophy. *Pacifism for the sake of pacifism is the height of arrogant selfishness when that belief prevents you from acting to save others from harm.* While he had no more love for war than any other Alderaanian, he had chosen to go into the military to be in a position to influence and change the military. *And when it became necessary to destroy it, I became a Rebel.*

In the Rebellion, he had seen and done things that Nyiestra could not have understood. He knew she would have done all she could have to support him and comfort him and help him deal with everything, but the fundamental changes in him meant that they would no longer have been suited to each other. At the most basic level, he accepted as true a concept that Nyiestra would have resisted with every neuron in her brain: There are some people who are so evil and capable of creating such misery, that killing them is the only way they can be dealt with. Grand Moff Tarkin, the Emperor, Darth Vader, Warlord Zsinj, Ysanne Isard, General Derricote, and Kirtan Loor were all beyond reasoned arguments designed to make them repent and abandon their evil ways.

The same events and experiences that would have sundered him and Nyiestra bound him and Winter. In many ways, his relationship with her astounded him because it was so wholly different from the one he had enjoyed with Nyiestra. Whereas they had done everything they could to minimize their time apart, he and Winter simply sought to make the most they could of the time they had together. Both of them had duties that kept them occupied and apart—and would continue to do so more often than not for the foreseeable future—yet the fact that each knew the other was out there somehow staunched what would otherwise have been a hideous emotional wound. He knew both of them—and probably everyone else from Alderaan that had been left alone—feared getting too close to someone in anticipation of losing them again. Despite that fear, they had grown close and provided an incredible amount of support for each other.

Ultimately, it had been Winter who suggested to him the perfect gift to memorialize Nyiestra, a woman she had never met or known.

Tycho found and purchased a perfect crystal sphere onto which had been acid etched the continents of Alderaan. Into the heart of this idealized version of the world he had called his own, he had Nyiestra's hologram imbedded. From within the depths of the world she had loved, Nyiestra smiled out at him, forever preserved, unchanging, and beautiful.

He keyed the comm unit and flicked on his IFF transponder. "I am Tycho Celchu, son of Alderaan, now orphan of the galaxy. I have come to this place of my birth to pay homage to who I was and those I knew. And those I loved and love still. It is my wish that when life abandons me, I am returned here to be among you, so that for eternity we may be together as we should have been in life."

He punched a button on his console, opening and purging the storage compartment in the X-wing's belly. Under the control of the R2 unit, the memorial capsule's compressed air jets pushed it forward till it emerged from beneath the nose of the snubfighter. A lump rose to his throat as the black oval capsule slowly began its trip into the swirl of stone that once had been Alderaan.

Tycho cleared his throat. "These gifts are but insufficient tokens of the love for you all that still burns within me." He hesitated for a second, then deviated from the formula he was supposed to speak to do his Return correctly. "This fighter is another. It bears the colors of the Alderaanian Guard and transmits their code. It is my pledge to you—not of vengeance but of vigilance. I hope you rest well knowing you will rest alone, because it is my life's work to see to it that no one else suffers as you have. I won't rest until this quest is complete."

He hit another button, closing the cargo compartment. The capsule continued drifting away, and he was tempted for a moment to blast it to bits with his lasers. He had no doubt that amid the debris, ships waited and searched for things to recover. The individuals who had located and brought in the *Another Chance* had been on a salvage mission of sorts, and countless were the stories of treasures rescued from the ruin of Alderaan.

Many of those treasures were shown to be forgeries, created and planted by confidence tricksters to prey on the Alderaanian community. Even nastier than they were the people claimed to have been from Alderaan—all rescued by miracle or coincidence—and who subsequently sought to insinuate themselves with families who had survived but had lost relatives. Because of the nature of the Imperial economy, a considerable portion of the wealth of Alderaan had survived the planet's destruction, making the survivors quite prosperous and, therefore, targets of opportunity for criminals.

He watched the capsule until it vanished into the swirl of debris. "Rest easy. I miss you all." He punched up the power on his IFF beacon and pulsed its transmission out in one grand confirmation of his vow, then shut it down, turned the X-wing around, and started the long trek back to Yag'Dhul and the war against Ysanne Isard.

12

Fliry Vorru fought the sense of nakedness that his abbreviated clothing inspired in him and braced himself for Ysanne Isard's tirade. "Yes, the diversion of the convoy has been confirmed by a number of sources. It is not the utter disaster you have made it out to be since Antilles is not holding on to our tankers, but is returning them."

"Returning them so we can refill them and he can take them again." Her diaphanous red gown swirled around her like a tornado. "You should have anticipated this sort of strike and taken steps to prevent it."

Vorru waved her suggestion away. "I *did* anticipate it and chose to ignore it. The amount of bacta taken was insignificant in comparison to both our supply and the demand for it. In fact, the loss of that bacta has provided me an excuse for hiking prices yet again, increasing our profits. I calculate our losses at between seventeen and thirty billion credits—an amount I will recoup by the end of the month."

"Bah! We lost more than just money when Antilles hit our convoy. We lost prestige and respect." She pointed a hand toward the sky. "We have people out there laughing at us because a dozen aging snubfighters were able to pirate bacta from us."

Vorru let his voice sink into a bass growl as he began to pace through her roomy office. "What we *lost* was insignificant and provides us an opportunity to cut Antilles off from his base of support. He stole the bacta and made a present of it to many of the worlds it was meant for anyway."

"My point exactly. He has earned their goodwill."

"But that will fade to bitterness when he cannot repeat his gesture." Vorru's splayed out fingers closed into a fist. "First, we will cut allotments to worlds to cover our losses. Second, we will delay shipments to worlds that accepted bacta from Antilles; and third, we will demand payment from those worlds as if the delivery had been made by Antilles on our behalf. Delinquent accounts will receive no more service from us."

Molten fury flowed through Isard's left eye. "You're giving me bookkeeping. I want blood."

Of course you do. Vorru's features sharpened. While Isard had been on Imperial Center—even hidden away after the Rebel conquest—her connection to that center of power had anchored her. She had been patient and prepared to be subtle. Here, on Thyferra, where the omnipresence of plant life and the languid lifestyle of the human masters of the planet made it the antithesis of Imperial Center, Isard seemed prepared to indulge her more *primal* urges.

"Please, Madam Director, reflect for a moment on how our current position mirrors that of the Empire prior to the death of our beloved Emperor. The Rebel attacks are tiny and really insignificant in every way, *except* as strikes against our prestige and image. You yourself have often said that destroying the Rebellion must come before the rebuilding of the Empire, and in this you have correctly focused on the core of the problem. This problem we face still because Antilles opposes us and must be destroyed."

Vorru opened his hands and spread them. "Our problems in dealing with him are significant at this point. We do not know where he is, so mounting a strike against him is impossible."

Isard folded her arms over her chest. "We will begin operations to locate him."

"Of course. I have already begun to spread word through the various smuggling networks and criminal organizations offering a substantial reward for reports on his operations. They will bear fruit soon, I am certain." Vorru allowed himself a smile. "Until then, by manipulating the price and supply of bacta to punish those who deal with him, we can vilify him and cut him off from his bases of support. To wage his little war against us, he needs supplies and allies. If Antilles were not who he is, we would consider him of no more importance than a pirate."

Isard raised a clenched fist. "I would still take steps to crush him. I will have my ships fly cover missions for our convoys."

Vorru hissed as if he'd been stung. "Be careful, Madam Director."

"You caution me? Don't overstep your bounds, Vorru, or you will be dealt with."

"I recall the fate of Kirtan Loor, Madam Director, and I have no desire to be trapped in the belly of the *Lusankya*." Vorru raised his open hands. "I merely wish to point out that if we accept full responsibility for the protection of our convoys, then Antilles will be our problem alone. This means our resources will be spread too far and will be too diluted to deal with him and his people."

Isard's chin came up. "You have an alternate proposal?"

"Certainly. We require the customers to protect our deliveries to their worlds, otherwise we deem their worlds too dangerous for shipments. We bring our convoys to certain destinations and demand our customers meet us and complete their journeys by themselves. If Antilles and his people hit them after the tankers leave our protection, they will anger a neutral party to their dispute. The Rogues will fight people other than our pilots, saving us personnel and equipment, both of which we no longer have in an unlimited supply."

Isard's right eyebrow arched. "This would also save us on shipping costs, increasing our profits yet again."

"True. It also allows us to prepare an ambush for the Rogues at a time and place of our choosing. Mind you, this will be later as opposed to sooner because we need time to let Antilles's actions utterly destroy his reputation. We want him to be cut off, with nowhere to hide, when we move to eliminate him."

Isard pursed her lips as she considered what he said, giving him more of a visual indicator of her mood than he had ever seen before. "The steps you are taking have merit, though the delay they necessitate annoys me. Finding myself impatient is also annoying. Antilles has managed to survive and even prosper during the time I should have dealt with him. Horn escaped from the *Lusankya*. Both of them, and their companions, have chosen to oppose me directly and openly, which has robbed me of the detachment I had when dealing with the Rebel opposition to the Emperor."

Vorru inclined his head slightly, impressed by her self-analysis. *She is loath to entertain fantasies about herself or her situation, no matter how inviting they might, in fact, seem. She has not lost her mind . . . yet. Whether or not she will is another thing.*

Isard stared off over Vorru's head. "The flaw Rogue Squadron has, a flaw the Rebellion has, is the fact that they have been able to overcome all the challenges thrown at them. Not since the days of Derra IV and Hoth have they known defeat. They are accustomed to winning, and this self-pride can be used against them." She nodded once, then focused on him. "Carry on, Vorru, continue your scheming. I will let them become accustomed to dealing with you and your methods, so when *I* strike, the surprise alone will be enough to kill them."

Wedge stood up behind his desk as Booster Terrik's bulky form filled the doorway to the station manager's office. "I appreciate your coming here so quickly, Booster. I know you wanted to spend some time with Mirax before she heads out."

The older man shrugged. "She's helping prep this Horn for his part in the mission. There's only so much of him I can take." Booster plopped himself down in a steel-frame canvas chair. "I think she took up with him to annoy me."

Wedge laughed and sat back down. "I'm sure it *does* seem like that, but I think there's a lot more there."

"CorSec has always wanted to steal our women."

Wedge arched an eyebrow in Booster's direction. "You can impart whatever motives you want to Corran, but you know your daughter better than that, my friend."

Booster frowned. "He's using those Jedi sorceries to addle her mind."

"The only person confused about his Jedi heritage is Corran." Wedge shook his head. "Luke Skywalker has been transmitting material about the Jedi to him to keep alive the possibility that Corran will train to become a Jedi, but Corran's a bit focused right now on getting at Isard and freeing her prisoners. He's almost obsessive about it—a trait you know something about."

Booster planted his massive hands on the arms of the chair. "If you want to scold me about disapproving of the man my daughter is seeing, the message is received. Anything else?"

"That wasn't my intention—that would be like teaching a rancor to dance. It probably won't work, you will get your head bitten off, and even if you do succeed, the result won't be very pretty." Wedge shivered. "Actually, I wanted to offer you the chance to pilot the *Mimban Cloudrider* on the run to Thyferra."

Booster sat back and brushed the fingertips of his left hand over his chin. The *Mimban Cloudrider* was one of the Thyferran tankers. Wedge had pulled the crew from it and, with Booster's help, had gotten identification files sliced together that listed Mirax, Corran, Elscol, Sixtus, and Iella Wessiri as the crew under various pseudonyms. Once in orbit at Thyferra, they could make planetfall in a shuttle and hook up with the Ashern. Wedge still needed someone to command the mission and thought Booster would be invaluable in that position because of his experience and instincts.

Booster lowered his left hand to the arm of the chair. "No."

"No? You'll be able to chaperone your daughter."

"She can take care of herself."

"You'll get to pilot a ship again."

Booster smiled and his body convulsed with silent laughter. "Closer, but still off the mark. The *Cloudrider* is too small. Too little to do."

Wedge frowned. "Wait a minute. When I got my freighter and started hauling cargo, weren't you the one who told me that being the master of my own ship and fate was the greatest thing to which I could aspire?"

Booster nodded and sat forward. "I did, but that was before Kessel. Five years in the spice mines changed me."

"Five years spicing would change anyone." Wedge frowned. "Don't tell me Kessel broke your spirit, because I flat refuse to believe it."

Booster's booming laughter filled the office. "Broke me? It would take more than no air and lots of work to break Booster Terrik. The mines could be a brain cracker for a lot of folks, especially the pols the Empire tossed in there. Others of us were content to wait our time out. Fliry Vorru, for example, is very patient, which makes him very dangerous. We knew the Empire would never let him out, but he was confident he'd be out someday. I knew I would get out, but the time there still ground on me."

The flesh around his eyes tightened, leaving the red light in his left eye burning like a laser in the darkness. "The time I spent in Kessel was unbelievably boring, Wedge. Monotony. Day after day the same things would happen with the same people. There was no night, no day, just shift after shift after shift. Prisoners might come and go, but that was it. Pain I could handle and fight against, but boredom? It was the enemy, and it had me mashed flat."

Wedge winced. "I can't imagine . . ." There certainly were times when Wedge would have welcomed less excitement in his life, but not year after year of it. *I'd have gone out of my mind.*

"When I got out, I made one trip on the *Pulsar Skate,* but the solitude of hyperspace reminded me too much of Kessel. That's why I retired and gave Mirax the ship. Now I travel and do deals for friends because it means I'm constantly meeting folks and getting to know them and learn about them. I'm trying to fill the void that Kessel left in me, and piloting *Cloudrider* isn't going to do that for me."

Wedge nodded. "I understand, though I wish it were otherwise. You've got skills I need." He sat back in his chair. "Having someone I can rely on doing a job that badly needs to be done would be a big help."

A smile slowly grew on Booster's face. "I have an idea for you that might serve both of us and cover up some loose ends."

"What do you have in mind?"

"Let me run this station."

"What?"

"Look, you have this station that's been a trade staple in this region for a very long time. You've got the Republic thinking it's been destroyed, which means your enemies think that, too, but ships that come in-system to make navigational adjustments can still see it here. You're fooling no one, and the fact that you've shut the station down to folks who have been here a lot means you're making them angry. That, in turn, means that someone is going to sell you out to Iceheart."

"We figured that."

"Well, you should also figure this: Pretty soon no one is going to want to be trading with Thyferra. You're giving away what Vorru wants to charge for. His only recourse is to cut off the bacta supply going to folks who deal with you. Once he does that, you're dead." Booster pressed his hands together. "On the other hand, if we open this station to trade, we start generating capital for this operation *and* we have people bringing us information and equipment. We develop suppliers who are in our debt because of this station—which means they won't want to betray you—and who bring the material here to us instead of having us go out and get it."

"And running the station would mean you'd be anything but bored."

"There's that, too."

Wedge closed his eyes and thought for a moment. He'd

known all along that the location of his base would get out, but Booster's idea of making the secret's preservation valuable to smugglers and traders did suggest it might last longer. *All the years the Empire searched for Rebel bases, it wasn't our trade partners who sold us out.* And the prediction of Vorru's action was pretty much what Wedge had figured Vorru's response would be. Wedge had been gambling that gratitude for the free bacta would keep trade channels open, but he agreed that supplying a profit motive would go much further in that regard.

He opened his eyes. "Okay, that works for me. What do we use as a cover story for why part of the station is restricted?"

Booster shrugged. "Does it matter? We can start all manner of rumors, from your desire to emulate Warlord Zsinj and carve out your own empire to your desire to build a force to wrest Corellia away from the Diktat or even that you and Isard are working a racket to spike the price of bacta. The greater the number of rumors the better, quite frankly, since they will armor the truth and result in folks bringing us information to further our plans—whatever they might be. As long as there is some mystery here, and folks smell profits in trying to figure it out, we'll be covered."

Wedge nodded thoughtfully. "I suspect that your taking this position means you'll be pitted against Vorru in this war to control trade and information."

"And that won't be boring at all." Booster's smile broadened to the edges of his face. "This will be grand."

"I hope you're correct." Wedge stood and stepped away from the station manager's chair. "Booster Terrik, this station is all yours. May the Force be with you."

13

The shuttle ride down to Thyferra from the *Mimban Cloudrider* left Corran a bit uneasy. A rising storm made the air turbulent and being strapped into a seat in the back made Corran want to scream. He glanced over at Mirax and saw she was having as much trouble as he was sitting still. *Either one of us could pilot this* Lambda-*class cargo shuttle through this storm front without this much bumping around.*

Mirax placed her hand over his and gave it a squeeze. "We'll get down."

"I figure. Crashing and dying wouldn't be nearly as interesting as the rest of this run." Corran closed his eyes and concentrated on regulating his breathing. He tried to convince himself he was doing that just to settle his stomach—and that he'd done such things countless times before for exactly the same reason. It was true, but he also knew his choosing to do it now was a result of reviewing the datacards Luke Skywalker had sent to him.

Corran admired Skywalker's ability to read him. Very little of the material sent had been dry, boring, procedural stuff—examples of the breathing exercises were pretty much the only things that fell into that class. By and large Luke had provided him with stories of Jedi Knights that pointed to their long tradition of law enforcement and their dedication to virtue and justice and not a little to the bold, heroic tales that had made the Jedi legendary throughout the galaxy.

The selection is perfectly focused to inspire me to join him. The problem with it was that Corran found it rather daunting. It also caused him to start second-guessing himself, which was something he seldom did and hated whenever he did do it. Before reading the Jedi material, Corran would have put the dread coiling his belly down to a reaction to the bumpy ride. Now he wondered if he wasn't anticipating some disaster through the Force, which in turn made him wonder if he was leading his friends into an ambush.

I know just enough about the Force to be dangerous— more so to myself than my enemies. He had really appreciated Skywalker including information about lightsaber maintenance and fighting styles. He'd gotten a chance to practice with the weapon in the *Cloudrider*'s galley and began to feel comfortable with it. He was notoriously bad when fighting against a remote—recalling his failure at picking off its stinging bolts made him shift uncomfortably in his seat—but four days of practice had made him feel confident enough with the lightsaber that he sincerely doubted he'd lop off any of his own limbs using it in a fight. *In my hands it's more of a lightbludgeon, but it will do in a close fight.*

The shuttle's wings creaked as the pilot began to retract them. The viewscreens on the interior of the shuttle's cabin showed a heavily forested landscape up through which occasionally thrust very inorganic stone and transparisteel towers. The buildings didn't look so much inappropriate for the setting as they did *alien* to it. Corran knew instinctively these were the human dwellings on Thyferra, because no Vratix could live in one.

Mirax indicated one particularly blobby building with a nod of her head. "I bet *she* lives there."

Corran hesitated for a second, wondering which *she* Mirax meant, but the cold anger in her eyes took the choices from two to one. Anyone else might have been pointing out where Ysanne Isard lived; but Mirax had no use for Erisi

Dlarit, so Corran knew it was Erisi to whom Mirax referred. While Corran had not been at all pleased to become a guest of Ysanne Isard's through Erisi's efforts, Erisi had engineered the destruction of a whole convoy of freighters specifically to kill Mirax.

Corran turned his right hand over and held Mirax's left tightly as the ship settled down on the landing pad. "Might want to throttle back there just a hair. You're probably right, but we're not going to go on a social call just to find out."

Mirax gave him a sweet smile. "I was thinking of sending a gift."

Corran returned the smile. "Ah, but how does one gift wrap a bomb?"

"Bomb?" Mirax shook her head. "Nope, too quick. I want her to linger."

"Remind me never to make you angry."

She raised his hand to her lips and kissed it. "You'll never do that, love . . . at least not more than once."

Corran and Mirax slid from the seats and followed the rest of the passengers out of the shuttle. It brought in crews from a half-dozen tankers parked in orbit around the planet, most of which were returning from runs they completed after the Rogues had hijacked their convoy. Of main concern for most of the crews was whether or not they'd be docked pay by their employers for making unauthorized runs. The majority opinion seemed to be that they would be because the Thyferrans never lost sight of the bottom line and were willing to cut costs anywhere and everywhere.

The five infiltrators did not appear to be that different from the rest of the crews going dirtdown. While Thyferrans owned and ran the shipping companies, they hired laborers from throughout the galaxy to actually do the work. On Thyferra these foreign workers were restricted to certain areas around the spaceport, but none of them seemed to find these restrictions that tough to bear. Most of the crews found the Thyferrans arrogant—the word *Imperial* was used to punctuate this point several times on the trip down—and preferred to keep with other spacers.

Once outside the shuttle, Corran picked up his luggage

satchel. He opened it and pulled out the heavy tool belt and looped it over his left shoulder. A big hydrospanner hung at his left hip. He picked the bag up with his left hand, leaving his right hand free to deal with his identity card.

Or the lightsaber. To disguise the weapon, he'd grafted the working end of a hydrospanner onto the butt of the lightsaber. One quick, smooth draw and he had a working weapon in hand. Elscol had pronounced his work useless and suggested he would do better being able to produce a blaster in a pinch. He'd replied that a blaster and hydrospanner don't look a lot alike.

A tall, slender Thyferran man with blond hair looked down his long, skinny nose at Corran. "State your name and the nature of your business."

Corran hesitated for a second and immediately felt heat flush up from within his jumpsuit. "Eamon Yzalli. I am here to wait for my ship to be refilled and head out again."

The Thyferran snatched the identity card from Corran's hand and ran it through a datapad's card slot. "Ship's mechanic?"

"Yes, sir."

"Do you always bring your tools with you when you come to a planet?"

"Well, sir, not always, sir, but I have a friend who might get me a berth on another ship so . . ."

The Customs official's eyes darkened. "You would not think of overstaying your welcome here and trying to go into business for yourself doing repairs, would you?"

Unless it's fixing your attitude, nope. "No, sir, never my intention, sir."

"Very well." He hit two buttons on the datapad, then swiped the card back through the slot. "Your provisional visa is good for a week. Remain longer than that and face criminal charges."

Corran looked down as he accepted the card back, refusing to meet the man's eyes. "Yes, sir. I understand, sir. You have been most kind, sir."

"Yes, well, be gone. Next."

Corran shuffled on past and into the spaceport's main

building. Its long, low shape, with softened edges and decorative elements clustered in groups of six suggested to him that the insectoid Vratix had designed and created the rectangular spaceport. The whole structure looked as if it had been worked around and between existing trees, with the roof being open to let some of them grow up through it. While clearly artificial, the two-story building showcased the natural beauty of what had been there before it had been created instead of trying to supplant and surpass the beauty of the native plants.

Inside the spaceport itself, Corran rejoined Mirax. Ahead he saw Elscol and Sixtus, off to the left he saw Iella. Their Ashern contact was supposed to meet them in the spaceport building, but no one appeared to be paying any of them any attention. There were backup contingencies in case contact could not be made for some reason, but Corran hoped they didn't have to fall back on them because they involved a lot of waiting and, in an emergency situation, sitting around waiting meant disaster.

Seeing that nothing was happening immediately, Corran guided Mirax over to a row of seats set beneath an overhead walkway servicing offices on the second level of the spaceport. The seats were also located fairly near a refresher station of which he wanted to make use. "Watch my stuff for me?"

Mirax nodded and sat while Corran piled his satchel and tool belt in the empty seat beside her. He started to step away toward the refresher station when its door opened and a stormtrooper with a blaster carbine slung at his right hip came walking out. *In that armor, how can they . . . ?* Corran realized he was staring, then turned away quickly. He realized that looked suspicious as could be, so he leaned down and smiled at Mirax. "What did you say, dear?"

The look of fear in Mirax's widening eyes and the reflection of a stormtrooper's helmet eclipsing her brown irises told Corran his attempt to look inconspicuous had failed utterly and completely. He felt a heavy hand land on his shoulder, straightening him up and turning him around. Belly to belly with the stormtrooper, he looked up into the black eye lenses and tried to smile. "Is there something I can do for you?"

"I know you. Identification card."

Corran's mind reeled. It had to be impossible for the stormtrooper to actually know him, then he realized the man may have been on the *Lusankya* and might have seen him there. *Then again I could just look like someone else.*

Anxiety began to build in Corran as he handed over his identification card. *Think, quick, what to do?* He forced himself to breathe normally. *First thing is to avoid panic. The identification is good and solid. It will hold up.*

The stormtrooper held it up and examined it forward and back. "It seems fine, but you're familiar, and I don't know anyone named Eamon. Come with me so I can check you out."

Fighting the urge to panic, Corran flashed on one of the Jedi stories. He settled a simple grin on his face and stared intently into the black recesses of the helmet. "I don't need to go with you."

"You don't need to go with me?"

Corran's grin grew. *Hey, it's working. I'm influencing his mind.* "I can go about my business."

"You can go about your business?" The stormtrooper shook his head, then grabbed a handful of Corran's jumpsuit front. "Your business is my business, void-brain." The stormtrooper's comlink clicked from inside the helmet. "This is Nine One Five, bringing one in."

The stormtrooper looked past him at Mirax. "She with you?"

Fear for her cleared Corran's brain of disbelief over his failure to warp the stormtrooper's mind. He twisted toward his right to get a look at her, letting his right hip hit the back of the seat containing his luggage. He let himself begin to fall back, using his weight to tear his clothing free of the stormtrooper's grip. His head went down and his feet came up, letting him somersault backward over the chair. As he did so his right hand grabbed the hydrospanner and slid it free of the belt. Landing on one knee, he brought his head up and looked at the stormtrooper.

Corran found himself staring into the barrel of the man's blaster carbine.

"Hydrospanner will work better if you have the heavy end pointed toward me, but it hardly matters." The storm-trooper's two-handed grip on the carbine kept his aim steady. "Come along with me or the janitorial staff earns its pay."

"Sithspawn!" Corran swore and hammered the floor with the hydrospanner's head. As the tool rebounded from the floor, and the head of the hydrospanner went bouncing off to the right, he thumbed the lightsaber on. The silvery blade sizzled out and swept up through the muzzle of the blaster carbine. The weapon's barrel fell one way, the storm-trooper's left hand another as Corran whirled to his feet and brought the lightsaber around in a slash at the stormtrooper's eyes. The blade burned through the helmet, filling the air with the pungent scent of melted armor and burned flesh.

The stormtrooper collapsed like an empty suit of armor. Someone in the spaceport threshold screamed, then Corran saw two stormtroopers stationed near the Customs officer come running. Two more appeared from in front of the space-port, entering the building closest to Sixtus and Elscol. She pulled a hold-out blaster from her bag and shot at one of them. He went down with a wound to the leg, and suddenly the whole building erupted with blasterfire as stormtroopers appeared on the elevated walkways on the narrow ends of the rectangular building.

Corran dove forward into the row of chairs and pitched them over backward. Mirax went with them and hunkered down beside him. She brandished the smoking ruin of the stormtrooper's blaster carbine. "I appreciate the rescue, but did you have to destroy his blaster?"

"Can't parry the bolts, so I just parry the weapon." Cor-ran ducked his head as crossfire from the far walkway nib-bled away at the chairs behind which they hid. Above them, the stormtroopers on the balcony directed their fire toward Elscol and Sixtus. Corran knew more folks than just Elscol were shooting, since he saw one stormtrooper across the way go down, but the Imps definitely had them outgunned and outmanned.

Unless I do something, what I started is going to kill us all. He leaned over, kissed Mirax full on the mouth, then smiled. "Stay here, I have an idea."

"Don't get yourself killed."

"What, and make your father's day. Not going to happen." *I hope.*

Lightsaber in hand, Corran ran low and fast toward the refresher station. He hit the door hard and cut inside as blaster bolts shattered tiles and burned into the duraplast door. He could all but hear the stormtroopers who had shot at him laughing about how screwed up his priorities were, and it struck him that a refresher station, especially in a public spaceport, would be a really ignominious place to die. *Which is why I don't plan to die here.*

He kicked open the door to one of the stalls, hopped up on the commode, and climbed up on the edge of the durasteel partitions. He stabbed the lightsaber up through the ceiling and made three quick cuts. A triangular section of ceiling crashed down and a shower of tiles from the floor of the refresher station above spattered down in its wake. Corran worked his way a bit further along the partition, then boosted himself up into the second-floor refresher station.

Emerging from the stall into the empty refresher station, he felt a terrible calm wash over himself. He'd felt it before, long ago and far away, on Talasea, when he'd engaged other stormtroopers in combat. *When I come out of here, the stormtroopers across the way will see me and warn their comrades. I've got five, maybe six seconds to get all of them. Any longer and I'm dead.* He shifted the lightsaber to his left hand, wiped his right hand off on his jumpsuit, then grabbed the hissing blade again. *I'm already dead, this is just to save my friends.*

He ripped open the refresher station's door and stepped onto the elevated walkway. One step out he brought the lightsaber around in a waist-high cut that caught the first stormtrooper in the back. He pitched forward, then rebounded off the guardrail, but Corran had already moved past him. In a continuation of the move that had taken the first man, Corran shifted his right wrist, raised the lightsaber, and used a backhanded cut to decapitate the second warrior.

That blow, though grandly struck to great effect, was a mistake and Corran knew it. Though it popped the man's head off and sent it flipping up through the air, it also allowed Corran's arm to carry too far back. Sliding forward toward the next stormtrooper in line—the third of the four he faced—he wasted a second bringing the lightsaber back into striking position. He tried a high, two-handed cut that should have split the stormtrooper from outside shoulder to inside hip, but the Imp had already begun to turn toward the attack and ducked it.

The stormtrooper lunged toward Corran, catching him with a shoulder in the ribs. The stormtrooper drove him back, slamming him into the ferrocrete wall. Corran felt something crunch in his chest, then he couldn't breathe. The lightsaber fell from Corran's hand as the Imp drove him again into the wall, pinning him there, crushing him. Corran stared into the black lenses of the man's helmet and heard low laughter.

The laughter died as the stormtrooper's comlink came alive. "Get clear, Seven Three, so I can shoot him."

The pressure in Corran's chest slackened for a moment and he knew he had only one chance for survival. As the stormtrooper withdrew, Corran kicked off the wall and knocked his foe into the guardrail. Launching himself at the man's head, Corran grabbed him and held on as the metal guardrail shrieked and bent. Overbalanced, they both whirled off the elevated walkway. Corran tried to twist around so he'd land on top of the stormtrooper, but with a short fall and no frame of reference, he only half-accomplished his goal.

He hit hard, his back slamming into the body of the first stormtrooper he'd killed. His rear end hit the ferrocrete floor, sending a jolt of pain up his spine, then the second stormtrooper smashed headfirst into the floor and his limp body crashed down on Corran, sandwiching him between their armored bodies. With his lungs burning for lack of air, he leaned back and found himself looking straight up into the muzzle of the remaining stormtrooper's blaster.

Unable to do anything but cough, Corran closed his eyes and prepared to die. He heard the whine of a blaster being fired, then felt a hammer-blow to his chest. It didn't hurt the way a blaster bolt hurt, but he knew he'd been hit. *I'm dead, I have to be dead.* As much as he knew that was the truth, he immediately felt a need to rebel and live. *Open your eyes. If you can open your eyes, you're not dead.*

Corran willed his eyes open and would have laughed if he could have. Standing over him he saw Bror Jace, a member of Rogue Squadron the Imps had killed well before Coruscant had fallen. Though he wished it otherwise, as his consciousness faded, Corran knew there was only one explanation for what he saw. *I am dying because only the dead can see the dead.* He knew that made little sense, but he was beyond caring as he realized the dead really have little use for logic as well.

14

Wedge shivered as he waited for the shuttle from the Twi'lek freighter dock at the Yag'Dhul station. His shiver had less to do with apprehension about the Twi'leks' arrival at the station than it did the temperature on the station. Lowering it by an average of five degrees was just one of the few changes Booster Terrik had made since he'd taken over.

Wedge slowly shook his head. Booster had long been legendary for being tightfisted. *He's left dermal ridge indentations on every credit that has passed through his hands.* While Booster was more than generous with his friends, in business he was shrewd and capable of saving money in any situation where he found himself. By lowering the station temp, and by refusing to heat unoccupied portions of the station, he lowered its operating costs rather significantly.

More important, by leaving the tapcafs and cantinas on the central levels warmer than any other place, he encouraged people to congregate there and patronize those establishments. Since the station's vendors were paying him a percentage of their profits *and* were funneling all their supply needs through Booster, the old man was making credits hand over fist.

Credits that are going to get us the things we need.
Booster had put the word out through his network of contacts that he'd taken over the station and deals were to be had and made there. Traffic to and from the station had begun to increase and while Booster told Wedge there were some suppliers he'd have to visit to make deals with, the vast majority of the items they needed would be delivered straight to them at Yag'Dhul.

The Twi'lek shuttle, an octagonal tube that lacked all the elegance of the Imperial *Lambda*-class shuttle, looked as if it had been extruded from the freighter. It moved sluggishly onto the landing platform. It settled down onto a docking collar, which rose up to meet it and formed itself to the ship's hull. Lights on the exterior of the collar went from red to yellow and then green, signifying an atmospheric seal had been achieved.

A lighted panel near the viewport through which Wedge was watching showed the progress of a personnel-mover heading out to the Twi'lek ship. Outside, slowly moving across the loading platform area, droid-driven grav-sleds approached the ship to begin to offload cargo. Wedge had no idea what Booster had asked the Twi'leks to bring, but he knew from his visits to Ryloth that an exchange of gifts was customary. He hoped the Twi'leks brought ryll so it could be shipped to the rylca production facility on Borleias and transformed into the medicine that was vital for curing the Krytos epidemic on Coruscant.

The personnel-mover started its trip back to the station's hub. Wedge walked over to the doorway where it would arrive and positioned himself in front of it. He tugged at the sleeves and waist of his jumpsuit. He knew it might have been good form to wear the Twi'leki warrior togs he'd worn on Ryloth, but they were designed as warm-weather clothes and Booster's habitat adjustments made it a bit too cool to wear them with comfort.

The doorway opened to admit an obese Twi'lek wearing a robe made from a shiny gold fabric and held closed by a thick red sash. A coral ornament secured a gold cloak at his throat and the cloak's reflected light jaundiced his pink flesh, especially the flesh of his lekku, which he wore draped over his shoulders. He clasped his black-taloned hands before his belly and executed a short bow.

Wedge returned it. "I am pleased to be able to greet you here, Koh'shak."

"It is my pleasure to accept the invitation of Booster-ter'rik to visit you, Wedgan'tilles." The bulbous Twi'lek moved through the doorway. "You recall Tal'dira?"

A second Twi'lek filled the doorway and had to bow his head to make it through. The black flightsuit he wore had been supplemented with a scarlet loincloth and cloak as well as a golden bandoleer running from right shoulder to left hip. The hugely muscled Twi'lek's lekku had been tattooed with a whole host of designs, the significance of which Wedge could only guess at. He wore a blaster on his right hip and Wedge knew from prior experience that the bandoleer concealed a pair of vibroblades.

"It is an honor to see you again, Tal'dira."

"And you, Wedgan'tilles." The Twi'lek warrior gave Wedge a smile full of sharp teeth. "Koh'shak will run off and find his trading partners, leaving warriors to speak among themselves."

Wedge nodded in the fat merchant's direction and Koh'shak immediately headed off toward the lift-tubes to find Booster. While Wedge looked forward to spending time with Tal'dira and learning why the warrior had come to the station, he regretted not being able to sit in on the conversations Booster and Koh'shak would have together. *They might not be warriors, but the battles they will wage to strike a bargain will be of epic proportions.*

Wedge waved a hand toward the threshold of the cantina on that level. "May I offer you the hospitality of the station?"

The warrior nodded. "You honor me."

"Say that after we get served. Our selections are rather limited here." Wedge led him into the darkened cantina and wove a serpentine path through small tables to an open booth in the back. The reserved hologram drifting above it proclaimed its glowing message in a multitude of scripts and stood almost as tall as a Jawa. Wedge held his hand over the holoprojector and let it do a quick scan of his palm. The message changed to one of welcome, then morphed into a bill of fare. Wedge sighed and slid into the booth. "Having a table held for me here is about the only benefit of command."

"Warriors must take pleasure in even the slightest of benefits, because death is ever our companion." Tal'dira sat opposite Wedge, interlacing his fingers and placing his hands on the table. His lekku flopped over inside his elbows. "You deserve more than this for your great victory."

Wedge raised an eyebrow. "Great victory?"

The Twi'lek chuckled in a manner that seemed almost menacing. "You took from Iceheart a convoy of bacta."

"It wasn't exactly defended very heavily."

"It matters not. You did what no one would dare to do—you struck at the Bacta Cartel. What you did is memorable and worthy of praise."

"Thank you." Wedge glanced at the serving droid that approached the table. "Corellian whisky for me, Whyren's Reserve, if you have it. Tal'dira?"

"This Whyr'rensreserve will suffice for me as well."

The droid beeped an understanding of the order and rolled away. Wedge smiled at the Twi'lek. "You did not come here to tell me what you thought of the raid against Iceheart."

"Ah, but I did." Tal'dira leaned forward and raised his hands so his chin could rest on his outstretched thumbs. "The galaxy is changing. I am not old enough to remember the prior Republican era, but I have heard tales of the Clone Wars. Since its birth, the Empire sought to maintain peace, but there was much conflict that they ignored, conflict in which a warrior could find a career and build himself into a legend. And then there was the Rebellion . . ."

The Twi'lek fell silent as the droid returned with their drinks. Wedge plucked the tumblers of the amber liquid from the serving tray and set one before his guest. Hoisting his own glass aloft he offered a toast. "To warriors and their legends."

Tal'dira nodded and added, "And to those skilled enough to become *living* legends."

Wedge touched his tumbler to Tal'dira's and drank. He let the whisky linger on his tongue for a moment, then let it trail fire down his throat and into his belly. He gave himself a moment to consider what Tal'dira had said and he thought he had a glimmering of where the Twi'lek meant the conversation to go. The thought that he might be right threatened to plant a smile on his face, so he deliberately narrowed his eyes.

"The Rebellion was very much a place where warriors were able to build reputations. Too many of them have become posthumous legends, but that was one conflict that favored the courageous and devoured the weak." Wedge kept his voice even, but found his words surprising him. It felt natural to refer to the Rebellion in the past tense, as if it were over even before the last bits of the Empire had been smashed. He realized that this thought was not wholly wrong, for the conquest of Coruscant had elevated the Rebellion from being a movement to being a government almost overnight. *That's a transformation I never thought I'd see.*

Tal'dira's black talons clicked gently against the duraplast tabletop. "It is my profound wish I had been possessed of the foresight to join the Rebellion."

Wedge shrugged his shoulders. "You had responsibilities as a Twi'lek warrior. I had no such responsibilities and could therefore join the Rebellion."

"True, but to acquit my duties to my people I should have opposed the Empire."

Wedge frowned for a moment. The political makeup of the Empire had been such that the nonhuman populations always knew they existed at the sufferance of the Emperor. For many of them, remaining unnoticed by the Empire seemed the best way to make sure they were not destroyed. Historically, the Twi'leks found negotiation and deal making preferable to direct confrontation, and this preference had served them well during the time of the Rebellion. They seemed to view both the Empire and the Rebellion as rival heat storms that would annihilate each other, leaving the Twi'leks in a position to thrive afterward. The victory of one side over the other had not been predicted—especially not the Rebellion's victory. *Tal'dira's lament is genuine, but the product of hindsight.*

"I would have been happy to have you fighting beside

me, and Nawar'aven has been a boon to my squadron, but you did what was required of you." Wedge smiled. "Until you put together those fighters I saw on Ryloth, I know you had very little in the way of hyperspace-capable ships native to Ryloth. I have to imagine the Empire deliberately suppressed such technology on Ryloth so they would not have to deal with you as a force."

"It is kind of you to say so."

"To even think otherwise would be to do you a disservice. While many think of Twi'leks as traders, I know you have a proud warrior tradition."

"But our warriors are unproven to the galaxy." Tal'dira waved a hand toward the half of the station above his head. "As you have said, to most of the galaxy Twi'leks are merchants like Koh'shak or criminals like Bib Fortuna. You have been to Ryloth. You know this is not true, but such is the impression that has been made on the galaxy. Thinking that sapient beings believe all of us to be merchants and thieves preys on my mind."

Wedge glanced down at his tumbler of whisky. "I thought the fighters you have created were impressive." The Twi'leks had taken a TIE fighter's ball cockpit and married to it the S-foils of an X-wing fighter. The S-foils were connected to a collar that allowed them to rotate independently of the cockpit, much in the way the cruciform stabilizers on the B-wing rotated around its cockpit. The design provided stability for the pilot and had proved very effective with the B-wing. "Their maneuverability, I would imagine, makes them very formidable."

Tal'dira straightened up and smiled with genuine pleasure. "The Twi'leki designation for them is *Chir'daki*. In your Basic it would be Deathseed. It recalls the spores of a parasitic fungus that invades a larger creature and destroys it. Most unpleasant, as would be facing our *Chir'daki* in combat."

Wedge sipped a bit more whisky. "They *are* hyperspace capable?"

"Indeed. The twin-ion engines are used for main propulsion. The engines on the S-foils are smaller than those in your X-wings, but they provide power for the hyperdrive motivators and shield generators. We have quad lasers for our weaponry—no proton torpedoes because we decided obtaining supplies of them might be difficult."

"Wise decision—proton torps and concussion missiles are the only things we're having trouble finding. Booster is using up a lot of favors to get them." Wedge gave Tal'dira a curt nod. "I envy you your ships."

"And I envy you your ability to win victories." Tal'dira played with his tumbler of whisky in a most unwarriorly fashion. "You have proven yourself time and again a most dangerous enemy."

Wedge glanced down for a moment and stroked his chin with his right hand. "It occurs to me, Tal'dira, that it would be a waste for your ships to go untested."

A light sparked deep in the Twi'lek's dark eyes. "Indeed, a great waste."

"Perhaps it would be possible for you and some of your pilots to join us." Wedge spread his hands open. "The work is dangerous, and we will find ourselves outcasts everywhere if we fail."

Tal'dira's lekku twitched nonchalantly. "Twi'leks have been outcasts before."

"Can you give me a squadron?"

The warrior nodded. "Fearful that pirates might prey upon Koh'shak's freighter, we shipped with a dozen Deathseeds and pilots. We would be honored to join your battle against Iceheart."

Which is what you wanted the instant you heard we were fighting her, but you could never have asked. You wanted to be invited. Wedge sat back. "I know you are aware of how serious this is, but there really are fairly grand problems here. If you join us, Iceheart could cut the bacta supply to Ryloth."

"Ryll may not be bacta, but it suffices for many of our needs." Tal'dira shrugged. "Twi'leks pride themselves on being hearty, and bacta is seen in some quarters as a means for the weak to survive. If we are deprived of it we will lose people, but if we do not oppose Iceheart and take our place in the galaxy, what is the reason for living?"

"And you know Iceheart isn't going to forgive you if we lose."

The Twi'lek smiled easily. "The implacable foe is the only one worth facing. If we know we have lost everything we will fight that much harder. Such are the battles worth winning and worth taking pride in."

Wedge raised his tumbler again and clinked it against Tal'dira's. "Welcome to the Bacta War, Tal'dira. Here's hoping Iceheart and her people choke on your Deathseeds."

15

The thing Corran hated the most about floating in the bacta tank was that he could see blurred figures outside the tank, but he couldn't communicate with them. Even when one or more got close enough to press a hand to the transparisteel window into the tank, he couldn't make out who was at the far end of the arm. He could guess, but since the room outside the tank was kept dim and lit mostly by a yellow-green glow from within the tank itself, confirming his guesses was impossible.

He had no way of knowing how long he'd been in the tank, but he found the duration of his stay both too long and too short. Pain in his back and guts had been overwhelming at first, but it subsided after a while. In its wake came a tingling in his legs, which was good since he'd not felt anything in them at first. Only after feeling returned to them did Corran allow himself to think about how badly he had been hurt and how close he'd come to death.

I probably broke my pelvis in the fall, then when the stormtroopers landed on me I broke my back and probably ruptured internal organs. Had bacta not been available, those injuries would have been fatal.

That realization sobered Corran and gave him a clarity of mind that allowed him to go back over what he had done at the spaceport. His two mistakes were very clear and gnawed at him. *I should have known better. I am not a Jedi. Trying to use Jedi methods without proper training is stupid, as I found out. I'm as bad as wannabe police—a Jedi vigilante. If Jedi techniques were just parlor tricks and illusions, the Emperor wouldn't have hunted all the Jedi down and had them destroyed. If these abilities are that dangerous, they shouldn't be used without proper training.*

While that line of thought made certain he'd never again try to warp the brain of a stormtrooper, Corran was not as harsh in his self-judgment concerning the fight on the catwalk. Lacking a blaster and pinned down by crossfire, to do nothing would have meant both he and Mirax would be dead. Escaping that trap required action and he'd taken action. His mistake in the fight had been the result of inexperience with the weapon he'd used. *I swung wildly, using more power than I needed. If I moderated things, kept the blade more under control, I could have gotten at least the third stormtrooper.* The fourth stormtrooper would have shot him, Corran had little doubt, but his attack would have all but eliminated half the threat to his friends.

A gentle tug on the breathing mask he wore caused Corran to look up. He saw a round hatch through which light came and a silhouette of a human head and shoulders in it. Kicking his legs, Corran made his way to the surface of the tank. He removed the breathing mask and hauled himself out through the hatch. The medtech there lowered a grate over the hatch and pointed Corran toward it. As he had done before, Corran stood on the grate as the tech used a water spray to wash the bacta residue from him and back into the tank. Holding his hands high, Corran turned slowly beneath the spray, then smiled as the tech tossed him a thick towel.

"How do you feel?"

Corran shrugged and wiped his face. "Pretty good. How badly was I hurt?"

The tech's face screwed up tight. "Pretty bad. You were in shock when we dunked you. Internal organ damage, broken pelvis, spine, and ribs—more quantity than quality of damage."

Corran nodded. "So I was in for, what, a week?"

"Two days."

"What?" Corran frowned at the tech. "I should have been in there much longer than that for those injuries."

The tech lifted his chin and gave Corran an imperious stare. "You are used to dealing with export-quality bacta, and Xucphra product at that, friend. The bacta here is more potent."

"Made by Zaltin *verachen*?"

The tech bowed his head. "Very good. If you will follow me, your friends are waiting for you."

Lacking clothes, Corran wrapped the towel around his waist and followed the tech down some stairs and through a doorway. The room beyond it was lit by a ghostly green glow coming from the transparisteel viewport that dominated the left wall. It looked back into the tank, the light from which allowed him to see further into the room than he had been able while in the tank. Low, long, well-padded day beds and high-backed chairs filled the rest of the room and had been arranged so anyone using them could keep an eye on his progress. Shadows shrouded the archway in the wall opposite the one he entered through.

As he came through the doorway, Mirax stepped forward and enfolded him in a hug. She kissed his lips, then his right ear. "I can't tell you how good you feel. I was afraid you'd not make it."

"And give your father the satisfaction?"

She laughed lightly. "I'll tell him that the Horn tenacity is, in fact, good for something."

Corran kissed the side of her face and held on tight. One of the most unnerving things about being in a bacta tank, with its temperature control and neutral buoyancy, was the feeling of floating in a void. If not for the touch of the breathing mask on his face, he would have had no connection to the outside world. Just being able to hold on to Mirax and feel her body through the thin material of her clothes brought him fully back into the world.

"You weren't hurt, were you?"

Mirax shook her head. "Nope, I kept my head down and came out in one piece." She grinned. "And I even managed to recover your lightsaber for you. It and your Jedi credit are safe."

"Great. Thanks." He released Mirax and gave Iella a hug. "Yet one more time you've had to watch me bobbing in bacta."

Iella smiled. "As long as you keep coming out whole, hale, and hearty, I don't mind."

"Thanks." Corran let her go, then nodded to Elscol and Sixtus. "Sorry to have inconvenienced you."

The big man just shrugged. Elscol's eyes narrowed. "The crossfire was a bit more inconvenient than this. We've gotten some work done while we've been waiting."

"And good work it has been." A tall, slender man came through the archway and gave Corran a once-over. "I'm glad to see you healed. You were in a bad state when I first saw you."

Corran hesitated. While he'd floated in the bacta he'd mulled over the identity of the man he'd seen standing above him in the spaceport. He'd looked like Bror Jace, but Corran knew that was impossible because Bror Jace had been killed by the Empire. Corran had decided that the man he'd seen was someone affiliated with the Zaltin corporation, as Jace had been, and perhaps was even closely related to Jace. That solution made perfect sense to him and seemed to satisfy all the facts in his possession.

But there's no mistaking that tone of voice. Corran's jaw hung open. "You *are* Bror Jace."

"Indeed I am." Jace bowed his head, then graciously waved Corran toward one of the day beds. "You'd like an explanation on why I'm not dead?"

Corran sniffed. "I've been reported dead myself. Those things happen."

Mirax slapped him playfully on the belly. "You're dying to know what happened to him, just like the rest of us."

"Well, if the rest of you want to indulge him, then I think the only polite thing for me to do is listen." Corran sat and adjusted the towel to preserve his modesty. "Go ahead, Bror, knock us out with the story."

Jace, whose blond hair picked up green highlights from the bacta tank, smiled easily. "I hardly think the tale engrossing enough for you to endure a second telling of it, so I beg your forbearance."

Corran glanced at Mirax. "You've heard this before."

"Yes, and I'd rather have him tell you instead of having you get it out of me later."

Corran winced. "Right. Okay, Bror, do it."

The Thyferran began to pace, clasping his hands behind his back. The short pants he wore and the thin shirt rustled with his movements—and Corran found the whole ensemble a little hard to reconcile with the pilot he'd known and competed with in his early days with Rogue Squadron. *The pacing is right, as is the imperious tilt of the chin, but the clothes are what kids wear.*

"I joined Rogue Squadron for a number of reasons, not the least of which was to maintain parity between Zaltin and Xucphra. This was important because Xucphra had Imperialistic leanings. They'd been the first of our two companies to be given an Imperial license to be an exclusive producer of bacta, establishing the cartel. Zaltin had been brought in by the Empire to serve as competition for Xucphra—Zaltin had no real desire to become part of the cartel, but the choice we were given was to join or be put out of business. In effect this was no choice, so we did what we had to do to survive."

Corran raised an eyebrow. That was as close as he'd ever heard any human from Thyferra being critical of the corporations with which they were affiliated. Despite the fact that Jace was attempting to paint Zaltin in a good light in comparison with Xucphra, the honesty was welcome and sparked in Corran a willingness to trust Jace further than he ever had before. *How much I trust him depends on the rest of this story.*

"The intention behind my joining the squadron was for me to become known and trusted within the New Republic. Zaltin officials had come to the conclusion that the Empire was doomed and wanted to make agreements with the New

Republic to provide bacta and the means to expand bacta production back along the lines of the system that existed before the cartel was created. Altruism was not their motivating factor—prohibiting the production, sale, and distribution of something is much more difficult than managing the same. The cartel only worked because of the Empire—with its death, the back of the cartel would be broken. The only way Zaltin could profit was to work out a deal with the New Republic which allowed us to oversee the expansion of production throughout the New Republic.

"Zaltin officials also realized that the Vratix, through their terrorist organization, the Ashern, would make a case to the New Republic for independence. They would ask for help throwing off the yoke of their human masters. Since bacta production is all but impossible without the Vratix, Zaltin began to court them. We supplied money and hiding places for them. We began an alliance that would eventually make Zaltin the agents for the Vratix in spreading bacta production throughout the galaxy, enriching us all."

Bror Jace stopped and closed his eyes for a moment. "The Vratix do not think the way we humans do. Whereas we would incorporate reports and data produced by someone into our plans, they incorporate such individuals into their planning groups. It is as if they don't disassociate the report from the person making it. Realistically, this is a societal way of ensuring the spread of information and stimulating more creativity within groups, though its efficiency can be questioned.

"The Ashern, who were being given reports on my impressions of the New Republic, required me to return to Thyferra to join their main planning group."

Corran nodded. "So you were sent a message telling you that your patriarch was dying."

"You remember. My course home was set by Captain Celchu. Erisi asked about it, and I told her my itinerary because I wanted her people watching for my return. In my trip I made one deviation—an unscheduled stop. I transferred from my X-wing to a freighter that brought me back here. Into my X-wing we placed a bomb meant to mimic the acci-

dental discharge of a proton torpedo. The X-wing was slaved
to a shuttle and dragged off toward Thyferra. We intended to
enter the system from quite a distance out, send the X-wing
in, then have it blow up where everyone could see it."

"But the Imps had an Interdictor Cruiser waiting for you,
thanks to Erisi." Corran scratched at his upper lip. "Reports
we got said there was no Imp debris where you died. I knew
something was up then, but I didn't think you'd lived. Did the
shuttle survive the ambush?"

Jace shook his head. "No, so we had no idea what happened until my family received a hologram from Commander
Antilles explaining the circumstances of my death. At that
point I'd already returned and had gone underground, so it
didn't really matter *how* I'd died as much as it mattered that
both the New Republic and Xucphra thought I was dead."

Mirax frowned. "Something just occurred to me—you're
the reason Qlaern Hirf came looking specifically for Wedge."

Jace nodded. "Wedge is intelligent, resourceful, and re-
spectable, so he was my obvious choice. Corran would have
been my second choice, but by the time we sent Qlaern Hirf
out, news of Corran's death had reached Thyferra."

"You would have sent him to me?" Corran wasn't certain he'd heard correctly. He'd never had the impression that
Jace had seen him as having the same attributes that he
ascribed to Wedge.

"Corran, though we established that I was a better pilot
than you, this does not mean I have no respect for your skills
or experience." Jace's tone of voice lightened ever so slightly.
"Your long association with the Empire's criminal class
means you understand a host of methods necessary for eluding authority and surviving, which were things I thought
would prove useful in keeping Qlaern safe."

"Thanks. I think."

"I meant that as a compliment."

"I'll remember that."

Mirax glanced over at Iella. "Too bad the bacta can't
cure annoying personality traits."

Iella shrugged. "Congenital defect, I'm afraid. Corran's
always been competitive and contrary."

Corran gave Iella a hard stare. "I always got along with you."

"Because you knew you'd lose if we ever went head to head where our skills overlap."

He could have protested her observations, but he knew it was more true than false. "Okay, you made your point." Corran forced a smile on his face. "Where do we go from here? What's been decided while I've been floating?"

Elscol folded her arms. "Sixtus, Iella, and I will be staying here—taking Jace's place in the Ashern planning councils because he'll be going back with you to liaise with the squadron. We're bringing in expertise on how to take a planet away from its government and how to deal with counterintelligence operations."

Corran looked at his former partner. "Are you ready for this?"

Iella thought for a moment, then nodded. "I'll probably get the cleanest shot of any of us at Isard. Diric's death still hurts, but if I'm to honor his memory, I can't do it by sitting around and mourning. You made that point very succinctly."

"Yeah, but here you won't be among your friends."

Iella smiled gently and caressed Corran's cheek. "True, but that means I've got fewer things to remind me of Diric and distract me."

"I don't think being away from friends would have made it any easier to get over my father's death, but I understand what you're saying." Corran winked at her. "Don't do anything stupid—especially in the name of revenge. Promise?"

"Sure, as long as you make the same promise."

"Done." Corran got up and gave her a big hug, then reluctantly let her go. Looking back at Mirax he asked, "So, what about the rest of us?"

"Our job here's done. We've delivered our charges, and we'll be safeguarding our liaison officer back to the base, so we're going home." Mirax smiled at him. "At least we'll be doing that as soon as we get some clothes on you, that is."

"As long as I don't have to use Jace's tailor, I'll be happy."

"What's wrong with what I'm wearing?"

"I hate shorts."

"On you, who'd notice?"

Jace's riposte stunned Corran, then he smiled. "I was thinking I spent a long time in the bacta tank, but I have a feeling that's going to be like nothing compared to the trip home. I'm glad you're alive, Jace. Life's been much too easy since you've been gone."

16

Wedge exerted the effort to wipe the smile off his face as his X-wing hurtled through hyperspace. Bror Jace's return from the grave had been a most pleasant surprise, both because he wasn't dead and because of the insight into Thyferra he provided. Zaltin had long kept tabs on Xucphra, and Isard had not changed procedures so much that Jace's intelligence reports had been completely invalidated.

He was very happy to have Jace back in the squadron. Zraii had put an X-wing together out of parts for Jace. The Thyferran had it painted red with green trim—the corporate colors of Zaltin—and had been checked out on it within three hours of his arrival at Yag'Dhul. Jace had been a hot hand in an X-wing when he was first with the squadron, and his time off had not seemed to dull his skill very much at all. *With as few pilots as we have, they all need to be sharp.*

Wedge had been less than pleased with learning that Corran had been injured on Thyferra. He'd have been angry with Corran except that the smaller man gave him a full report on what happened, including an analysis of his mistakes. Corran had been quite frank concerning what he had done, reminding Wedge of Corran's attack on stormtroopers on

Talasea. *When Corran finds trouble, he never seems to have difficulty just diving in, especially when the lives of others are at stake. Nice trait to have in a friend.*

Information Jace had brought with him set the basis for the run the squadron had headed out on. Isard had initiated escort service for the bacta convoys, moving them to centralized locations where the client worlds would come to get their bacta. Wedge saw immediately that if he hit the covered convoys he'd be in serious trouble, but Jace's people had initiated an operation to get them some of the bacta anyway. The Ashern had sliced new code into the navicomps on three of the freighters that would produce a course deviation in the final leg of the trip. The freighters would fly out from under their cover and be in a position for the squadron to make off with them. The navicomps would remain useless until the squadron sent them the key code or until the crew stripped the computer down and reloaded all of the software.

Wedge knew the operation was chancy, but to refuse to go after the ships would mean that the Ashern's effort had gone for naught. The risk of the operation had to be weighed against the good that could be done with the supplies of bacta the ships carried. Halanit could still use more, as could several other small settlements that found the Thyferran price prohibitively high. More important, Coruscant needed more bacta to supplement the rylca treatments for the Krytos virus.

He couldn't discount the possibility of a trap entirely, but for the Imps to ambush him meant they would be leaving another of their convoys open. The freighters that were coming to him were from a small convoy that was being watched over by the *Victory II*-class Star Destroyer *Corrupter*. Though the smallest of the ships Isard had in her fleet, it carried two TIE squadrons, equaling his force, and bristled with enough weaponry to be able to lay siege to whole planets.

Complicating matters, Wedge knew less about its Captain Ait Convarion than he wished he did. Convarion was supposed to have served both at Derra IV and Hoth before being given the *Corrupter* and being sent off on suppression missions—government-sanctioned campaigns of terror against populated worlds on the Outer Rim. Convarion was rumored to be calculating and cruel, with a penchant for quick action that had won battles despite the odds being against him. That was a combination that could cause a lot of trouble for the squadron.

If Convarion knows in advance of the defection, we could be in severe trouble. If he has to deal with having three missing ships from his convoy upon his arrival at the Rish system, he'll be searching for an atom in a nebula. Depending on the reluctance of the freighter crews to follow us, we'll need a maximum of an hour to move the convoy farther on. If we have been betrayed, we'll have to jump back out of the system as fast as possible . . .

Wedge glanced at his primary monitor. ". . . and hope against hope that Isard hasn't convinced any Interdictor cruisers to join her side." He shook his head and sighed. He knew he was worrying about events that were very low on the scale of probability, but the chance of a problem still niggled at him. He knew he'd have felt better if he'd been in on planning the operation from the first, but he wasn't in a position to refuse the help the Ashern offered.

"I'll just make the best of this situation and hope Captain Convarion isn't as sharp as rumors make him out to be."

A pinpoint of black expanded up and engulfed the snubfighter as it reverted to realspace in a system with a red dwarf star surrounded by a dust disk. Three bacta freighters hung in space just above the plane of the disk. The captains had oriented the ships so their bellies pointed inward and the two dorsal turbolasers they sported overlapped their fields of fire.

Wedge opened a comm channel. "One and Two Squadrons, S-foils in attack position." Both the X-wings and the Deathseeds responded to his order, causing their stabilizers to split and lock. The fighters spread out on their previously assigned approach vectors, but they held back from closing with the freighters.

He shifted the comm unit over to the frequency the Ashern indicated the Thyferrans used. "This is Wedge Antilles. I have two squadrons of fighters here. We intend to have your cargo. If you cooperate you will be given a course, be able to drop your cargo, and then go back home unharmed."

Nervous tremors shot back through the voice that answered him. "Antilles, we were told that if we went with you, we'd be destroyed. We have family back on Thyferra."

That comment sent a chill down Wedge's spine, but he fought against the ideas it planted in his head. "Your families will not be harmed. Isard can't kill families of pilots and expect any more shipments of bacta to go out. It's a bluff that I have to call. If you decide not to go back to Thyferra, I'll help you get your people to safety. You're going to lose your cargo, you might as well save yourself some pain."

One of the tankers began to move away from the others. Mynock, Wedge's R5 droid, tagged it as *Xucphra Rose*. "This is Bors Kenlin in the *Rose*. We're yours, Antilles."

"Kenlin, don't go. You have a wife back on Thyferra."

"Isard will be doing me a favor if she kills her." The *Rose* drifted further from the other two ships. "Where am I going?"

"Stand by, *Rose*." Wedge shifted his comm unit over to the squadron's tactical frequency. "Nine, you and Ten and your two Deathseed friends will escort the *Rose* to Halanit. Isard has threatened dependents on Thyferra if the crew goes along with us, so find out who their people are so we can transmit the data to the Ashern and try to save them."

Corran's voice came back strong. "As ordered, sir." Two X-wings broke from formation and made a quick flyby on the *Rose*. In the first pass they downloaded to the *Rose*'s navicomp the course for their run to Halanit. As they came back around, the *Rose* moved on the exit vector with them and two Deathseeds fell in behind. In the blink of an eye all five ships went to lightspeed and vanished.

Wedge looked back at his monitor again. The remaining ships were *Xucphra Alazhi* and *Xucphra Meander*. Wedge suspected the first voice he'd dealt with was on the *Alazhi*. Since the ship was named after a key component in bacta, he assumed the captain had seniority over the other two. Wedge shifted his comm unit back to the Thyferran frequency. "*Meander*, what is your decision?"

A woman's voice answered him. "*Meander* is unconvinced the crew will be safe from Isard's reprisals."

"*Meander,* your cargo will be bound for Coruscant. If you can't lose yourself there, you can obtain transport to anywhere you want to go from there. I guarantee you that your cargo will alleviate an incredible amount of suffering."

Xucphra Meander began to drift away from *Alazhi.* As it did so, the *Alazhi* began to roll to bring its turbolasers to bear on *Meander.*

Wedge shifted over to his tactical frequency. "Three and Four, neutralize *Alazhi.* Five and Six, pick up *Meander* and head to Coruscant."

Gavin and Shiel broke their X-wings out of the formation and sprinted in at the *Alazhi.* They kept their fighters moving in a grand spiral, which made them very difficult to track, especially as they dipped below the turbolasers' ability to depress sufficiently to shoot at them. Green laser bolts shot out in pairs at the incoming fighters, but they always came in above or below the X-wings.

Coming up on a turn in the spiral, Gavin's fighter rolled and spat laserfire at the freighter. One quad burst hit the ship's hull right in front of the turbolaser battery, then two more caught the battery in the side. Fire tracked up the blocky battery, blasting away at the armor plates sheathing it. Molten globules of armor rocketed off through space, then an explosion filled the battery with fire and ripped it apart.

Shiel's run on the aft battery proved just as effective, stripping the freighter of its offensive weaponry. The two fighters began to orbit the *Alazhi,* flashing past the cockpit one after another. Well away from them Rhysati, Inyri, and their two Twi'lek companions led the *Meander* off toward Coruscant.

Wedge adjusted his comm unit and tightened the beam to focus on the *Alazhi.* "*Alazhi,* you are defenseless."

The man who had first answered him again spoke, but anger had replaced nervousness in his voice. "We can and will oppose you, Antilles. This is piracy. But we have a standoff here, because you only have fighters—you can't board us. If you shoot us up, you or we will destroy the ship and you lose the cargo. You got some of what you want. Go away. Leave us alone."

He has a point—we can't board the ship. I hadn't expected Isard's threat to the crew's families. I'd thought, given that we harmed no one last time, that we would have cooperative crews. Wedge thought for a moment, then forced an edge into his voice.

"Be advised, *Alazhi*, that the same software that allowed us to bring you here will, when the correct signal is sent, purge your ship of atmosphere and slave itself to our navicomp data. Your choice is not whether you come with us or not, but whether you do so alive or dead."

He let that sink in for a moment or two. *If they call my bluff, I let them off so they can tell others that we didn't kill them. It'll win us some goodwill, perhaps.* "Your decision, *Alazhi*?"

Fear had returned to the captain's voice. "You'd kill us just to get this bacta?"

"I'd kill you to get the bacta to those who need it. Isard unleashed a disease on Coruscant that kills ninety-five percent of the victims who go untreated. Which should I count as more valuable: the lives of a dozen freighter crewmen or the lives of billions?"

"You'll help our families?"

"You have my word on it."

Silence fell for several heartbeats, then the *Alazhi*'s captain spoke in a distant whisper. "I hope you know what you're doing. *Alazhi* is yours."

Wedge went back to the tactical frequency. "Gavin, *Alazhi* is yours to shepherd on her rounds."

"I copy, Wedge. Transmitting data to *Alazhi* now. See you later." Gavin's X-wing swung out and around to head toward the exit vector. The two Twi'leks swooped in, taking up positions on either of the *Alazhi*'s flanks while the Shistavanen curled around and came up in the freighter's wake.

As the *Alazhi* came about to starboard and began its run up to lightspeed, a vastly huge white dagger thrust itself through the fabric of space on a course that cut in at the freighter's line of flight. Dread bubbled acid into Wedge's throat as the *Corrupter* reverted to realspace and opened up with its weaponry. Waves of green turbolaser energy washed down from the Star Destroyer's port batteries. While not made for engaging snubfighters, firing at point-blank range the gunners could hardly miss. The flank Deathseeds evaporated in a cloud of green plasma. The turbolaser fire eroded all the sharp lines from Shiel's X-wing, reducing it from a sleek fighter to a fluid blob that slammed into the aft end of the *Alazhi*.

A second volley of fire from the Star Destroyer focused itself on the bacta tanker. In an instant the entire ship glowed orange, then the bacta storage tanks exploded one after another. The superheated bacta sprayed out and instantly congealed into delicate sheets of ice that mocked the violence of their birth. Similarly the transparisteel and quadanium-titanium alloy plates used in the freighter's manufacture twisted and flowed, tearing away and exploding outward, before they congealed into a warped mockery of what the freighter had once been.

Of Gavin, Wedge saw nothing.

"Condition Critical. Exit the system now on Critical vectors. Go! Go!"

Asyr's voice pounded into Wedge's ears. "Wedge, what about . . ."

There's nothing left of Gavin. "Go, Asyr, go now. Waiting around is just going to get you killed." Wedge hauled back on his stick and punched his throttle up to full. He glanced over to his left and saw Asyr's X-wing hanging off his S-foil. "Three seconds to lightspeed."

"I copy, Wedge."

Wedge hit a button on his console and made the jump to lightspeed. The stars elongated, then sucked him into a tunnel of white light, but he felt as if he left his guts back in the system with the *Corrupter*. It had always been the plan to scatter and flee if *Corrupter* showed up, but to do that after taking losses made him feel horrible. *Four more are dead because of me.*

Part of him immediately rebelled at that thought, seeking to place blame elsewhere. If the *Alazhi*'s captain had not hesitated, then everyone would have been out of the system before *Corrupter* arrived. If Isard had not threatened the crews with the safety of their families, everything would have gone well. *If Senator Palpatine hadn't been greedy, this situation never would have existed.*

Wedge closed his eyes against the omnipresent light of hyperspace. "What happened back there is my responsibility. The operation had risks, but all operations have risks. Blaming myself for what happened isn't going to do me any good. What I need to do is learn from the situation because Convarion is very good."

He punched up a data request and got Mynock to break down the entry and exit vectors of the various ships, then had them overlaid on the system diagram. As the astromech did so, Wedge got his first glimmer of understanding. *Corrupter's entry vector appeared very fortuitous because it angled in on Alazhi's exit vector, but it really was the same entry vector the freighters used to arrive in the system.*

Wedge whistled slowly. What that bit of data told him was that Convarion had waited at the previous transit point, had tracked the exit vectors of all the ships in his convoy, then had his people do an analysis of them. The three ships that deviated from the planned course were discovered, their course plotted, and the *Corrupter* came after them. *Whether the freighters were hijacked or just had a poor navigator, Convarion came after them, intent on destroying them. His ship arrived in-system and shot immediately.*

A chill crept into Wedge's body and puckered his flesh. "Iceheart has never been one for compassion, and now she has a ship's captain who shares her contempt for it. We're lucky we only lost four of our pilots. I had hoped this war would be quick—I knew it would be dirty. We're going to have to be quicker and dirtier, and with Convarion and Iceheart opposing us, that's not going to be an easy task."

17

The sound of a thousand individuals stamping their heels and coming to attention echoed through the *Corrupter*'s hold as Fliry Vorru followed Ysanne Isard from the belly of the shuttle. Vorru looked out over the straight ranks of sailors and stormtroopers and allowed himself a smile. *Such a display of Imperial might I've not seen since before I was sentenced to Kessel. The Rebels may own Imperial Center and may have proclaimed themselves a New Republic, but they will never know Imperial splendor like this.*

At the base of the gangway, Isard paused and offered her hand to a small, lean man in a black uniform. The rank insignia he wore on his jacket's left breast bore only six color tabs, but the fact that he also wore two rank cylinders told Vorru he was a Commander, not a mere Captain. Even so, because of his position of command on the ship and Imperial tradition, addressing him as Captain would be proper. *And the way he genuflects before kissing Iceheart's proffered hand shows this Convarion is nothing if not proper.*

Convarion met Vorru's offered hand with a strong grip. The man's sharp features, thick black hair, and blue eyes all combined to grant Convarion an intensity that surprised

Vorru. *I had thought all such fire-eaters had been killed at Endor. This man is ambitious and, therefore, dangerous. If he were my subordinate, I would have him killed.*

"Pleased to meet you, Captain Convarion."

"And you, Minister Vorru." Convarion's mouth smiled, but any pleasure failed to register beyond the boundaries of his lips. "I am honored that you would deign to notice my ship and our exploits."

Isard, wearing her scarlet Admiral's uniform, glanced back at him with faint amusement in her eyes. "You have shown initiative, Commander, and I always notice initiative. I should like to inspect your ship, if that is possible, but first I would speak with you in private."

"Of course, Madam Director." Convarion bowed, then pointed to an aisle through the middle of the bone white ranks of stormtroopers. "My wardroom is this way."

Vorru trailed behind Convarion and Isard. He noticed that Convarion matched his pace to that of Isard and that she, in reaction to this, varied her gait and caused Convarion to do the same. Convarion's face gave no sign he noticed what was going on or if he was annoyed by it or not. He merely looked up at Isard with rapt attention on his face, not sycophantically hanging on her every word, but receiving what she said as if it were advice worthy of his most sincere consideration.

Vorru suppressed a smile as he watched Convarion operate, because he knew the man had to be trying to balance two conflicting scenarios in his head. By sending the *Corrupter* after the errant ships, Convarion had succeeded in ambushing an Antilles operation and scattering his forces. By Convarion's estimate Antilles lost a half-dozen ships, including several of the Uglies, known as Deathseeds by the Twi'leks who created them. Just knowing that some Twi'leks had thrown in with Antilles was valuable information itself, and Convarion would have been due some reward for just bringing that tidbit back from his mission.

On the other hand, he had left the majority of his convoy uncovered and open to attack. Antilles had still gotten away with two ships and Convarion had destroyed another bacta freighter on his own initiative. His report had stated that the freighter was moving in conjunction with the pirates and did not acknowledge his initial hail, so he considered it hostile and destroyed it. Such decisiveness was the sort of thing Isard appreciated, but the loss of a bacta freighter was a high price to pay for it.

The hatch to the small wardroom closed behind Vorru, trapping him in there with Isard and Convarion. Vorru moved to the end of the room far from the door and seated himself at the corner of the rectangular black duraplast table that dominated the room. Convarion hovered closest to the far narrow end of the table, ready to take his place at the head of it if Isard did not wish that position for herself.

Isard remained standing just inside the hatchway and stared at Convarion. "Your discovery of the deception concerning the freighters was impressive, Commander."

"Thank you, but it was no more than should be expected from any of our personnel. I chose to wait for all of my ships to be away because the Rebels used the tactic of misjumping ships in the case of the bacta convoy that Warlord Zsinj ambushed at Alderaan. I had to assume that same tactic might be used again. Because of *Corrupter*'s speed, I could arrive in synch with my ships at their destination even if I delayed leaving. I had my navigators plot the outbound vectors for my ships and noticed three were off course. We plotted possible stopping points along that route and proceeded after them. It was a fairly basic pursuit operation."

Irritation flared in Isard's molten left eye. "And destroying the *Alazhi*, was that no less than I should expect from our personnel?"

"As I explained in my report—"

"As you *lied* in your report." Isard's eyes narrowed. "Analysis of your ship's data records show your gunners opened fire three seconds after reversion. A signal went out to *Alazhi* five seconds after reversion, and the volley of shots that destroyed *Alazhi* came eight seconds after reversion. You chose to shoot regardless of their response."

Convarion's face constricted, pulling flesh taut over his cheekbones. "I shot in response to contingencies I had worked out prior to our arrival. *Alazhi* was alone, which meant the other ships had already been captured and moved. *Alazhi* had been disarmed and damaged. Because it was surrounded by hostile snubfighters and was moving in conjunction with them, I had to assume it was under their control. I was aware of your policy of punishing collaborators, and I chose to implement it immediately. Punishment delayed is punishment stripped of connection with the crime that triggered it. While *Xucphra Alazhi*'s crew will not have a chance to learn from their mistake, other crew of other ships know the policy is not an idle threat."

"So you chose to implement a policy without asking my permission?"

Convarion nodded. "I did."

"And you are prepared to take full responsibility for doing so?"

A slight hesitation marked Convarion's reply. "I am."

The down-turned corners of Isard's mouth rose. "Then you will execute the families of those crewmen on the *Alazhi*. We brought them with us in the shuttle."

Color drained from Convarion's face. "If that is your wish."

"What I *wish*, Captain Convarion, matters not." Isard strode toward him and plucked the rank cylinder from the right side of Convarion's tunic. "What I *order* is all that matters. What initiative you take must be within your mission parameters, it must not exceed them. Do you understand me?"

The naval man nodded, but Vorru detected a stiffness to his motion signifying resistance. Elements of the Imperial military had never accepted Isard's de facto running of the government, which was why many of them proclaimed themselves Warlords and created their own little empires. Those who had remained loyal, either to her or the concept of the Empire, still could bristle when she gave orders.

Convarion's head came up. "It is your *order*, then, Madam Director, that I kill the families of the crew of the *Alazhi*?"

Isard's head briefly flicked toward Convarion, but Vorru

doubted Convarion caught her slip. "That situation has been dealt with already and does not need your attention. I have another task for you. Minister Vorru, your briefing."

Vorru pointed to the chair at the head of the table. "Please be seated, Captain Convarion. As you know, bacta is a precious fluid that is produced in limited amounts and only available from us, here, on Thyferra. All bacta in the galaxy is produced under our license and is sold with our approval. If you need bacta, there is only one place to get it.

"At least, that was the situation until Antilles and his people pirated the first convoy. What do you think they did with that bacta?"

"It is rather clear they didn't sell it, since that is the obvious answer to the question." Convarion shrugged reluctantly. "I have no idea what they did with it."

"They gave it away. Much of it went to Coruscant, but we anticipated that." Vorru pressed his hands flat against the tabletop. "Because they used our ships and our crews to transport the bacta, we know where it ended up. We have shorted future allotments to various worlds to make up for the bacta they were supplied by Antilles, and we have charged them for that bacta."

Convarion's expression eased. "And they have paid?"

"Some have. Some have refused to do so." Vorru smiled. "This presents us with a problem."

Isard leaned forward, posting her arms on the table. "If some do not pay, we appear weak and others might balk at paying us. If they do not pay, they are as much thieves as Antilles and his people."

"So you have a policy you are going to order me to implement."

"How perceptive of you, Captain." Vorru nodded solemnly. "We have a list of the worlds that received stolen bacta. We have eliminated those worlds that have paid us, have made arrangements to pay us, or have sufficient resources to be able to pay us. We are left with a handful of target worlds that are too poor to afford the gift Antilles gave them. You will select one of them and take our bacta back."

"And if there is no bacta to recover?"

Isard straightened up and smiled mostly coldly. "If the bacta is used up, it will have granted them health. You will take it back again."

Convarion nodded. "It will be done."

Vorru raised a hand. "Not so quickly, Captain, there are some special caveats for what we want you to do. First and foremost, you will be taking along with you two companies of the Thyferran Home Defense Corps and one squadron of their fliers to carry out the work that needs to be done."

"But my Imperial troops will be much more efficient . . ."

"Indeed, but we want the Thyferrans to see the crimes of these worlds as crimes against *them*, not against Director Isard. We want the Thyferrans to get their hands dirty. If they are acting with us, they become complicit in our activities. They will make themselves targets for Antilles, which will bind them more tightly to us. By making them administer the punishment to these worlds, we give them an even greater stake in seeing that we remain here to help defend them, and we give them a reason to defend themselves."

Convarion's eyes narrowed. "You sound as if you truly think Antilles and his rabble can actually topple you."

"Nonsense!" Isard dismissed that supposition with a wave of her hand. "There will come a point, however, when the New Republic considers what it is going to do about us and our control of the bacta supply. They have refrained from causing trouble so far because they are reluctant to dabble in the internal politics of worlds. To do so would split their Republic, since a number of worlds that declared independence and have joined them still have their Imperial officials in place running things. Warlord Zsinj has further distracted the New Republic, but once he has been dealt with, they will again consider us."

Convarion nodded. "If our client states are afraid of losing their bacta supply, they will not press for the Republic to do something about us. And if the Thyferrans back us fully, the New Republic would have to stage an invasion of Thyferra to oust us."

"Precisely."

Vorru let Isard's comment echo in his ears, but he was not as confident of it as her voice suggested she was. Discounting Antilles entirely was a mistake, and one Isard should have known better than to make. While Vorru believed the Antilles threat could be controlled and minimized, the only way it could be eliminated was by killing Antilles and destroying his power base. The network of contacts Vorru had in place to gather information about Antilles was just beginning to report data to him, but so far it had been useless in trying to locate Antilles or figuring out what his long-term intentions were.

Vorru opened his hands and smiled at Convarion. "So, will you follow orders and punish a world for dealing with Antilles?"

"Shoot me the datafiles on the target worlds and I will get back to you with plans for dealing with them in two days." Convarion stood. "You may select the final target or leave it up to me, at your discretion. I would ask only one thing in return."

Isard arched an eyebrow at him. "And that is?"

"As you said before, my initiative is limited by my mission parameters." Convarion half-smiled. "If you want the lesson to be learned by the maximum number of people, do me the favor of defining my mission as broadly as possible."

18

In many ways Iella Wessiri could not believe she had decided to come along on the mission after all. She understood how important it was to undertake, and how much good it might do for the Ashern cause, but at the most basic level she opposed it. *It's murder, nothing less.*

When Elscol had proposed the operation, she'd used the euphemism *sanction* to describe what they would be doing to one of Xucphra's higher-ups, Aerin Dlarit. Dlarit, an older man, had been appointed a General in the Thyferran Home Defense Corps. In the day-to-day operation of the THDC he deferred to Major Barst Roite, but Dlarit strutted about in his uniform at a host of social functions. Local media had shown him any number of times assuring his fellow Xucphrans that the Ashern were under control and that happy days were on the way.

"He's made himself an obvious target." Elscol had opened her arms to emphasize her point. "If we take him out we will rock Xucphran society to its foundations."

Iella had protested the whole idea. "Dlarit is hardly a military target in any real sense. He's a fop. We can undercut him by hitting other targets and making his assurances lies."

"We could, but hitting such sites still doesn't bring the nature of war home to the people. We need to frighten them, deeply."

"And hitting military targets won't do that?"

"Eventually. This will be faster."

Iella frowned. "Wouldn't just shooting random people accomplish the same thing?"

Elscol shrugged. "Probably. It's a backup plan."

"You can't be serious." Iella looked at the smaller woman in utter disbelief. "That would be murder. *This* is murder, for all intents and purposes. You can't kill innocent people."

"Look, Iella, there are *no* innocent people here." Elscol planted fists on her hips. "Over the years I've helped dozens of worlds liberate themselves from the Imps, and part of each fight is making the populace wake up to what's really going on. People assume that if they say nothing and do nothing they're not involved in the fight, but the fact is that their apathy is a tacit vote of support for the status quo. They have to be made to see that by making *no* choice they have indeed made *a* choice. When they understand that, they begin to think about those choices, and we make choosing the Imps out to be a very bad choice."

Iella's head came up. "Black Sun used to use that same rationale to justify murdering all sorts of folks."

"There's a difference between Black Sun and us."

"Oh, do tell."

"Black Sun was all about greed and selfishness." Elscol looked around at the humans and Vratix gathered in the room. "We're fighting for freedom, for the right to live the way we want to live. We're fighting for the only thing worth fighting for."

"And if these people want to be ruled by the Empire?"

"They can consider our action an eviction notice." Elscol's brown eyes narrowed. "You come from a law-enforcement background where you were out to protect the innocent from the ravages of the criminals. You could do that without resorting to this drastic an activity because you had the weight of the government behind you. You had a justice system that would reinforce the will of the people. I understand that and respect it. By the same token, I also know that you saw criminals out there that you knew could only be stopped by a blaster bolt.

"That's what we're up against here. Dlarit might seem harmless, but he's helping prop up a system that keeps the Vratix in virtual slavery. He's propping up a system that means billions of individuals suffer needlessly from diseases because they cannot afford the cure. He's got the blood of everyone who died because of a lack of bacta on his hands, as well as that of the families of the *Alazhi*'s crew."

Iella had nodded. "I can't deny the validity of what you're saying about Dlarit. Add to it the fact that his daughter spied on the Alliance for the Imps and got Corran captured. The problem still is that I'm uncomfortable with assassinating him, especially in his home."

"The act has much more impact there. We'll make a hologram of the execution and start circulating it. That will get our point across, and fast, too."

"And it will make us into ghouls. What about Dlarit's staff and his family? What do we do if they find us there?"

The muscles at the corners of Elscol's jaw bunched. "Blasters do have stun settings."

Iella had raised an eyebrow. "You sound as if you would kill his children, too."

"Erisi's his daughter—Huttlings grow up to be Hutts."

"But leaving his minor children alive would show us to be capable of mercy for those who realize the error of their ways, correct?" Iella had looked hard at her. "Correct?"

"It'll make the operation more difficult, but it can be done." Elscol had looked around the briefing room. "Any other philosophical objections, or can we get to planning?"

There were none, so Elscol immediately moved into planning the assault. *And what a job she did.* Her experience in planning and executing operations showed through in how she broke down the Dlarit estate's security setup. Iella had attended countless CorSec Special Operations briefings about raids on criminal strongholds, and Elscol's presentation was the equal of any of them in detail and foresight.

To everyone's surprise, including her own, Iella agreed to join the group of a dozen Ashern commandos volunteering for the operation. Elscol, Sixtus, and three of his Imp Special Naval Operations comrades formed the core of the group. Iella, two Vratix, and four humans—all four of them Zaltin refugees—filled out the rest of the team. Each commando was issued a blaster, a blaster carbine, dark clothing, a comlink, and a light armored vest with armored plates that covered them from throat to groin, front and back. Iella knew the armor would be almost useless for stopping a blaster bolt, but even deflecting it from the body's midline meant the wound might be survivable.

Iella hunkered down behind the bole of a huge akonije tree. The humidity in the air helped retain the day's heat, and the vest made her none too comfortable. Even so, the slight whisper of a breeze helped cool her. *But it also hides some noises and creates others, keeping me on edge.* She blew a wisp of her light brown hair back out of her face and peered ahead into the darkness.

Barely visible as hulking shadows, Sixtus and his companions worked their way forward through the rain forest that sheltered the Dlarit estate. The estate itself was set on a small knoll at the foot of high mountains that had once been part of an extinct volcano. Holograms of the estate taken in daytime looked incredibly beautiful, with the natural stone building rising up out of the surrounding jungle like a small volcano itself. Huge waterfalls cascading down the mountainous backdrop added the last element to transform the estate into a paradise.

They also provided the means for entering the estate. Most travel to and from the estate took place by airspeeder. Forty-five kilometers of a twisting, single-lane track connected the estate to the main throughway to the south, but several gates interdicted it, and a number of narrow passes between natural rock outcroppings made for perfect ambush points if an invasion were attempted along it. Likewise, a ring of well-hidden Comar Tritracker Air Defense batteries meant approaching the estate in an airspeeder without authorization could be suicidal. Various sensor arrays positioned around the estate also monitored likely avenues of approach through the rain forest.

Slicing into the planetary computers and making use of Zaltin surveillance satellites, the Ashern team had pulled down realtime holograms of the estate and the thermal images of the guards on their rounds. They also found the placement of the sensor devices in the rain forest and noted the human patrols tended to concentrate on the side of the estate facing the mountains and the waterfalls. After studying the specifications for the sensors in use around the estate, they realized that the sensors on the mountain side of the estate had been muted so the movement of water and the sound from the falls wouldn't constantly be triggering alarms.

Entering the estate, they made their approach from the far side of the mountain and ascended to the summit by dusk. Once darkness fell, they descended, keeping as close to the waterfalls as they could. They sped their descent by rappelling down beneath one of the longer falls, letting the curtain of water hide them from the estate's sensors. Once at the base of the mountains, they moved in along the fringes of the sensors' range, cutting a labyrinthine path through the jungle.

The SpecNav troops led the way. Though they were as big as stormtroopers, Sixtus's men were deceptively swift and deathly quiet. Iella was more than happy they were on her side. As scary as facing stormtroopers might have been, fighting against these men would have been worse. At one point they had been selected to join the Imperial Navy's most elite fighting unit, and the product of their skills proved that choice had been a wise one.

Iella heard a single click over her comlink, so she hurried forward, remaining low. She reached Elscol's side and looked off in the direction where the smaller woman pointed. Silhouetted against the lights from the house she saw two Thyferran Home Defense Corps guards wandering along. Elscol tapped her finger twice against her comlink and huge shadows rose up to eclipse the guards. Iella heard no screams or shots being fired, but another double-click played over the comlink, indicating the guards had been neutralized.

The rest of the group moved up to the edge of the clearing around the estate. Barely twenty-five meters separated them from the mansion solarium. Iella dropped to one knee next to one of the guards and felt for a pulse in his neck, but her hand encountered a sticky wetness that told her all she needed to know. *The sound of a stun shot being fired or the light from the blue burst could have been seen. These men had to die.*

Elscol tapped two of the SpecNav soldiers on the shoulders and they sprinted forward across the lawn to the shadows beside the solarium. Iella found herself holding her breath, waiting for a reaction from the house. A single click from the comlink told her the SpecNavs felt safe. Elscol sent them a double-click, and Iella prepared herself to run.

The SpecNavs pulled an electronic device from an equipment satchel and slapped it over the solarium's door lock. Iella saw lights on the device flicker and shift color, then five of them all burned green at the same time. They went out after three seconds at which point one of the SpecNavs pushed the door open. Another double-click came through the comlink, and Iella was up and running.

With each step she braced herself for a shot from the darkness, a burning red bolt that would hit her, lift her up and send her flying across the yard. She'd seen it happen to others before, more times than she could remember. The look of surprise on the victim's face as confident immortality dissolved into dismay and despair haunted her. *In death, especially violent death, no one ever looks pretty.*

She made it to the door and passed through, then cut to the left and hugged the wall on the other side of the doorway into the main house, opposite the first SpecNav trooper. After her, came Elscol; then Sixtus. They both ran through the doorway, then double-clicked an all clear so Iella and the SpecNav moved up. Other members of the team fanned out through the mansion's lower floor and secured it without incident.

Elscol and Sixtus moved up the stairway to the main floor. Iella followed them up and found the main floor dark save for a muted yellow light coming through one open doorway further along the main hallway. The darkness didn't sur-

prise her terribly much—the raid had been timed to reach the
estate halfway between midnight and dawn to take advantage
of the fact that most people would be asleep. That a light was
still on seemed odd, but carelessness couldn't be ruled out.

*Nor can someone's working late. That's supposed to be
Dlarit's office.* Iella crept forward cautiously. Though only
ten meters separated her from the lit doorway, she took two
minutes to make it that distance. At the edge of the doorway
she tilted her head and got a quick glimpse into the room.
What she saw prompted a smile and made her double-click
her comlink and invite the others forward.

She strode into the office and shook her head. Wearing
his finest Thyferran Home Defense Corps uniform, Aerin
Dlarit sat sprawled in a high-backed chair behind his desk.
The holoprojector plate built into the desk displayed a meter-
tall replica of a monument featuring a larger-than-life statue
of Dlarit atop a pedestal. The hologram slowly rotated in the
air, complete with a throng of miniature well-wishers gasping
and applauding at its base.

Elscol drew her blaster pistol and dropped her voice to a
whisper. "Get the holocam up here. He dies a monument to
his own ego and misplaced trust in the Empire."

Iella laid a hand on her arm. "Wait, I have another idea.
One that may work even better."

"He has to die."

"With what I have in mind, he will, but a thousand times
over." Iella drew her own pistol and clicked the selector lever
over to stun. "We've already killed two guards, so they know
we're serious. Trust me, this will work."

"If I don't like it, he dies anyway."

Iella smiled. "You'll like it. We'll get more play out of it."

Iella explained, and Elscol balked until Sixtus cracked a
smile. That swung Elscol over, so Iella fired one shot into
the sleeping General, then set to work. The party exited the
estate the same way they'd come in, and though burdened as
Iella was carrying away General Aerin Dlarit's dress uniform,
the journey seemed not nearly as hard as before.

19

Commander Erisi Dlarit's TIE Interceptor dropped from the belly of the *Corrupter* and let gravity seduce it down into Halanit's atmosphere. The cant-winged craft bucked a little as it entered the frigid planet's atmosphere, reminding Erisi that the Interceptor would surrender some of its maneuverability to friction and drag. Maneuvers she could pull in the vacuum of space would get her killed below.

The Rebels refer to these fighters as squints, *but in atmosphere I prefer to think of them as* winces. From the moment Ysanne Isard had appointed her to lead the Thyferran Home Defense Corps aerospace wing, Erisi had lobbied hard to equip her two squadrons with X-wings. While slower and slightly less agile than the Interceptor, the X-wing's shields and ability to use proton torpedoes in addition to its lasers made it a superior fighter.

It mattered not at all how eloquently I argued, what facts I used, Iceheart would never have agreed to my request. Erisi realized her own sense of superiority had collided full on with Isard's need to see anything and everything Imperial as better than anything the Alliance had to oppose it. *Isard sees herself as the pinnacle of Imperial excellence and demands that ev-*

*erything else rises to her level. What I or others know counts
as nothing to her because we are not up to her standards.*

Erisi really couldn't blame Isard for treating the Thyferrans and the THDC as the Empire's stupid, inbred cousins.
Though the *Corrupter* had already been en route to Halanit
when the Ashern raid took place, word of it had been communicated to the ship. Her cheeks burned as the image of her
father slumped naked in his chair exploded in her mind. Mor-
tifying in the extreme, the incident meant that the *Corrupter*'s
Imperial crew felt no reason to hide their contempt for the
THDC personnel on board.

The fact that her father had been involved hurt her
deeply. What made it even worse was that Iella Wessiri had
been identified from the hologram. The Imps took that as a
sign that Antilles had entered into a full alliance with the
Ashern, but Erisi read more into Iella's participation. *Iella
caused my father to be embarrassed so as to get at me, to
avenge herself for my betrayal of Corran and the rest of the
Rogues. This was a message directed at me by her—a private
declaration of war.*

Erisi glanced at her monitor and snarled into the comm
unit. "Four, close the formation up." Behind her four Interceptors came a quartet of the double-hulled TIE bombers.
Her Interceptors were nominally flying cover for the bombers, though once they dropped their thermal detonators and
proton bombs to open up the main colony, the Interceptors'
mission changed to engaging ground targets and suppressing
fire at the stormtrooper-laden shuttles that would follow.

The TIE bombers swooped down through the air and
spiraled in on their target. Erisi and her flight came around to
follow them in. She couldn't help but remember countless
training exercises where she'd used an X-wing to stoop like a
hawk-bat on such lumbering craft. *Two would be dead in my
initial pass and the others would die as they attempted to flee.*

Below her, the bombers began their runs. The thermal
detonators fell lazily from the bombers as if harmless. Their
explosions flashed golden light through the glacier and bled
up into the great gouts of steam they produced. The light
breeze below quickly cleared the steam off, revealing a hole

roughly a kilometer around and nearly half that deep. Steaming water pooled in the bottom of it, and Erisi knew the thermal detonators had cleared the glacier down to the transparisteel canopy that protected the Halanit colony from the harsh climate of their world.

The bombers' second pass eliminated the canopy. The high-yield proton bombs shattered the transparisteel shield, fragmenting the sheets at ground zero. A shock wave rippled through the double-walled barrier, ripping whole transparisteel plates free from both layers as it went. The warm air from beneath the shield rushed upward, blowing debris up and out, then condensed in the frigid air. At the same time, around the hole's jagged edges, cold air poured down into the colony.

Rolling her Interceptor up on the port stabilizer assembly, Erisi spiraled the fighter down in through the hole the bombs had created. The chasm into which she flew stretched out above and below her fighter like the grandest of Coruscant's boulevards. Long suspension bridges linked both sides of the chasm at various levels and quickly icing-over waterfalls splashed their way down into the depths in front of her. Lights from hundreds of viewports dotted the chasm's depths with yellow circles and squares.

Erisi hit the triggers on her lasers. A stream of green laser darts scored a ragged line along one face of the chasm, piercing the viewports and reducing them to darkness. As she shot, she glanced at her primary monitor, waiting for the missile warning alarm to be activated. *It's going to be missiles or turbolasers, and if they're going to use them, it'll have to be now.*

She continued her flight deeper and deeper, strafing targets as she went. One line of fire scattered a crowd on a balcony. Another swept across a foot bridge, chasing a man who foolishly thought himself faster than a laser bolt. Nearing the bottom of the chasm, she chopped her throttle back and pulled up in a loop, but not before filling the ice-crusted pools below with enough laser energy to start them boiling.

She knew, with the canopy being breached and the ichthyoculture pools having been transformed into giant stewpots that the Halanit colony was dead. Those who didn't freeze to death would starve—each a terrible way to die. She realized that her old comrades in Rogue Squadron would be horrified at the carnage, as she would have been if the Empire had carried this attack out on Thyferra, but she felt no remorse for the people doomed by her action.

They were already dead. Their need for bacta had been desperate, because without it their marginal colony could not survive. They could not afford bacta because their colony was so poor, hence anyone with enough neurons to form a synapse would have seen that the only sensible thing to do was to abandon Halanit or choose a method of exploiting the world to generate enough money so it could sustain itself.

I have no obligation to save the stupid from themselves. Even if we had given them bacta, another crisis would have wiped them out. The fact that they refused to face reality does not make it incumbent upon me to shield them from the disaster they so fervently court. Erisi's eyes narrowed as she started a strafing run back toward the surface. *And they compounded their stupidity by consorting with thieves and using bacta for which they could not pay.*

Despite the lack of fire defending the colony, she knew they were anything but a defenseless, inoffensive community. Their accepting the bacta from Wedge and the others was the equivalent of stabbing a knife into the Thyferran economy. If Thyferra allowed them to do what they did, other worlds would similarly duck their obligations. Other individuals would emulate Wedge, and pirates would swarm over the bacta convoys. The rightful reward for providing a vital fluid to the galaxy would be denied to Thyferra in an attack as destructive as the one she was mounting.

Rocketing up through the hole in the shield, Erisi rolled out and began a long elliptical orbit over the breached shield. "Interceptor One reporting. No hostile antiship fire in evidence."

"We copy, One. The Captain congratulates you on your run and requests you join him for the march through the colony."

"I copy, Control. As ordered." Erisi smiled. *We've shown*

Convarion that THDC pilots are not the incompetent nerf-brains he thought we were. Now he will show me how powerful stormtroopers are so I won't forget who is superior to whom. Not that I ever could, but I shall say nothing. Convarion would never believe himself to be my subordinate anyway.

Gavin didn't realize it was an explosion that had awakened him until a second and third blast sounded. He threw off thick layers of blankets—his Tatooine upbringing guaranteed that he felt cold even in Halanit's hot baths—and snarled as he thrust his feet into cold boots. He fastened them, then stood and strapped on his blaster belt as Farl Cort appeared in the doorway of his room. "What's happening?"

Before Cort could answer, Gavin's ears popped with the change in the colony's air pressure. Air began to rush out of the room, tugging at the hem of Cort's cloak. The little man's face went ashen. "They've breached the shield."

Gavin grabbed him before he could fall. "Who's they?"

"Imperials, I guess. There's a Star Destroyer in orbit."

"Sithspawn! You should have gotten me up when it arrived." Gavin wanted to pound his head against the wall. He had been certain that he'd been careful enough to hide his trail so the *Corrupter* couldn't follow him. When it showed up at the convoy hijacking, he'd immediately broken his flight and dove away from it. The *Xucphra Alazhi*'s bulk shielded him from the destroyer's turbolasers. He knew he was dead unless he exercised the only option available to him, a jump to lightspeed, which he did blindly.

He held the jump for fifteen seconds, which were the longest fifteen seconds in his life. Jumping blind into hyperspace was about as stupid as making fat jokes around a Hutt, and nearly always as fatal. Coming out of hyperspace, he made a quick read of the area and had his R2 unit plot another short jump. He put his ship through a series of seven such small jumps, doubling back and forth, then took a long jump out toward the Rim. He landed on a small planet, got into and out of some trouble there, and then began his run back to Yag'Dhul.

Because astronavigation had never been his strength, he was limited in his choices of destinations. To make the trip back as quickly as possible, making a long run to Halanit was his best route because, from there, the trip to Yag'Dhul could be accomplished with several short hops. He also thought there might be an off-chance that Corran and Ooryl wouldn't have left Halanit by the time he got there. Traveling to Halanit would run him pretty much out of fuel. He hoped the Halanits would give him some in return for the bacta they'd been given, and with Corran being there he was certain they would fuel him up.

Despite Corran's absence, the Halanits had been more than happy to give Gavin fuel, but the problem was that they needed to synthesize it first. The process of refueling his fighter was to take two days, during which they tried to make him feel as much at home as possible. On a world sheathed in ice, with abundant amounts of water and a cuisine based on fish, making a Tatooine native feel at home was not easy.

And now Corrupter *has tracked me here, so I repay their hospitality with death.* Gavin growled incoherently, then stopped and forced himself to think clearly. He thumbed on the comlink clipped to the lapel of his flightsuit. "Jawaswag, give me a system start, now!"

His R2 tootled something back at him.

"I don't care, just do it. Turn on the fuel pumps and suck their synthesizer dry if you have to. Gavin out." He lifted Cort away from his slump against the wall and set him on his feet. "Get me to the utility hangar, now!"

Cort's brown eyes unglazed. "Utility hangar, yes. Come, it's on the other side of the chasm."

Cort led Gavin from the apartment he'd been given and out into one of the subterranean corridors running toward the chasm. Screaming people had begun to fill the corridor, but the small man deftly cut through them. Gavin shouldered his way through the thickening crowd and caught up with Cort as they reached the walkway across the chasm.

Gavin grabbed the back of Cort's cloak and yanked him

back out of the way of a green laser bolt. More of them played out in a line across the walkway, chasing down and burning the legs from a running man. The man's screams were swallowed by the whine of a TIE Interceptor as it streaked past and he rolled from the walkway to fall to oblivion.

"Now, go!" Gavin's shout carried above the screeching of the other Interceptors strafing the chasm. Gavin started running, letting his long legs devour the distance. He let every ounce of panic he felt fuel his run, and he knew he was running faster than he ever had before. His lungs burned and his breath steamed, but the echoed whines of Interceptor engines wouldn't let him stop until he reached the far side and the safety of the tunneled corridor.

Cort arrived two steps after he did, adrenaline having lent him speed enough to almost match the taller man's pace. Cort moved into the lead, cutting and weaving through corridors and down ramps until they came out into a huge subterranean cavern with a huge steaming lake, two bacta-storage cylinders, a variety of old Zenomach and other tunneling devices, and Gavin's X-wing.

His fighter had been painted gold, with light red-orange crescents creating a scalelike pattern. Near the front of the fighter, a mouth had been painted with large, white, daggerlike teeth; the proton torpedo launching ports had become the pupils of eyes. When asked how he wanted his X-wing decorated, he'd chosen to make it over in the image of a krayt dragon, the most fearsome predator on all of Tatooine.

He turned back to Cort. "Look, this is my fault. They're here after me. I'll take off and lead them in a chase away from here. Get your people into defensible positions and hold out. These tunnels will make it tough on stormtroopers, so they'll withdraw when I'm gone."

Cort shook his head. "We have no weapons."

The plaintive tone in his voice punched Gavin straight in the heart. "I never should have come here." He drew his blaster and pressed it into Cort's hands. "Take this, do what you can. I'll do something."

Gavin ran to his X-wing and clambered up on a mole-miner to boost himself into the cockpit. Cort disconnected the refueling lines, then backed away and tossed Gavin a salute. Gavin returned it, then pulled on his helmet and fastened his restraining straps. He left his life-support gear on the floor of the cockpit, disdainful of the time it would take to pull it on. *If I go down out there, I'm dead anyway, so it doesn't much matter.*

He cut in the repulsor-lift generators, retracted the landing gear, and feathered the throttle forward. The X-wing headed toward the retracting metal doorway built into the mouth of the cavern. Beyond it, Gavin saw a translucent glowing wall of white that he realized was snow that had drifted in against the door. He thumbed his fire-control to lasers and linked them for dual fire, then hit the trigger. The snow barrier evaporated, so Gavin kicked his throttle forward and shot out into the Halanit sky.

Keeping the X-wing low enough to skim the drifts, he headed out in a long loop through a valley that curved around to the north. Three kilometers out from the cavern he rolled up on the starboard S-foil and began to climb. As his sensors began to pick up Imp fighters, he reached up and flipped the switch that brought his S-foils into attack position and locked them.

A glance at his fuel indicator told him he had ten minutes for fighting before he made his run out of the system. Halanit itself created a fairly insignificant gravity shadow in hyperspace—he needed to get away from the gas giant around which it orbited. *No problem—ten minutes is more than enough time to make the Imps angry enough to chase me.*

Jawaswag beeped at him and Gavin smiled. "You're right, the Imps are flying in formation. They want to make this easy. Acquire One, Two, and Three." With the sensor signature of each locked into his fire-control computer, Gavin kept his fighter on the deck and closed to proton torpedo range. That course had him flying directly at the rising column of smoke and steam coming from the holed canopy.

"Jawaswag get me a sensor record of all this, visual and everything."

The droid hooted his assent.

Gavin waited until he hit the outer fringes of range, then popped his weapons control over to proton torpedoes. He set them for single fire, then acquired the first Interceptor. His head-up display went from yellow to red and the R2's keening wail filled the cockpit. He hit the trigger, shifted to the second target, got a tone, and fired a second torpedo.

The first torpedo lanced up from the snowy landscape and smashed full into the Interceptor's cockpit. The subsequent explosion shredded the Quadanium solar panels, sowing chaff and debris in the path of the other two TIEs. The second torpedo blasted into the left wing of its target, snapping it off, then exploded right behind the cockpit. The Interceptor just disintegrated, its scattered pieces clipping the last Interceptor.

That squint immediately heeled over in a roll and dove for the planet. Gavin tried to get a lock on it, but it fell too quickly. Slight adjustments to its course told him it was still under power, but he doubted the pilot could recover from that sharp a dive. *He's going in.*

Gavin braced for the explosion and fireball as he came up over a little crest, but the Interceptor didn't crash. Instead it plunged in through the base of the steam plume and into the chasm that was the heart of the Halanit colony.

No one gets away that easy. Gavin switched back to lasers and brought the X-wing up in a lazy loop that he took over the top. The black hole in the planet's white blanket loomed before him like the mouth of a krayt dragon. He ignored the spark of fear in his guts and evened out the power to his shields. *The people of Halanit might be defenseless, but I'm not. Now you pay for the fun you've had.*

Erisi spotted the two *Lambda*-class shuttles flying down. Their wings began to retract as they prepared to land near the colony's surface entrance. She brought her Interceptor around and vectored in toward the landing site. With the flick of a switch she cut in her repulsor-lift coils and extended the Interceptor's landing gear, even though she expected them to sink into the snow. *Nice to have a ship with the hatch on top.*

She keyed her comm unit. "Bascome, you have command of the flight. Continue to orbit but do not make another chasm run unless it is specifically requested of you."

"As ordered, Commander."

The first shuttle landed and disgorged two squads of stormtroopers in their cold weather gear. The stormtroopers dashed into the opening of an ice cavern the colony used as a shelter for visitors' personal spacecraft. Red lights flashed from within, bathing the snow with the color of blood, then some black smoke slowly drifted up through the narrow opening.

Looks like they're in. Erisi waited for the second shuttle to land before she popped the hatch on her fighter. The cold immediately cut through her flightsuit; yet despite it, she removed her heavy helmet. The sweat in her hair froze immediately, but she ignored it. Climbing up out of the hatch, she slid down the curve of the cockpit and found the snow crust sufficiently solid to bear her weight. Leaving her blaster in the shoulder holster she wore, she strode across Halanit's frozen face and fell in beside the black-clad Captain Ait Convarion.

The Imperial officer acknowledged her presence with a nod she felt was calculated to be mildly dismissive of her even though she towered over him. Sandwiched between stormtrooper phalanxes, they wordlessly made their way into the ice cavern and to the heat-lock beyond it. The doors had been blasted open, and the rush of warm air filled the cavern. Steam and smoke hovered in a low cloud, trapped by the cavern's roof.

Convarion preceded her into a rough-hewn tunnel, stepping over the sprawled body of a civilian. They continued on until they reached a vista point at one end of an elevated walkway bridging both sides of the chasm. Stormtroopers held both sides of it, with the pair guarding that end bringing their blaster carbines up across their chests when Convarion appeared.

Fists planted on his hips, Convarion surveyed the damage. Screams echoed through the chasm, chased by the piercing whine of blaster fire. Red lights lit previously dark transparisteel viewports and red laser bolts reached out to knock fleeing figures from some of the other bridges.

Convarion looked back over his shoulder at Erisi. "You were unopposed in here?"

"Yes, Captain, we were. Flying in here was not easy, but we made our passes without mishap."

"Good. Wouldn't want your people to get bloodied in their first engagement." He waved his right hand around to take in the whole of the colony. "My stormtroopers will neutralize the major pockets of resistance, then your people can come down and finish things up."

Convarion's condescension could have been cut with a vibroblade, but Erisi chose to ignore it. "As you will, Captain Convarion. Those of us from Thyferra much appreciate your diligence in helping us prosecute those who would victimize us."

The scream of an Interceptor diving into the chasm overrode Convarion's reply. As it passed the bridge, a pair of red laser bolts pierced the ion-engine exhaust vector system, spraying half-melted louvers out in its backwash. The Interceptor began a roll that ended in a brilliant explosion as it hammered one of the lower walkways. The ferrocrete decking undulated out away from the impact point, crumbling with the wave front. It held for a moment or two, then, piece by piece, began to rain stone into the depths.

As terrifying as that was, it was nothing compared to the sight of the X-wing swooping through the chasm. Painted like a brutal, fearsome creature, it appeared more like a predator seeking prey than a war machine piloted by the enemy. Without being able to identify the pilot as he flashed past, Erisi knew it was one of her old squadron-mates.

And she knew the only way she would survive was to get back to her Interceptor and shoot him down.

Gavin flew past the collapsing walkway and saw a hail of laser bolts streaking past him from all angles. *Small arms fire. No real threat.* He smiled grimly, pulled back on his throttle to reverse his thrust and cut in his repulsor-lift coils. He flipped the X-wing's lasers over to single fire, then applied enough rudder to bring the fighter's nose around toward his tormentors. He leveled the fighter out, killed his thrust, then let the repulsor-lift coils propel him up through the chasm.

Using his rudder pedals, he turned the ship left and right. He dropped his crosshairs on the stormtroopers shooting at him and returned their fire. Whereas their laser bolts skipped harmlessly off the X-wing's shields, his shots proved to be anything but harmless. It wasn't that they were sufficiently powerful to pierce a stormtrooper's armored chestplate as much as they evaporated it, and most of the person beneath it.

Part of Gavin rebelled at the slaughter. The storm-troopers had no chance of survival facing him, but they did not break and run. They stood their ground, giving their lives for the dead creation of a dead Emperor. *They gain nothing from this. Why? Given enough time, I will kill them all.*

Gavin slowly nodded. *Right, they're buying time. The Corrupter is scrambling more TIEs. If I stick around, I'm not leaving.*

He kicked his throttle in and sped up his ascent. He still sprayed knots of stormtroopers and concentrated a lot of fire on the uppermost region, trying to get the one black Imperial uniform lurking amid a squad of stormtroopers. Most of them went down, but he couldn't tell if he got the officer or not. *Analysis of the sensor data may answer that question. I hope so.*

Realizing he had done all he could for the people of Halanit, Gavin accelerated the X-wing and launched it through the hole in the transparisteel shield. "They'll pay, Cort, they'll pay dearly for this." Rolling out to port, he pointed his fighter west and began his run home.

Erisi pulled the Interceptor's hatch shut and dropped into the pilot's seat as the X-wing jetted up and out through the shield hole. She pulled on her helmet and strapped in, then went for an engine start.

Both refused.

Diagnostics scrolled over her primary monitor. *Reactor chambers are too cold for a start.* She punched up a directory of systems software, then worked her way down through a hierarchy of choices until she got to a list of emergency overrides. She glanced at her weapons display, then picked a program that drained the energy from her lasers into the reactor cores to warm them enough for a restart. She waited until the temperature had climbed sufficiently, then restarted the engines.

The twin ion engines roared to life and sent a gentle *thrum* through the cockpit. Erisi shunted energy back into recharging the lasers, then cut the repulsor-lift generators in, retracted the landing gear, and throttled up to head after the X-wing. Coming up and around, she dropped her Interceptor on his tail, but saw he already had ten kilometers worth of lead over her. *Even with the Interceptor's greater speed, I won't catch him before he escapes the atmosphere and goes to lightspeed.*

Erisi reached over and punched up a broad band frequency selection for her comm unit. "Fleeing X-wing, this is Commander Erisi Dlarit of the Thyferran Home Defense Corps. Land at once or be destroyed."

"Erisi?"

She recognized the voice immediately. "Gavin? Listen to me. You have to stop. If you don't, they'll get you."

"Don't you mean *you'll* get me?"

Erisi smiled. "No, the Imps will get you. Surrender to me and I can protect you from them."

"How should I do that? Give you my override codes so I end up like Corran?" Gavin's laughter stung her ears. "You want me, come get me."

"I would if you weren't so intent on running." By shunting more energy to her engines, she could increase her speed, but her lasers would have no power to shoot Gavin when she caught him. *If I had proton torpedoes, on the other hand . . . Iceheart is a fool.* "I never would have thought you a coward, Gavin."

Gavin laughed again. "A year ago, maybe even three months ago, you could have gotten me to turn back with that taunt, but not now. I'm not nearly as stupid as you'd need, for me to engage you while *Corrupter* comes around and cuts me off."

"Rationalize your cowardice any way you want, Gavin." She knew she couldn't get him to turn around, so she tried to hurt him as their ships left Halanit's atmosphere. "Run away so you can come back later. Know you've doomed the people of Halanit. And know I'll kill you when next we meet."

"You'll pay for what you've done here, Erisi." Emotion filled Gavin's words, pinching their tone. "For you, getting out of this alive will be impossible."

"Impossible is what Rogues do best."

"Yeah, but you were never really a Rogue, were you?"

Kilometers began to scroll up impossibly quickly on Erisi's range finder as the X-wing ran up to lightspeed and entered hyperspace. Erisi watched it vanish, then pulled back on the Interceptor's yoke and looped the fighter back toward Halanit. *No, I was never a Rogue, Gavin. I never relinquished my grip on reality.*

She smiled as the *Corrupter* came into view around the curve of the moon. "I know where the true power in the galaxy is, and I know that if you keep trying to defy the impossible, eventually you fail. *This* is your time to fail."

20

The feeling in Corran's gut was as cold as Wedge's narration of the holographic imaging from Gavin's X-wing. At various points in the presentation Winter hit keys on the datapad connected to the holoprojector. The image froze, then the computer enlarged and enhanced an image from the background. *They're all of dead bodies—dead civilian bodies.*

Corran shivered and felt Mirax gently rub her hand along his spine. *I was there not a week before this happened. I probably talked to some of those people, ate with them, joked with them.* Corran realized that, as he had with his comrades in CorSec, he had mentally prepared himself for losing friends who were in the squadron. All of them accepted the risks of warfare and all of them had the same things at stake. Riv Shiel's death had surprised him, but he was able to tell himself that Shiel had died well, in combat, just as he would have wanted to go.

The people of Halanit however . . . He shook his head. "They were never meant to find themselves in that situation."

Mirax leaned heavily against him. "I know, but Isard put them there, you didn't."

The glow panels in the small briefing room came up, in

no way easing the severe expression on Wedge's face. "First I want to state publicly that, in my opinion, Gavin could have done nothing more than he did at Halanit. While he has felt he somehow led the *Corrupter* to Halanit, we know that isn't true. Halanit stopped asking anyone but us for bacta after our first run, and the tanker pilots knew where they had dropped off a supply. It was easy for Iceheart to tag them as a target—I'm fairly certain she would have found out who we had supplied no matter how we got the bacta to the worlds, but we could have made it tougher for her. The fact is that Iceheart has publicized what happened at Halanit to frighten others into paying Thyferra for the gift of bacta we made to them."

Wedge's brown eyes narrowed. "Since Gavin's departure, there has been no direct communication from Halanit. According to the messages Iceheart has sent out, the *Corrupter* initiated a planetary barrage that expanded upon the damage the bombers and stormtroopers had inflicted. It is my assumption that no one was left living in the colony. I'm fairly certain that after all was said and done, the place was sown with mines and other boobytraps to kill survivors or rescuers."

Nawara Ven's braintails twitched. "So you're saying we're not going to try to save any of the people there."

Wedge shook his head, his reluctance to forgo such a mission thick in his voice. "We do not have the ships we need to help them. If even one-tenth of the individuals there survived, that would dwarf our transport capabilities. I do know the New Republic is sending some ships to Halanit, but they don't expect to find survivors either."

He opened his hands. "I know that's not easy for any of you to hear. Innocent individuals have suffered because of something we did, but what we did meant they lived just that much longer. Had we not acted, that colony would have been dead weeks ago. We kept it going that much longer. We were able to lift a blanket of oppression and misery from them, and this disaster cannot devalue what we did. Iceheart made choices that raised our conflict to another level."

"She has to pay." Gavin hammered a fist down onto the

arm of his chair. "Iceheart and Erisi and all of them have to pay."

"And pay they will." The edge sliding into Wedge's voice brought Corran's head up. "Ysanne Isard has forgotten the lesson she taught the Rebellion by giving us a sick Coruscant. She's forgotten that our strength is our freedom and her weakness is her link to the sources of production for bacta. We can go anywhere and be anywhere, but she's limited. She is limited in how much she can cover, so we can hit her where she's open and run when she has our targets protected."

Inyri Forge raised a hand. "But we ran this time, and she hit an innocent world. How do we prevent that from happening again?"

"Two ways. First, with Booster's help, we'll deal the bacta we capture to traders and let them sell it. The price is high enough for them to accept the risks. We can have them undercut Isard's prices or we cut them off from future shipments. In return we can get the arms, munitions, and spare parts we need to continue doing what we're doing. We'll insulate places by allowing them to deny knowing where the bacta came from and we'll make traders very happy with us. The traders become a cutout for us and Isard can't complain too loudly about them because if she does, she loses access to the supplies she needs to maintain her forces.

"Second and more important, we have a score to settle with her. Thyferra has dozens of small bacta-producing colonies out there. We're going to pick one and destroy it. The mission will be dirty and dangerous. What bacta we can't haul away we'll destroy. And we'll let her know that we'll continue to hit her colonies every time she takes her war to an innocent party."

He brought his hands together. "There are analogies that can be drawn between Halanit and Alderaan, and I wish neither incident had happened. What's important to remember is that both worlds died because evil has been allowed to run unchecked. In our pleasure at defeating the Empire, it's all too easy to ignore the nasty bits and pieces of its evil that survived. The New Republic is out hunting down Warlord Zsinj. I'm sure, out there, somewhere, there are still people who will yet come forward to overthrow what we've done and try to reestablish the Empire. This war is really far from over, but if we don't realize that and act accordingly, there will be more Alderaans, more Halanits.

"All of us *have* tried to keep this idea uppermost in our minds, but we saw a diminished Isard as a diminished threat. I know I was doing that, not consciously, but I still was doing it. No more." Wedge's hands folded down into fists and crashed against each other. "Isard is killing innocents, extorting money, enslaving the Vratix, and holding prisoners we want freed. Each and every single thing we do from this point forward is going to be part of the plan to bring her down."

"However." Wedge's voice took on a huskiness. "This war isn't going to be over fast. After this strike at a bacta colony, we'll be moving into a protracted conflict where we'll be more pirate than we are army. It will be exhausting but, as long as she doesn't get her hands on an Interdictor Cruiser, we'll be able to stay ahead of her and wear her down. We'll frustrate her and make her impatient. Then we'll have her."

Corran found himself smiling. Wedge was correct in that without an Interdictor Cruiser to prevent the X-wings from running and hiding in hyperspace, Iceheart's navy would be ineffective against them. *We're okay unless someone jumps in on top of a ship the way the* Corrupter *did. Barring that, we can fly in, shoot off a bunch of proton torpedoes, take out some freighters, and flee before Iceheart can stop us. As long as we don't run out of torpedoes, we should be fine.*

Wedge's head came up. "Tycho and I are working with Bror Jace on compiling a list of viable targets for our punitive strike. When we have a selection made we'll convene another meeting and begin planning of the operation. Until then, your time is your own, but stay here on the station. We'll go when we have a plan in place, and I'm hoping that will be sooner than later. Thanks. You're all dismissed."

Corran sat back for a moment, then let Mirax tug him to his feet. "Lots to think about."

She nodded in agreement and slipped her left arm over his shoulders. "I don't know about you, but I want a drink and something to eat. Do you want to hit a tapcaf?"

"Sure. How about the Hype?"

"Food's better at Flarestar."

"Actually the service is better at Flarestar, but I prefer the decor at Hyperspace." Flarestar tended to be rather dark and quiet, while Hyperspace was as brilliantly lit as its namesake. "The mood I'm drifting into isn't one I want to aid and abet with dim light."

Mirax gave his shoulder a squeeze. "Lead the way."

They walked to the station's core and took the turbolift up to the first of the docking ring's decks. Hyperspace's well-lit opening beckoned to them from opposite the lift. The decor consisted mostly of pinks, yellows, and white jumbled together in an odd, asymmetrical manner that Corran found somehow comforting. He'd decided it was that the color selection was repulsive, but the strange angles and mixing prevented any of it from being overwhelming. The Trandoshan who ran the place seemed to have a quasi-mystical respect for shape and form, often seating people in the tapcaf in a way that accentuated the establishment's visual chaos.

They followed the large sauroid to a corner booth big enough for the entire squadron. Corran considered it wishful thinking on her part. The booth was far enough away from the other patrons that he felt he could talk with Mirax without surrendering privacy, so the Trandoshan's choice suited him perfectly. A motley silver-and-gold 3PO droid came over to take their order, then bounced off to fill it.

Corran picked at a chipped area of the duraplast table's edge with his thumbnail. "Wedge made some good points in there. I think he's right that all of us had really stopped thinking about the seriousness of what we were doing. Face it, since Blackmoon, aside from me, the squadron had really lost no one. I showed back up and that helped reinforce our feeling that we were invincible. Tycho joined us, then Bror reappears, and we're suddenly reinforced by some of the best pilots the Rebellion ever had."

"The unit *has* felt more relaxed." Mirax shrugged. "I think that's only partly because of the successes you've had. You *are* good, but I think you've all underestimated your opposition. Sure, Isard had to run, and she's trapped herself on Thyferra; but she's still tough. Captain Convarion is very aggressive. *Avarice*'s Captain Sair Yonka is very smart and calculating—the antithesis of us Corellians because he does care what the odds are and does everything he can to maximize his chances of survival. He's spent much of his career on ships in the Outer Rim chasing down pirates and protecting convoys, so he understands very well what Isard has him doing.

"The *Virulence*'s Joak Drysso is a stalwart Imperial. I think he's working with Isard as much to strike back at the Rebellion as he is for any other reason. I was talking with my father, and it's his guess that Drysso will move over to take command of the *Lusanka*—assuming, of course, Isard was in command of it to this point. Drysso's Executive Officer is Captain Lakwii Varrscha, so she'll be moved up in his place. I had to outrun her when she was commanding a Customs corvette. Tactics weren't innovative—standard Imp, utterly by the book—but tactics for an Imperial Star Destroyer have never really been subtle anyway."

Corran nodded as the serving droid put tumblers of Corellian whisky in front of them, then accompanied it with a steaming, tentacled mass of noodles and thin-sliced vegetables drenched in a green sauce. "Thanks, I think." He glanced at Mirax as the droid retreated. "Is this what we ordered?"

"I think so." She stabbed a fork into it, twirled it and lifted a dripping noodle coil to her mouth. She chewed for a moment, then swallowed. "Unrecognizable, but not inedible."

"Your enthusiasm is underwhelming." Corran poked around the food with his fork, speared something crunchy and popped it into his mouth. The sauce seemed a bit hot, but it was flavorful and cleared his sinuses, so he decided against complaining. "Not bad. I also think you're right on in pointing out that we have been underestimating Isard and her people. Part of it is because Erisi joined them—I think we have a vested interest in seeing her in a negative light. That could easily be a fatal mistake. We need our edge back, and I think Wedge is going to beat that idea into our brains from this point forward."

Corran looked up as Ooryl entered the tapcaf and waved him over. The Gand hesitated for a moment, looked back out into the concourse, then nodded. As he made his way through the jumble of tables, Corran saw three other Gands trailing in his wake, like mynock splitlings drafting off their parent. Only one of them equaled Ooryl's size—the other two probably massed as much as Ooryl but wore most of it around their middles. *I wonder how that works with an exoskeleton?*

Ooryl stopped at the edge of the table. "Greetings Corran and Mirax. It is Qrygg's honor to present to you three Gands from Qrygg's homeworld of Gand. They are Ussar Vlee, Syron Aalun, and Vviir Wiamdi."

The larger of the three bowed his head. "I speak for all three of us when I say we are most pleased to make your acquaintance."

Though the Gand's speech had the guttural tones and clicks of Ooryl's normal voice, Corran found himself having a hard time comprehending what was said. He knew he should have understood it easily—it was only a greeting—but the use of personal pronouns surprised him. *Ooryl explained long ago that Gands considered it the height of presumption to use personal pronouns to refer to themselves, because it arrogantly assumes the listeners know who the speaker is. Only after having done something so memorable that such an assumption can be made can a Gand refer to himself as "I."*

Mirax covered for Corran. "We're very pleased to meet you as well. Ooryl is a good friend, so we are honored to meet his friends."

Ooryl quivered for a second. "Qrygg is sorry for your misinterpretation because Qrygg knows it is Qrygg's fault, Mirax. These Gands are not Qrygg's friends. They are *ruetsavii*." Ooryl's mouth parts closed for a moment, then snapped back open. "In Basic they would be something like observers or examiners, but more than either."

Corran raised an eyebrow. "They're your superiors?"

The taller Gand—Vviir Wiamdi by order of introduction—exaggerated the shaking of his head. "We have been sent by the Elders of Gand to watch Ooryl Qrygg. We are to chronicle Qrygg's existence and to criticize it. It is a great honor."

Ooryl doesn't seem to think it's that great an honor by the look of him. Corran smiled. "If there is any way I may be of assistance to you, please do not hesitate to let me know what I can do. Ooryl and I have spent much time together, and he's saved my life more times than I care to remember."

All three Gands nodded their heads sagely, but Corran was uncertain he was reading their body language correctly. *I'm not sure I can read them at all, and I doubt I'm going to get a good explanation from Ooryl.* Corran looked over at Mirax, but she didn't seem to be any more confident of her judgment of the Gands than he was. *One more thing to learn about, which is why this galaxy will never be dull.*

Corran pointed to the open area in the booth. "Would you care to join us?"

Ooryl shook his head. "Now it is time for Qrygg to interface with Zraii and tend to Qrygg's X-wing. After that, the schedule allows for dining."

Vviir bowed his head again. "I beg your forgiveness for this interruption. We will watch you interact with Qrygg at a later date." He turned and led the procession back out of the tapcaf with Ooryl drawn along in the trio's wake like an X-wing tractored to a freighter.

Mirax raised an eyebrow. "What was all that about?"

"Not a clue."

"And Ooryl's not going to tell you anything, either." She pointed in their direction with her fork. "I've never heard of, let alone seen, a group of Gands wandering around together. Very odd."

Corran shrugged and attacked his food. "Twi'leks have joined us, and now we have some Gands with us. I don't understand it, nor do I *need* to understand it. I just hope Iceheart gets as confused by it as I am."

21

Under other circumstances Wedge Antilles thought he might have liked Qretu 5. The ring of asteroids surrounding the planet that provided his people with cover against ground-based early-warning systems had looked wonderful in the night sky in all the holograms he had studied. The world's moist and warm climate encouraged the growth of lush green foliage, over the tops of which Wedge's X-wing whisked at dizzying speed. Mountains upthrust by colliding tectonic plates also hid the fighters from their target, providing the personnel at the Q5A7 Bacta Refinement Plant no warning about the impending attack.

Wedge's force was flying in at a strength of twenty-four—two squadrons' worth of snubfighters. The three losses to the *Corrupter* had been replaced by the Gand *ruetsavii* and their curious ships. The Gands flew heavily modified TIE bombers. The Quadanium solar panels at the front had been cut on the diagonal bias like those of TIE Interceptors and had a central cutout to provide the pilot with peripheral vision. The bomb delivery system in the secondary hull had been scrapped in favor of a concussion missile launching system with a six-missile magazine, then a hyperdrive motivator and shield generators had been added. Two lasers completed their weapons array. While the Gand bombers were still slow, the shields were strong; and Wedge found the ships preferable to Y-wings for the long-range raid they were making.

He had not intended to have the Gands come along on the mission, but Ooryl had insisted they would anyway since they were *ruetsavii*—and what exactly that meant Wedge was as yet uncertain. In the preliminary and simulator runs they made on the mission, the Gands had proved very competent and skillful, though Wedge thought Ooryl could outfly all of them.

Wedge checked the chronographic readout on his main screen, then glanced up at the horizon. *The mountains are right where they're supposed to be. Over the rise and the valley should take us right in on target.* Pulling back on the X-wing's stick, he brought his fighter up so the sun rising at his back could illuminate his X-wing. He reached up with his right hand, flicking the switch that brought the S-foils into attack position, the keyed his comm unit. "Rogues, we go in. *Chir'daki,* stand by."

Tugging his stick to the right, he kicked the X-wing into a barrel roll to starboard, then leveled out and began his run through the valley. The mountains rose up off both S-foils but were far enough away that Wedge didn't feel as cramped as he did on the Death Star trench run or even the conduit mission on Borleias. His onboard computer matched the terrain to the mission map it had in memory, sounded a mild drift alarm and Wedge corrected the problem almost unconsciously.

Wedge thumbed the controls over to proton torpedoes and linked the fire of both launch tubes. He kept his hand easy on the stick, nudging the craft this way and that, then shot out over the edge of a three-hundred-meter-tall cliff. As he rolled, he saw a black valley dotted with lights and brought his fighter around on a heading for a large dark block with flashing red and yellow lights on each of its corners. His targeting crosshairs dropped into the shadowed outline and he pulled the trigger.

Two proton torpedoes shot out on tongues of blue flame

and streaked away at the building. They hit barely nanoseconds apart and detonated just after punching through the ferrocrete wall. Their subsequent explosions vomited argent fire out through their entry holes, then through the roof and out the windows on the upper three floors. The roof collapsed in on itself, leaving the fire on the building's interior lighting up the night like magma in a volcano's heart.

With a flick of his thumb Wedge shifted the X-wing over to laser fire and left it firing single shots in sequence. Triggering a burst of fire, he sent a hail of red laser bolts burning through the night. His shots tracked over the main refinery building and down through the darkness. Something he hit exploded brilliantly, sending a red-gold fireball into the air. It imploded but still bumped him around as he flew through where it had been, then he was over the bay and starting a long loop over Qretu 5's largest ocean.

As he came around he got a chance to look back at the Q5A7 plant and felt his stomach fold in on itself. The cliff wall and the waters of the bay reflected the light from the burning refinery, magnifying it and spreading it all over the valley. The X-wings that had come in behind him had similarly launched proton torpedoes at ground targets. The missiles, which were powerful enough to put quite a dent in an Imperial Star Destroyer, blasted apart unarmored buildings. Lasers filled the night like lightning strikes, melting roads, setting trees on fire and exploding anything even vaguely incendiary when they hit.

Though the targets they had specified had been strictly industrial, collateral damage was inescapable. At least one bright fire burned in what should have been a residential complex for plant workers—clearly one of the proton torpedoes had overshot its mark—and Wedge didn't know if the ground target his lasers had destroyed had been droid-driven or if it contained innocent bystanders. Coming in prior to dawn had been an attempt to minimize the presence of innocents in the target zones, but even minimal involvement of noncombatants meant some of them would die.

Part of Wedge didn't want to care because the raid was meant to make Isard pay for Halanit's destruction. That raid had been collateral damage through and through, but murdering Thyferrans, Vratix, and assorted resident alien workers would hardly make Isard atone for what she had done. The only pain she would feel would be the loss of bacta and her ability to produce it. *To her, those we kill are reason enough for continuing her predations, whereas those innocents she kills are just punishment for our misdeeds.*

Another part of Wedge wanted to abort the Twi'leks' run on the valley. The damage done had been rather ample. The Deathseeds would only be able to strafe the ground, sowing more terror in the populace, but probably not doing much to further cripple the refinery. *What has already been done should be enough, but I know it isn't.* He keyed his comm unit. "*Chir'daki,* you are good to go."

He got a double-click acknowledgment from Tal'dira, then Corran's voice broke in. "Lead, I have multiple eyeball contacts coming up off the deck to the north."

"I copy, Nine. Seven, you have command of the ground op. Two, Nine, and Ten, on me to deal with the intruders." Wedge hauled back on his stick and brought the X-wing up in a loop. Rolling out to port, he saw Asyr pull up on his starboard S-foil while Corran and Ooryl joined him to the left. "How many, Nine?"

"Eight, sir."

"I copy. Engage at will, but save your last two torpedoes." Standing off and shooting the TIE fighters down with proton torpedoes would be the safest means of defeating them, but Wedge wanted to save some torpedoes in case they ran into a heavy ship as they tried to get away. *As nearly as I can tell all of Isard's capital ships are five hours or more distant from here, but if one shows up I want to give it a barrage that will keep it off us long enough for us to escape.*

The intervention of Thyferran Home Defense Corps pilots had been anticipated. Their intelligence reports about Qretu 5 had indicated the placement of such troops on the world, though after Gavin had described burning three of them down on Halanit, there was open debate as to whether or not the THDC pilots would dare come up and fight. Eight starfighters were enough to discourage someone from bringing their own freighter into Qretu 5's spaceport and demanding it be filled with bacta or to protect freighters going out to or coming back in from a convoy.

Isard didn't anticipate our coming in to this place in such strength and with the intention of wreaking total havoc. Wedge linked the fire on his lasers, pairing them, and evened out his shields fore and aft. A pair of missiles from his port sizzled through the dawning sky and impaled distant specks of black. Twin stars twinkled for a moment before the sound of the explosion collided with his fighter, then Wedge was on the TIEs and firing.

Two bursts of laser fire bracketed one of the TIE fighters. The first pair of bolts liquefied one of the hexagonal solar panels, immediately pitching the fighter into a decaying flat spin. The second pair lopped off the upper half of the remaining solar panel, adding a loopy, wobbling element to the spin. The wounded TIE dropped from the sky like the asymmetrical rock it resembled and exploded on impact with the ground.

Pulling back on the stick, Wedge brought the X-wing's nose up until it pointed away from the planet. He let the climb bleed off just a little of his speed, trading it for altitude, then he came back over the top and started back down into the fight. He selected one target and began to close, but it died in a quad burst of laser fire, so he ruddered the nose to the right and swooped in on a TIE angling for a deflection shot at Asyr's X-wing.

These pilots know nothing. Coming in from above and in front of the TIE fighter, Wedge knew he should have been easy to spot. The TIE pilots had clearly focused in on getting Asyr, to the exclusion of everyone else. While that kind of focus and concentration might be useful in all sorts of endeavors, in a fighter pilot without situational awareness, it was suicide.

Wedge knew, from looking out his canopy and studying his sensors, where his other fighters were and where the dwindling supply of TIEs was. He couldn't feel their presence in the way Luke described being able to fix people and machines in relation to himself through the Force, but he did have a sense of where they were. This situational awareness meant he would know if a TIE had begun to close on him and would be able to take the appropriate response, from calling for help to outmaneuvering the other pilot.

Without it I would have died hundreds of times over. Applying a little rudder, Wedge tracked his crosshairs over to cover the TIE and tightened up on the trigger. Four red lances of light converged, melding into one, then skewered the fighter's ball cockpit. The ion engines exploded, spinning the solar panels away like sabacc cards. Flaming debris sprayed out like sparks in the wake of a passing meteorite, igniting a fire in the foliage below.

Mynock trumpeted triumphantly.

Wedge glanced at his main sensor screen. "That was the last of them, true." He activated the comm unit. "Nine, take Ten and swing over the spaceport. Suppress ground fire if you get any and report all clear."

"As ordered, Lead."

"*Chir'daki* One to Rogue Leader."

"Go ahead, Tal'dira."

"*Chir'daki* pass complete. We had secondary explosions in the vehicle sheds and machining shops."

"Good going, Tal'dira. Stand by for phase two of the operation."

Tycho's voice entered the frequency. "Wedge, I have someone on the deck complaining. Claims to be the plant manager."

"I copy, Tycho. Tell him to evacuate the whole area and consider a career change. Resistance means we grid the surrounding town and start melting parts of it."

"As ordered, Wedge."

Looking back at Q5A7 and the surrounding area, Wedge saw a lot of fire and rising columns of dense smoke to greet the dawn. Some small ships had set out from the bay's marina and ground vehicles were beginning to fill the coastal roadway heading north and south. *Those who can get away are— those who can't will just wait in fear.*

"Lead, this is Nine. The spaceport is clear. No hostiles and the traffic-control tower is empty but intact."

Wedge smiled. "You got close enough to determine that, Nine?"

"Whistler has good distance processing equipment from stakeouts, Lead. He's never been wrong before."

"I copy. Stay covering the spaceport."

"As ordered, Lead. Nine out."

Wedge punched up a new frequency on the comm unit. "Rogue leader to Taskforce Bantha."

"Bantha here, Wedge. We can spot the city by the fires from up here."

"I don't doubt that at all, Booster. It could have been nastier but Iceheart only had eight vape-bait pilots here. They're gone, so it's safe to have the freighters come in."

"Our pleasure. Incoming."

Wedge smiled. During the two weeks the squadrons had trained for the raid, Booster had arranged for a convoy of independent freighters and smugglers to meet with him, Mirax, and the *Pulsar Skate*. He told them he'd get them all the bacta they could haul provided they would keep what they earned as a credit against his future demands. Some balked, but most came along, even though Booster demanded they slave their navicomputers to the *Skate*'s and fly blind with him to their destination. When they arrived in the system and took up positions in the asteroid rings around Qretu 5, Wedge and his people began their run.

Wedge brought the fighter's nose up until it eclipsed the burning town and started another turn over the ocean. Regret for the damage done to nonindustrial targets began to eat at him. *My parents died when a pirate took off from the fueling station they ran, igniting the station. Down there could easily be another kid who has just lost his parents in a blast we caused. I know what we are doing is right and even necessary, but that doesn't lessen the pain or dull the horror of the people on the ground. I have to believe that opposing Isard and insulating billions of people from her evil is a great good, a vital good, but I can never let myself think that it justifies inflicting pain on innocents. It may well explain why it had to be done, but it can never justify it.*

Even as revulsion for the fire and damage began to fill

him, sanity provided a means for draining it off. *The key difference between us and Isard is that she fully intended to do the most harm to the most people. We did not. We chose our targets well, we set the attack for a time when casualties would be minimized, and we have made no attempt to attack targets of opportunity like the ships or landspeeders fleeing the town. We exerted as much control as possible to keep the strike as clean as we could.*

Wedge smiled. *Then again, it was said that the Emperor's throne had been molded of good intentions. We must take responsibility for what we've done on the ground and repair what we can. If not, we do by negligence what Isard does in malice.*

He keyed the comm unit. "Booster, when you're on the ground, establish a contact so reparation claims can be forwarded to us. I want survivors and orphans taken care of."

"This isn't the Gus Treta station, Wedge."

"I know, but the kids on the ground don't have you to see them through the hard times, do they?"

"I copy, Wedge. It will be done."

"Good." Wedge glanced again at the city, but the dawn had dulled the brightness of the flames and showed him how much of the area had gone unharmed. "Booster, make sure they know we hit Q5A7 to hit Isard, and we'll only be back if it's apparent she's dependent upon them again. Tell them we're death itself for our enemies, but the best of friends to have for allies. I'm sure they can figure out for themselves how to join that latter class."

22

Mirax Terrik gave the rakishly good-looking man a dazzling smile as she stepped into his office. "Talon Karrde, pleased to meet you again. I don't know if you'll remember me . . ."

Karrde returned her smile, his pale blue eyes sparkling. "I could hardly forget you, Mirax Terrik. Because of your efforts, those cases of Alderaanian wine cost me well more than I had expected to pay." He took her right hand and gently kissed it—his black moustache and goatee tickled her hand and fingers.

"I didn't realize you were the other person bidding for them."

"But if you had, you'd not have fought any less tenaciously for them." Karrde shrugged easily enough that Mirax was almost willing to believe he had dismissed the matter. "What you cost me I put down as the fee paid for a lesson in dealing with exotic items. If you weren't in the business of hauling things for the Rebellion, I might have had a chance to test what I learned against you again."

"And my girl would have made you pay even more in your next meeting." Booster Terrik rested his big hands on Mirax's shoulders. "I would have expected you to be using something bigger than an old hollowed-out asteroid for your headquarters, Karrde. You can afford it."

"Pleased to see you again, too, Booster." The hint of a smile played across Karrde's lips. "As for this asteroid, Tapper found it, but before he could exploit it he ran into some Imperial problems. After our groups merged, he brought it to my attention. We're using it until we find something more suitable."

Quelev Tapper came around from behind Booster and stood next to the chair to the left of Karrde's massive desk. "While most of the ore has been mined, there's enough metal in the rock to give sensors trouble." Though as slender as Karrde, and almost as handsome, Tapper's manner contrasted sharply with Karrde's polite grace. "It will do in the interim."

Karrde opened his hands and indicated the pair of chairs facing the desk. "Please, be seated."

Mirax accepted his invitation and looked around the office as she sat. The chamber's stone walls had been smoothed to an obsidian glassiness, but still had a significant texture in the bumps and recesses the mining process had left behind. The room's furnishings—characterized by Karrde's desk— were heavy and blocky, more of an industrial grade than they were elegant. Despite that, however, the artifacts and items displayed on shelves and atop tables, did provide an air of sophistication to the surroundings. Mirax noted on the sideboard a cut-crystal decanter full of a pale green liquid and four goblets, prompting a smile.

Karrde's gaze followed hers and he gave her a slight nod. "Might I offer you some of the wine I paid so dearly for? The best is a dry green from Aldera."

Mirax nodded. "Please." She glanced at her father.

Booster perched in his chair as if it were a slender pole and he was a bird topping it, but he nodded. "Thank you."

Karrde poured from the crystalline decanter. It looked to Mirax to be of Quarren manufacture. She knew from the styling it came from Mon Calamari, but the purple tint to the glass told her the Quarren had made it, not the Mon Cals.

Quarren crystal rarely makes it off Mon Calamari. Karrde definitely fishes for items with a very wide and fine net.

She accepted her glass of wine from Karrde, then raised her glass with the others as Karrde offered a toast. "May the bargaining be as sweet as the profit and the next deal not long in coming."

In tasting the wine Mirax found it very dry, but surprisingly tart without being truly sour. "Perfect with game."

Karrde sat at his desk and nodded. "I've heard it said this vintage was originally intended for a banquet featuring krayt dragon."

"Oh? What happened, too much wine and not enough krayt?"

"No, too much krayt and not enough hunter." Karrde held the glass up and let light sparkle through the wine's receding legs. "The wine was ordered prior to the hunt. The dragon got the hunter, and the widow used the vintage at the memorial service. The wine won praises and since has been a very popular vintage. This particular year was considered very good, but the wine laid down the year of Alderaan's demise was supposed to be even better."

Booster cleared his voice. "It's amazing what you know, Karrde. I'm very impressed. I was wondering if your encyclopedic knowledge includes where I can get some supplies I need."

Karrde's blue eyes narrowed slightly. "*You* need or things Wedge Antilles needs?"

"They're things that are needed, Karrde." Booster brought his hands together. "Let's trim some parsecs off the course of this conversation, shall we? You know I think of you like the son I never had."

Karrde snorted. "Like the son you never had killed."

Mirax suppressed a laugh, and her father smiled. "True, I've not forgotten how you managed to pick up pieces of my network while I was harvesting spice on Kessel. That did anger me, but it also convinced me that Mirax was right in wanting me to retire."

"Yet here you are bargaining for Antilles and his band of mercenaries."

Booster frowned. "They're not mercenaries."

"No?"

Mirax shook her head. "Actually, to be mercenaries, they'd have to be *paid*. They're doing what they're doing because of obligations they feel to the Vratix and others."

Karrde shot a glance at Tapper, then the two of them shook their heads. "Idealists cause a lot of trouble in this galaxy."

"Just remember it was one of those idealists who killed Jabba."

"Good point, Booster, but I've got no desire to end up like Jabba."

"Nor will you." Booster sipped more of his wine. "Wedge and the others may be idealists in some respects, but they're also practical when they need to be, and I'm here to put that practicality into terms you can understand and respect. What I'm looking for is missile- and torpedo-sensor packages, launch-tube assemblies, and a supply of proton torpedoes and concussion missiles."

Mirax noted no reaction by Karrde, but Tapper's eyes widened quite a bit.

Karrde raised his hand to cover a yawn. "I've heard that you made a mess of the bacta refinery on Qretu 5."

"Care to know how much bacta we hauled away?"

"I have my estimates. I also know where you sent a great deal of it."

Mirax smiled. "It doesn't take a genius to know we've shipped a lot to Coruscant."

"But it will take a genius to get the rest of it, eh?" Karrde set his glass of wine down. "What sort of numbers are you looking at with your equipment?"

Booster leaned back in his seat. "Three hundred launchers and sensor packages: fifty should be snubfighter systems, the rest can be capital ship systems. Right now I want two thousand proton torpedoes and a thousand concussion missiles, though I expect those numbers to change."

"Upward, of course."

"Of course."

Karrde's expression sharpened. "You going to be arming your freighters, Booster?"

"Try taking one of them off and find out, Karrde."

Talon Karrde smiled broadly. "I'm a smuggler, not a pirate."

"Thin line between them." Booster thrust his chin forward. "Pirate steals from his suppliers, smuggler just cheats them."

"You've distilled that difference to its essence, Booster." Karrde sat back in his chair. "You'll be paying with bacta?"

Booster nodded. "Not a problem, I assume?"

"Not really. The price now is so high that much of what I would be trading for is being sold to buy bacta from the cartel. Oddly enough, with the New Republic somewhat strapped for liquid capital, military surplus and munitions are actually dropping in price. It's a buyer's market. I shouldn't be telling you that, of course."

Mirax laughed. "Except you know we already know that, *and* you want to rub in the fact that you'll be gouging us on the prices."

Karrde's eyes glittered with amusement. "She's very sharp, Booster. You should be proud."

"I am. You can get us what we want?"

Karrde nodded. "Not all at once, of course."

"Installments are fine." Booster glanced at a thumbnail, then looked back up. "Delivery will be a bit peculiar. We'll arrange for exchanges at various places where your ships will offload material for us. We'll be transporting it to our final destination ourselves."

"Not that you don't trust me."

"But we don't trust you." Booster smiled. "I know you've already learned more about our operation than I wanted you to, and I also know that Vorru is trying to learn as much about us as he can. I don't want you to find we're a commodity you can trade to him for a profit."

Karrde held his hands up. "So far I have avoided taking sides in the civil war, and I see this as a simple extension of it even though Antilles has resigned from the New Republic's military. Since the cartel really isn't interested in selling bacta to me, and since you need my services, it isn't going to do me any good to sacrifice you to them."

"Provided we still are a profit center for you."

Karrde frowned. "Booster, you make it sound like I don't value our history together."

"Oh, I think you do, and the history of your making a profit off me is what you value."

Mirax raised an eyebrow. "The fact that either one of you would sell the other for a bucket of warm dewback drool isn't really germane here. Betting against Wedge Antilles's abilities lost Iceheart the Imperial homeworld and sent her packing for Thyferra. Talon, you're too smart not to back him, especially since his victory will break the cartel and open up the bacta trade. A little gratitude toward you from the Ashern rebels won't hurt when distribution is set up."

"Point taken." Karrde picked up the datapad on his desk and punched a few keys. "I'm going to have you liaise with Melina Carniss on the delivery details."

Booster frowned. "Carniss? I don't know her. Never heard of her."

"She worked for Jabba on Tatooine. She filled a niche that would have been in the middle of his security apparatus, but she was Jabba's own agent. Formally, she was his dance coordinator. Good head on her shoulders. She understands a lot of the business, but is a bit shy on experience." Karrde stood and waved his left hand toward the doorway. "Here she is. Come in, Melina, my dear. This is Booster Terrik and his charming daughter, Mirax."

Mirax shook the woman's hand and returned her smile. Several inches shorter than Mirax, Melina wore her dark hair in a rather short cut. It accentuated a white stripe that started with scar tissue near the corner of Melina's right eye and shot straight back beyond her ear. Her green eyes and full mouth made her pretty and the way Tapper looked at her suggested he was smitten.

"Pleased to meet you both."

Karrde waited until Tapper slid a chair from over by the wall beside his own and Melina seated herself before he continued. "Melina, you'll coordinate shipments of material to

Booster. He'll give you the details. The cargo and the delivery points will be hazardous, but we'll not charge him our normal rates for such things. He's part of our family—albeit a rather distantly related one."

She nodded. "I understand."

Mirax smiled. *Great, this means what we don't pay for transport we will pay for the cost of the items. And Karrde said it was a buyer's market.*

Karrde looked up from his datapad. "Is there anything else you need, Booster?"

Tapper laughed. "Perhaps he wants *Another Chance* or the Death Star's womb. I mean, as long as your aim is to break the Bacta Cartel, you might as well go in for other things you can't get."

The brow over Booster's artificial left eye rose. "It's important in this business for you to be able to tell fable from fact and wishing from thinking. From what I've heard, about six months before I got out of Kessel, just after the Imps hurt the Rebels at Derra IV but before they ran them off Hoth, some treasure hunters searching the Alderaan graveyard found *Another Chance* and turned the ship and its arms over to the Rebels. That's fact. The location of the shipyard that built the Death Star is likely a fact as well, but it's one I don't know and it's my *wish* that it's a fact that went to the grave with the Emperor. I don't *think* that's likely.

"Now it's Iceheart's *wish* we won't break the cartel and destroy her power." Booster smiled coldly. "I *think*—no, I *know*—she's not going to get her wish. Her fall will not be fast, and it won't be bloodless, but it's coming. Count it as fact."

Tapper raised his hands. "Sorry, I meant no offense."

"And none was taken." Mirax patted her father on the arm and felt the tension begin to flow out of him. "My father just wanted to make sure that you knew betting against Wedge was a mistake."

Karrde pressed his hands flat against his desktop. "A lesson we have all learned, I am certain. Now let us attend to the details that make sure we all profit from it."

23

Corran Horn felt tired enough from the recent raid and run home that he knew he should just turn in, but the idea of hitting the small suite of rooms he shared with Mirax didn't appeal. On his approach back to the Yag'Dhul station he'd gotten a message she'd recorded saying she was taking her father out on another trip to finalize arrangements for supply shipments. She expected to be gone for three days.

Which means I'm alone when I could use a good hug and some sympathy. Corran knew what was happening to him, and he wanted to fight against it, but even by trying some of the breathing exercises Luke Skywalker had recommended to him, he had a hard time putting a dent in his downward emotional spiral. *It's like flying into a fireball. You have to hang on and hope you come out in one piece on the other side.*

The fourth anniversary of his father's death had snuck up on Corran and ambushed him. A lot of hydrogen had been melted into helium in a lot of stars since his father's death, but the memory of holding his father's dead body in his arms had the immediacy of an event that had occurred moments before. Corran could still feel his father's weight pressing against him. The man's stillness, the stink of blood and blaster-burned flesh, the screams of those in the cantina, including his own, all pounded in on him.

The previous year, things had not seemed to be so bad to him, but he'd just started with Rogue Squadron at that time, so he had a legion of distractions to dull the pain. He also realized that his liaison with Mirax and meeting her father made it tougher on him. Though he loved her and wouldn't give her up for anything, Corran couldn't help feeling that his father would have felt betrayed by his love for Mirax. While he knew his father would have accepted her eventually, the fact that he didn't have his father's approval gnawed away at him.

Getting to see Booster and Mirax together compounded the problem. Corran was happy for Mirax that her father was around because the love they shared was obvious enough that a blind Givin frozen in carbonite could have seen it. She was lucky to have her father, and he was equally lucky to have her. As much as Corran wanted Mirax to be happy, what she shared with her father reminded him of what he had lost. *I thought the void inside me had been filled, but it had just scabbed over and is now plenty open.*

On top of that, the next step in the evolution of the Bacta War was pushing him to the limit. Wedge had teams, from full squadrons down to single two-ship flights out harassing the Bacta Cartel. The whole strategy was to hit and run, which worked exceedingly well. Because the Thyferrans scheduled their bacta shipments it was possible for the Rogues to show up, force the Star Destroyers to scramble their fighters, pop off some proton torpedoes to take out a few TIEs, then scatter. He knew the strategy had to be frustrating for Iceheart's people, since they were taking losses here and there without killing any of the Rogues; but it wasn't much better for Corran or the rest of Wedge's people.

Engaging in a straight-up fight with even a *Victory*-class Star Destroyer like the *Corrupter* would be suicide for a squadron of X-wings. It was true that the large Star Destroyers were not particularly good at defending themselves against snubfighters—hence the development of the *Lancer-*

class frigates—but even accidentally shooting down one or two X-wings would hurt the Rogues significantly. Conversely, aside from repeated proton torpedo salvos, there was no way snubfighters could cripple or destroy a Star Destroyer. If the whole squadron fired a salvo of torpedoes at the same time, they could certainly bring the Star Destroyer's shields down, but any captain worth his rank cylinders would roll the ship to present undamaged shields and keep shooting. If all his shields were stripped away he could still go to light-speed before another torpedo could hit.

Corran had no wish to commit suicide in an attack on a Star Destroyer, but cutting and running made him feel . . . *criminal.* He knew that was stupid, but he figured the judgment was based in the fact that Wedge hadn't given anyone a clear timetable concerning when they would move into the war's final phase—the phase where Iceheart left Thyferra and the Bacta Cartel would be broken. *If I knew how long we were going to run, I could see it as a tactical advantage. Right now it seems as if we're doing something so we won't be doing* nothing.

Realizing he had no desire to be alone, he headed for the tapcaf known as Flarestar. He hoped other members of the squadron would be there, though the chances of that were slim. Ooryl seemed to spend most of his time with the *ruetsavii.* Nawara Ven and Rhysati as well as Gavin and Asyr Sei'lar spent most of their time being couples. Tycho and Wedge were either on missions or planning yet other missions. Bror Jace and Corran had never been close, while Inyri Forge and the Sullustan Captain Aril Nunb had discovered they shared a passion for obscure games of chance like contract sabacc and double-draw fendoc. As stunning as they were as pilots, their ability to separate other gamblers from their credits was so remarkable that two of the ships in the Rogues' growing collection of freighters had joined the fleet to pay off bad debts.

Corran smiled to himself as he entered the Flarestar's darkened interior. *Inyri's sister Lujayne would just tell me I was holding myself back from getting to know the others, but I'm not sure it's that simple. I'm just without my close friends—Mirax, Iella, Ooryl—and not really of a mood to make new friends.*

"Corran! Corran Horn, come on over here."

Corran's smile grew at the sound of the man's voice. "Pash? What are you doing here?" He cut between and around tables and gave the taller, slender man a friendly, back-slapping hug. "Normally you aces fly your A-wings through this system so fast I didn't think you even saw us here."

Pash pulled a chair over for Corran, then pointed at one of the quartet of pilots already seated at the table. "Linna caught an unstart in one of her J-77 engines just as we swung through the fringes of Yag'Dhul's atmosphere. We called in an emergency and put into the station here. Zraii said he can fix it up—looks like a micrometeorite chewed up the alluvial compressor."

Corran nodded. "That blows the pressure in the reaction chamber, and the engine pops out of synch with its twin. X-wing's damper system prevents that from happening."

Linna, a blond woman with a mouth just a bit too wide, snorted. "Sure, if you want to be piloting something that should be in a museum. Speed is what will keep a pilot safe and the A-wing has plenty of speed to burn."

Corran looked at Pash. "You let your pilots talk like that?"

The red-haired man shrugged. "Children. What can I do?"

"You can explain to them that going faster doesn't mean they're flying better."

Linna and the other three A-wing pilots regarded Corran as if he and Pash had just taken public loyalty oaths to the Emperor. "If you can't handle the speed, you're not much of a pilot."

Corran shook his head. "Pash, you were just hoping I would walk in here, weren't you?"

Pash laughed lightly. "Actually I was waiting for Wedge or Tycho, but I figured you'd be up to the challenge. I know you know of times when speed wouldn't have helped at all."

Corran nodded. "Or hurt."

"Sure, as if such a time could exist." Linna grabbed a half-full pitcher of Lomin-ale, filled her mug, and topped it with foam. "Speed can't hurt."

"Oh, the innocence of youth." Corran took the mug from in front of her and blew off the foam. "Let me tell you about this time we were on a mission and we got jumped by a *Lancer*-class frigate. If I'd been in an A-wing, well, Rogue Squadron would have a lot more dead on its rosters and Isard would still own Coruscant . . ."

Though he knew the news he had would make Ysanne Isard happy—in and of itself a feat worthy of monuments—Fliry Vorru kept any sign of it from his face as he entered her office. He intended to surprise her so he could gauge her disposition. The weather becoming hotter and the inclusion of daily rainstorms that hit in the early afternoon had combined with the pressure from Ashern strikes to make Isard more than disagreeable.

Antilles and his antics had further exacerbated the problem. Their hit-and-run tactics were costing the cartel in both credits and prestige. Each raid cost the cartel one or two TIE fighters, which really amounted to insignificant losses, *if* someone had access to a TIE fighter production facility. Sienar Fleet Systems had numerous starfighter factories scattered throughout the galaxy, *but they neglected to put one here, on Thyferra.* As a result, the cartel had to trade for replacements with the likes of Supreme Warlord Harssk and High Admiral Teradoc. They gratefully accepted bacta in return for the fighters, but the scorn that came with each delivery could drive Isard into furious tantrums.

When Isard turned to look at him and smiled, Fliry Vorru felt something cold and serpentine slither through his abdomen. "Ah, Minister Vorru, do come in. I was hoping we would have a chance to speak, and here you arrive before I need send for you."

Glad he had saved himself from being summoned, Vorru nodded graciously and returned a smile of his own. "I have information I think you will find useful and even pleasing."

Isard's scarlet diaphanous outfit rustled as she took a seat in a high-backed chair. "Good news is most welcome, Minister Vorru. Would you be seated? Refreshment?"

There is something going on here I do not understand. Have the Ashern poisoned her somehow? "Perhaps I will give you my report and you'll have a chance to reconsider your offer, Madam Director."

Isard's eyes widened. "You can't think me so capricious that I could rescind my offer because you've overestimated what you want to tell me, can you?" She waved away any reply before he'd even made an attempt to open his mouth. "My news is good enough to make me offer you something to drink. Give me your news, then you shall have mine and you can see if you want to drink with me."

I knew one of us would be surprised here, but I didn't expect it would be me. He nodded slowly. "As you will, Madam Director. Our main problem in dealing with Antilles and his people is that they are striking at us and running quickly because there is nothing to hold them back. They have no attachments to the systems they are hitting. We arrive, they launch proton torpedoes or concussion missiles, then they scatter like shrapnel from a proton mine."

Isard nodded, her smile not having shrunk a millimeter. "This has been the course of things to this point. I trust you have found a way to change this."

"Two aspects of it, yes." Vorru lifted his chin. "My network of spies has begun to produce information. I have yet to find out what the location of Antilles's base is. He and his people are being very cautious, but I have no doubt we will discover it in time. Until then I have uncovered two very important pieces of information: Where they are getting their munitions and, more to the point, where the next shipment will be placed in the hands of the Antilles group."

"Really?"

The hint of falsetto in her voice didn't escape Vorru, but he did not consider it important at the moment. "It is true, Madam Director. A woman working for Talon Karrde had previously been employed by Jabba the Hutt. Subsequent to his death she spent a couple of years in abject poverty on

Tatooine. Karrde took her in and has helped her get back on her feet, but her taste for fine things has never been satisfied—nor has her ambition. Karrde appointed her to liaise with the Antilles people—Booster Terrik, in fact—an old friend from Kessel."

"Fascinating. Karrde's name is not unknown to me, though I would not have thought his organization of sufficient size to meet Antilles's needs."

"Carniss indicates Karrde's operation is larger than anyone suspects. Karrde prefers to maintain a low profile to escape trouble with authorities. Booster Terrik placed a huge order for munitions and equipment, which Karrde is meeting in installments. Karrde's people are shipping the supplies to a rendezvous point, then Terrik is taking them back to Antilles's headquarters."

Isard sat forward. "Does Carniss know where that is?"

"No, but I have been given the location of the rendezvous point. They will be making the transfer in the Alderaan system."

"They probably draw some sort of ephemeral strength from visiting the site of Alderaan's sacrifice."

"Undoubtedly so, Madam Director. What is important is that Antilles will have his fighters and his freighters there. If we divert our warships to Alderaan we can ambush the Antilles group and destroy them."

Isard's eyes narrowed, but her smile did not die and this contradiction confused Vorru. "No, Minister Vorru, I'm not going to send all my ships in case this information is false. I don't doubt you or your source, but Antilles might catch wind of our ambush and refuse to show up. He could even hit a bacta convoy and subject us to yet more ridicule. No, I won't have that."

She held up her right index finger. "I do know what I will do. I will send Convarion and the *Corrupter*. He's ambushed them once and can do it again."

Vorru shook his head. "But if you only send the *Corrupter*, Antilles and his people will scatter as usual. We will accomplish nothing."

"No, Vorru, we will accomplish everything." Isard

laughed aloud, her voice full of triumph. "While you have woven a net of spies to catch Antilles, I have been searching for the means to kill him. I have found it, and in twelve hours it will be here and ready to join Convarion as he goes for the kill."

Vorru frowned. "I don't understand."

"It is rather simple, Minister Vorru." Isard's smile became cold. "At great expense I have leased from High Admiral Teradoc a ship, the *Aggregator*."

Vorru's jaw dropped. "An Interdictor Cruiser."

"Exactly." She clapped her hands together. "When it arrives at Alderaan and powers up its gravity well projectors, Antilles and his ships will be trapped. There will be another sacrifice at Alderaan—another victory there for the Empire to celebrate. What do you say to that?"

"I say, Madam Director, I *will* accept that drink you offered"—Vorru smiled—"and raise a toast to victory."

24

Wedge's X-wing reverted to realspace above the plane of the elliptic in the Alderaan system. Spread out in a flat disk, the rubble that had once been Alderaan looked like the crumbs left behind after the cutting of a *ryshcate*. He slowly shook his head. *Dying only once isn't nearly enough punishment for the Emperor to atone for this evil.*

Mynock beeped with each ship entering the system. The Rogues in their X-wings had come in first and oriented themselves toward the Graveyard. The most likely threat to them would come from there, from pirates or others hidden amid the debris. *Some of the chunks are large enough to screen even a Star Destroyer.* If there *was* one there, the plan was clean and simple: The X-wings would target it with a full salvo of proton torpedoes, giving the other ships a chance to run.

The dozen freighters Booster had rounded up came in next with the *Pulsar Skate* in the lead. Moments after reversion they made course corrections to get themselves pointed toward their exit vectors. The *Chir'daki* came in last and split their squadron up so each freighter had a fighter escort. If trouble erupted, the Twi'lek and Gand squadron could reassemble and screen the escaping freighters from any TIEs or other snubfighters, then head out themselves.

Wedge glanced at his screen and saw the names of the various ships in his fleet scroll up. Green letters indicated they were all set to fulfill their part in the mission. *At least we've gotten here in one piece. Now we need Karrde to do his job.*

Booster's grudging respect for Karrde counted for a lot with Wedge. He'd actually met Karrde years earlier, back in the days before he joined the Rebellion. Wedge had owned a freighter and was hauling cargo all over the Empire. Karrde had inquired if Wedge wanted to move some cargo for him, but Wedge had turned down the offer. He'd heard nothing bad about Karrde and that had set him back a bit. *No negative rumors means too little is known about the man, and I wasn't inclined to trust him as a result.*

Since joining the Rebellion, Wedge had not run across Karrde, but he didn't doubt Karrde's ability to produce the weapons and equipment they needed. *The fact that Booster went to him first is proof enough that Karrde is genuine and can be trusted to deal straight with his clients.* The munitions, launchers, and sensor systems would give them what they needed to complete Isard's downfall.

"Lead, this is Seven."

"Go ahead, Tycho."

"Wedge, I'm getting anomalous contacts from the Graveyard on my IFF frequency."

Wedge frowned. The Identify Friend/Foe system involved the identification beacon all ships carried. It sent out a signal that other ships picked up, telling them the name of the ship and its identification designation. Smugglers often had two or three IFF modules that they could swap in and out to run under clean names. Contacts on the IFF frequency were simple rechecks of a ship's identity. *And if Imps are waiting in the asteroids it's an unbelievably stupid way to tip us to their presence.*

"Tycho, is it the same signal over and over again?"

"Seems so. You thinking an automated beacon of some sort?"

"You *are* running an Alderaanian code. Perhaps there is

an old system traffic satellite in the asteroids wanting to check you for Alderaan control."

"Probably. I'll punch up the gain on my passive sensors and see if I find anything in that direction."

"I copy." Wedge looked at his main screen as Mynock began beeping again. "Heads up, people, we have incoming traffic."

A string of freighters entered the system, led by a ship tagged *Starry Ice* by the IFF system. A half-dozen ships drifted in behind *Ice,* staggering their positions so strafing runs along any one particular vector would pick up only two targets. Because Karrde's ships were bigger than most of the freighters Booster had collected, the smuggler only needed half as many to deliver his goods.

A man's voice broke in on the comm channel. "This is Quelev Tapper for Karrde. We've gotten the initial payment for this lot and you've got fifty million credits still in your account. In another month we should have another thirty percent of your order ready."

Booster responded to him over the comm channel. "Fine with us. Begin the transfer."

One of the freighters began to move forward, but as it cruised in right below the *Ice,* a huge patch of space went from black and star-strewn to white, angular, and deadly. The Interdictor Cruiser's bulk eclipsed a massive slice of the Graveyard. The sight of its quartet of domed gravity well projectors caused Wedge's stomach to fold in on itself. *The cruiser will stop us from running into hyperspace, but it's far too weak to engage us by itself. It's going to be carrying a dozen TIEs at best, and the freighters can maneuver out of the effective range of its guns. Going after two squadrons of snubfighters, half of us with proton torpedoes, means this cruiser has gotten itself into a fight it really can't win.*

Before Wedge could begin to issue orders, two things happened. The first, the lighting-up of a red warning light on his console, was something he expected. It told him that the Interdictor Cruiser had powered up the gravity well projectors and that none of the ships in the system could jump to hyperspace to escape. *Not a wise move to trap us here.*

The second thing squeezed an icy fist around his heart. One third larger than the Interdictor Cruiser, the *Corrupter* appeared to interpose its bulk between the cruiser *Aggregator* and the snubfighters. Its turbolaser batteries and ion cannons immediately began spraying green-and-blue energy bolts out toward the waiting freighters. Wedge knew instantly the barrage was untargeted, meant more to inspire panic than do damage.

As TIE fighters started pouring from the Destroyer's belly, Wedge immediately started snapping orders to his people. "Booster, scatter freighters. Move! Tal'dira, give me a flight to orient on me and another to orient on Tycho. Use the others to vape those TIEs, but don't close with *Corrupter*. Rogues, slave your torpedo targeting to my signal. Transmitting now. Tycho, I go first, then you follow."

"I copy, Wedge."

Wedge's droid, Mynock, shrieked furiously as Wedge punched the throttle forward and drove straight at the *Victory II*-class Star Destroyer. "Shut up, Mynock. Distract me with your screaming, and we'll both end up dead!" The droid fell silent, and Wedge promised himself that if he survived the run, he would get the droid's memory wiped and rename it something suitably heroic.

Though the droid lacked courage, his assessment of the current situation was dead on. *And worth screaming about.* The Destroyer and cruiser carried, between them, three squadrons of TIEs. Wedge's confidence in his people knew no limits, but the Rogues were standing off to shoot their proton torpedoes, which left the Twi'leks to fight against the TIEs. The chances that some TIEs would get through to harass the freighters were overwhelming.

The TIE threat was the least of the problems they faced in the system. The only way to counter the *Corrupter*'s threat was for the X-wings to hit it with a spread of proton torpedoes. The squadron, firing double shots, could pump out twenty-two proton torpedoes. *If* they hit—and missing a nearly kilometer-long ship was tough—they could blow through the shields and do some damage. Wedge would fly in close to target the ship for the first volley, then have Tycho follow up for a second, hopefully catching the *Corrupter* without shields in place. *If the second spread hits the Star Destroyer in an unshielded area, it could rip it apart. We'll get damage on the first spread, but it will be the second that knocks it out.*

Wedge pushed all power to his forward shields as he hit a wall of TIE fighters six kilometers out from the *Corrupter*. Once past them he evened his shields out with a flick of his thumb and then started draining his lasers of energy and pumping it into his shields. At two and a half kilometers he would get a firing solution for the *Corrupter*. He'd hold it until his squadron had launched, launch himself, then pull up and out. "Coming up on targeting. On my mark. Five, four, three, two, one. Get ready."

The targeting reticle on his head-up display went red. "Mark!" Wedge pulled the trigger on his stick, launching two proton torpedoes. Launch report after launch report from his squadron scrolled up on his screen. *Hey, even the Gands got off two concussion missiles.*

Preparing to break off and run, Wedge glanced at his sensors and saw four TIEs in his rear arc. Realizing that pulling up and away would allow them to pounce on him, Wedge rolled his X-wing to port, then took the snubfighter down in a long loop that would carry him below the *Corrupter*'s hull. *If they want to come after me, they get to brave their own fire, too.* Juking right and left, Wedge bounced the fighter back and forth between streams of turbolaser fire.

A brilliant incandescence blossomed above him. The proton torpedoes slammed into the *Corrupter*'s shields all along the ship's length. The shields acted like huge, invisible parasols to ward off the fierce energy unleashed by the proton torpedoes' detonations. Roiling plasma curved up and around, following the arc of the *Corrupter*'s port shields as if some energy creature were trying to take a bite out of the ship. Then several torpedoes arrived late and pierced the shield at its heart, causing it to collapse. The tardy torpedoes and two concussion missiles pounded the destroyer's hull, blasting apart armor plates and crushing turbolaser batteries.

"Beginning my run now!"

Wedge felt a moment's joy at the collapse of the *Corrupter*'s shields, but it died as the big ship began to maneuver. It rotated in space above him, executing a roll that swapped up for down and presented the squadron with its undamaged starboard shields as a target. *Convarion knows we have a limited supply of proton torpedoes. If he survived this salvo, we've got one last shot to take him down. If he repairs his shields and rolls again, we're done, because then he can take all the time he wants to come after us.*

Wedge keyed his comm unit. "Corran, set up for the third run."

"I copy, Wedge. Lots of eyeballs out here."

"Here, too." Wedge pulled back on his stick and brought his X-wing up between the *Aggregator* and the *Corrupter*. He got a good look at the damage the torpedoes had done to the Destroyer and saw fire in the ship's interior. He knew bulkheads had already been sealed and the fires would go out as soon as the atmosphere drained away. *So it's time to see if I can add to the problem.* He started to angle in at the *Corrupter,* but green laser bolts slashed past him from behind, causing him to break off the run, roll, and dive.

Tycho's voice boomed over the comm unit. "On my mark. Five, four, three, two, one. Get into firing position."

Right. The pair of TIEs on Wedge's tail had no intention of letting him set up on the *Corrupter.* Wedge chopped his throttle back, then reversed his thrust and ran it up to full. The TIE fighters immediately closed and snapped off quick shots, then bypassed him. Hitting the right rudder pedal, Wedge brought the X-wing's nose around on the track of one of them. Switching over to quad-fire lasers, he hit the trigger. Three of the bolts hit the TIE. Two lanced through the cockpit while one boiled away a corner of a solar panel. The fighter immediately went into a flat spin and arced out toward the system's outer orbits.

More rudder brought the X-wing around to point back up at the *Corrupter.* Wedge killed his reverse thrust and started it forward as Tycho said, "Mark! Fire now!" Wedge thumbed his fire control over to missiles and got a lock, but never pulled the trigger. *Sithspawn! What is that?*

A ship the size of a *Carrack*-class light cruiser ranged up from the Graveyard, cutting in past the *Aggregator*'s stern and in at the *Corrupter*'s bridge. The ship's white nose was separated from the bloodred after portion by a big black stripe slashed on the diagonal across it. Wedge realized he'd seen that color scheme on a ship before, but he didn't connect it with Tycho's X-wing until the cruiser opened up on the *Corrupter* with its weaponry.

Five heavy turbolasers and ten laser cannons poured scarlet energy into the Destroyer's unshielded hull. The laser cannon shots skittered across the white surface, stippling it with black marks and exploding turbolaser batteries. The heavy turbolasers concentrated their fire on the Destroyer's tower, burning through the hull on deck after deck.

Wedge kicked his thrust in at full and rolled his X-wing so he put the Graveyard over his head and the Destroyer's hull beneath his fighter. Off his starboard S-foils a silvery glow built as the first of the proton torpedoes hit. The energy storm they created splashed up and around the edges of the shield. Wedge pushed the X-wing lower, skimming it along the Destroyer's hull. *Just like being back in the trenches.*

Wedge jinked the ship as turbolasers and the starfighter behind him tried to target him, then hauled back on his stick. The aiming reticle for his proton torpedoes had burned red for the entirety of his flight, but Wedge held back until his true target sank down into the reticle. He saw one Imperial officer standing in the middle of the bridge viewport and watched his mouth open in surprise.

Wedge hit the trigger.

A pair of proton torpedoes stabbed through the transparisteel viewport, filling the bridge with blue fire, then detonated. The bridge's blocky outline plumped and softened for a second before the aft port corner blew out, vomiting golden fire. Backblast sent smaller golden geysers back out through the forward viewports, but Wedge pulled up between them, then rolled and dove past the Destroyer's aft.

"Tycho, hit the cruiser!"

"I copy. On me, Rogues. Beginning my run now."

Coming up over the belly of the Destroyer Wedge got a

good look at the battle. Sporadic turbolaser and ion cannon fire came from the *Corrupter*, but far more numerous were the escape pods exploding from its hull. The *Aggregator* tried to shoot at the snubfighters, but most were using the dying Destroyer as a shield as they approached, and the *Aggregator*'s commander seemed reluctant to shoot in that direction.

The light cruiser came back around and made a run across the *Aggregator*'s stern. The ships exchanged fire, but the Interdictor Cruiser could only bring a few of its weapons to bear on the other ship. Neither ship did significant damage to the other, though the *Aggregator*'s starboard shields did go down.

"On my mark, launch torpedoes. Mark."

On Tycho's command the X-wings launched their missiles. Blue pinpoints of fire blossomed from various points around the Graveyard and shot in at the Interdictor Cruiser. The red light on Wedge's console went out as the ship's commander shunted power from the gravity well projectors to his shields. *That's the move to make, but did he do it in time?*

Most of the proton torpedoes, beginning with the two Tycho launched, slammed into the port shield. They exploded into a silvery firestorm that billowed up and out, then pressed in on the shield. Unlike the *Corrupter*'s shield, however, the *Aggregator*'s did not collapse all at once. Gaps appeared at a couple of points, allowing a handful of torpedoes to skip through and blast into the ship's hull. Armor plates peeled away like dead, dry skin and secondary explosions ripped gaping holes in the Interdictor's hull.

Without waiting to pick up TIE fighters or escape pods, the *Aggregator* suddenly jetted forward. On Wedge's console, the range finder scrolled off numbers; then the cruiser vanished into hyperspace. *Running was his only choice.*

Wedge glanced at his sensors and saw no hostile fighters near him. Safe for the moment, he keyed his comm unit. "Tapper, don't run very far. Booster, report on your fleet."

"We're all still here, Wedge. We took some hits from TIEs, but shields mostly held so we're all operational."

"I copy, Booster. Rogues and *Chir'daki*, protect yourselves, but hold back from killing anyone who isn't being actively hostile for a moment." Wedge glanced back over his shoulder. "Mynock, scan comm frequencies and get me the command frequency the TIEs are using. I also need the escape pod frequency."

The droid's muted beep acknowledged the command, and data began to scroll up on the main screen.

"Thanks." He punched up the frequency for the TIE fighters. "Imperial pilots, this is Wedge Antilles. You have a choice: get killed here, stranded here, or surrender. If you want to surrender, power down your weapons and engines. If you're moving under power we will consider you hostile. We've got no more reason to want you dead than I would hope you have to be dead."

A lone male voice came back over the comm unit. "Captain Ardle from *Corrupter* here. We're Thyferran Home Defense Corps pilots. Does that make a difference in your offer?"

"Is Erisi Dlarit flying with you?"

"No, sir. I was in her command, but was picked to head up one of the two squadrons coming here with the *Corrupter*. Mostly trainees. I've got eight left. The *Aggregator*'s squadron only has four left and they're THDC, too."

"I copy, Captain Ardle. Follow the instructions I gave you and you'll not be hurt."

"What about the escape pods?"

"We'll recover them, too."

"And the *Corrupter*?"

Wedge switched his main screen to a plot of ship positions in the system over time and set his viewpoint from within the Graveyard. "The *Corrupter* is currently not under power and is drifting down into the Graveyard. Inside two hours the Graveyard's asteroids will chew it up into unrecognizable bits."

"Oh." Ardle sounded subdued. "Alderaan has its revenge on the Empire."

"And exacts revenge for Halanit. We don't have the tractor beams to pull it back up, and I sincerely doubt it could be made operational again. Running as fast as possible to Coruscant we couldn't get anything back here in time to save it."

Wedge knew the run to Corellia would be shorter, but he expected no help from his homeworld and the Diktat. "The *Corrupter* is gone."

"I copy, Antilles. I'll give the order to my people, and we'll wait to be rescued."

Wedge switched over to the escape pod frequency and repeated his offer of rescue, then arranged with Quelev Tapper for his ships to pick up as many pods as they could and exact whatever ransom they wanted from the passengers. Tapper sounded more interested in getting the TIEs and their pilots, but Wedge declared them "prisoners of war" and refused to let Tapper have them.

"Okay, Antilles, I'll let it go, but only because I know you'll be buying spare parts for those TIEs from us before too long."

"That's probably truer than I'd like to admit, Tapper. Have a safe trip home."

Tycho's voice broke through on the comm frequency. "Wedge, I have a situation."

"Yes?"

"Remember that cruiser that took a piece out of the *Corrupter*?"

"Kind of hard to forget it, isn't it?"

"Well, it was the source of the IFF queries earlier on. It appears to think I'm the *Another Chance*. It has identified itself as the *Valiant*, and now it wants to know where we're going to go from here."

Wedge brought his X-wing around so he could see the light cruiser again. There it hung in space, three hundred meters of lethal starship. *Having it as part of our fleet would be very good, but how can we convince it to join us?* "Tycho, any sign of intelligent life on board?"

"Ah, Wedge, it thinks I'm an Alderaanian war frigate, so I think we can rule out intelligence. If I had to guess, I'd assume this cruiser was slaved to *Another Chance* as an escort. They got separated and it returned here to wait for *Another Chance* to show up. I arrived with the IFF code, started broadcasting targeting information, and it did its job."

Wedge nodded. "I copy. I think I need you to take it back

to our base. Emtrey, if I recall his introductory monologue, is supposed to know the rules, regs, and procedures of over six million military organizations past and present. Perhaps he can figure out a way to communicate with the *Valiant* so we can make full use of it."

"Got it. Do I leave now, or wait and escort the rest of you back?"

"We'll go together." Wedge smiled. "Victory like this deserves a parade, and I'd be happy to have you and your cruiser in the lead."

25

Corran Horn dropped into the seat beside Mirax at the black round table in the briefing room. He felt bone weary from the fight at Alderaan, which surprised him because he'd actually not shot down any of the eyeballs. Because he had been waiting for fire orders to send proton torpedoes at the larger ships, all he could do was evade their attacks. While the pilots had been clearly green—a fact that 66 percent losses on their part made abundantly clear—their lasers still burned hot and could have vaped him had he not outflown them.

He took Mirax's left hand in his right beneath the edge of the table. "Sorry I couldn't cover the *Skate* out there."

Mirax gave him a smile that helped energize him. "I'd have felt safer, but that would have spoiled Booster 'One-Man-Army' Terrik's fun. He manned the laser cannon and was a general hazard to any eyeball peeking at us. He says he winged a couple of them."

Corran gave her hand a squeeze, then looked up and saw Booster glowering at him from the other side of the table. *If looks were lasers, he'd be more than winging me right now.* "I'm glad there weren't more in the way of complications. Your father looks ready to rip something apart with his bare hands—like me."

"Being ambushed by Imps has him in a bad mood. We'll be heading out soon for a meeting with Talon Karrde concerning security."

"The leak came from his people?"

Mirax nodded. "My father thinks so. I want you to look over some stuff on it for me—give me your professional opinion about this spy thing."

"Ah, sure, Mirax, glad to, but you should remember from the Erisi thing, I'm not that sharp on spotting spies."

"This one isn't that good." Mirax gave him a wink. "Let me know what you think. We'll see if Karrde concurs."

Wedge and Winter entered the room, followed closely by Tal'dira, Aril Nunb, and Tycho. Winter sat down at the datapad built in at the far end of the table and hit some keys. A holographic image of the Yag'Dhul station hovered over the holopad in the center of the oval table. Wedge took a position at the head of the table, Tycho sat between him and Booster, and Tal'dira took the seat at Booster's left hand. The Sullustan seated herself to Mirax's right, facing Tal'dira.

Wedge covered a yawn, then leaned forward on the end of the table. "I apologize for asking you here to this debriefing so quickly after your return, but I want to talk about what happened in the Graveyard while details are still fresh in our minds. We have two issues to discuss: the arrival of the Imps and what to do with the *Valiant*.

"Before that, however, I want to thank each of you for your action and the action of your people at Alderaan. There is no question about it—we got very lucky at Alderaan. The *Valiant*'s appearance and action hurt both the *Corrupter* and the *Aggregator*. Even so, it was the discipline of our people that provided us the opportunity for such luck to come into play. If it weren't for your *Chir'daki* pilots covering Tycho and me on our runs, we wouldn't have been able to do what we did to either Imp ship."

The Twi'lek's braintails twitched strongly. "Your praise is most appreciated, Wedgan'tilles. The loss of two of my pilots is grave, but nothing in comparison to what all of us would have lost were our leadership not so clear thinking in a time of trouble."

Tycho nodded in agreement. "It was your torps that vaped the *Corrupter*, Wedge. Zraii's going to waste a lot of paint adding it to your display of kills."

Wedge shook his head. "Look, your shots hurt it, I was just in a position to pinpoint a target. Imps have forever dismissed the threat our torps are to their ships. You'd think, after losing two Death Stars to X-wings they'd learn, but their ignorance is our margin of safety."

Corran smiled. "So you'll order Zraii to pull the kill from your X-wing?"

Wedge hesitated, then smiled sheepishly. "Let's not go too far—it *was* a good pair of shots." His eyes narrowed. "Convarion got what he deserved, especially in getting the tables turned on him. The fact that he was able to show up, *and* had an Interdictor Cruiser with him is most disturbing. Winter, any idea where the *Aggregator* came from?"

Winter tucked a lock of white hair back behind her left ear, then hit several keys on the datapad. The image floating above the table shifted from that of the station to the triangular form of an Interdictor Cruiser. "The *Aggregator* was last noted as part of an anti-Rebel taskforce led by High Admiral Teradoc. Intelligence on him—at least the intel I'm able to access from here—is sketchy. Most of his duty stations were Rimward. He was diligent in his duties and virulently anti-Rebel, but beyond that unremarkable. He was *not* at Endor and remained nominally loyal to the Empire until Coruscant fell."

As nearly as Corran knew, Teradoc's history was not unique. A few brave individuals declared themselves Warlords as soon as they heard of the Emperor's death, but many of the others—especially those in the military—remained loyal to the Empire. Sate Pestage, an Imperial Advisor, held power for six months until a cabal of Imperial Advisors ousted him from power. Most of the military backed this group because it seemed disposed to taking action. It was only after Ysanne Isard supplanted them that members of the military began to grab for power themselves. Even so, a fair number of military leaders and politicians proclaimed their loyalty to the Empire until Coruscant fell.

At which point they had to fend for themselves, since they no longer had access to the bureaucracy that made the Empire run. While there were administrative areas and sectors that held themselves together—a tribute to the resourcefulness of their Grand Moffs—Corran expected that within two years nearly three-quarters of what had once been the Empire would be under the New Republic's control.

Winter looked up from the datapad. "If I had to guess how Isard got her hands on the *Aggregator,* I would guess she traded bacta for it. The fact that the *Aggregator*'s TIEs were being flown by Thyferran Home Defense Corps pilots suggests that Teradoc is running low on trained personnel. With a supply of bacta he can keep them alive a bit longer. Without unlimited Imperial resources, he's having to conserve people the way we did."

Booster narrowed his eyes, both electronic and natural. "I'd also read into the pilot change a lack of confidence by Teradoc in Isard. Right now you have to figure that Teradoc is getting gigabytes of stories from the *Aggregator*'s crew about how we ambushed the ambushers. I think if I have my people start asking around what someone is willing to pay for a slightly used Interdictor Cruiser, word will get back to Teradoc. He'll assume we're suggesting we're planning on capturing the next one he loans to Isard, so he won't be free with his ship."

Wedge nodded. "That's worth a try. From this point forward we're going to have to assume, however, that it is possible another Interdictor Cruiser could jump us. Actually, we have to assume it is probable that we might be jumped again. We'll continue hit-and-run attacks and will just have to make our exchanges more covert. We can do that by having the incoming freighters guided to a location of our choosing, which means they won't know where they're going until the last minute."

Mirax raised her right hand. "Perhaps you can't remember back when you were hauling cargo, but I'd never go to a rendezvous without knowing where it was."

"Good point, but I suspect Quelev Tapper can convince Karrde that we're trustworthy."

Booster laughed. "Continue paying in advance, and Karrde will believe it."

"That we'll do." Wedge straightened up. "Remember, we've now eliminated one of Isard's four ships."

"Sure," Corran sighed, "but it was the smallest of them all."

"Agreed, but Ait Convarion was probably the most aggressive of the commanders Isard had working for her. He knew how to fight a Star Destroyer—what chances you could take with it and what chances you couldn't. He expected us to scatter and we didn't, which is why he died. The commanders of the larger ships are likely to be more conservative." Wedge smiled. "The Empire's boldest Admirals died at Yavin. Regardless, both *Avarice* and *Virulence* are the newer-model *Imperial*-class Star Destroyers, deuces—so they carry six squadrons of TIEs. No matter how good or bad their commanders are, they can overwhelm us."

Corran smiled. "With targets."

"Yes, but targets that shoot back." Wedge shook his head. "Impstar deuces have a crew of nearly forty-six thousand people, if you count the troops they carry in the mix. They have a lot of fire power. Granted that it's not terribly well suited for use against snubfighter squadrons, but an Impstar deuce will take a lot more pounding than a victim like the *Corrupter* before it goes away."

Tycho nodded. "The one thing we have going for us in this regard is that a big ship has a lot more things that can go wrong with it than a smaller ship—maintaining our X-wings is easy compared to maintaining an Impstar deuce. Isard is going to have to be using them to run with convoys, and if we keep hitting them, the Impstars are going to have to be on a near constant state of alert. That will take its toll."

"But will they wear out before you do?" Mirax looked from Wedge to Tycho, Tal'dira, and finally Corran. "Even before this last operation, you were pushing yourselves very hard. Tycho's right, repairing an X-wing is easier than repairing a Star Destroyer, and I don't doubt we can do things to spike the prices on crucial parts for Isard's ships by buying them up ourselves, but replacing any of you or your people is going to be impossible."

Corran knew that she was asking the right question, but she was missing clues to the answer. "One advantage we have, Mirax, is that Isard's forces have to react to us. They always have to suppose we're out there, whereas we only have to deal with them when we *are* out there. It will be rougher on them than it is on us. We can't keep this up forever, but we won't have to." He looked at Wedge. "Right, Commander?"

"I hope so, Corran." Wedge folded his arms across his chest. "I like the idea of buying up some critical parts. Turbolaser focal lenses, power couplers, and the like. Better yet if we can find junk and get it to the other side, that would help a lot."

"I'll see what I can do on that count, Wedge."

"Thanks, Booster." Wedge frowned. "I also gather you're going to speak to Karrde about how the Imps found us at Alderaan?"

A braintail twitched its way toward the center of the table. "How do we know the information was not transmitted from our side to Isard's people?"

Booster looked over at Tal'dira. "Our freighters were slaved for the jumps to the *Skate*. I didn't tell my people where we were going. Wedge told you fighter jocks where we were going in your mission briefing, but that was only forty-eight hours before the run. The *Aggregator* was given over to Isard five days before the strike, and the pilots on it were run through mission-specific briefings about twelve hours after the ship arrived. Karrde had the information about our run a good two standard weeks before that, which means the data squirted from his people to the Imps."

"Besides, if one of Booster's people betrayed us, Isard would have showed up here with the *Lusankya*." Corran tapped a finger against the tabletop. "Presumably, that's information Karrde doesn't have."

"Nor information he'll get from me *or* my people." Booster snarled directly at Corran. "My people are good people, Horn. Decidedly trustworthy."

Aril Nunb chittered in Sullustan for a second, then translated to Basic. "Booster, Corran did not mean to suggest your people are untrustworthy—he stated as much by noting we were not attacked here."

"I know what he was implying, Captain Nunb." Booster's frown deepened. "He's CorSec, through and through, *and* a Horn on top of that. He assumes no one who's ever moved a little contraband can be trusted."

Corran wanted to protest that he hadn't meant what Booster thought he did, but he had to admit to himself that, deep down, he was suspicious of the smugglers Booster had working on hauling supplies for them. *In the past it would have been simply because they were smugglers, and anyone who has once crossed the border between lawful and lawless is likely to do it again and again. Because of that, they can't be trusted, at least they can't from the point of view of someone who is lawful. Now, because I'm an outlaw, I know that isn't exactly true, but I didn't suspect Erisi until too late, primarily because she was one of us. Because that fact made me blind to her treachery, I want to avoid falling into that same trap again.*

He looked over at Booster. *Of course, he'll never believe that.*

Wedge rapped a knuckle on the table. "Enough, Booster. Aril's right, and no matter *what* Corran might or might not think about your people, I know it's nothing you've not already thought a dozen times over about each of them. We're in a tenuous situation here, and caution is vital for all of us. The fact is that the leak probably did come through Karrde's people. Booster, I want you to sort that out with him."

"Consider it done."

"Good. You'll let me know what Karrde says." Wedge looked up at Winter. "Last topic: the *Valiant.* Any luck in learning anything about it?"

"A lot of luck, actually." Winter smiled heartily. "The *Valiant* is an Alderaanian *Thranta*-class War Cruiser. All of them were supposed to have been destroyed when Alderaan disarmed, but it seems as if *Valiant* and two other War Cruisers—*Courage* and *Fidelity*—were refitted with robotic controls and slaved to accept commands from *Another Chance*. They were its escorts. One of them would fly into the system before it, another would fly with it, and the third would take another course to draw off pursuit. The trio of ships would change off, and some of the damage on the exterior of the ship suggests it ran off more than one pirate raid on *Another Chance*. If Emtrey can talk it into opening up its logs we'll be able to confirm that idea."

Wedge gave her a big grin. "That's a lot of information for so little time to research the ship."

Winter's hair spread out in a white veil across her shoulders as she shook her head. "Most of it is information I remember from reading histories when I was younger and by correlating little bits of data I picked up in the Organa household or when I worked with Princess Leia aiding her father. When the *Another Chance* was recovered, it was clear that a massive power surge had fried circuits, including the controllers for the external communication arrays that allowed ship-to-ship communication. Since *Valiant* queried Tycho's X-wing when it broadcast the *Another Chance*'s IFF code, and followed his lead in picking targets, the *Valiant* was clearly assigned to protect the *Another Chance*. Three War Cruisers and a War Frigate frequently comprised a patrol in the Alderaanian fleet, so I concluded there must have been three War Cruisers. The *Valiant* and the other two were the last three built in that class, were commissioned, and then were immediately decommissioned. Unlike the other ships the Alderaanians had used in the Clone Wars—which were scrapped and melted down into peace medals that were presented to the crews and surviving families as mementos—there were no records of scraps being sent out to crews. Nor are there records of crews having served on them, so I have concluded that they were immediately refitted with droids to accompany the War Frigate *Another Chance*."

Booster's jaw hung open. "You remembered all that and figured it all out?"

Mirax laughed. "Winter has a holographic memory. She

remembers everything she sees, hears, or experiences, including that dumb look you're giving her."

Booster snapped his mouth shut, then shook his head. "Then remember this: Never have children."

Wedge snorted out a quick laugh. "Crumbs don't fall far from the Hutt's mouth, Booster."

"Thanks a lot, Wedge." Mirax gave him a hard stare, but softened it with a smile.

"Sorry, Mirax. Winter, what are the chances that *Courage* and *Fidelity* are still out there?"

"Won't have any way of estimating that until we get a look at *Valiant*'s inner workings. Emtrey thinks he can find a way in, and he now has Whistler helping him slice some code. Zraii is nearly shedding his carapace over a chance to work on the *Valiant*, so my guess is that they'll have it open and functioning to our satisfaction within a couple of weeks."

"That's something, then." Wedge glanced at Booster. "You want the *Valiant*, or is it too small for you?"

"I'm sure you can find someone else who is better suited to commanding it." Booster forced a yawn. "Overseeing a crew of droids would be more boring than I care to imagine. You should give the job to that protocol droid of yours."

Corran laughed. Trying to visualize Emtrey on the bridge of a ship issuing commands produced ridiculous images in his mind. "By the time he informed his crew of his qualifications, they'd mutiny."

Wedge and the others who had worked with Emtrey joined Corran in laughter. Wedge ended his laugh with a cough, then cleared his throat. "I think Emtrey is better suited to be an Executive Officer, not a Commander. I do think, however, we've got someone who has the skills we need and could get more out of a droid crew than anyone else." He reached out with his right hand and touched Aril Nunb on her left shoulder. "You've flown more than fighters. Interested in commanding a War Cruiser?"

Her deep red eyes widened in surprise, then she nodded. "That's a job I can handle. I may need Emtrey to help me."

"He's all yours." Wedge gave her a nod, then smiled at the others. "Okay, I think we've got some directions in which we can head and some operations to plan. We got lucky this time, but from here on out, we manufacture luck. The good we'll keep and the bad will go to Isard. She missed her best chance to kill us off, and I see no reason to give her another one."

26

The apathetic mask Fliry Vorru had fitted onto his face cracked. He'd managed to keep his expression utterly impassive as Ysanne Isard dressed down Erisi Dlarit. Both women had maintained rigid control at first, wielding civility and titles with razor-kiss efficacy. Polite phrasings bottled up vitriol; but Vorru knew if he'd tossed a pair of lightsabers between them, they'd have minced each other in a nanosecond.

Then Ysanne Isard had said, "High Admiral Teradoc has withdrawn the *Aggregator* from my service and that is *your* fault!"

Erisi exploded. "*My* fault? What algorithm did you use to calculate that conclusion? *Sir.*"

"The calculations were simple enough that I would have thought *any* provincial mind could have grasped them." Isard's eyes narrowed as her hands balled into fists. "*Your* pilots were on both the *Aggregator* and the *Corrupter*. It was your pilots who were supposed to deal with the snubfighter threat. They failed, costing me the *Corrupter* and now making me the laughingstock of the galaxy. Teradoc had the gall to say to me that he'd only lend me toys if I would promise they would not return broken! The Emperor would have had his guts for floss over such a remark. Because of you, I am subject to such indignities!"

"Begging your pardon, but the orders placing *my* pilots on those ships came from *you*. I asked you to use our Elite pilots for the mission, but you picked a green unit."

"Their evaluations—reports *you* prepared—were outstanding."

"Yes, but they'd not seen combat before." Erisi's blue eyes burned intensely. "You sent them out after a unit that is arguably the best fighter squadron in the galaxy."

Isard raised an eyebrow. "Even with your participation no longer needed or welcome?"

The sniped quip seemed to pass unnoticed by Dlarit, but Vorru had no doubt she'd cataloged it. "My Elite Squadron is the equal of Rogue Squadron. If you had sent us after them, Teradoc would be prostrate before you, begging you to accept his allegiance. He is laughing because you destroyed three squadrons, because you didn't heed the warning he offered by refusing to send his own pilots against Antilles."

Vorru saw Isard preparing for a counterargument and knew if Isard were not checked Erisi might pay with her life for her frank audacity. In the space of a heartbeat, he examined his options. If he said nothing, Isard would destroy Erisi Dlarit, throwing the Dlarit family into further disrepute. The fact that the Ashern had humiliated her father clearly fueled her desire for retribution on the forces arrayed against the Bacta Cartel. She had wanted to fly on the mission to Alderaan, but Isard had refused that request. To turn around and then blame Erisi for the mission's failure was frustrating enough that Erisi might wish for death.

Intervening on her behalf would open him to Isard's wrath, but the price might be worth it. Erisi and her family still had considerable influence within the Bacta Cartel. If Isard had to be removed, having Erisi as an ally might make such an operation possible and certainly would smooth over the consequences of it on Thyferra. *I could even claim to the New Republic that I joined Isard specifically to work against her from the inside like this.* The idea that the New Republic would have to accept him as the leader of the new Bacta Cartel broadened the grin Erisi's defiance had put on his face.

"I think, Madam Director, you cannot discount the fact that the Rogues clearly had planned ahead against the eventuality of betrayal. Granted an Alderaanian War Cruiser is an antiquated ship, but coupled with the X-wing squadron's strength, it was enough to make Captain Convarion pay for his recklessness."

Isard rotated her head around to glance at him over her shoulder. "You presume Convarion made a mistake to blind me to the fact that *if* our operation was betrayed to Antilles, it was doubtless through a spy you have failed to locate."

Vorru caught Erisi's eye, and in a moment he felt he had earned her gratitude. Part of him began to list the various ways she could make it more manifest. Because of her beauty and strength, the idea of a physical union to consummate their alliance in opposition to Isard came to mind, but he dismissed it. He had no doubt it could happen—and might well happen yet—but their need for each other had higher purposes than sating lust. *If we are to be allies, our first conjunction must be full of purpose and confirmed by reason, not dictated and muddled by emotional involvement.*

Vorru knew he could fall victim to Erisi's charms, because she realized that it was possible to play to his vanity and desperation. He had always been vain, but he had kept it in check. His age attacked both his vanity and ambition, reminding himself that he had little time to accomplish all the goals he had set out for his life. His time on Kessel had gotten him no closer to the heights he had once seen as his due, and now he knew that unless he acted quickly, his chances of even approaching them would wither and die.

"That possibility cannot be discounted, of course, Madam Director—nor can it be proven, as you are well aware. The fact is that Antilles has been very cautious throughout his career. That he has lived this long is ample proof of that. The precaution taken against our interference could have been nothing more than a concern over whether or not he could trust his trading partner."

Isard turned so she could watch both him and Erisi. "Yes, his trading partner. I want Karrde dealt with."

Vorru shook his head. "Under no circumstances. If we treat Talon Karrde any differently than we do now, he will realize we have an agent among his people, and we lose a very valuable resource. Moreover, Karrde's loyalty can be bought. We will have him when, if, and however we want him."

He opened his hands. "As for your assertion that Commander Dlarit is to blame for the failures of her pilots, this, too, is disingenuous. Her pilots were inappropriately matched against Rogue Squadron. Captain Convarion always believed the appearance of his vessel would strike terror into the hearts of his enemies. He expected them to panic and run precisely because they ran the first time he ambushed them. Antilles has not lived this long by repeating mistakes. Convarion should have insisted on having the best pilots possible flying with him. He did not, because he assumed their contribution to his victory would be incidental."

Isard brought her head up. "Ah, well, then it seems I am wrong about everything!" The rising ironic tone in her voice did nothing to hide her anger. "Perhaps you would like to tell me how things are going to go from now on and what we should do about them."

Vorru smiled and took a half step toward Isard as he turned to face her. "I would guess, despite the possession of the War Cruiser, Antilles and his people will continue their"—he glanced at Erisi—"as the pilots so colorfully put it, 'hit-and-hype' raids. In actuality you've seen those raids are minimally effective. I would imagine they will also try to infiltrate some of the tanker crews so they can hijack more shipments. Our losses—and we will have some—should be minimal."

Isard's eyes half-closed. "*Minimal* losses to us will still be enough to let them finance their war against us."

"True, but the fact is that time runs in our favor, not theirs. We have a number of ways to deal with them, but their threat will not be ended until we locate their base and destroy it."

Isard pressed two fingers against her lips for a moment.

"The elimination of their base has always been the way to deal with them. What other plans do you have in mind?"

Vorru smiled hesitantly. "The prime method of eliminating their ability to fight against us is for us to open up our storage wells and make an abundance of bacta available."

"No!" Erisi and Ysanne looked at each other in surprise as their joint denunciation of that suggestion echoed loudly through the room. Isard shook her head. "That would kill the price of bacta and loosen the dependency of others upon us."

"Agreed, but we can survive the momentary weakness, Rogue Squadron cannot. The strength of the bacta price is their strength. Take it away, and they are left penniless. Karrde won't speak with them. They will be unable to maintain their spacecraft and will no longer appear to be friends worth protecting. Make bacta abundant, offer a reward to bring Antilles and his people in, and hint that bacta will remain abundant if they *are* captured or betrayed to you and Antilles is done."

Even as he outlined the plan, Vorru knew Isard would reject it. *It is the easiest and most bloodless of the plans needed for getting rid of Antilles. She will reject it because it does not satisfy her sense of revenge. She wants him to suffer, not wither. I doubt she recognizes she should reject it because of the backlash she will suffer among the Xucphra people when their standard of living crashes.*

Isard slowly shook her head. "Antilles has defied me directly and has killed one of my Destroyers. I want him dead, I want Horn dead and the others, but I want them to know I was the hand behind it, not market vagaries. Moreover, relinquished power is power that is not easily recovered. Next."

"The other plan is the current one—a plan that requires vigilance and patience. We keep seeking information and then pounce when we know where he is." Vorru shrugged stiffly. "The problem with this plan is that it is frustrating, since we cannot act until we know where he is based. That could take three months, six, a year."

"Unacceptable." Isard shook her head adamantly. "I am not going to sit back and allow Antilles free rein while I just wait. This situation cannot be allowed to mature further. We need action. I want to kill something, and I want to use *her* pilots to do it." Isard pointed an unwavering finger at Erisi. "If your pilots are truly elite, killing something should not be beneath them."

Vorru felt a cold shiver run down his spine. *Halanit was a disaster, yet she would repeat it.* "Madam Director, a raid right now would be a waste of people, parts, munitions, and goodwill."

"But it will show High Admiral Teradoc and that fool Harssk that they should not trifle with me and laugh at me. And what need have *I* of goodwill? Do I not own all the bacta there is? Others should please *me* with their actions, not seek to be pleased by me."

Vorru held his hands up. "There is no question you have power others would do well to respect, but attacking another place like Halanit will inspire more fear than you want."

Isard gave Vorru a predatory smile, all sharp tooth and pitiless. "But fear is exactly what I want, Minister Vorru. However, I take your point. I will still have my attack, and Commander Dlarit's people will do it, but we'll spare off-worlders for the moment."

She blithely turned her attention on Erisi, and the Thyferran woman paled. "You will plan a mission that punishes the Ashern for their boldness in resisting me. Their antics have been hardly damaging, but I want them to know that to defy me is to court death. Find something—a munitions dump, a rebel camp, a sympathetic village, anything. Find it and destroy it. No warning, no mercy." She smiled. "No question who the true power here is."

27

Mirax Terrik found herself surprised by the delighted smile on Talon Karrde's face. A crescent lined with white teeth split his moustache from his goatee and gave him the rakish air of a space pirate. What surprised her was not that Karrde could smile so handsomely, but that he dared to, given the scowl on her father's face. *Karrde can't be ignorant of my father's temper, so he thinks he's anticipated our trouble.*

Karrde, alone in his cabin, waved both of the Terriks to chairs. "I'll dispense with greetings because I suspect you'd doubt my sincerity after what happened at Alderaan." Karrde came around to the front of his desk, then leaned back on its edge, crossing his long legs.

Mirax sat in the chair she'd been offered, but her father remained standing. He rested his hands on the back of his chair, then leaned forward to bring his eyes down to Karrde's level. Mirax knew the posture well—her father lowered his head like a thirst-mad bantha preparing to sprint to a watering seep. She'd seen other creatures begin to cringe as Booster did that, but Karrde did not.

"Karrde, I've been over the details again and again. I've checked my people." Booster tapped Mirax's shoulder with his thumb. "I've even had her CorSec suitor look some material over to check this out."

Mirax covered her reaction to her father's statement. Booster had asked *her* for advice about making a final check on his security records, and *she* had brought Corran in on it. Booster had not been pleased when he found out that "CorranSec" had gone over things, but he accepted Corran's conclusions. *Now he makes it sound like he solicited Corran's advice. We're going to talk about this.*

Karrde held a hand up. "I know what you're going to say."

"Yeah?"

"I think so." Karrde's eyes actually twinkled. "You'll tell me that the leak to the Imps came from my organization."

Booster's head came up. "You knew?"

"Not before the fact, no. I had no idea. Afterward, though, it was rather obvious." Karrde shrugged. "Melina Carniss sold you out."

Booster straightened up to his full height. "Have you killed her, yet?"

"No. I didn't want to precipitate action that could not be reversed."

Booster chuckled deeply. "You are studying her to find her connection to Isard."

"Actually I wanted to see how far she had spread Isard's influence in my organization; but, yes, I have been watching her." Karrde folded his arms across his chest. "Now that you're here, I thought I would allow you to determine how you want to deal with this situation. Shoving her out into space would probably be the most expedient method of killing her. I heard about a renegade band of Twi'leks who used to run electricity through a vat of bacta, torturing their victims to the point of death, then turning off the electricity and allowing the bacta to heal them up."

Mirax swallowed against the bile rising in her throat. "Easier just to let the word get out that Melina was a binary-agent: She sold the Imp ambush to us just the same way she sold us to Isard. Let the bacta witch deal with her."

Karrde nodded. "I also have a Wookiee in my employ who could . . ."

Booster shook his head. "No, no Wookiees. Armpits are convenient for lifting corpses and moving them to dump sites."

"I'll loan you any weapon you want to deal with her. I have things from all over, including a recently acquired Sith lanvarok that promises to be truly elegant, *if* I've figured out correctly how it's supposed to work." Karrde frowned. "But you're not left-handed, so that will complicate things."

Mirax raised an eyebrow. "You really have a lanvarok?"

"Yes, do you have a buyer?"

"A collector."

"Good."

"And he's left-handed."

"Even better."

"If you will give me details on the lanvarok and authenticate its Sith origins . . ."

Booster cleared his voice. "We have current business to discuss before you get going on this deal."

"Of course, Booster, of course." Karrde smiled. "We can holograph the lanvarok in use and that should help spike the price . . ."

Booster shook his head. "No."

"You prefer another method for dealing with traitors?"

"I do." Booster smiled broadly. "I want you to keep her alive and working."

Karrde frowned. "Why?"

"I have my reasons."

"Not good enough, Booster. You'll have to do better if you want her to stay alive. She betrayed one of my customers to an enemy, causing harm to my customer, my people, and my reputation. She has to die."

Booster's protestations confused Mirax. She looked up at her father. "Why do you want her to live?"

Karrde's eyes narrowed. "I believe, for one thing, your father will suggest that with Carniss still in place, Isard won't try to infiltrate a new spy into my organization."

Booster nodded. "Better the Hutt you have tagged than one you don't."

"Agreed, Booster, but I'm still afraid I can't accommodate you in this."

"What?"

"Oh, please, don't act so incredulous." Karrde shook his head gravely. "I can't have her threatening my customers. It's bad for my reputation and bad for morale and puts me at a serious disadvantage in my business dealings. She's going to die."

"You gave me a choice of how she dies."

"Old age is not one of the options I had in mind." Karrde waved away Booster's comment. "No, she has to die. There is no retreating from this point."

"No?" Booster arched an eyebrow over his artificial eye. "I have more things to buy. I can always take my business elsewhere."

"If I had a credit for every time I heard that sort of empty threat, *I* could buy and sell Thyferra and Isard a dozen times over." Karrde snorted. "I believe our old business is concluded. Now about that lanvarok . . ."

"Don't be so anxious here, Karrde." Booster slowly smiled. "You've got our munitions business already—though that *could* change. This is something more."

"It would have to be special if you expect to buy Melina's life with it."

"I think it is. I was going to give it to Billey—pitch some work his way for old times' sake."

Karrde nodded. "Dravis, the new guy working for him, is good."

"So I've heard, but you're better."

Karrde smiled. "So I've heard."

"Anyway," Booster growled, "I want a gravity well projector."

Mirax covered a smile as Karrde coughed and regarded her father with disbelief. *So you can be surprised, Karrde. Not easily, but possibly.*

"A gravity well projector?" Karrde shook his head. "Billey can't get it for you."

Booster nodded. "It's impossible to get one, I know, but I could use it, and so I thought I'd start asking. If you can't do it . . ."

"Reverse thrust there, Booster. I just said Billey couldn't get it."

"You can?"

Karrde lifted his chin. "Easily."

"Sure. That's the deepest bucket of sithspit I've ever heard being sloshed about."

"I can, and I will, and it will cost you." Karrde's eyes narrowed. "But giving me that purchase order doesn't get you Melina Carniss's life."

Booster smiled. "Does it give me six months of her life?"

Karrde closed his eyes for a moment. "Two months, but she'll be isolated from most of my operations."

"I see. I also need parts for a squadron of TIE fighters. I want some Y-wing ion cannons and circuitry refit kits that will allow me to put the cannons in the starfighters."

"That's custom work. It'll be expensive." Karrde looked at the fingernails on his right hand. "And it will get you another month of Melina's life."

Booster leaned forward, his fingertips digging into the plush cushioning of the chair's back. "Take it out of the money you'll make selling our bacta hauls."

Karrde laughed as he shook his head. "You're selling me bantha hides before you've killed the bantha, Booster."

"I'd ask you to trust me on this one, Karrde, but I know *that* would take more credits than buying Carniss's continued survival." Booster frowned. "We have ops planned that will pull in bacta. Locate the items and wait for us to deliver before you order them. We'll sell the bacta to you at seventy percent of the galactic average price."

"Fifty percent *and* you'll leave the Coruscant market open to me."

The chair's nerfhide covering squeaked as Booster's grip tightened. "The bacta we deliver there is being used to fight the Krytos virus. That's pure charity *and* a stopgap that's preventing the spread of the virus off Coruscant. It's not a profit center."

Karrde's face hardened. "Every place is a profit center, Booster. You know that." He raised a hand to stop Booster's growl from growing into an argument. "I'll donate freely seventy percent of the allocation you'd have delivered to the world, but the other thirty percent I'll use to feed the black market demand. You have to know that you're already losing nearly forty percent to the black market now, after delivery, so I'll get more where you want it to go."

"And that gives me a stay of execution on Melina Carniss?"

Karrde nodded. "Her life is in your hands."

Booster glanced down at the deck, then slowly nodded. "You're a bastard, Karrde."

"Quite possibly, but you know you'd have let me keep thirty-five percent of the bacta to sell on Coruscant if I'd pressed you for it."

Booster's head came up. "Perceptive, too."

"Thank you."

Mirax, who slowly shook off the shock the frank bargaining had sparked in her, frowned. "Why didn't you push for as much as you could get?" Karrde hesitated, and Mirax could see his decision to answer her question was a struggle for him. *He plays things so close to his vest that he's reluctant to let someone else see how he works.*

Some of the amusement drained from Karrde's face. "I'm going to turn the Coruscant black market work over to Billey. I don't think he and Dravis could handle thirty-five percent of the supply you'll bring me. No reason I should give them enough of a supply to allow the bottom to drop out of that market. Thirty percent is enough to suit me and them."

Booster smiled and gave Karrde a nod. "Keep it up and I'll take back the bastard remark."

"What, and make me earn it some other way?"

"Good point. I want to still work with Carniss to set up our rendezvous, but we're going to plan them in a way that will prevent Isard from ambushing us again. I'll give her a circuit of worlds to travel on. When your ships come into a system they'll be told to proceed with the journey, or they'll be met by our people and the exchange will take place. Isard can't cover all those locations *and* her bacta convoys."

Talon Karrde smiled. "A rendezvous circuit, I like it. You know where you'll meet them; and if the system looks wrong, you know where they will go next, so you let them go. Very good."

"I think it will work. It will keep Carniss busy *and* frustrate Isard."

"So you have a use for Carniss in the future?"

"Perhaps." Booster smiled. "How soon can you get me that gravity well projector?"

"A month. Maybe two."

"Good." Booster extended his hand toward Karrde. "I can't say it was a pleasure doing business with you, but I've spent more time doing less with fewer results in the past."

Karrde shook Booster's hand. "It's a good thing you're retired, Booster. I wouldn't like having to split the galaxy between us. Please, don't leave quite yet. I'd offer you my hospitality."

Booster smiled. "And you want to talk to Mirax about the lanvarok."

"Indeed," Karrde laughed, "it's a very good thing you're retired."

28

Iella drew her knees up to her chest and settled her arms around them, then sighed. *Diric would have found this place fascinating.* Softly muted moonlight glowed green through the room's skylight. It managed to make the spare room seem warmer and more inviting, despite the lack of amenities.

Human amenities, she corrected herself. *To the Vratix this would be next to luxury.*

The Vratix who still lived in harvester tribes were scattered over the face of Thyferra, living in villages much akin to the one in which Iella and the Ashern rebels had sought refuge. The buildings themselves were created out of an air-dried mud and saliva mixture that the Vratix slathered on a twig and branch lattice. While not as strong or durable as ferrocrete, the towers and tunnel houses, if unmaintained, could still last as long as five years.

In the past, before the Vratix became civilized, the elemental dissolution of their dwellings would force a migration to a new area, carefully allowing their previous territory to recover from their habitation. Likewise, in the past, the Vratix themselves had provided the saliva and had done the mixing to prepare the mud. Now they used a domesticated branch of a similar species, the knytix, to create the mud for Vratix masons. The knytix, which resembled the Vratix—though smaller, blockier, and less elegant in form—were kept as pets, as work animals, and Iella had heard, as food for special occasions. When she had said she could never eat a pet, a Vratix had explained that pets were offered as a gift to those the family wished to honor, it became apparent that the level of their sacrifice showed the depth of their respect for the individual to whom the offer was made. That certainly made the practice more understandable, but she still couldn't imagine eating a creature a young Vratix once called Fluffy or its Vratix equivalent.

Though eating knytix could have easily been seen as a primitive practice by a barbaric society, the Vratix clearly were anything but. The Vratix village consisted of several towers that rose up into the middle reaches of the gloan trees. Concentric circular terraces with little walls at the lip gave each tower the look of a stepped pyramid, though the rounded foundation made it more elegant. Huge arching bridges connected one tower to another and were all but hidden by the thick forest foliage.

Vratix artistry was not limited to the architecture. The green skylight had been made by a Vratix artisan who chewed various rain forest leaves into paste, then fashioned it into a film thin enough to allow light to pass through. It appeared delicate in the extreme, yet was strong enough to ward off rain and survive other climatic conditions.

The stems and veins of the leaves formed a complex and chaotic network that looked visually attractive, but Iella knew that was not its primary purpose. Because both light and sound took time to travel to the eye and ear, respectively, the Vratix considered them secondary and deceptive senses. What one saw or heard was always something that had happened in the past, but what one could feel with the sense of touch, that was immediate and present in real time.

Reaching out she let her fingers play across the inside of the circular skylight. Her gentle touch conveyed a legion of different textures, some soft, some smooth, and others rough or sharp. She likened the progression to that of the music in a symphony, except that in choosing which way to stroke the surface, she could determine what she felt and in what order. *If I were worried, soft and smooth would soothe me, whereas if I were manic, sharp might caution me.*

Similarly, a whole variety of textures had been worked by the mason who had created the room she had been given. The walls had gentle ridges that swelled like waves on an ocean. They swirled into spirals and opened on smooth voids that encouraged placid tranquillity. The raised platform on which she slept had been cupped like a crater to hold her in, yet the sides and walls nearby were sleek and almost slippery to the touch. Near the doorhole, raised bumps warned of potential harm and the need for caution.

"They've thought of everything."

"Not quite." A hand reached up and grabbed the sill at the bottom of the door, then the tendons and muscles tensed in the arm attached to it and Elscol pulled herself into view. "The Vratix were nice enough to give us some footholds for climbing up here, but I'd still prefer a rope ladder."

Iella laughed and helped pull the smaller woman into the room. Because the Vratix's hind legs were so powerful, leaping up to the doorholes of rooms set well above the ground was simple. The need for stairs never developed, so Vratix architecture never included them. Visiting humans were normally housed in public areas, but advertising the presence of Ashern agents was not a good idea, so they were secreted away in rooms that were difficult for humans to move into and out of.

"Sixtus isn't with you?"

"No. He's out wandering through the rain forest." Elscol shrugged and adjusted the blaster on her right hip. "I've known him for years now, and there are just times he has to drift away. I suspect the Imps did some nasty stuff to him and his people when they trained him to be Special Ops and occasionally he has to fight it."

"Never had anyone exactly like him in CorSec, but I understand the need to get away. What's going on? Change of plans?"

Elscol shook her head. "Nope, we'll leave here after

dark, as planned, and move to the next haven. Just seeing us here seems to be good for Vratix morale. I don't really have any sense of how good the Vratix will be in combat, but they're fighters at heart."

"You mean at pulmonary arch."

"Doesn't have the same ring to it, does it?"

Iella shook her head. "No, not really."

Elscol smiled and seated herself on the foot of Iella's bed. "Well, doesn't matter. Armed with vibroblades, force pikes, or blasters, we can get enough Vratix that we can overwhelm humans in Xucphra City. Some of the Ashern indicate their training cadres are swelling in our wake. We come through, they get more volunteers. Sixtus has specified benchmarks for training, and it looks like we'll have our force in a couple of months."

"I'd feel better about them if we ever got to see their warriors in action."

Elscol nodded. "Agreed. From what Sixtus has said, though, because bacta and healing is so much a part of Vratix society, for a Vratix to become a warrior and cause harm is a very solemn decision. The Ashern, as you know, sharpen their forearm claws and paint themselves black. The former is for fighting, but they paint themselves black so they can remain in the shadows, hidden away to protect the other Vratix from what they can and will do to win freedom."

"Well, their reluctance to be violent explains why they haven't just risen up and slaughtered all the humans on the planet." Iella sighed. "It's too bad they have to resort to war to win the freedom they never should have lost in the first place. I hope we can remain free long enough for the Ashern to be ready to fight. How long do you figure we have until Isard storms us?"

"Good question. Me, I'd have done it in a heartbeat before we embarrassed General Dlarit, but she's trying to keep the populace happy. If the Xucphra folks see white armor in bulk on their world, they're going to figure she's got no more use for them, and I suspect they can cause a fair amount of trouble for her." Elscol sat back, leaning against the wall.

"Of course, Isard has more trouble than just us. That's what I came to tell you. News from the front."

"Yeah?"

"Yeah. And good news, too."

Iella dropped to the circular chamber's floor and sat cross-legged. Twisting her blaster belt around so she was more comfortable, she smiled up at Elscol. "What did you hear?"

"The *Corrupter* is no more."

Iella's jaw dropped. "What? How?"

"Isard tried to ambush Wedge and the others. Apparently, Wedge had a surprise waiting for them. A steady diet of proton torpedoes put the *Corrupter* down. No word of squadron losses—at least none that are reliable. Data came from a tap on Xucphra corp news, so it all has an Imp spin."

"Still, if they're saying the *Corrupter* was destroyed, that means its loss was the least of the problems Isard has." Iella clapped her hands. "Maybe this mission isn't going to be suicidal."

Elscol's face closed down. "We're a long way from getting out, Iella, but getting shot up isn't going to get you and your husband reunited."

"What?" Iella tried to cover her surprise at Elscol's comment because when she heard the words she knew part of her had been considering the mission in exactly that light. "I never . . ."

Elscol leaned forward and rested her elbows on her knees. "Hey, do I look like some Xucphra clerk who's going to believe everything you say? No. I've been where you are. I lost my husband to the Imps back on Cilpar, and part of me wanted to die with him there. I took off after the Imps for revenge, but always in the back of my mind was the feeling that when I died we'd be together again. Wedge saw that in me and saw the urge for self-destruction grow in me. When he kicked me out of Rogue Squadron, well, that woke me up; and I began to see a lot of things."

Iella's head came up. "Are you saying there's no life after death?"

"I'm saying it doesn't matter." Elscol held her two hands

out, palms toward the ceiling. "On one hand, if there isn't an afterlife, you'll be remembered for the things you did while you were alive. On the other, if there *is* an afterlife, you'll be able to share all you did with those who died before you. Either way, living as long as possible and doing the most you can is the only way to go. I decided I didn't want to be known here or in the afterlife for having quit. I don't think you do, either."

Iella frowned. "You're right, but sometimes the pain . . ." She clutched her hands against her breastbone. "Sometimes it hurts too much to live."

"Nonsense." Elscol's dark eyes sharpened. "Pain's the only way we know we're alive."

"What?"

"If the afterlife is supposed to be special and wonderful and blissful—and there aren't many theologies that suggest otherwise—then it follows that pain's the only way you know you're alive. Not letting the pain get to you, not surrendering to it, that's the way you continue living." Elscol brought her hands together, then glanced down at the floor. "It still hurts me, too, at certain times of the year, but I don't let it overwhelm me."

"I haven't let it overwhelm me, either."

"No, you haven't. You're strong, Iella, real strong." Elscol gave her a half-grin. "It's just that as things get going tougher, in the moments when stress is off, you'll start to feel the pain. Fight it."

Iella slowly nodded. What Elscol had said made perfect sense to her. While involved in an operation, the stresses of the operation would push everything else into the background. When the stress slackened, she tried to recover a sense of well-being, and would invariably harken back to her time with Diric. The joy would melt into melancholy, then that would congeal into sorrow and pain. *I'd come to a point where surrendering to the pain would be more simple than fighting the Imps and everything else.*

She realized that she'd not faced this problem before because when Diric had been taken by the Imps there was always a chance that he would be released and they would be able to continue their lives together. Hope had shielded her against despair and the pain of her loss. *Circumstances are different now, but I'm also a different person than I was. I will survive and fight the pain.*

She looked up and was about to tell Elscol the same thing, when a howling shriek filled the air and sent a tremor through her tower room. *No mistaking that for anything else—TIE fighters are coming in.* She dove for the doorhole and lying there on her belly stared out at the Vratix village. Other brown-gray towers were all but invisible in the thick foliage of the rain forest until green laser bolts illuminated them and began setting trees on fire. The bolts hissed through the air, igniting a rain of flaming branches and leaves falling on buildings and the forest floor.

Elscol hunkered down beside her with blaster in hand as the TIEs made another pass. Trees split as if they had been struck by lightning. Their boles exploded, spraying the rain forest with fiery hardwood splinters. Impaled Vratix and knytix twitched on the ground or limped along, black blood streaming from their wounds. In other spots, heavy bits of tree fell, crushing Vratix and pulverizing the walls of houses.

"Sithspawn!" Elscol bounced a fist off the floor. "We've got nothing that can stop them. They're just slaughtering Vratix for the fun of it."

"It's not fun for the Vratix." Iella watched as the Vratix began to flee. The whole tableau took on an unreal air. Part of it came from the Vratix leaping high into the branches of trees surrounding the village to escape. If Iella had allowed herself to forget how sophisticated the Vratix could be and just see them as insects, then she was watching a whole swarm of Corellian gluttonbugs clear-chew a forest. They moved in a mass, leaping away as bolts rained down on them, exploding and pitching body parts in every direction.

The most surreal element in the whole scene was the lack of wailing from the victims. The Vratix vocalized no sounds as they fled. They grasped each other and remained close, clearly taking security in the sense they trusted the most. *But that's what's getting them killed. Massed together like this makes them terribly vulnerable to the strafing runs.*

"Elscol, we have to do something."

"What? These blasters aren't going to bring down a starfighter, even if they don't have shields." Elscol coughed as the breeze wafted smoke toward them. "The only thing *we* can do is try to get out of here."

"Agreed." Iella looked out again, bracing to duck away from more aerial fire, but as the echoes of the last TIE's shriek died, no new one rose to take its place. Instead the whine of blaster fire started at the north end of the village. She looked in that direction and saw figures in white moving into the burning village. "Stormies."

Elscol laughed and checked the power pack on her pistol. "Not hardly. Look at the armor and how they wear it. Most of them are too small for it. They're Home Defense troops all dressed up for this operation."

"How can you be sure?"

"You think real stormies would raid a jungle village wearing white?"

Iella hesitated. "But on Endor, in the forest there, reports I heard . . ."

"Trust me, Iella, they learned from that mistake. Getting drubbed by a Wookiee and a bunch of Ewoks convinced them to institute some reforms." Elscol pulled herself into the door-hole and leaped out. "C'mon."

Iella followed, making the three-meter drop without injury. Running forward, she caught up with Elscol at the wall that edged the rooftop where they stood. As Elscol swung her legs over the top of the wall, Iella raised her blaster pistol and sighted in on one of the advancing troopers.

Elscol gently slapped her thigh. "Save it, you'll never hit from here. Too far."

Iella glanced down and grimly closed one eye. "Too far for you, maybe." Her head came up and she sighted in on a group of three troopers. She centered the gun on the middle one, fired, then snapped a shot off at the other two. The first shot hit the target square on the left breast, then glanced up off the armor and burned through his throat. The second shot pierced the left eyepiece on the second trooper, spinning him around like a top before he went down. The last shot missed its intended target, passing over the trooper's head by a couple of centimeters, but only did so because the first trooper's body had knocked him off balance and he was falling.

Elscol looked up with wide-eyed amazement at her. "A head shot at this range?"

Iella shrugged, then tapped the rear sight. "Shoots high." She sat on the edge of the wall, then leaped down to the next level and remained crouched at the foot of the wall. Elscol landed beside her. A few red blaster bolts bloodied the smoke in their direction, but none came even close to getting them. "They don't know where we are or where those shots came from."

"And because they aren't Vratix, they'll have a hard time jumping up here to find us." Elscol smiled and crept forward toward the edge of the terrace wall. "I can hit from this range."

Iella came forward carefully, ducking as a fleeing Vratix leaped past. At the edge of the terrace, she saw the troopers moving into the village, shooting into the doorholes on the ground level. Scarlet backlighting sometimes silhouetted a Vratix form. More often than not it seemed as if the blaster-fire started the tower's lower rooms burning. *There is no searching, this is just a mission to destroy this place.*

Angered beyond the point of caring about anything, Iella rose from her crouch and began shooting at targets. Elscol rose up beside her, laying down a pattern of fire that sent the troopers scurrying for cover. Iella looked over at her, and they both knew seasoned troops—real stormtroopers—never would have shied from blaster pistol fire. A few of the troopers were down and still, and yet more thrashed in pain on the ground. Iella wanted to feel compassion for them, but their cries for help were her greatest ally. *If the wounded infect the rest with a desire to avoid death, they'll break and run.* At the same time she acknowledged that the troopers' running was her only chance at survival.

Iella ducked down as scattered return fire headed in her direction. She popped a fresh power pack into her blaster pistol and pressed her back against the wall. Though the wall itself was smooth, Iella felt anything but placid at the moment. "Well, we've gotten their attention so the Vratix can flee."

Elscol ducked back beneath the edge of the wall. "You realize it's just a matter of time before they call for one of the starfighters to come back, don't you?"

Iella slid further along the wall, then nodded. "I guess we finish them quickly, then."

Elscol raised an eyebrow. "Your suggestion for Dlarit made me think you might not have the stomach for this kind of fight. I'm glad to be wrong."

Iella came up and triggered off two more shots before the troopers shifted their aim to shoot back at her. She dropped back down, uncertain if she'd hit anything and disturbed by what she saw. "Bad news. They've got a squad moving to flank us."

The smaller woman shrugged as if Iella had reported she felt a light drizzle starting to fall. Elscol checked her power pack and smiled in the near silence that reigned in the village. "We can give up, or we can fight our way through them."

"I don't see surrender as an option."

"Nor me." Elscol tucked a lock of brown hair behind her left ear. "On three we're over the wall to the last terrace. We go forward, take some shots, then over again and at them."

"Frontal assault?" Iella shook her head. "I may be dead and not know it, but I'm not crazy."

"They're scared. We sprint to their line of cover, then we start vaping them close in. CorSec had to train you for that sort of fight and I've gotten used to it, too."

Iella thought for a moment. From the base of the wall to the trees and rubble the troopers were using was only twenty-five meters. *Shooting like mad to make them keep their heads down, it might just work.* "I'm game."

"Let's do it." Elscol rose into a crouch. "One, two, three!"

With her left hand on top of the terrace wall, Iella came up and over, then dropped the eight feet to the next terrace. She hit, rolled, and sprinted to the next edge. She vaulted it in tandem with Elscol and landed solidly. She shoved off the wall with her right hand, then brought the blaster around to spray shots at the troopers crouching twenty-five meters away. Her hastily snapped shots didn't hit any of them, but they dove for the ground as if she were a Star Destroyer commencing a planetary bombardment.

As she raced forward, cutting right and left, she waited for a target to show himself so she could drop him with a clean shot to the head or belly. *Belly would be better. He'll scream.* She waited for the screams, waited to hear the troopers she was approaching start to scream in terror. She started to scream herself, hoping to spark her foes into panic.

Suddenly one of the troopers did stand. She brought her pistol around, but he leveled his blaster carbine at her and triggered a burst before she could shoot him. She saw a trio of sizzling scarlet energy darts fly at her and for a second considered it nothing short of miraculous that they had missed. Then she felt the tug on her left thigh. Her world whirled, and her chin dug into the moist loam at the base of a gloan tree. She snorted dirt from her nostrils and wondered what had happened, then the first wave of pain hit her.

Iella rolled onto her back and glanced down at her left thigh. Crusted black flesh surrounded a hole oozing blood. Biting back a scream, she unbuckled her blaster belt and pulled it off. She pressed the holster against the wound, then wrapped the belt around her leg and refastened it. Pulling it tight almost made her faint, but she struggled against the darkness nibbling at the edges of her sight.

She didn't think she'd blacked out, but as the world lightened again she found herself looking up at a trooper standing over her. He was saying something, but she couldn't focus on the words. All she could notice was that the armor seemed over-large on him, with the breastplate covering half his stomach and the helmet resting firmly on the armor's collar.

The trooper gestured with his blaster carbine, but Iella still wasn't able to understand him. She tried, but an odd whirring sound eclipsed his words. An angular shadow dropped down behind him. Iella heard a horrid snapping and crunching as the trooper began to telescope down toward the ground. He twisted around, his legs going limp, allowing Iella to see the ragged parallel wounds slashed down through the back of his armor.

Standing behind him, with claws dripping blood, a black Vratix warrior drew his arms in toward his thorax. His head bobbed once, then his powerful hind legs straightened, propelling him up and out of her sight. If not for the ravaged corpse of the soldier at her feet, she would have had no proof of his intervention.

Her mouth hung open as she looked at the trooper's body. *Those claws sliced through that armor with the ease of a wampa filleting a tauntaun. No way all the bacta on this world could close those wounds.* She leaned back against the trunk of the gloan tree, somehow finding comfort in the roughness of its bark. She heard screams that sounded far distant, more whirring, and other crisper sounds she never wanted to identify.

"Iella!"

She looked up. "Sixtus! Have you found Elscol?"

The large man nodded, then bent and scooped her up in his arms. "She twisted her ankle and got pinned down. How are you?"

"Hurt, but I should live."

"Good. I'll get you clear."

Iella tried to point back toward the troopers. "But they're out there. Another group, flanking us."

Sixtus shook his head. "The Black-claws got them all. It won't make up for the Vratix dead here, but it should start making the Xucphrans scared." His eyes narrowed. "When they find their people dead, they'll have a hard time sleeping."

Iella winced against the pain. "Wait."

"No, the Ashern have a base camp with some makeshift bacta tanks."

"No, not that." She shook her head to clear it. "Look, don't leave the bodies here. Take them away, far away. Just have the troopers disappear. Not knowing will be worse than knowing. Take our bodies, too, hide them. Don't let Isard know how badly we were hurt."

Sixtus smiled. "That's odd."

"What?"

"Your lips are moving, but I'm hearing the kind of things Elscol would say." He stepped over a thick gloan branch and continued down a narrow jungle trail. "I'd not have thought you capable of thinking that kind of thing."

"One thing I know, Sixtus, is that a high body count doesn't mean victory, it just means a lot of folks died." Iella tipped her head back toward the village. "A lot of people died there, but not knowing the true story will give our enemies something to think about. If they decide they don't want to fight because of it, we win."

29

Captain Sair Yonka of the Imperial Star Destroyer *Avarice* looked back and forth between the two suits of clothes the silver protocol droid held up for him. To the right he had a conservative black suit, cut along vaguely military lines. He knew it would make him look powerful and might even inspire fear in some people. *That is not always a bad thing,* he reflected, *but not wholly appropriate in this instance.*

The other suit was completely civilian, and he would have chosen it in a heartbeat except that it was a bright crimson. *Just what Isard wears.* Despite the fanciful styling, including the fringes at the hem of the jacket and along the sleeves, the bloody color and memory of Isard robbed the suit of its playfulness. That suit, because it was flashier than the black, would be more noticed, but people might miss him altogether, remembering only the clothes. *This is not a bad thing either, and desirable right now.*

He shook his head. "Let me think about it some more, Poe." He waved the droid away, but not before he caught a distorted mirror view of himself on its breast. Tall and slender, his black hair and bright blue eyes combined with strongly chiseled features to win the admiration of many women and the jealousy of their men. The touch of white creeping in at his temples had prompted him to grow a black goatee—something that was strictly against Imperial regulations, but not being in the Imperial service anymore, he had no fear of flouting those regulations.

While the warped reflection did not describe his outsides, it certainly did match how he felt inside. Yonka turned and walked out onto the balcony of his twenty-sixth-floor suite at Margath's. Strains of music drifted down from the 27th Hour Club, but it washed over him without effect. Even the sight of three moons hovering above the placid ocean, two ivory and one blood red, failed to register as anything more than yet another planetary night sky.

Leaning on the balcony rail, Sair Yonka slowly shook his head. He had the distinct feeling he was in the wrong place at the wrong time, but that oppressive sensation was one he'd lived with for longer than he could remember. While the Emperor was alive, he was able to hide within the protective shell of the government's legitimacy. *I knew what I was doing was right in someone's eyes. Patrolling the Rim, keeping pirates away from raiding worlds like Elshandruu Pica here, that was a mission no one could deny was necessary. That Rebels were often classified as pirates and dealt with harshly meant nothing. It was fairly common among pirates to call themselves Rebels to justify their predation on Imperial outposts.*

Since the Emperor's death he had clung to his role as a defender of the Empire to justify what he had been called upon to do. He added to that a very real desire to see to it that his people were not ordered into some futile fray at the whim of some self-appointed Warlord. Zsinj had tried to recruit him, but Yonka had steadfastly refused to take any orders except those coming from Coruscant. He bound himself to Ysanne Isard, because she seemed the best bet for dealing with the Rebels. *Her focus on destroying them,* then *reestablishing the Empire seemed to make the most sense to me.*

Then she went and lost Coruscant. Yonka bounced a fist off the railing. He'd followed her orders and helped her establish her presence on Thyferra, but that was before he heard about the Krytos virus. He appreciated her sense of pragmatism in dealing with the Rebels, but the virus targeted all sorts of folks who never so much as raised their voices in support of the Rebels. Her use of the virus meant she was capable of *anything* and that scared Sair Yonka.

The fear did not surprise him as much as the depth of it did. He knew she had operatives in his crew and had no doubt they'd strike at him were she to give the appropriate orders. Defying her was something that would have to be done—he knew that. *But not yet. Escorting convoys is nothing new to me or the* Avarice. *Perhaps if we're given a mission like the destruction of Halanit I will balk. Until then, a confrontation has no merit.*

He sighed. He had Isard on one hand and Antilles's Rogues on the other. An Imperial Star Destroyer Mark II, like the *Avarice*, had little to fear from a squadron of snubfighters. He acknowledged that their use of proton torpedoes could, in fact, hurt his ship, but his own pilots were very good and his turbolaser crews repeatedly drilled in antiship and antitorpedo fire missions. He had no doubt his ship could hurt the Rogues, but, he suddenly realized, he wasn't certain how much he wanted to hurt them.

They have no choice but to see me as a threat—as the most significant threat Isard has for them. He'd read the performance reports from the *Virulence* ever since Lakwii Varr-scha had taken over as Captain. They were not impressive in the least. The *Virulence*'s fighters scrambled slowly against Rogue threats and had never even come close to downing any of the Rogues. While his ship had yet to kill any of them either, they did drive them off faster, preventing them from getting off second and even third proton torpedo volleys against the convoys.

He shook his head again and forced thoughts of the Rogues and Ysanne Isard from his mind. The *Avarice* orbited through the night sky above, forming a dart-shaped silhouette as it passed before the bloody moon. *It's up there, as are all my worries, while I am down here. I came here to relax, so I shall do so, though not so many others would find this situation relaxing.*

Elshandruu Pica's Imperial Moff, Riit Jandi, had married a woman nearly forty years his junior. Yonka had known Aellyn Jandi years before on Commenor. They had grown up together and had slowly begun to realize their attraction to each other when he won an appointment to the Imperial Naval Academy. He lost track of her until, much later, he had come down to pay his respects to the Moff after rooting out a band of pirates that infested the system's asteroid belt. Once he and Aellyn laid eyes on each other, their feelings were rekindled and, for the past five years, they'd carried on a secret affair.

Kina Margath, owner of the hotel in which Yonka was staying, had befriended Aellyn Jandi and agreed to help her conceal her affair from the Moff. Rumors were spread that Yonka came to Margath's to romance Kina. Aellyn used her influence with the Moff to get favorable treatment for Kina's casino and hotel operations, and Yonka always managed to haul a goodly supply of exotic liqueurs and beverages from the worlds he patrolled to Elshandruu Pica, enabling the 27th Hour Club to meet its boast of being able to supply any drink a patron could name.

Yonka turned away from the railing and, looking back through transparisteel viewports, watched the droid brush specks of lint from the two suits he had been shown. *A choice based on my mood is not the way to go. I should dress to make an impression. Aellyn will like either suit, but I won't be wearing clothes very long in her presence, so her tastes do not matter.* He slowly smiled. *What others think is important. Her husband, for example, what would he like to see me wearing?*

"Poe."

The droid turned to face him. "Sir?"

"Please arrange for the repulsor limo to be ready in an hour. It will take that long for me to refresh myself and dress."

The droid nodded as best he could. "You have made a decision on what to wear, sir?"

Yonka laughed and strode back into the suite. "Poe, I have indeed. This affair is not without danger—the wrath of a Moff is not often survivable." He stroked his goatee with his right hand. "If one is going to dress for death, can blood-red ever be a wrong choice?"

Because of his position half a kilometer due east of the planetary Moff's oceanside cottage, Corran saw the repulsor-lift limousine approaching first. The driver had it speeding along, which would have made it a difficult target for a blaster rifle shot, but he wasn't sideslipping or changing height to make such a shot impossible. *No fear of ambush, which is good.*

Corran turned on the comlink clipped to his helmet and tapped it twice with a gloved finger. A single click came back, confirming Wedge's reception of Corran's warning about the limo's approach. Corran watched for any more vehicles following. Their briefing suggested Yonka wouldn't be bringing his own security detail, and that the Moff's wife regularly eluded hers; but the chance that her husband had others watching her or Yonka had to be covered.

He waited for one minute, then slowly started working his way back to the rendezvous point. Like the other Rogues on the mission—save Ooryl and the other Gand accompanying them—he wore some of the stormtrooper armor they'd gotten from Huff Darklighter. The dark blue color Darklighter had stained it so it matched his personal security force's uniforms blended perfectly into the night. He carried a blaster carbine, wore a blaster pistol on his right hip, and had spare power packs for both on his belt. He clipped his lightsaber to the back of his belt, so it dangled down like a stubby tail, out of the way but accessible if he needed it.

Of course, on this mission, if I need it, we're in deep Huttdrool. In theory, it was a quick hit and run. Though Yonka didn't know it, Kina Margath had long been a Rebel agent on Elshandruu Pica. Poe, the droid serving as Yonka's valet, had once been part of Rogue Squadron's staff. Once Wedge put out feelers to learn more about the soldiers in Isard's employ, a complete rundown on Yonka's affairs came back, providing the basic information for the mission.

If any more than one or two shots get triggered, we've

done something very wrong. So far it had gone completely as expected, and Corran didn't like that. On such missions—the same sort he'd performed dozens of times when with the Corellian Security Force—nothing ever seemed to go as planned. In going after Yonka, the most likely glitch would arrive in the form of the Moff's own squad of stormtroopers, and that was a serious complication. *Exfiltration under fire is not going to be fun.*

Even though he knew that outcome was a distinct possibility, Corran didn't have a bad feeling about the mission. Prior to his learning he was the grandson of a Jedi Master, he would have put the lack of dread down to his rather foolish and rash belief in good luck. He'd always trusted his feelings about things, but he'd never questioned the mechanism that generated those feelings. To him they just existed, and he had learned to abide by them or deal with the consequences.

Now he knew that his feelings were really based on sensations he was getting of and through the Force. Before they were intangible and even though he gave them weight, others did not. Now, because of Luke Skywalker, the Force had gained credence. Others would accept what he felt as if it were a true measure of what was happening.

That frightened Corran—especially after the disaster on Thyferra. *I don't know enough about the Force and what it means to rely on it. I certainly can't let others use what I feel as a crutch. If I'm wrong, they'll pay for my mistake. I won't have that happen.*

He reached the rendezvous point in a little ravine slightly northeast of the cottage. Corran crouched between Ooryl and Rhysati, across the way from Gavin, Wedge, and the tall Gand named Vviir Wiamdi. The other two members of the team waited in Picavil's spaceport with two X-wings, ready to cover their escape if things got messy. *Bror Jace and Inyri Forge will be able to down anything the Moff can put in the air, but if we need them I'm sure the* Avarice *will scramble fighters, and then we're stuck.*

Wedge looked up at Corran and nodded. He tapped Corran and Rhysati on the knee and pointed off toward the right. Ooryl and Vviir were directed left, leaving Wedge and Gavin to go straight in at the open garden doors and into the back of the cottage. Wedge tapped his chronometer, then held up two fingers.

Two minutes to get into position, then we go. Corran nodded and followed Rhysati. He still felt good about the mission. *Let's hope that holds true. Let's hope the only surprise is that which appears on Yonka's face.*

Sair Yonka let himself into the cottage and nearly dropped the magnum of Mandalorean Narcolethe he'd brought to share with Aellyn. The door clicked shut behind him, muffling the sound of the repulsor limo's departure—not that he could have heard it past the thunder of his heartbeat in his ears. He had enough presence of mind to prevent his jaw from dropping open and instead crafted a smile that flashed white teeth at her.

Though neither as tall or slender as he was, Aellyn shared with him black hair. She wore hers long, so it descended well past her shoulders and lay gently along the swelling of her breasts. The gown she wore had been woven of a wispy fiber that had been dyed a midnight blue. It covered her from thin shoulder straps down to her ankles and glowed electrically where the light hit it, yet proved sheer enough to tantalize him with visions of what it sheathed. Her blue eyes sparkled with mischief, promising much and summoning most pleasurable memories to his consciousness.

The slight breeze from the garden brought the scent of flowers to his nose and teased playfully with the skirts of her gown. Her glance darted toward the open doors and the darkness beyond. Yonka fondly recalled having made love with her in the garden, beneath the canopy of stars and the trio of Elshandruu Pica's moons. His smile broadening, he set the Narcolethe on the side table next to the door and extended his hand toward her.

For a half second, primarily because the dark blue of the armor matched perfectly the color of Aellyn's gown, the two blaster-toting figures entering through the garden doorway seemed appropriate. Only when Aellyn opened her mouth to scream and the second figure shot her did he realize they were not part of any surprise Aellyn had cooked up for him. Even so, the blue hue of the stun shot that hit her still seemed somehow in keeping with the theme of the evening.

Yonka raised his hands. He heard the comlink clipped to the leader's faceplate buzz, but he could make out none of the words. The man nodded, then reached up and removed his helmet. Despite the sweat pasting brown locks to the intruder's forehead and the edges of his face, Yonka immediately recognized the man. *It can't be . . .*

Yonka felt his chest tighten, yet fought to keep his voice even. "You needn't have had her shot, Antilles."

"Wouldn't do to have witnesses, would it?" Wedge nodded toward her without letting his blaster waver from Yonka's direction. "We could have killed her, but unnecessary bloodshed is not something we revel in. In fact, we don't like it at all."

Eliminate me, and you assume my ship won't function at all well. Yonka found himself flattered, but he was too much of a realist to allow vanity to lift his spirits. "One man does not mean much on a starship."

Wedge smiled. "You underestimate your worth, Captain Yonka. Like it or not, as you go, so goes the *Avarice*."

"Killing me will only have a minor effect on the *Avarice*."

"I agree, Captain Yonka."

"Yet you have come to kill me."

"Kill you?" Wedge shook his head. "I've come to offer you a deal."

Yonka blinked in amazement. "Deal? What kind of deal?"

Antilles positively beamed. "A deal that starts with making you a very rich man."

30

Fliry Vorru strode slowly down the ramp from the belly of his *Lambda*-class shuttle then stopped midway as he saw Erisi Dlarit waiting for him at the edge of the landing pad. She wore a smile that seemed inviting, though her blue eyes seemed focused distantly, well beyond him. He found both her smile and presence pleasing, but his natural wariness prevented him from drawing any true enjoyment from either.

He nodded in her direction and began walking again, this time not fighting gravity but allowing it to make his step more brisk and lively. "Commander Dlarit, so nice of you to greet me."

Erisi easily returned his nod. "My pleasure, Minister Vorru."

Vorru matched her smile. "Did I detect a hint of wistfulness in your expression as you waited here?"

The hint of a frown threw a twitch through her brows, then she shook her head. "No, no, I just thought it rather ironic that a man as dangerous as yourself should be content with piloting so docile and meek a ship."

"Meek?"

"I would have seen you flying an Interceptor, certainly, or a gunship, not a *Lambda*-class shuttle."

Vorru nodded. "Ah. I'm afraid, though, this is anything but a normal shuttle. I have made a number of modifications that make this ship far more lethal than it appears to be."

"I see. I should have expected such clever deception from someone as intelligent as you."

"You refer to me as clever and intelligent." He shook his head. "I fear you've found my weakness, Erisi. Flattery will win you much."

"How much to make you willing to act as a shield for me during another tantrum thrown by 'She Who Cannot Be Defied'?"

Vorru smiled up at her, then offered her his arm. "Even you, most beautiful Erisi, could not flatter me that much. You were summoned, too?"

"Yes." Erisi's voice sank into a harsh growl. "The convoy that the *Avarice* had been escorting appeared back in-system, though three tankers were missing."

Vorru nodded as they walked through the tall gray corridors. Isard's vehement demand that he return to the capitol immediately had not been accompanied by any explanation, but more interference by Rogue Squadron seemed to be the only thing that could make Isard so angry. "What was Captain Yonka's explanation of their loss?"

"I don't believe he offered any." Erisi shook her head. "As nearly as I can determine, the *Avarice* did not return with the convoy."

Vorru shivered, and the hair at the back of his neck began to rise. "Could Antilles have gotten the *Avarice*? He does have the Alderaanian War Cruiser."

"I don't believe he could have, even with the War Cruiser. There have been no reports I know of that indicate any battle took place out there. You, Minister, would have better sources in that regard than I."

"Call me Fliry, Erisi. Compatriots in Iceheart's rage should not use titles between them." Vorru punched a turbolift button and stepped into the box when the doors opened. "As nearly as I know, all things have gone perfectly with the *Avarice*. Captain Yonka made his rounds, visited his mistress on Elshandruu Pica—he's seeing the Moff's wife, though the

Moff believes he's bedding the owner of a local resort. The *Avarice* left orbit on schedule and continued the circuit as it was supposed to."

"Clearly something went wrong, Fliry." Erisi gave his arm a little squeeze as the turbolift stopped its ascent. "Now we just have to determine who will catch the blame."

Vorru reached out and punched the emergency stop button on the lift before the doors could open. "I have the turbolifts regularly swept, so I know we are safe for the moment. I ask you this, realizing I now place us at more risk than ever before. Do you feel, as I do, that Madam Director Isard is not viewing the same reality we are?"

Erisi's eyes narrowed. "Do I think she is insane?"

"Yes."

"Quite." Erisi twisted around and faced him fully. "Antilles consumes her. If he is not dealt with shortly, she could destroy Thyferra. This is not to say I doubt her ability to eliminate Antilles—she is most dangerous in that regard."

"But you would be in favor of having contingency plans that guarantee the survival of the Bacta Cartel no matter what happens to her."

"Exactly. You've read my mind."

"Only because our thoughts run in parallel." Vorru again hit the emergency button and the door slid open. "Let us bravely face out fate and deal with the future it presents us."

As they neared Isard's doorway, Vorru held a hand up, stopping Erisi. He preceded her into the room and bowed politely in Isard's direction. "I came as quickly as I was able, Madam Director." He half-expected her to jump all over him, but as she turned, she just nodded.

Isard brandished a holoprojector remote control, then let a thin grin tug at the corners of her flatline mouth. "Good, Commander Dlarit is here, too. I only need do this once." She stabbed the remote at an unseen receptor and suddenly Captain Sair Yonka appeared life size, standing before her. "This is a wonderful display of treachery."

Yonka's figure bowed to the room. "Madam Director Ysanne Isard, I regret not being able to bring you this message personally, but not that much. In the time I have been associated with you I have found you to be sociopathically self-centered, prone to irrational and impulsive reactions to situations, and prey to a preference for appearance over substance. I have no doubt these affectations were seen as skills by the late Emperor, and indeed may have enhanced your ability to comply with his orders, but by no means are these the traits that make for great, or even *adequate* leadership."

Vorru killed the impulse to applaud. The fact that Sair Yonka wore a black suit of military styling, yet lacking any military insignia, struck Vorru as appropriate. Yonka was not abandoning his military background, just severing his connection to Isard. *The first mynock to flee a ship burning into an atmosphere.* Yonka's tone of voice—even, but full of conviction—sharply contrasted with the fury clearly building in Isard.

"I have, upon reflection, come to the conclusion that further service to you would be to condone and support an evil that perhaps would seem insignificant when grouped with the Emperor, Darth Vader, and Prince Xizor. I sincerely doubt, however, the billions of victims who have suffered because of you would be so sanguine about you. I hereby resign your service and renounce allegiance to you and what you represent. The same goes for my crew, save those loyalists you had aboard the *Avarice*. When informed of the new order of things, they hijacked a *Lambda*-class shuttle and forced us to destroy them."

Yonka clasped his hands behind his back. "I know your intent will be to hunt us down and exterminate us. There is no doubt that with the *Virulence* and *Lusankya*, you could do just that, but you won't get that chance. Most of my career has been served in the Outer Rim—I know of worlds and systems that you could never find. Seek out the *Avarice*, and you will leave yourself vulnerable to enemies who can destroy you."

The image faded to gray static, then evaporated, leaving Isard staring back toward Vorru. "You once told me he had a mistress, this Captain Yonka."

Vorru nodded. "On Elshandruu Pica."

"Have her killed." Isard spoke softly, surprising Vorru

with her ability to keep her anger from coloring her words. "And any children she has, any siblings, any family."

"And not *his* family?"

Isard snorted harshly. "I got this hologram three hours ago. Extermination of the crew's families began then. Do recall, as Director of Imperial Intelligence, I have been through this routine before. I happened to notice the information on Yonka's mistress was not in his file. You were not collecting it for your own purposes, were you, Minister Vorru?"

The small man half-lidded his eyes. "Merely awaiting confirmation before I committed anything to bytes, Madam Director." He opened his hands innocently. "I just wonder at your desire to go after his mistress. You don't imagine she influenced him in this decision, do you?"

"No, of course not." Isard folded her hands together. "She dies to cause him pain. Have her death holographed—I will play it for Yonka as I work on him."

"As you wish, Madam Director." Vorru bowed as he replied to her, but inside he felt only contempt for her. *Aellyn Jandi will be far away and out of your grasp because it will frustrate you, Iceheart.* "The *Avarice*'s departure puts us in a curious position. Our ability to guard our convoys has been halved, unless you plan to take the *Lusankya* out of orbit and press it into that duty."

An eyebrow arched over her red eye. "And leave Thyferra vulnerable to an attack by Antilles or an uprising by the Ashern? You think me more mad than Yonka did."

"Hardly that, Madam Director, just a person faced with difficult decisions."

"This is why I have you to advise me, Vorru." Isard glared at him, her gaze burning a blush onto his face. "You are correct—we cannot guard our bacta convoys *and* prevent an uprising here. Moreover, if we do nothing, Antilles will get bolder and might convince a number of worlds to throw in with him so they can take by force what we are afraid to ship out. That would destroy us. In the face of this I see only one clear choice."

Vorru half-closed his eyes. *She won't surrender, so there must be some new atrocity she is planning.*

Isard slowly smiled. "I believe it was you, Minister Vorru, who noted that we could not destroy Antilles until we determined where his base was. Your reports in regards to the search for that base, I have been told by you, have been fruitless because Antilles and his people are very cautious in how they accept goods from outsiders—only the people he trusts are allowed to come all the way into his base."

Vorru nodded. "That is the problem, Madam Director."

"No longer. Antilles could operate without taking chances because we gave him time to do so. I intend to deprive him of that time. The Rebels always worked best when no pressure was placed on them and they were allowed to operate on their own time scale."

"You have found a way to make him act faster?" Erisi's questioning tone underscored Vorru's own thoughts. "Threatening an innocent world might do it, but to move sufficient forces there to do such a thing would leave Thyferra vulnerable."

Isard barked a small, triumphant laugh. "You've not seen it, neither of you. I have found a way to pressure Antilles *and* make Thyferra *more* secure. I put together an analysis of the bacta production here and determined that the bacta industry needs only one point eight million Vratix to operate all the facilities we have at one hundred percent efficiency. This means there are a million surplus Vratix on the world. I have ordered the round-up and internment of a thousand Vratix a day for the next thirty days. At the end of that time I will have them all killed and begin collecting two thousand a day. I will continue in this manner until we have downsized our worker population or Antilles tries to stop me."

Isard's smile marked how proud she was of herself for coming up with the plan, and Vorru found himself inclined to agree with her. Its simplicity and elegance made it a plan that could be implemented immediately, and the deadline factor meant Antilles would have to react. *This could bring him out after us and, if it does, expose his base to our ships.*

Erisi raised a hand. "Madam Director, I am assuming you will present this policy and plan as something for Thyferran consumption only—making it appear as if it were being used as a means to suppress the Ashern. To challenge Antilles openly would be to raise his suspicion. He is not a stupid man, so he will be careful, but there is no need to make him think things through one more time."

Vorru immediately chimed in. "An excellent suggestion, Madam Director. If news of the program comes from locals it might appear as if you were trying to keep it a secret. Antilles will certainly feel the pressure to intervene. An added benefit is that we will have increased chances to pick up on Antilles's local covert communication network and disrupt it."

"Indeed, those *are* added benefits. While I would hate to have it thought I was cravenly trying to hide information from Antilles, I could affect an air of disdain, as if the whole thing were, like him, beneath my notice." Isard opened her hands, then pressed them together, fingertip to fingertip. "I approve of your amendments to my plan. We implement it tomorrow."

Vorru smiled. "I will alert my operatives to be especially attentive to any of Antilles's activities."

Erisi mirrored his smile. "And my people will be ready to pit themselves against the Rogues, either here or at their lair."

"Excellent." Both of Isard's hands curled down into fists. "A month. Antilles has a month yet to live. Then, once he is eliminated, the Empire will rise again and the natural order of things will again be established."

31

Fatigue made Corran's eyes feel as if Tatooine's twin suns had settled into his skull. He knocked at the doorjamb of Booster's office, but refrained from leaning heavily against it, lest he fall asleep on his feet. He and Ooryl had made a run to Thyferra, hitting some interim systems along the way to make it impossible to backtrack them to Yag'Dhul. A direct trip would have taken them twelve standard hours—their course added another twelve to the total. While he had managed to get a little sleep while in hyperspace, the trip left him feeling like he'd spent the last two days in the belly of a Sarlacc.

Wedge, seated in front of Booster's desk, looked up. "You could have stopped to get a meal before you reported in, Corran."

Sure, and have Booster presume I can think only of myself when I've been on an important mission like this? "Not hungry, Wedge. The news kind of killed my appetite."

Booster arched a white eyebrow above his artificial left eye. "You were able to confirm the reports from Thyferra, then?"

Corran nodded. "According to communication intercepts, approximately two weeks ago Iceheart initiated a program in which she's gathering up a thousand Vratix a day and is planning to execute them when she has thirty thousand total. At that point, if Ashern resistance to her regime has not ceased, she'll collect more."

Wedge's voice dropped into a low growl. "She finally thinks she's found a way to draw us out."

Corran shrugged slowly. "I monitored public announcements and privately coded messages from Iella and Elscol. Everything seems to indicate this program is a domestic one only. There has been no mention of us or what we've been doing."

Booster barked a harsh laugh. "You think she would say anything directly to motivate us? That would make us suspicious of a trap."

Corran frowned. "So since she said nothing about us, it *is* a trap designed to catch us? You must have a conspiracy theory program working overtime on your datapad, Booster."

Wedge sat forward and held a hand up to forestall Booster's reply. "Doesn't matter what Iceheart intended—though I do think Booster is more right than you are here, Corran—the fact is that we have two weeks to prevent her from slaughtering thirty thousand Vratix. Conspiracy or no, trap or no, we have to act."

"I wasn't saying we shouldn't act, Wedge." Corran shook his head to clear his mind. "I'm just saying it's not an obvious attempt to provoke us."

"CorSec always did miss the obvious." Booster snorted with disgust, then hit a couple of keys on the datapad centered on his desk. "Do we initiate things?"

"Can we?" Wedge's brown eyes narrowed. "Where do we stand on the refits?"

"The sensor and targeting units are all in place. If we use the crews from the freighters we have hanging around here, I can have the launchers ready to go inside a week." Booster looked up. "Karrde even has our last shipment of concussion missiles and proton torpedoes ready to go. An hour after I send him a message via the HoloNet, his convoy should be assembled. We can have it here within a day, with missile batteries and torpedo magazines fully loaded twelve hours later, if all goes well."

"What about the gravity well projector."

"Got it, and it's being installed now."

"Good. Let's get things going. Call Karrde and set up a rendezvous for twenty-four hours from now." Wedge glanced up at Corran. "Will you be ready to lead a flight out to escort them in by that time?"

Corran hesitated, not certain what he heard was really what Wedge said. "Escort them in?"

"I'll make it thirty-six hours—let him get some sleep."

"Fine, Booster, that should work."

"Wait, wait, wait." Corran held his hands up. "You really intend for me to lead Karrde's convoy *here*? We aren't going to work out some transfer thing?"

Wedge shook his head. "No. Time is of the essence."

"But, Wedge, sir, begging your pardon, if we do that, then Isard will know where we are. The *Lusankya* and the *Virulence* could be here just twenty-four hours after we get back with the convoy." Corran frowned and rubbed a hand over his wrinkled brow. "I thought Booster determined that someone in Karrde's organization provided Isard with the data to set up the Alderaan ambush. You're practically inviting Isard here."

Booster smiled. "No practically about it, Corran, we *are* inviting her here."

"But you can't do that! Even if this station were bristling with missile launchers, there's no way we could take down a Super Star Destroyer and an Impstar deuce."

Wedge shook his head. "I understand your protest, Corran, but you're not privy to the plans Booster, Tycho, and I have put together for dealing with Isard and her fleet. You do know we've been taking her forces apart bit by bit, which certainly was part of our overall plan, but we had to make decisions about what to do if Iceheart forced our hand, and she has."

"Then tell me what the plans are so I don't think you've lost your minds."

"Can't do that, CorSec." Booster flipped his datapad

closed with a click. "You're going to go out and get the convoy and bring it here. If Isard decides to act early and take our pilots hostage, she can't torture out of you information you don't have."

Wedge nodded in agreement. "And I need you to lead the escort flight because Isard and her agent would not believe we were on the level if you or Tycho or I did not bring the flight in. I don't want to cut you out like this, but the less you know, the less you can reveal."

Corran felt his flesh tighten around little goose bumps and a wave of weariness wash over him. "I hear what you're saying, Wedge, but are you certain this is going to work?"

Booster roared with laughter. "Certain? Certain? Of course he's not certain. The man who would only bet on certainty has no guts."

"I have plenty of guts, Booster, but I don't like risking them, or my life, or the lives of my friends, if I don't have to. Certainty, or as close as I can get to it, is what I want."

"And you call yourself a Corellian?" The big man snorted derisively as he sat back in his chair. "No wonder you joined CorSec."

"What's *that* supposed to mean?"

"I thought it was obvious, CorSec. If you had the guts for life—if you were even to *imagine* yourself worthy of my daughter—you wouldn't have spent your life in service to the Empire's puppet. You played it safe when men with real courage were out there defying the government."

Corran's fatigue melted as his anger grew. "Oh, you're going to use the smugglers are really patriots story to excuse your greed? Let me tell you something, Booster Terrik, you can think of yourself as a noble scoundrel if you want, but the fact is you were out for money when you were running shipments, nothing more. The fact that you didn't pay taxes on what you imported, the fact that you broke laws, might mark you as some sort of protester against the government in the eyes of some, but I know the truth. You were just a criminal—not as violent or bad as some others, but a criminal just the same. And those taxes you didn't pay were the kind of taxes that build roads, maintain spaceports, and educate kids.

What you did was deny them their due, and provide the contraband that allowed organizations like Black Sun and Hutt bands to thrive on our world."

Corran thrust a finger directly at Booster. "And as for being worthy of your daughter, I'm the worthiest man you ever met. Every gram of character you think you have, she *does have*. And brains, too, and courage. And even you, Booster Terrik, don't want to see her hooking up with a man who has your morals and standards."

Booster rose from behind his desk, his hands balled into fists. "And if you were the man you think you are, Corran Horn, you'd not have abandoned her on Thyferra."

"Abandoned her?" Corran's mind flashed back to his mad dash into the refresher station and his fight with the stormtroopers. *I didn't abandon her.* "You want to talk abandonment? I left for five seconds to save her life. You left her for five *years*, Booster, or have you forgotten your vacation on Kessel?"

"A 'vacation' your father got for me, Horn."

Wedge stood abruptly and posted a hand in the middle of each man's chest. "All right, stop it. Right now." He gave each of them a little shove and Corran let himself be propelled back toward the doorway. Wedge turned to Booster, shifted both hands to the larger man's shoulders, and forced him down into his chair.

"Listen to me, Booster—and you'll listen because you don't want to find yourself in the situation of having Mirax say this to you: Corran Horn here is one of the smartest, skilled, and courageous men it's been my privilege to know. He escaped from a prison that makes Kessel look like a resort world with hourly shuttles in and out. He's gone and done things on missions that put him at risk because those things save the lives of others. If not for him, Coruscant would still be in Imperial hands and I, as well as your daughter, would be dead or Isard's slaves.

"When you arrived on this station, you said you thought I would have protected Mirax from the likes of Corran." Wedge shook his head. "The real story is that I was overjoyed when they became friends. Mirax needed someone as stable as Corran because she's never really sure where you are or what's happened to you. And Corran, he needed someone with Mirax's curiosity and fervor for life because he'd been cut off from everyone he knew and trusted. Both of them were gyros that needed to be spin balanced, and they did that for each other."

Before Corran could begin to grin triumphantly, Wedge whirled and stabbed a finger into his chest. "And you, my friend, need to get some perspective here. You're seeing Booster as your father's old enemy, and your father isn't here to put him in his place. Well, you aren't your father. Their fight isn't your fight, and you can't stand in for your father in it. And you should be smart enough to know Booster doesn't have a problem with you because you were Hal Horn's son— he's got the same problem with you that every father ever had with any man romancing his daughter. She's the best thing that ever happened to him."

Corran nodded. "She's the best thing that ever happened to me, too."

"Right, which means the two of you have more in common than either one of you would admit. Now the both of you better think on this: Mirax loves both of you, so unless you think she's got no taste or character judgment at all, you better figure you both are worthy of each other's respect." Wedge folded his arms and positioned himself so he could see both of them easily. "I don't expect you'll ever get to the point where you actually *like* each other, but, when you're both acting like adults, you'll be above this sort of bickering."

Corran looked up and met Booster's stare openly. *Waiting to see if I break, aren't you? Waiting to see if I knuckle under.* In a nanosecond Corran resolved never to give in, never to change his opinion of Booster. While all Wedge had said was true—*and made damned good sense*—Corran had been raised with his father's rivalry with Booster Terrik. *If I do give in, I've betrayed my father.*

Or have I? Corran frowned as he thought about his father and the life his father had led. Hal Horn had lived for years with the knowledge that he was really the son of a Jedi and subject to the extermination policy the Empire had put in place concerning Jedi. His father could have done anything to make himself safe. He could have retreated to the hinterlands of some backwater world and become a hermit, but he chose not to absent himself from the duty his father—fathers, really—had acquitted. A Jedi helped maintain the peace and uphold the law. Hal Horn did the same thing as best he could by working with CorSec, no matter that his duties might expose him to the Emperor's Jedi hunters.

Corran suddenly realized that his father's rivalry with Booster Terrik had not been personal. Hal Horn had pursued Booster because Booster broke the law. Yes, the fact that Booster evaded him repeatedly did frustrate him, but the basis of his pursuit was always the same. *He didn't let it get personal. I have and in that I've betrayed my father.* He glanced down for a moment and thought about some of the exercises Luke Skywalker had urged him to try out. *By making things personal—Kirtan Loor and Zekka Thyne—I have betrayed the Jedi traditions my father, in his own cautious way, tried to instill in me.*

Corran's head came up as he stepped forward and extended his hand to Booster. "You're not my enemy. Never have been. I'm not yours. For the sake of your daughter, the people we've got to save, and the memory of my father, I don't want to fight with you anymore. Doesn't mean we won't disagree—perhaps even violently at times—but you don't deserve my ill-will."

Surprise slowly blossomed on Booster Terrik's face. He started to say something, then stopped. His hand came up and engulfed Corran's. "Normally I'd be angry that I had misjudged you so badly, but you've reinforced just how good a judge of character my daughter really is. And you're right, we'll disagree and I can guarantee it'll be violent, but that's okay. We're Corellians. We can do that."

Wedge dropped his hand on top of theirs. "Good. You know, the Imps on Coruscant used to call two Corellians together a conspiracy. Three they'd call a fight."

"More fools they, then." Corran smiled. "Any Corellian knows three of us together is a *victory*. It's time we remind Iceheart and the rest of Imp holdovers of that very fact."

32

Corran glanced at the chronographic display on the X-wing's main monitor. "Whistler, confirm that we're ten standard minutes past the time for the rendezvous."

The R2 unit blatted out an annoyed tone.

"Fine, so I won't ask you to confirm how late they are anymore—at least not every minute." Corran forced himself to exhale deeply and tried to draw in some of the inner peace that Luke indicated such a cleansing breath should bring in its wake. He failed, and that just heightened his frustration. Despite accepting the mission, he had not liked having to be the one to draw Isard's agent into Yag'Dhul. While he knew the deception Booster and Wedge had planned would certainly make the discovery of their base appear to be serendipitous, every second Karrde's people were late allowed the image of a Thyferran taskforce appearing to pounce on them grow in his mind.

It wouldn't have been so bad, but Corran had not come alone. Gavin, Rhysati, and Inyri flew X-wings to give him a complete flight, and Mirax had come along in the *Pulsar Skate*. None of them knew how dangerous their mission might be—and Corran granted that the odds of their ending up dead on this mission probably were no greater than they were on any other—but he still would have felt better if he could have told them what was really going on. *Of course, that would mean I'd have to know what was going on.*

A light flashed on his communications console. He punched the button beneath it. "Nine here."

"*Skate* here, Nine." Mirax's voice sounded good to him and immediately began to take the edge off his frustration. "So, as long as we're waiting, you want to tell me what you said to my father?"

Corran frowned. "How do you know about that?"

"Well, I could say that you talk in your sleep, but you don't." The light tone in her voice conveyed the image of her smiling face to him. "When we headed out, my father shot me a private message. Normally he says I should make sure you take good care of me. This time he said I should keep my eye on you and follow your lead. Bit of a difference there."

"Yeah, just a bit."

"So?"

"We had a talk."

"Are you going to tell me what was said, or am I going to convince Emtrey he needs to spend more time around you?"

"Hey, no reason to trot out the turbolasers here." Corran hesitated for a moment, then sighed. "Your father and I had it out. He said I'd abandoned you on Thyferra . . ."

"What?!"

". . . and I accused him of having abandoned you when he went to Kessel."

"What?! You really told him that?"

"Yeah, then I told him that you were everything he wanted to be and that the last person he should want interested in his daughter was someone who held himself to the same level of morality and responsibility he did."

"And you still have your arms and legs intact?"

"Your father isn't exactly a Wookiee, Mirax." Corran forced a laugh. "Besides, it was about that point when Wedge intervened."

"Ah, that explains why you're both still alive."

"Right. Wedge pointed out that since you love the both

of us, we've got a lot more in common than we do in conflict. He said, in essence, that we should grow up and start acting like adults."

Mirax laughed lightly. "I bet that went over well with my father."

"He listened, and the two of us were prepared to get back into it, but I let things bounce around inside my head and I realized I was disliking your father for the wrong reasons. Somewhere inside I figured it was my duty to my father to continue his rivalry with your father, then I realized my father hadn't let it get personal. He might have hunted your father with a bit more gusto because your father didn't make it easy, but he didn't hate Booster. By allowing myself to do so, though, I was really going against everything my father had tried to teach me."

"I can understand that." Mirax's voice softened. "And it kind of bothers you that your father never told you who your grandfather really was, doesn't it?"

Corran thought for a second, then nodded. "I guess it does, but not in the sense that I would have expected. Part of me thinks I should feel betrayed because he kept that secret from me, but I don't, really. In keeping it from me, he kept me safe. What I didn't know I couldn't reveal. I still don't know if Grandpa Horn helped other Corellian Jedi families hide, but if one had been found out, more could have been discovered. And my father really did try to instill in me the code of honor the Jedi espoused. He also taught me to trust my instincts and hunches, which are glimmers of whatever talent I have.

"Where it bothers me is that, knowing my father, he had to have been inordinately proud of our heritage. He must have wanted to share it with me and would have, I suspect, after the Emperor died, but Bossk killed him before that happened. I would have thought he'd have come up with a way to get me the information if anything happened to him."

"What about your grandfather, Rostek Horn?"

"He's on Corellia, under the Diktat. I haven't had a chance to communicate with him. Perhaps when this is all over, that's an option. Still, I would have liked to hear my father talk about his father."

Whistler tootled.

Corran glanced at his monitor. "Whistler, what do you mean by 'All you have to do is ask'?"

The droid hooted at him.

"Okay, so the statement is self-explanatory. What will happen if I ask?"

Whistler piped a triumphant tune.

"What's Whistler saying, Corran?"

"Just a second, Mirax." Corran reached out and ran a finger beneath the letters glowing on his monitor. "I guess I shouldn't be surprised, but I am. My father encrypted a holographic file and loaded it into Whistler. Apparently he did this back when I joined CorSec—though Whistler says the message was recorded well before that—in case anything happened to him. Whistler says he was instructed to play the file for me at any point where I asked about it *and* could provide the encryption key. I'm going to assume the key is either Nejaa Halcyon or my father's true name, Valin Halcyon."

Even as Corran explained to Mirax what the droid was telling him, a chill puckered his flesh. He felt as if his father were reaching back out of the grave to touch him, and he marveled how his father had anticipated Corran's eventually learning enough about his heritage to find the file of value. Before he had ever heard of Nejaa Halcyon, Corran would have put his father's foresight down to luck or even coincidence, but he knew the Jedi believed in neither. *My father knew that someday I would want this information, so he prepared a way for me to get it.*

That realization opened a whole new den of Hutts, with every one of them a criminal kingpin. He thought of Luke Skywalker's invitation to join him and train to become a Jedi Knight. *Did my father create this file in hopes that I would do just that?* Because the file had been created well before the Jedi's reemergence had been confirmed, Corran knew his father couldn't have anticipated the Jedi's invitation to him. *Or could he?* Regardless of that, had his father intended his message to inspire Corran to learn more about his heritage?

The droid chirped out a question.

"No, Whistler, save the message. Now's not the time to look at it."

"Why not, Corran? We've got time to kill."

"Because, Mirax, I don't have time to consider all of the questions it might raise."

"Such as?"

"Such as making me reconsider my answer to Luke Skywalker. Perhaps what my father has to tell me in this message will make me realize I *should* be learning to become a Jedi Knight. That decision would force other decisions, and some of them I don't want to make—primary among them a decision to leave you to go off and study the ways of the Force. My other responsibilities—to the squadron and the prisoners we're going to free—likewise make such a decision difficult. Right now I need to be able to focus on what I'm doing."

"So you won't play the message?"

Corran shook his head. "Not right now, certainly not until the Thyferran situation is over."

"What I hear in your voice, Corran, is that you might not ever play it."

"You know me very well, love." Corran closed his eyes for a moment and swallowed against the lump in his throat. He reached up with a hand and pressed the gold Jedi Credit against the flesh of his breastbone. "This hologram is the last thing my father has left me, but he never would have done it if he thought it would completely disrupt my life."

"Can you be sure of that?"

"Yeah. If it was something I had to hear, for my own good, Whistler would never have been instructed to wait until I asked to hear it." Corran laughed, and that eased the tightness in his throat. "My father trusted me to make my own decisions and deal with the consequences."

"That trust, Corran, is the last thing your father left you. It's a most precious gift indeed, and one well suited to you."

"Thanks, Mirax." Whistler shrilled a warning, prompting Corran to look at his monitor. A dozen ships popped in from hyperspace in an arrow formation and headed straight for the Rogue escort. "Whistler, pull manifests from each of the ships, then see if stated mass and performance profiles match." He hit a switch on his comm unit, bringing him online with the Rogue's tactical frequency. "Three, Five, and Six, fan out and pull life scans on the ships. If any of those ships are packed with more crew than we expect, I want to know about it."

Corran waited five minutes for the other X-wings to gather the data and for Whistler to crunch it all down. The various freighters appeared to be massing about as much as they should for their stated cargoes, and none of them was loaded down with troops, so Corran assumed the convoy was legitimate. "The convoy is secure from my standpoint, Mirax."

"I copy, Nine. This is *Pulsar Skate* to *Empress's Diadem*. You've been cleared for continuation of the journey."

"I copy, *Skate*. Feed us the coordinates and we can get this thing moving."

"Coordinates for exit vector, jump duration, and speed on their way."

Corran watched the data stream flow across the bottom of his monitor and wondered what Melina Carniss was making of it. He imagined she'd be disappointed because the first jump was just a short hop to a dead system. From there they'd get another exit vector that would put them on a straight line for the Yag'Dhul system, but the speed and duration data would suggest they were going to another system well beyond Yag'Dhul. *She'll be anticipating calling in a strike on Folor in the Commenor system.*

Corran smiled as he thought about the surprise the convoy would be in for during their journey. The speed that was being set for them would allow them to slip past the Yag'Dhul system in hyperspace, but Booster had thought of a way to end their journey prematurely. The gravity well projector he'd gotten from Karrde and had grafted onto the station would create enough of a gravity shadow to pull the convoy out of hyperspace. The premature end of the flight would deliver the goods where they were most needed and would be a trick clearly meant to conceal the location of the base from outsiders.

Which ought to be enough to make Carniss think secrecy is still important to us. Corran dearly wished he knew the full extent of Wedge's plan to deal with Isard's forces, but he respected the security provided by the compartmentalization of such information. *I doubt I'll know everything that goes on unless or until this is all over and I get debriefed.*

Corran brought his X-wing around on the appointed exit vector and chopped his throttle back to 51 percent of thrust. In hyperspace, the X-wings were twice as fast as the freighters, save Carniss's *Diadem* and Mirax's *Skate*. By dropping his thrust to just over half, the X-wing would arrive in-system just before the freighters and could head off any ambushes.

The other X-wings pulled up off his S-foils. "Nine to *Skate*. Escort is ready to head out."

"Lead on, Nine, and be careful."

"As ever, *Skate*. Wouldn't want your father to be disappointed in me."

33

Melina Carniss managed to keep a smile on her face and a light lilt in her voice despite being anxious to leave the Yag'Dhul station. "No, Mirax, no need to apologize. I've enjoyed your company over the last two days. I would have felt quite out of sorts and lonely had you not taken me under your wing."

Mirax smiled. "I'm glad you feel that way. I am sometimes accused of being somewhat smothering."

Somewhat? Lady, you could smother a Givin, and they don't need to breathe. "Again your company was appreciated. And let your father know I'm sure Karrde won't have a problem with my having been kept here awaiting payment. He's very understanding that way."

Mirax stepped back away from the turbolift opening. "See you on the next trip."

"I'm sure. Good-bye." Melina remained smiling even after the door closed. *Be just like her father to have security holocams set up here in the turbolift. I have to maintain the charade until I'm back aboard* Diadem.

Carniss had hoped to be away from the Yag'Dhul station as quickly as possible, but the delay in payment meant her ship was the last of the convoy to leave. Despite being a huge station, Yag'Dhul's docking bays were mostly in use, requiring a piecemeal unloading of the convoy. That delay meant the shipments couldn't be verified, hence the reason payment was late. Mirax's insistence that she leave *Diadem* and enjoy the station's facilities meant she had no chance to send a message out to Thyferra to report the location of Rogue base.

While it certainly was Mirax's fault that she'd not been able to make her report sooner, the fact was that she didn't really want to make it until her ship was outbound anyway. Her navicomputer had worked out the time it would take for Iceheart's taskforce to arrive at Yag'Dhul from Thyferra. Had she sent out the coordinates when she arrived, she would have been trapped on the station and killed along with all the others. *While Iceheart appreciates my information, I don't doubt I'm seen as expendable.*

Carniss exited the turbolift and cut between two battered freighters on her way to her ship. The motley collection of freighters and fighters reminded her of the force Karrde had said had been used to take Coruscant from Isard. *Except this force is lacking Star Destroyers and Mon Calamari cruisers.* Most of the ships looked as if they had been cobbled together from scrap salvaged from Endor or Alderaan. *Isard's* Virulence *could defeat this fleet all by itself.*

She walked up the ramp on her modified Corellian YT-1210 light freighter, the *Empress's Diadem*, and closed it behind her. The disk-shaped ship had a pair of blaster cannons in a turret mounted above and below a boxy concussion missile launch tube assembly that fired into the ship's aft arc. *What I can't outrun I can discourage from chasing me.*

"Peet," she shouted at her pilot, "get us off this station and bound for Corellia. We have business on Selonia. Once you compute the route and have the times, let me know. I'll be in my quarters."

"As ordered, Captain Carniss."

Melina headed back to her quarters and sealed the hatch behind her. Because space was at a premium on the freighter, her cabin was small, yet not without luxuries. Included among them was a small refresher station which meant she did not have to use the facilities shared by the rest of the crew. Since she was the only woman on board, the concession had a practical side to it, as well as serving to remind the crew of her superior status.

She opened the central drawer on her datapad desk and pulled it all the way out. On the back panel she slid aside a finger-length wafer of duraplast, revealing a small cavity. From it she pulled out a slender, silver capsule approximately the size of her smallest finger. She put it on the desk, then returned the duraplast wafer and the drawer to their proper places.

From her personal gear she got two small batteries and a transparisteel flask with a chrome bottom and capped with a chrome tumbler. She worked two screws loose on the bottom of the bottle and pulled the base off. Into the hollows in the base she snapped the batteries and the capsule. She fastened the flask's base back on the transparisteel bottle, then tossed the whole assembly into the refresher station's bowl and evacuated it.

The flush of disinfectant washed the flask down into a holding tank. As the *Diadem* came about on its exit vector, the pilot hit a switch that dumped the holding tank's contents out into space. The fluid immediately froze into a mass of blue ice that slowly began to drift in toward the system's sun. It would be months before the debris finally evaporated in the solar engine.

The sudden drop in temperature around the flask immediately started the capsule issuing orders. A tiny port opened in the tip of the flask's cap and a spark from the batteries ignited enough of the Savareen brandy to burn the flask free of the ice and jet it away. At the same time, a panel on the bottom of the flask opened up to expose electromagnetic sensors that started feeding system data to the capsule.

The capsule itself was really the heart of a probe droid. Stripped of the armor and devices necessary to let it enter an atmosphere and operate in a hostile environment, the droid took up a minimum of space and could easily function on batteries for a dozen hours. Its mission was simple: pinpoint the location of the system in which it was dropped, locate a hidden HoloNet transmission station, and pulse out a tight-beam message conveying that information to the station. The automated station would, in turn, deliver that information through the HoloNet to Fliry Vorru within seconds of its reception.

With the sensors, it mapped the sky and compared the configuration of stars with what would be available at various systems in the galaxy. While a complete catalog of systems would have required far more storage than the probe droid possessed, Vorru and his people had ruthlessly eliminated systems that lacked habitable worlds, had settlements that were insufficiently developed to help maintain the Rogues and their ships, or that otherwise appeared to be inappropriate.

Within an hour of beginning its mission, the probe droid found a match in its star catalog. It knew it was in the Yag'Dhul system. It oriented itself so it could pulse its message out to a clandestine HoloNet transmission site, but found an obstacle in its way. It did pick up comm frequencies emanating from the obstacle and also saw how many stars it blotted out of the sky, but had no way to identify it as a space station. It did catalog the item's presence, then it jetted up to a point where it could locate the relay station.

Once it found its target, the droid pulsed its message out. It continued to do so for the next three standard hours before a meteorite shattered the transparisteel flask and reduced the droid to so much junk orbiting Yag'Dhul.

Wedge looked out over the assembly of pilots in the station's amphitheater. They all looked eager, which was good, but that surprised him. When he began the briefing he expected their hungry expressions to melt into disappointment. "So, there it is: within the next twenty-four to thirty-six hours we anticipate the arrival of Isard's *Lusankya* and *Virulence* here at Yag'Dhul. We've already begun an evacuation of the station, with our ships taking up a position on the edge of this system. Their position provides a clean exit vector to

Thyferra, which is where you will be going along with them. Is that understood?"

Nawara Ven raised a hand. "Forgive me, Commander, but do you think having all of us fighters scramble and then run away will fool the Thyferran commanders?"

Bror Jace turned in his seat to look at Nawara. "If they were Thyferran commanders it wouldn't, but these are Imps. They're used to imagining that Rebels run at the sight of them."

Wedge smiled at Jace's answer. "Just as you've been simming a lot of antiship attacks, we've been simming the likely reactions on the Thyferran command level. We're pretty certain they'll believe our retreat, especially when we jump to lightspeed on a vector bound for Thyferra. Captain Drysso will assume, in our desperation to save the station we're going to strike at Thyferra. Because our snubfighters are twice as fast as the *Lusankya,* we'll have twelve hours there to batter Thyferra unopposed. He knows he can't beat us back there, so he'll finish our station off, then come after us."

Corran frowned. "What if his people pick up on the fact that we rendezvous with our freighters before we head out?"

"Still no cause of alarm for him. The *Lusankya* still outguns our entire fleet. More ships just provide his gunners with more practice." Wedge shrugged. "I know there are dozens of unanswered questions you have right now because I've been fairly vague about our overall plan and have just concentrated on your roles in what is going to happen. Your squadron leaders have more specific orders on which they will brief you at the appropriate time. Right now I just wanted to let you know that action is imminent, so you should take care to put your affairs in order and prepare any holograms you want sent in case of death."

Gavin smiled. "But you're not going to leave those things on the station here, are you?"

Wedge laughed. "No, we'll have them sent to Coruscant. Make no mistake about it, people, this won't be easy. A lot of us won't be coming back. There will be a terrible price to pay to liberate Thyferra, but an even greater one if we don't liberate it. We'll be taking a lot of risks, but we have no choice because this will be our best chance to destroy Isard. If we fail now, it could very well be that no one else will ever dare to oppose her."

Asyr let a little growl rumble from her throat. "So failure is not an option, eh, Wedge?"

"Not for us, Asyr, not by a long shot."

Fliry Vorru looked at the data scrolling up through the air above his holopad. Beyond the glowing green numbers he watched Erisi Dlarit study the information. "Rather ingenious of them, wasn't it, my dear, to choose the Yag'Dhul station as their base. You might have guessed."

Erisi nodded once, curtly. "I *did* guess and did some checking of my own. The station was ordered and reported destroyed. Pash Cracken signed the report indicating the station had been destroyed, so perhaps I should have been suspicious."

Vorru waved her remark away. "Don't berate yourself, Erisi."

"No, Madam Director will do that for me, won't she?"

Vorru smiled. "Ah, you know her so well. She does seem to visit injustice upon you with fair frequency. I think that is a situation that should change."

Erisi arched an eyebrow over an ice blue eye. "What did you have in mind?"

"See if your reasoning parallels my own. It strikes me that after the *Lusankya* is sent off to destroy the Yag'Dhul station, someone in the New Republic is going to have to take notice of how much firepower she possesses. While Zsinj has been more of a direct threat—and is why the New Republic fleet is out there hunting him down and, with any luck at all, destroying him—Ysanne Isard has succeeded in raising her profile rather considerably. The New Republic will be forced to deal with her sooner or later, and I'm inclined to think they will opt for sooner."

The Thyferran pilot nodded slowly. "I follow you so far."

"It strikes me that my position here is no longer going to

be profitable. I have managed, in my position, to set aside a certain amount of credits that would be sufficient, say, to purchase a planet. I would require a loyal staff and even a wing of pilots to keep my rivals at bay."

"I see. And would you be requiring my services as a pilot or my *company*?"

Vorru bowed his head in a salute. "Your services as a pilot would be most valuable to me. Your *company*, on the other hand, would be invaluable to me. I leave the choice of role to you, to be modified as you wish."

"Very well, I shall start as the commander of your pilots." Erisi clasped her hands at the small of her back. "How do you see this defection being accomplished?"

"After the *Lusankya* and the *Virulence* return from destroying the Yag'Dhul station, we will head out on the *Virulence* on an inspection tour of facilities. There will be an accident, we will disappear. It can be arranged."

"Then arrange it." Erisi looked around and toward the viewports displaying the planet's lush greenery. "Iceheart will find a way to destroy this world I love. I have no desire to be here when that happens."

"Nor do I, Erisi dear, nor do I."

34

Corran reached across the table at Flarestar and took Mirax's hand in his. "Thanks."

She gave his hand a squeeze. "Buying dinner was no big deal."

"That's not what I'm thanking you for." Corran glanced down at the table, then back up at her. "Seeing you sitting there I remember the first time I saw you, back on Talasea."

Mirax smiled. "Yeah, the lighting is dim enough in here to resemble that world."

He chuckled. "I was remembering how beautiful you looked then and how beautiful you are now."

"And I remember you cut a rather dashing figure in your flightsuit, then I had to go and spoil it by bringing our fathers' rivalry into things."

"But we got over that fast. Then I was remembering our last conversation on Coruscant before we headed out to conquer a world." His smile shrank somewhat. "And then I ruined what we were heading for by getting captured by Isard."

"Yet another crime for which she should pay."

"Agreed." Corran sat back as a serving droid started

clearing platters from their table. "A huge chunk of what gnawed at me while I was on the *Lusankya*, was knowing you thought I was dead. I didn't want to presume that my disappearance would have hurt you that much, but I knew how I'd have felt were our situations reversed."

Mirax nodded solemnly. "And now, in less than a day, we'll be tossed again into a fight where we both might die . . ."

Corran shot her a wry grin. "You wouldn't be trying to turn this into a 'sleep with me tonight because tomorrow we may die' thing, would you?"

"Me?" Mirax demurely pressed a hand against her breastbone. "Perish the thought. I'd never think of taking advantage of you like that—despite having bought you a lavish meal."

"Oh, no?"

"No."

"Why not?" Corran sniffed. "Am I not good enough for you?"

"You are that, but, as I recall, you're also already sleeping in my bed."

"Good point. It does sort of make this kind of seduction rather moot."

"True, but the flirtation is fun."

"I agree there, too." Corran smiled and tightened his grip on her hand ever so slightly, doing his best to make sure he didn't feed the pressure building in his chest into his hand. "And I can't think of anyone I would rather flirt with and be seduced by than you. In fact, I think we should make it permanent."

Mirax's brown eyes grew wide. "Lieutenant Corran Horn, are you asking me to marry you?"

"Look, I know this might seem abrupt. I mean, I know we've been living together since my return from the grave, but with all our missions and trips and everything, I'd guess we've not had more than three weeks in the last four months where we've actually been able to spend time alone with each other. Despite how hectic and chaotic things have been, what I do know is that I want more time to spend with you. I know that

I'm never going to find someone for whom I feel more than I feel for you."

"That's true, because if you did, I'd see to it that you stopped feeling altogether." Mirax squeezed his fingers. "Are you sure about this? Don't you want to talk to Iella about it?"

"She'd tell me I've been an idiot for not asking you to marry me sooner. She and Diric were as close as any two people I've ever seen; and despite the pain she's been through, I don't think she'd have surrendered one moment of their happiness together to make her feel better. For as long as I've known her she's had a habit of predicting how many weeks my relationships would last, and she was always on target. With us, no prediction."

"Always did think she was smart." Mirax held her right hand up. "One last thing, Corran: You realize that I'm not walking away from my lifestyle or my father. The Mirax Terrik you get is the Mirax Terrik you know."

"I think your father and I have an understanding, but even if we didn't, you'd be worth it. Realize I'm not going to change either."

"Wouldn't have it any other way."

Corran arched an eyebrow. "So?" He could feel his heart pounding in his chest. "Will you marry me?"

Mirax lifted his hand from the table and kissed it. "Yes, I will, Corran Horn."

The tension in him exploded in a nervous laugh that freed a single tear to roll down his cheek. He slipped his hand from hers, then pulled off the gold chain and Jedi medallion he wore. "This station isn't a good place for finding jewelry and I didn't want to ask Zraii to machine up a Quadanium ring, so all I have to offer you is this." He held the medallion out by the chain, but Mirax refused to take it.

"Corran, I know how much that medallion means to you. It's your good luck piece. I won't take it, especially just before the coming assault."

"Mirax, you've just agreed to marry me. Any luck left in this thing has clearly been drained. You're the most important person in the galaxy to me, so if this will keep you safe, or even if it will remind you of me, it's better off with you than hanging around my neck."

She accepted it from him and stared down at the medallion resting in her palm. She ran a thumb over Nejaa Halcyon's profile and slowly smiled. "Do you think our children will look like him?"

"Better him than your father." They both laughed. "At least for the boys, that is. If our daughters look like their mother, I'll be as pleased as possible and as protective of them as your father is of you."

Mirax looped the chain over her head and let it slip beneath her clothes. "I'm going to find you something that's just as special as this is. Maybe I'll talk to Zraii about fabricating something for you, something you'll never forget."

"Like what?"

"A ring, maybe, made from the *Lusankya*'s hull. It held you captive the way you hold my heart captive."

"You're good, Mirax, very good."

"I'm the best, Corran, and you always push me to excel."

He smiled. "So, when do we break the news to your father?"

Mirax paled slightly. "The *when* comes after the *how* I think. Give me some time to figure that out. We can tell Wedge, though, and some of the others, but that can wait until tomorrow. We have other things to do tonight."

"Such as?"

"You, Corran Horn, have asked me to marry you, I have accepted and I intend us to do everything right in our marriage." She stood up from the table and dragged him up after her. "Toward that end, there are certain things I think we should practice until we perform them perfectly."

Fliry Vorru found it easy to read the emotions running through the two ship captains. The briefing Ysanne Isard was giving them clearly frightened Captain Lakwii Varrscha. Though the woman stood taller and was more muscled than Ysanne Isard, she lacked the vitality that gave Isard her commanding presence. That the woman had risen so high in Imperial service marked her as competent, but Vorru felt her rise had much to do with the fact that she had hitched her career to that of Joak Drysso and his rising star had dragged her along to the limits of her abilities.

Joak Drysso, in contrast to Varrscha, was small and blocky, with prematurely gray hair that was matched by the color of his goatee. Despite his diminutive stature, he had an air of menace about him. Were it not for the perspective supplied by his surroundings, Vorru could have imagined him being a stormtrooper standing a hundred meters distant—lethal and not given to surrender.

Isard had chosen to wear her red Admiral's uniform for the briefing, despite the heat and humidity. "There it is, then. You will be attacking an *Empress*-class space station. The armaments and shielding are minimal, though the chance that some upgrades are in place cannot be overlooked. The Yag'Dhul system is twenty-four hours from here. I expect the station to be destroyed and you to return here within sixty hours from now. Are there any questions?"

Drysso nodded sharply. "I have to wonder, Madam Director, at why you are sending both the *Lusankya* and the *Virulence* on this mission. The *Lusankya*, as well you know, has more than enough firepower to obliterate the station. In addition I have twelve squadrons of TIE fighters at my disposal, which is more than enough to overwhelm Antilles's paltry forces. Even Minister Vorru's most generous estimates of the Rogue strength gives us a two to one advantage in fighters, and as good as the Rogues might be, they cannot hope to prevail against us."

Vorru cleared his throat. "You have forgotten the Alderaanian War Cruiser?"

"Its firepower is negligible. A Super Star Destroyer can absorb all the damage it can do and still destroy it at leisure. I will designate two squadrons of TIEs to keep it off me. There is no need for the *Virulence* to come with me on this mission. Moreover, its departure from Thyferra puts this world at risk."

Isard blinked. "At risk? From whom?"

"Antilles and his people. Recall, his X-wings are hyperspace capable. If they bolt when we arrive, they will be able to come here and have twelve hours to fly missions against positions here before we could possibly return."

Vorru frowned. "Toward what end? Antilles can't take this planet without troops."

"But he has them, Minister Vorru, in the Ashern rebels."

Isard waved their exchange away. "No matter—any gains they made in your absence would vanish when your return."

"Leaving the *Virulence* here would prevent even minimal gains." Drysso stroked his goatee. "While I have the utmost respect for and confidence in Captain Varrscha, her ship is not required on this mission."

"Nor is it required to safeguard Thyferra." Isard smiled slowly. "I have the Thyferran Home Defense Corps to ward off the Rogues, if they do what you say they will. What few of them the THDC allows to survive will be useless to the Ashern rebels. We can easily hold out for twelve or twenty-four hours—whatever it takes for your return. And the *Virulence* will be going with you to guarantee your return. Ait Convarion made the mistake you are making in underestimating Antilles. Convarion paid for his arrogance with his life."

Drysso accepted Isard's warning without a flicker of reaction. "I assure you, Madam Director, the *Lusankya* will return from Yag'Dhul victorious."

"I trust this will be the case, Captain Drysso, otherwise you'll have no reason to return here at all." Isard nodded solemnly. "You will find the consequences of failure most disagreeable."

Isard shifted her attention to Captain Varrscha and Vorru waited for the *Virulence*'s commander to collapse. "Captain Varrscha, you understand the mission as it has been given to you?"

"Yes, ma'am. The *Virulence* is to offer all aid and assistance to the *Lusankya* to complete its mission. I will execute Captain Drysso's orders instantly."

"Ah, I see." Isard's eyes narrowed. "You have served as Captain Drysso's subordinate officer for years now, yes?"

"Yes, ma'am."

"Following his orders is admirable, but what would you do if you thought he was making a mistake?"

"I don't understand the question, ma'am."

Anger curled its way through Isard's voice. "Are you capable of taking the initiative, Captain? If the *Lusankya* were suddenly faced with a threat, could you act to head that threat off without an order from Captain Drysso?"

"Yes, ma'am."

"Very good, Captain." Isard strolled over to where the other woman stood, her voice dropping to the level of a growled whisper. "Understand this: The *Lusankya* is more valuable than you or your ship. Its preservation is vital for our continued success here at Thyferra. You will do whatever you must to see to it that the ship returns here. Captain Drysso may consider your presence to be that of an observer, but I consider you a shield between the *Lusankya* and disaster."

Isard spun away from her and addressed all three of the individuals in the room. "If Antilles knows we are coming, he will have something prepared to oppose us. Even if he has not anticipated us, I do not think he will be helpless. He will be desperate, and desperation can inspire people to great feats of heroism. In desperation there is danger for our forces, so you must be careful. If your victory costs us too much, we could be in jeopardy."

Drysso's face became a resolute mask. "Victory will be mine, Madam Director."

"Those are famous last words, Captain Drysso." Isard snorted derisively. "Do your best to see you do not join the teeming mass of failures for whom those *were* the last words."

Iella Wessiri snapped the trigger assembly for her blaster carbine back into place and tightened the bolt to secure it. She picked up a power pack to slam it home, but stopped when Elscol Loro crouched and squeezed through the opening to the Vratix den they shared. "News?"

The smaller woman nodded. "All leaves have been canceled for crew from the *Lusankya* and the *Virulence*. Within six hours or so they should be under way."

"No convoy is forming up?"

"Nope, this is clearly a strike mission."

Iella frowned. "You mean *the* strike mission."

"Isard does appear to be dancing to the tune Wedge has called." Elscol shrugged. "I just hope Wedge can pay the synthesizer jockey when the bill comes due."

"He took Coruscant. Freeing this rock isn't going to be that much tougher."

"Yes, but Isard *wanted* the New Republic to have Coruscant. She's being a bit more possessive about Thyferra."

"True." Iella set her carbine down, then hit several buttons on her chronometer. "Well, this news puts us on the clock, then, I guess. Forty-eight hours after the *Lusankya* leaves Thyferra, Wedge and the others will be here. You've already told Sixtus we're on?"

"He and his taskforce are already heading to their staging points and expect to be in position to liberate the detention center when they get our signal."

Iella caught a funny note in Elscol's voice. "And you'd still like that signal to be a lift-truck bomb being flown into the Xucphra administrative headquarters to blow it up, right?"

"Call me silly, but I don't see why risking injury in an assault so you can capture Isard is preferable to scattering her constituent atoms all over the place with a bomb. And don't give me the justice line again."

Iella shook her head. "Look, I know how evil Isard is—she turned my husband into a mockery of himself. I'd like nothing better than to shove a blaster up her nose and melt her brain. I wouldn't consider it murder—"

"Nor would anyone else."

"—But her death isn't the point. Stopping her is. Even more important than that is to let her be tried in a court of law for her crimes. It's vital to let people know that the laws have purpose and that evil people *will* be held accountable for what they do."

Elscol frowned. "And a bomb doesn't do that?"

"A bomb is just more anarchy. Killing her that way will allow people to say she had to be kept quiet or important people would have been revealed to be collaborators. Blowing her up allows people to say she really escaped the blast. The lack of a trial, because she won't be held accountable for all of her crimes, means people can begin to think she wasn't so bad. Twenty years from now, thirty or fifty, there could be a neo-Imperial movement that holds her up as an example to be emulated. Blowing her up will make her a martyr, but a trial will show her up as a monster, warts and all."

Elscol chewed her lower lip for a moment, then shook her head. "Well, I hate to admit it, but you're actually making some sense. I must need a vacation."

"We *all* need a vacation."

"Okay, we'll find some resort on a world where the Empire is just a nasty rumor, *if* we survive this assault of yours."

"*When* we survive it, you mean."

Elscol smiled. "Right, *when* we survive it. I hope, though, you aren't expecting me to go in there with my selector lever on stun. Ain't going to happen."

Iella retrieved her carbine and slid a power pack home. "If it shoots back, I'm shooting to kill. With Vorru, Isard, or Dlarit, I'll go for a stun shot, but only if that's not going to get me or anyone else killed."

"Your plan calls for more finesse than the bomb, but I guess we can make it work."

"We will." Iella nodded solemnly. "Two days until Thyferra regains its freedom and Ysanne Isard loses hers."

35

Captain Joak Drysso let a low sinister laugh fill the dark hollow of the ready-room on the *Lusankya*. He recalled with holographic clarity the image of the *Executor* plunging into the heart of the half-completed Death Star at Endor. He'd known at that point that the battle was lost, so he'd taken his *Virulence* and fled from the battle. *I always knew I would have another chance to crush Rebels.*

He didn't believe for an instant the fiction that Antilles and his people were outcasts from the New Republic. Theirs was obviously a mission meant to keep Isard bottled up until they could deal with her—and Antilles had done a good job of keeping her attention on him. Had he not preoccupied her, she might have seen the wisdom of creating an Imperial Combine, bringing together the various Warlords out there to put an end to the New Republic. It would have been very successful, he was certain of that, and she could have even led it because she possessed what everyone else wanted: Bacta.

Isard's short-sightedness in this regard didn't surprise Drysso, primarily because she thought like a politician, not a warrior. Isard took great delight in being subtle and tricky, then when she decided to wield a hammer, she did it in a very clumsy manner. Sending Convarion out to destroy Halanit was a wasted gesture. An assault shuttle and a squadron of TIEs could have laid waste to that settlement. The attack did nothing but salve her ego and anger Antilles.

He would have handled things entirely differently. Drysso had agreed a strike was necessary, but he would have gone after Corellia and brought the Diktat to heel, adding Corellia and its shipyards to the Iceheart Empire. That would supply them the means of building more ships. He would have then badgered Kuat into making a similar deal, giving him access to those shipyards. *And then on to Sluis Van. Once I have those three sites under my control, I can strangle the New Republic by restricting trade—without ships and shipyards, nothing moves between stars.*

Drysso had chosen to stay with Isard because he thought she represented the best chance at reestablishing the Empire, and because she had the most legitimate claim to the throne itself. He had supported her decision to abandon Coruscant—*a world that does not provide the means to wage war is worth little in a war*. The New Republic's conquest of it *did* hamper the Rebellion, and Isard's possession of the Bacta Cartel put her in a very powerful position in the galaxy.

Unfortunately, her power is embodied by this ship. Drysso caressed the arms of the command chair in which he sat. *Only through this ship can she project her power to other worlds, command their compliance and punish their defiance. Now this ship is mine and thus is her power ceded to me.*

The comlink clipped to his jacket beeped. "Drysso here."

"Captain, five minutes to reversion to realspace."

"On my way to the bridge." Drysso stood and strode from the ready-room to a turbolift for the short ride up to the bridge. As the lift slowed, he composed himself, setting his face with a stern expression. The door opened and he immediately strode out onto the Captain's walk. "Report, Lieutenant Rosion."

The Chief Navigator looked up from the pit where he worked. "We're coming in as scheduled. The station is in orbit around Yag'Dhul, occupying an orbit outside of that of the largest of Yag'Dhul's three moons, with its position always opposite that moon. We are coming in on the only good entry vector that won't run us afoul of the world, its moons, or the system's sun. The station should be clear for an attack once we close into range."

"Very good." Drysso glanced over at his communications officer. "Ensign Yesti, when we revert to realspace, please inform the *Virulence* that we expect it to come in below us at a range of twenty kilometers. Inform Captain Varrscha she is not to power her weapons up except under my direct order."

"As ordered, Captain."

Drysso continued to walk forward until he reached the viewing station. The light tunnel through which the ship sped began to break down into long shafts of light. They, in turn, resolved themselves into unwavering gemstones set in a black blanket. Directly ahead of the ship's distant prow, the system's sun burned brightly. Yag'Dhul and its moons appeared as colorful spheres hanging in space. Silhouetted against Yag'Dhul's gray face, the space station appeared to be little more than a cross—insignificant and defenseless.

"Captain, we're showing signs of snubfighter deployment at the station."

"Very well, tell Colonel Arl he is free to deploy his fighters in a defensive screen. Have you spotted the Alderaanian War Cruiser yet?"

"Negative," reported Drysso's aide. "We are clear for a hundred kilometers around us, and *Virulence* is reporting similar clearance."

"Push the sensor sphere out to two hundred kilometers, Lieutenant Waroen, and keep scanning the fringes of the system for that War Cruiser. Time to engagement?"

"Ten minutes to range."

"Bring our shields up to full."

"As ordered, sir."

Drysso stroked his goatee as he watched the station grow larger. The scrambling of the station's snubfighters did not surprise him. That was the only reaction they could have, which is why he countered with deploying his fighters in a screen. It would be difficult for the X-wings to work their way through his screen and, while engaging in dogfights, all but impossible for them to maintain the sort of unit cohesion needed for a crushing volley of proton torpedoes to be launched at his ship. While proton torpedoes and concussion missiles were certainly a danger to his ship, they were only a danger in vast quantities—far more than three dozen snubfighters could possibly deliver.

"Captain, the snubfighters are going to lightspeed."

"Thank you, Waroen. Please confirm they are outbound for Thyferra."

His aide's surprise rang through his reply. "Yes, sir, that's it exactly."

"Good. They will arrive there after twelve hours in tiny cockpits, short on fuel and sleep. The Thyferrans can deal with them. We'll make certain they have no place to return to."

Light laughter greeted his comment, then the communications officer raised his voice above the din. "Captain, we have an incoming message from the station."

Drysso turned and pointed to a holoprojector pad to his left. "Please, Ensign Yesti, route it here." As the image began to resolve itself into that of a tall man with one artificial eye, Drysso raised himself to his full height. "This is Captain Joak Drysso of the *Lusankya*. Your fighters have deserted you."

"I sent the fighters off to play with something more their size." The tall man's hologram posted its fists on its hips. "I'm Booster Terrik, and this is my station. Your rate of closure puts you five minutes out from your preferred range for this sort of operation. I'll give you those five minutes before I destroy your ship."

"You're rather bold, Terrik, for having a station with minimal shields, a half-dozen laser cannons, and ten turbolaser batteries."

Terrik's image laughed. "We've made some modifications to the station." The figure nodded to someone outside the image area.

Drysso felt the *Lusankya* rock a bit. He immediately signaled for Yesti to cut off the transmission, then he snarled at his aide. "What happened?"

"They powered up a gravity well projector. It's projecting a cone of energy in our direction. It can't hurt us—the bump was just our own gravity-keeping generators adjusting the gravity on the ship. We have no damage or injury reports coming in."

Drysso frowned. The only thing the gravity well projector did was prevent them from turning and going to light-speed while still in the cone. "Lieutenant Rosion, compute hyperspace solutions for me."

"That will be difficult, sir. Because of Yag'Dhul's density, the array of the moons, and the gravity cone, we're severely limited in our choices. All we can do is run away from the plane of the elliptic until we escape the current constraints on us, then head out. If you want us to return to Thyferra, our best bet would be get free, take a short jump to the edge of the system, and then head back on our entry vector, since that is the fastest route to Thyferra."

Something else is going on here. "Lieutenant Waroen, shift assets to scan the edges of the system along our entry/exit vector."

"Yes, sir."

Drysso turned to watch his red-haired aide work. The young man's pale complexion drained further of color. "Sir, I have a small taskforce on the system rim. It is composed of snubfighters and freighters and maybe a larger ship."

"An ambush?"

"Perhaps, no, wait. Sir, the ships are outbound toward Thyferra. Exit speed is consistent with that of the freighters or our own ships."

Drysso nodded, then turned back toward the viewport. His assessment of Antilles's tactics had been correct: the man opted to send part of his force to Thyferra. The fact that the freighters had been waiting at the edge of the system indicated that Antilles had indeed anticipated their strike. *Even with freighters and the War Cruiser in support of his operation, he can do little to hurt Thyferra. His troops will be tired because of the journey and unable to fight well. Moreover, once I destroy this station, I can return to Thyferra. I will arrive shortly after he does and pounce on his forces, destroy-*

ing them. The gravity well will buy him some time, but not enough.

Drysso pointed to the holopad. "Yesti, open a comm channel with the station. Lieutenant Rosion, bring us to range and have us hold there, please."

"As ordered, Captain. Engines, all stop."

Terrik's image appeared again on the *Lusankya*'s bridge. "I notice you have stopped, Captain Drysso. Do you have surrender on your mind?"

Drysso smiled. "I do. Yours."

Terrik's anticipatory smile faded into puzzlement. "I guess you think we don't want to fight. Believe me, we do." Again he gestured to someone outside the image area and a much heavier tremor shook the *Lusankya*. "As your people will tell you, we've just powered up all of our tractor beams and have them on you. You can try to break free, but if you do, I've got to see a man about a guarantee he gave me."

"You better hope he works fast. Rosion, engines full back. Break those locks."

"Can't, sir. Helm is sluggish and those beams are very powerful."

Drysso snarled at Terrik. "You give me only one choice."

"Good. The terms of surrender are . . ."

"No, you fool, my choice is your complete destruction. Weapons, all bear on the station. Fire on my command!"

"Emperor's black bones!"

Drysso whipped around and spitted Lieutenant Waroen with a harsh stare, but his aide remained engrossed by a monitor and missed it. "What is happening, Waroen?"

"Sir, we have multiple proton torpedo and concussion missile sensors locked onto us."

"How many?"

"Many, sir, over three hundred." Waroen looked up. "We're dead, sir."

Drysso turned back to the viewport and imagined the rippling fire of three hundred proton torpedoes and concussion missiles smashing into his forward shield. Under that onslaught it would collapse and the missiles would begin nibbling away on his ship. *And that's only the first volley.* The subsequent volleys would consume the *Lusankya* utterly and completely.

With Drysso's vision of disaster came the crumbling of his plans for the future. The *Lusankya* was the key to everything, but he'd been tricked. Antilles had anticipated the strike at the station. He had set up a trap to destroy the Super Star Destroyer. *Even if I do shoot and eliminate some of the launchers, some of the tractor beams, all that will get away will be a severely damaged ship.*

Drysso hesitated and that hesitation should have lost him his ship and his dreams.

Two kilometers off his bow, the *Virulence* lanced upward, eclipsing the station. All of a sudden the Imperial Star Destroyer began to shrink, but it was only when he saw stars flashing back into sight at the corners of his vision did he realize why it was disappearing. *They're not destroying my ship, we're speeding away from the station—engines are still at full reverse. The* Virulence *broke the locks by interposing itself between us and the station.*

Drysso smiled and tasted sweat in the corners of his mouth. *We're free of the trap Antilles laid for us. He thought he had found a way to destroy us, but he did not. Now we get to spring a trap on him.*

The *Lusankya*'s Captain turned to face his bridge crew. "Rosion, plot a course back to Thyferra, as fast as we can get there. Yesti, send *Virulence* our thanks. Tell them their sacrifice will be remembered—a sacrifice that allowed us to destroy Wedge Antilles and hasten the Empire's rebirth."

Waroen looked up at him, disbelieving. "We're not going to help them, sir?"

"They're just doing their duty, Lieutenant." Drysso's mouth soured with the fear of ever engaging the station. "We now go to do *ours*."

36

By the time the *Lusankya* reverted to realspace, Captain Drysso had constructed a complete rationalization for his actions. He knew it was just that: a thin fabric of facts, circumstances and lies that would probably crumble under Isard's scrutiny. The fact remained, though, that he needed an explanation, and it was the best he could come up with.

It all started with the premise that Antilles's station would kill the *Lusankya*. This he knew and had the sensor reports to back it up. Isard herself had made it very clear that preserving the *Lusankya* was vital, so disengaging when given the opportunity to do so was the only choice he had. With the station being as heavily armed as it was, the only prudent course of action would be to cordon it off and let the inhabitants starve until they chose to surrender.

Once disengagement had been mandated, the next course of action had also been obvious. He had sensor reports to indicate Antilles, the War Cruiser, and dozens of freighters had headed out for Thyferra. That was a much larger taskforce than Isard had anticipated being used against Thyferra. Only by returning home at flank speed could the *Lusankya* be in position to destroy that taskforce. In fact, it seemed rather obvious, that without the *Lusankya*'s help, the Thyferran Home Defense Corps would be overwhelmed.

He had no choice but to return to Thyferra.

He realized that abandoning his TIE fighters at Yag'Dhul could be criticized, but he could even explain that away. The TIEs were meant to supplement the *Virulence*'s defenses—the fighters could track and shoot down missiles before they could strike the Imperial Star Destroyer. He also expected them to get in close enough to the station to destroy launchers and then complete the destruction of the station. That his pilots were dead if both the station and the *Virulence* were destroyed meant little to him—they had their duty to do just as he had his. If he remained to pick them up, he would have been destroyed.

Standing before the bridge viewport, he anticipated reversion into a battlefield. As the light tunnel melted away into a scattering of stars, he saw the green-and-white ball of Thyferra above him. No X-wings swooped about. No TIEs filled the void with green laser fire. He saw nothing out of the ordinary, just freighter traffic and a few system patrols.

Drysso slammed a fist off the transparisteel viewport. He'd been had by Antilles. The feint at Thyferra had drawn him off, causing him to sacrifice the *Virulence*. *The Rogues probably abandoned the station except for a handful of volunteers who were willing to trade their lives for that of the* Virulence. *The convoy I saw heading away from Yag'Dhul probably moved to another base—a base we'll have to search out, all the while enduring more hit-and-run attacks by the Rogues.*

Lieutenant Waroen's voice cut through the cocoon of mortification closing around Drysso's mind. "Captain, we have an Imperial Star Destroyer reverting to realspace twenty-five kilometers to our aft."

How did Varrscha get the Virulence *out of there?* Drysso looked over at the holoprojector pad. "Yesti, open a comm channel to that ship. Captain Varrscha, how did you get away?"

It took him a moment to recognize the holographic image facing him, but when he did he felt a cold hand tighten around his heart. "Captain Drysso, I fear you've mistaken my *Freedom* for your *Virulence*." Captain Sair Yonka smiled at him. "Don't say you're happy to see me—you won't be."

"Captain Drysso, the *Freedom* is deploying snubfighters, X-wings and Uglies."

Drysso stopped before he ordered his own nonexistent fighters into battle. "Contact the planet and have the THDC's squadrons scrambled. I want all their fighters up here protecting me. Helm, bring us about to engage the *Freedom*." He pointed a finger at Yonka's image. "I don't think, sir, when all is said and done, you will be happy that *I've* seen *you*."

The abundant undergrowth around the Xucphra corporate headquarters provided Iella and her people the means to get within twenty-five meters of the back entrance. They had expected to walk up to it, set a little lock-popping charge on it, blow it open, and be inside before much of an alarm could be raised. Ten meters along the corridor beyond the transparisteel door they'd be in the building's security center and would be able to control alarms and access to corridors and turbolifts.

But now there are two stormtroopers standing guard at the door. At first glance they looked to be the genuine articles, but Iella noticed they chatted back and forth quite a bit. *THDC banthas in rancor clothing.* Even so, the strip of open ground she needed to cover was enough that the guards, no matter how poorly trained, should be able to cut her down. Because they had been prepared for a close assault, none of her people carried a blaster rifle, just carbines and pistols, so killing both of them from cover was impossible. *We might hit them with carbine shots at this range, but the armor means we don't have a guaranteed kill.*

She needed a diversion, but the only real option she had was to use an explosive charge to distract them. The problem with that idea was that if it didn't kill them, they'd undoubtedly report the explosion, providing more of an alert to the forces inside than she wanted. She reached for her comlink to ask Elscol to divert some of her people to help out, when a TIE fighter screamed overhead at treetop level.

As a second and third TIE screeched past, Iella saw the door guards look up and point at the starfighters. One even took his helmet off to get a better look, tucking his headgear under his arm. Without a second thought Iella stood and strode from the undergrowth in their direction, shielding her carbine from sight with her body and turning her head to likewise watch the starfighters fly past.

A full dozen of the fighters roared out of their hangar, letting Iella know Wedge and his people had finally arrived. *Now if I can just do my part.* She looked up at the guards, smiling at them, as she reached the base of the stairs leading to the door.

" 'Scuse us, ma'am, but you can't be here." The helmet-less guard leaned his blaster carbine against the wall and began to fumble with his helmet again. "Restricted area."

"Oh, sorry." Iella reinforced her smile, then brought her blaster carbine up. She scythed fire back and forth, burning holes in the white plastoid armor over the guards' chests and bellies. The helmet fell from lifeless hands and bounced down the ferrocrete stairs as she ran up past it. She stepped over the body of one guard, then leveled her carbine at the door's lock and triggered a burst of scarlet fire that vaporized it.

Before she could push the door in with her foot, two Ashern Vratix reached the landing. With their powerful legs they kicked the guards' bodies off the landing. Brandishing blaster pistols fitted with adapters to accommodate their thick-fingered hands, the Ashern warriors bulled their way through the door and stalked down the hallway.

The security station's duraplast door crumpled beneath a Vratix kick. The Vratix went in, and lurid blue backlighting accompanied their assault. Iella arrived at the doorway seconds behind them and went in with her carbine ready, but all three of the Xucphra security police were out. Two had never even had a chance to draw their blasters and all three lay in pools of steaming caf.

"Definitely picked the wrong time to be taking a break. Secure them so they won't be a problem when they wake up."

Two human resistance fighters complied with her orders while a third dropped into the chair at the center of the building's security console. "Can you shut this place down, Jesfa?"

"Can a Vratix jump?" The dark-haired commando pointed at the twin banks of four monitors atop the console. "These provide views of various sites around the building— one for each of six floors and the two towers. I can see everything and," he added as he settled his fingers on the keyboard, "from here I can shut everything down. This is the same system I used to use when I worked security for Zaltin."

"Good. Lock everything down except for one turbolift. Secure the shuttle hangars in the towers and open up the main entrance."

"Consider it done. I'll shift my comlink to Tac-two so I can keep you apprised of anything I see."

Iella smiled. "Do that, but don't be surprised if they shoot the holocams out. I would."

She patted him on the shoulder, then fished her comlink out of her pocket. "Hook to Blade, we're in. The way is clear for you."

"On our way, Hook." Elscol sounded happy for the first time Iella could remember. "Good work."

Erisi Dlarit's anger at having her squadron last in the long line of Thyferran Home Defense Corps fliers heading out to engage the Rebels made her tighten her grip on the Interceptor's controls. Might Squadron, a group of green pilots that shared hangar facilities with her Elite Squadron, had been scrambled immediately. *They take their name to mean strength, but we've always considered it the answer to the question "Will they fight?"*

She'd had to place a call to Isard's office to find out why her pilots had not been called up, but no one there answered. Exercising the discretion her position gave her, Erisi immediately scrambled her own squadron. *Better we're destroyed in space than destroyed on the ground.*

The instant she became airborne, Erisi pulled tactical data from ground control and didn't like what she saw. An

Imperial Star Destroyer and an Alderaanian War Cruiser were moving to engage the *Lusankya*. The Imperial Star Destroyer had rolled and was flying along so its hull was perpendicular to that of the *Lusankya*. This would allow the Impstar's port gunners to be shooting down the top of the Super Star Destroyer. The Alderaanian War Cruiser worked back toward the *Lusankya*'s aft; and once it worked its way in past the system's freighter traffic, it would be able to attack the larger ship's engines.

The snubfighters deployed by the Impstar were closing in formation on the *Lusankya*. The THDC fighter squadrons coming up to oppose them were not flying together, but were strung out so the Rogues would engage them piecemeal. *That's suicidal.*

Erisi punched up a tactical frequency on her comm unit. "Elite Lead to Virile Lead. Slack your speed and let Might Squadron join up with you."

"No can do, Elite Lead. We have our orders."

"Consider them countermanded. Make sense, this is Rogue Squadron you're facing."

"And it's Rogue Squadron we'll be killing. For the glory of Thyferra."

Erisi popped her comm unit over the tactical frequency the Elites used. "Stay tight, Elites. We're going for the Rogues. Let's hope our comrades tire them out."

Wedge watched the tactical feed coming from the *Valiant* and felt a cold chill creep up his spine. "What are they doing? Why are they coming in at us like that?"

His R5 unit whistled curtly.

Wedge glanced at his monitor and smiled. "That was a rhetorical question, Gate. You wouldn't have sufficient data to be able to calculate an answer." After his last outing, Wedge had let the techs wipe Mynock's memory and upgrade his software. Because of the modifications Zraii made on the droid, he also learned the droid's designation had been changed to R5-G8, which he just truncated into Gate. "Give me a check on the transponder."

Another quick whistle announced it was in full working order.

Wedge keyed his comm unit. "Thirty seconds to the first wave of TIEs. Remember, our goal is to get at the *Lusankya*, not to spend our time dogfighting up here. Kill what you must, but keep with the mission. Two, stay with me."

"As ordered, Lead," came Asyr's reply.

Wedge flicked his lasers over to dual-fire mode, picked a target among the incoming TIEs, then waited for his aiming reticle to go red. As it did he tightened up on the trigger, letting two bursts of fire go, then dove away from the hissing green laser fire splashing against his forward screen.

His maneuver prevented him from seeing what happened to his target, but Gate dispassionately flashed the message "Target eliminated" in bloodred letters at the bottom of the monitor. *Maybe Mynock wasn't really that bad.* Wedge glanced at his sensor readouts and saw only a pair of TIEs in his wake. *Everyone got one, nice shooting.* He decided to leave the other two for the Twi'lek *Chir'daki* pilots following them in.

Gate hooted at him.

"Thanks, Gate, I've got thirty seconds to the next TIE wave." He opened the tactical comm channel. "Tighten it up, Rogues. Two more squadrons, then we should be clear to go in."

37

Corran suppressed a laugh. "Only two more flights, Lead? I count five, including one of squints."

"Agreed, Nine, but there is a two-minute gap between three and four, and another two minutes between five and the squints. I thought we could use that time to down the *Lusankya*. With your permission."

"Granted, Lead."

Corran hauled back on his stick as the second TIE flight came in, then barrel-rolled to starboard and came over the top. The X-wing pointed itself straight at a pair of TIEs that broke to follow his climb, but his inversion brought him in below their flight arc. One of them tried to pull a quick loop to bear down in on him while the other tried to force his TIE fighter down into a dive to spot Corran again.

Corran triggered two quad bursts of fire at the diving TIE. Two of the four laser bolts in the first shot missed, but the other two seared scars along the bottom of the starboard hexagonal wing. The second burst struck the bottom of the ball cockpit, slicing off the bottom third of it and severely warping the fighter's structural elements. The twin ion engines ripped free of their supports and blew through the cockpit canopy, then exploded.

Corran rolled away to port to escape the blast, then hit the right rudder pedal and brought the X-wing's nose around to starboard. The looping TIE came out of its maneuver and spitted itself on his aiming reticle. It went red, and Corran triggered a shot at it. All four laser bolts converged on its starboard solar panel and punched through to the cockpit. Corran saw a brief flash of light, then the TIE started a corkscrew down toward Thyferra.

"Ten has the next flight, Nine."

Corran tucked his X-wing back in behind and to port of Ooryl's fighter. The Gand rolled his X-wing up on the port stabilizers, presenting the incoming TIEs with a very narrow profile to shoot at. Corran aped his maneuver and watched as four TIEs separated themselves from the rest of the formation to come after Ooryl. He glanced at his sensors.

"Whistler, why didn't you say we were getting ahead of the rest?"

The droid hooted a quick response.

"I would too have listened to you." Corran keyed his comm unit. "Ten, we're all alone here for a bit."

"Ooryl understands, Nine." Corran caught an edge to Ooryl's voice he couldn't recall hearing before. "Ooryl has them."

Ooryl has them? That sounds like something Jace or I would say.

Ahead of him, Ooryl triggered a quick burst of quad fire that hit a TIE in the cockpit canopy and blew the engines out the back of it. A little etheric rudder shifted his aim point to port, then a second shot disintegrated another TIE's port solar panel. Ooryl rolled out to port, then dove below the remaining TIEs.

Sithspawn, that's great flying! Corran inverted his X-wing and pulled back on the stick to follow Ooryl's dive, but by then the Gand had started his fighter around in a grand loop. Corran rolled again to follow, but a sharp bleat from Whistler made him glance at his aft monitor. "Ten, your playmates are on my tail."

"Ooryl copies, Nine. Continue on your arc."

"Continue? They're coming up fast."

"No longer."

Up ahead Corran saw Ooryl's X-wing tighten its arc impossibly quick, swapping nose for tail in the space of two hundred meters. The ship remained inverted, so Corran couldn't see the cockpit, but he could imagine the Gand's mouthparts moving apart in his imitation of a smile. "Ready to break on your mark, Ten."

"Go to port, Nine. Mark."

Corran rolled to port, then, as Ooryl had done, he reversed his thrust. Instead of looping the ship, Corran applied rudder until his nose swung back along the path he had just traveled. He came about just in time to see Ooryl melt the wing off another TIE.

Its wingman dove abruptly away from the Gand's trap.

"Great shooting, Ten. You've got a hot hand."

"Thank you, Nine."

"Three flight, want to tighten it up here?"

"As ordered, Lead." Corran started his thrust pushing his fighter forward. "Come on, Ooryl. We've got a big target now."

Captain Drysso watched the holopad's display of the battle. "Helm, *Freedom* is trying to slash over the top of us. Roll us so we can track her."

"Captain, if you do that, we'll expose our ventral surface to the snubfighters."

"I know that, Helm." Drysso looked over at the beefy man heading up his gunnery command. "Guns, use our ion cannons on *Freedom*. I want that ship."

"Captain, Guns copies your order, but requests you reconsider."

Drysso's eyes narrowed. "We have more ion cannons than that ship has guns, Lieutenant Gorev. I want it, and you'll give it to me. I don't want to destroy it unless necessary. Antilles got one of our Impstars, now we'll have one of his."

"What about the snubfighters and the War Cruiser?"

"Use our concussion missiles. Use all our turbolasers and heavy turbolaser batteries."

"The snubs are too small for turbolasers to track them. The War Cruiser is in our aft, so my missiles are having difficulty finding firing solutions."

"By all that's Imperial, you'll find solutions, Lieutenant Gorev, or someone else will be in your position, do you understand?" Drysso's hand rose with his voice. "Understand me, people. This is a *Super Star Destroyer*. A handful of snubfighters and a ship a tenth of our size cannot hurt us. Do what you are told and victory will be ours!"

Fliry Vorru had seen the TIE Interceptors flash past the viewports of his office and knew the time to make his escape from Thyferra had come. *My shuttle is hyperspace capable. I run suborbital to the far side of the planet, wend my way clear of obstructions, and vanish.* He collected a fistful of datacards and tucked them inside his tunic.

He reached the door to his office and found it wouldn't open. He quickly punched a security override code into the locking mechanism, and it opened. In his outer office he found two stormtroopers and his secretary trying to open the door to the hallway.

"Stand back. Elicia, please do yourself a favor and duck behind your desk. When they come for you, tell them horrible stories about me, and they will protect you." As the blonde did as she was told, the stormtroopers came to attention. "You two will conduct me to my shuttle hangar in the east tower."

Vorru punched a security override code into the lock, and it opened as well. Stepping into the hallway, he pointed out the security holocams at either end of the hallway. "Destroy them."

With a volley of shots his guards complied with his order and Vorru realized they were just Home Defense Corps personnel. *Of course, the amount of clattering their armor makes could have told me that.* He waved them on after him and quickly worked his way toward the east end of the building, shooting holocams as they went. "Since the locks only respond to security override codes, we have to assume the Ashern are in the building. They will control the turbolifts, so we'll be using stairs."

Vorru ignored the grumbles from his escort and got them to the east tower without meeting any resistance. *So far, very good.* He forced one of them to precede him up the stairs and had the other one follow, but the precaution proved unnecessary as they saw no one and nothing while they climbed up two floors. They emerged from the stairwell on the hangar level. "Down around the corner, to the right. Hurry, I hear the engines powering up."

This did not please Vorru, since he had intended to pilot the shuttle himself—primarily because he was the only pilot he wanted to know his final destination. The fact that the shuttle had already begun to power up meant someone else had decided to use his means of escape, which created a huge set of complications to be dealt with. Vorru's displeasure with the situation bled into his words, causing his guards to sprint on ahead of him and around the corner to the hangar.

A volley of scarlet blaster bolts sent the armored guards tumbling back down the hallway. They slammed into the wall and rebounded, but were hit by a half dozen more shots before they landed on the floor. One laser carbine came spinning across the floor to trip Vorru up. He crashed down hard, but bit back a curse and thereby saved his own life.

From the ground he had a narrow view of the hangar and the cloaked forms of two of Isard's Royal Guards walking from the doorway over toward his shuttle. *Isard! She's using my shuttle to escape. How dare she!*

Vorru snatched up the blaster that had tripped him, then sprinted into the hangar. At point-blank range he shot both of the men in scarlet armor in the back, then dove for cover as the shuttle's laser cannons sprayed the hangar with bolts. He felt the hot backblast of the shuttle's maneuvering jets as it lifted off, then emptied the blaster's power cell by pumping shot after shot into the vanishing shuttle's shields.

Vorru tossed the useless blaster aside and rose from the floor. "She probably thinks I'm stuck here, but I'd have been as stupid as she is if I only had one bolt hole." He toed one of the Royal Guards, then flipped the body over and pulled the blaster carbine it had been lying on from the floor. "I will survive this, Ysanne Isard, if for no other reason than to make you pay for the trouble you've given me."

As Corran's X-wing raced in on the *Lusankya,* the Super Star Destroyer began to roll. "Lead, what do we do?"

"Stay on target. We may not be edge-on anymore, but we can hit the guns from below. Commence weave, thirty seconds to firing position."

Corran rolled his fighter to starboard, opening up some room between himself and Ooryl. He pulled back on his stick and nudged it to port, throwing the X-wing into a spiral the pilots referred to as a weave. The fighter's movements were not wholly regular, making it all but impossible for the *Lusankya*'s gunners to get a good shot at them. *Of course, one good shot with those heavy turbolasers and all the bacta in the galaxy couldn't help me.*

The *Lusankya*'s heavy weapons filled the void with countless bolts of green laser energy. The shots spiraled out as crews tried in vain to target the incoming snubfighters. Corran studied the bases of the cones, mentally recording the location of each battery. *Those are what make this mountain of metal dangerous. Destroy them and it's just a big box in space.*

Despite the spiral, getting a target lock on the *Lusankya* was not hard at all. Corran shifted his weapon's-control over to proton torpedoes and linked them for dual-fire. The box at the center of his head-up display went red immediately and Whistler sounded a constant tone indicating target lock. "Good, Whistler, good." He punched a button on his communication console that started green, then quickly shifted to red.

"Nine has double-lock. I'm firing."

"Launch, Nine, then get clear."

"As ordered, Lead." Corran pulled the trigger on his stick and watched two proton torpedoes streak away at their target. "Pull the *Lusankya*'s fangs and hope we don't get gummed to death on the way out."

38

Drysso stared down at his aide. "How many incoming torpedo tracks, Lieutenant Waroen?"

"Twenty, sir."

Two per X-wing. Survivable. "You see, only twenty."

"Wait, sir. I have twenty-four."

"No matter."

"Now I have forty, no, eighty. Eight zero."

Drysso's jaw dropped as he saw a nova flare blossom up over the horizon of his starboard bow. The shields held for a second or two, then collapsed. Warning sirens started shrieking on the bridge as multiple torpedo and missile hits exploded six kilometers away on the ship's bow. The brilliant fire gnawed at the clean lines of his ship, shattering armor plates and triggering dozens of secondary and tertiary explosions.

Even before the tremors reached the bridge, Drysso started shouting orders. "Waroen, kill those sirens. Give me damage control reports. Guns, what have you lost and why haven't you gotten me the *Freedom* yet?"

Waroen's voice rose above the din. "Captain, we have full bow shield collapse."

"How did they get that many missiles off, Lieutenant?"

"Sir, I don't know, sir."

"Sithspawn! Find out how!" Drysso watched as the *Freedom* fired down at the Super Star Destroyer. Salvos of red turbolaser bolts pulsed out from the smaller ship, savaging the *Lusankya*'s unprotected bow. Vaporized armor immediately condensed into metal clouds that hid the full extent of the damage done, but Drysso had no hopes that his bow would look like anything but a blackened, battered lump. *Still, that damage is nothing compared to what we can do.*

Over a hundred starboard ion cannons fired back at the *Freedom* in a display so massive it appeared as if sheets of blue energy had erupted from the *Lusankya*'s side. The Imperial Star Destroyer's shields imploded, leaving azure lightning to skip and arc all over the ship's surface. Drysso saw secondary explosions ripple through the smaller ship's port gun decks, letting him know the *Freedom* had been badly hurt.

"Captain, I've lost fifteen percent of my starboard firepower."

"Thank you, Guns. Lieutenant Waroen, where did those missiles come from?"

"The freighters, sir, they're launching missiles that appear to be using the starfighter telemetry to target us." Waroen glanced at his monitors. "Sir, I can reestablish the bow shield, but it will lower our protection elsewhere."

"Do it, Waroen. Guns, forget the *Freedom*. Kill the freighters." Drysso clasped his hands at the small of his back. "The freighters are our main threat now. Kill them, and this battle is over."

Tycho Celchu rolled his X-wing to port, then pulled back on his stick. He cruised in on the tail of a TIE fighter and pulled the trigger. Two bursts of dual-fire lasers shot out, stabbing deep into the engine assembly. He rolled quickly to starboard and dove, clearing the exploding TIE's blast radius.

"You still with me, Eight?"

Nawara Ven's voice came back a little less calm than Tycho would have wanted. "With you, Seven, just barely."

"New flight, Eight, then our second run on the *Lusankya*. You take lead."

"As ordered, Seven."

Tycho throttled back a bit to let Nawara Ven pass him, then he sideslipped to the left and took up a position in Nawara's port aft arc. Coming back off the first run on the Super Star Destroyer, the X-wings had boiled into the fourth TIE flight. Between them and the Twi'lek *Chir'daki*, the TIEs never had a chance. As they closed on the fifth flight, it lost unit cohesion as four of the pilots pulled away and headed back toward the incoming Interceptors.

"Only eight out there, Nawara. Choose your target carefully."

"Got one in mind, Seven." Nawara's X-wing remained straight and level as it raced in toward the TIEs.

Tycho began to wince. *Head-to-head is usually a winner for us, but it burns some shields. In this environment, I'm not so sure that's wise.*

Nawara's X-wing snap-rolled up onto the starboard stabilizer foils, then fired four dual bursts of lasers at its target. The first two missed wide, as did the TIE's return fire, but the last two hit the TIE dead on. Two of the bolts sheered the starboard solar panel in half while the other two peeled back the flesh of the cockpit. The TIE started a crazy tumble through space, and suddenly Tycho found himself through the line of TIEs and clear to run on the *Lusankya*.

"Lead, Seven and Eight are going in."

"I copy, Seven."

Tycho rolled left to give Nawara more room, then put his ship into a weave. Coming in at the *Lusankya* from the front, he dropped his aiming reticle on the blackened portion of the ship's bow. Guttering flames indicated places where the ship was leaking atmosphere. Tycho picked a particularly bright torch as his aim point. He shifted over to missiles and immediately got a keening target lock tone from his astromech. Seconds later he got a red light from his telemetry transponder.

"Double-lock for Seven. Two away." He pulled the trigger, sending two proton torpedoes streaking on jets of blue flame at the *Lusankya*. From all around the larger ship other blue lights suddenly ignited and began to cruise in toward the point Tycho had targeted.

From the very beginning of their operations, Wedge and Tycho had agreed that the only way they could defeat the *Lusankya* was to overwhelm it with proton torpedoes and concussion missiles. The problem they had was that to do the job correctly they would require twelve or more X-wing squadrons—squadrons they didn't have. Taking a lesson from the conquest of Coruscant, they decided that freighters equipped with launchers and missiles would give them the launching platforms they needed. By slaving the freighters' missiles to the X-wing telemetry, they eliminated the need for target acquisition sensors on the freighters—the use of which would have immediately designated the freighters as targets for the *Lusankya*.

To prevent anyone from figuring out their strategy, Wedge had Booster buy launchers, munitions, *and* sensor units from Talon Karrde. Reluctant to buy something and not use it, Booster hooked the sensors up to the station, noting that just lighting them up would be enough to make even the *Lusankya* think twice about engaging the station. As their plans evolved, Booster agreed to stay behind and make the *Lusankya* think it had been trapped while the Rogues left the system, rendezvoused with Sair Yonka's *Freedom,* and rode the rest of the way in relative comfort to Thyferra. The freighters moved on in to set up the ambush while the *Freedom* waited at the fringes of the system for the arrival of the *Lusankya*.

Tycho's missiles exploded against the ship's shields, but they buckled quickly enough as the rest of the missiles locked into his telemetry hit the ship. Nawara's shots likewise raced in, sowing explosions over the ship's surface. Other Rogues continued the assault on the ship's starboard gun decks, destroying turbolasers, ion cannons, and concussion missile launchers. *If we can kill* Lusankya's *ability to strike from one side, our ships can operate with impunity.*

Toward the other end of the Super Star Destroyer, Tycho saw the Alderaanian War Cruiser *Valiant* pour fire into the ship. The *Lusankya*'s tail guns exchanged shots with the *Valiant*, but Aril Nunb's droid crew managed to maneuver the smaller ship so shots impacted against shields that were still strong. The Super Star Destroyer's aft shields appeared to be holding, but the *Valiant*'s constant battery had to be draining energy that could have been used elsewhere to great effect.

Rolling to port and diving, Tycho sailed his fighter beneath some return fire and noticed the *Lusankya* had begun to strike out at the freighters. They presented a diverse choice of targets and began to scatter as the big ship turned its guns on them. *Evasive maneuvers, as per orders, but that's going to make missile launching tougher.* He glanced at his monitor. *Only two missiles left anyway, enough for one more run.*

He checked the location of the Interceptor squadron, but saw it had not closed as quickly as anticipated. "Lead, Seven is set for one more run."

"Negative, Seven. The squints have picked up a lamb and are running it clear of here. You and Nine, with your wings, are to pursue."

Tycho's astromech flashed a quick scan of the shuttle onto his monitor. "Shuttle is positive for one lifeform. You think that's Isard?"

"Like as not. She's not getting away. Go, Tycho, go."

"I copy, Jesfa." Iella crouched and quickly ducked her head around the corner. She jerked her head back and rolled away as three blaster bolts gouged a divot out of the ferrocrete wall. *That was closer than I have any interest in getting in the future.*

Iella keyed her comlink. "Your report was dead on, Jesfa. Keep telling me what holocams he's killing and we'll get to him."

Elscol came running up and dropped to one knee at Iella's side. "What have you got?"

Iella jerked a thumb at the corridor. "Trapped rat, it appears. Your people secured the stairwells?"

"Yeah. He's trapped here on the fifth level." Elscol gave

Iella a half-smile. "You want us to evacuate innocents, or do we just track this guy down?"

"Let's get him."

Elscol waved a team of two men and two Vratix forward. "We have a live one. Be careful."

Two of Elscol's people took up positions at the mouth of the corridor. Their efforts to look down it produced no fire, so they gave the all-clear signal. The two Vratix then rushed forward to flank the only door in that hallway and then checked it. They indicated it was locked. Elscol and Iella went running down the hall to its end and crouched there, preparing to glance down either branch after their quarry.

Iella pressed her back against the corridor's left wall. She started to nod to Elscol, inviting her to check her end of the corridor first, but she saw movement back the way she had come. The duraplast door exploded out into the hallway as blasterfire chewed it in half. Two bolts caught the Vratix on the right side of the door in the abdomen, spinning him further into the corridor. As the fire swung back through the doorway the second Vratix took a pair of shots to the thorax, dropping him to the floor with his sextet of limbs twitching.

The two men at the far end of the corridor came running up and rushed the doorway before Iella or Elscol could call them off. The second man in straightened up abruptly, then flew back into the corridor all loose-limbed and burning from a trio of shots to the chest.

Of the first man Iella only saw booted feet that jerked twice, then lay still.

"Jesfa, get me a six-man team up here now." Iella looked over at Elscol. "We wait, right?"

"For that guy to escape? If he got in that room, he knows override codes. He could have a secret turbolift in there and be on his way out."

"I doubt it." Iella keyed her comlink again. "Jesfa, have them bring concussion grenades."

Smoke drifted out of the doorway, then a blaster carbine came sailing out of it and clattered to the floor in the midst of the dead commandos. "I give up."

Iella and Elscol exchanged glances, then Iella snapped a command. "Come out with your hands in the air."

"Do I recognize that voice?"

Iella's jaw dropped open. *Fliry Vorru?* She slowly smiled. "Vorru? I'm expecting those hands raised."

The small white-haired man appeared in the doorway and gingerly stepped between the legs lying therein. "Ah, Iella Wessiri. Someone I can trust to do the right thing."

Elscol stood and leveled her blaster carbine at the man. "You want the right thing? I have justice in a clip right here for you, murderer."

Iella reached up and laid a hand on Elscol's carbine. "You can't. He's surrendered."

"Surrendered? He just burned down four people."

"More crimes for him to be tried for."

"Exactly." Vorru smiled rather smugly. "I'm sure the people of Thyferra will want to try me, *if* the New Republic will let them."

Iella frowned as she stood. "Oh, once the New Republic is through with you, the Thyferrans will have their chance."

"I hope you're right, Iella, because I know the Thyferran people have a strong sense of justice." Vorru's hands slipped down to the level of his shoulders. "Of course, since I know which of the New Republic officials have been hoarding bacta and I know the backdoor deals made by member states to get bacta, well, I suspect this is information they won't want to have come to light."

Iella laughed. "You think you're not going to pay for your crimes because you'll make some political deal?"

"Alas, Iella, that is the reality of the situation."

Iella sharpened her laugh and her expression. "You're assuming, of course, that I don't have my own brand of justice in mind. I wanted Isard because she killed my husband. If I can't have her, you'll do." She raised her carbine and pointed it at his head. "One shot and a lot of crime files are closed."

Vorru brought his hands together and applauded her. "Nice bluff, but I've read the Imperial and Corellian files on you, my dear. You could never shoot me."

"True." Iella lowered her blaster. "But she can."

Elscol's single shot caught Vorru in the throat. It pitched him against the doorjamb, from which he rebounded and fell on top of his blaster.

"Nice shooting."

Elscol looked down at her blaster. "I don't remember setting this weapon on stun."

Iella smiled. "I do, when I stopped you from shooting him the first time."

Elscol frowned. "Why only stun him? Why the charade?"

"Vorru always likes being in control. He was expecting you to burn him down—it would have been his victory because you would have killed a man who had surrendered, and that would make you as much of a murderer as he is. Once he realized I was out here, he decided to play another game. He was in control until the last second, when I let you shoot him."

The other woman nodded, then snapped her carbine's selector lever off stun. "What he said, though, about paying for his crimes is probably true. The New Republic will make a deal with him."

"Sure, if they get a chance." Elscol smiled. "The Rogues pulled him off Kessel. We can always dump him back there. No deals, only justice."

Elscol laughed aloud. "You know, you keep this up and you might convince me there's more to do with unreconstructed Imperials than kill them."

"Let's work on it, Elscol, but only after Thyferra is free."

39

Captain Sair Yonka picked himself up off the *Freedom*'s bridge deck and staggered to his feet. He swiped a hand at his forehead—it came away bloody so he tore a strip of cloth from the tail of his tunic and jammed it against the wound. *Antilles, you paid me a lot, but it wasn't enough.*

"Someone give me a report on what's going on out there. Lieutenant Carsa?"

"Carsa's dead, sir. His monitor blew up in his face."

"Are we blind then, Ensign . . . ?"

"Issen, sir. No, sir, not blind. The *Lusankya* has been hit again by torps and missiles, but it's beginning to shoot at the freighters. We're being left alone."

"Then it's not all bad news." Yonka leaned against a bulkhead. "Helm, can we maneuver?"

A pained voice called to him from the depths of the bridge. "We've lost fifty percent of our maneuverability, Captain. We can roll, but speed and turns are going to be tough. I can muster enough to get us out of here, though, sir."

"Weapons, what's our status?"

"We've still got most of our port weapons, sir, but starboard weaponry is shot. No realistic judgment about repairs."

"What's the status of our shields?"

A bald man punched a button on a console, then clapped his hands. "Shields are coming back up. I've got seventy percent of power. They'll hold while we run away."

Sair Yonka shook his head. "We're going nowhere. Lieutenant Phelly, roll us so we can bring our starboard weapons to bear."

"Begging your pardon, sir, but we're not being paid enough to die here."

"Then let's make sure we don't die." Yonka flung his arms wide open. "We all knew that staying with Isard would get us killed. We also knew that if we left her service, she'd hunt us down right after she killed Antilles. Now we've got to kill the *Lusankya* here, or it will kill us someplace else. This isn't about money, it's about our survival, our freedom."

He pointed out the main viewport. "Out there you have people in freighters and snubfighters pounding on that behemoth. They're gnats compared to the *Lusankya*. They can sting it, but they can't kill it. That job is up to us and we're going to do it because if we have to die, it isn't going to be dying while we're running. The Empire's dead—we all know that—so this is our buy-in to whatever follows it."

Wedge saw the *Freedom* begin a roll as turbolaser fire lanced from the *Lusankya* at the freighters. One salvo caught a disk-shaped Corellian light freighter and snapped it in half. He saw shields glow and shrink as other ships got hit by one or two shots, but none exploded. He knew that was more luck than skill, and that a lot of the freighters weren't going to survive to the end of the battle.

"Lead to Two, time for our last run."

"Negative, Lead, I have a TIE on me."

"Coming, Two."

Wedge pulled back on his stick and brought his fighter up into a loop, then rolled out to starboard as Asyr's X-wing shot past. A TIE streaked by, hot on her tail. As Wedge dropped in behind him, the TIE fired a volley of shots that pierced Asyr's aft shield. Something at the back of her fighter exploded, then she rolled down and out of sight.

"Two, report."

Asyr didn't answer his call. "Gate, assess damage on Two."

The droid beeped a response, but Wedge ignored the information filling his secondary monitor. *Got something to do first.*

The TIE rolled to starboard then started to climb. Wedge pulled his X-wing into a steep climb, then snap-rolled starboard and powered the fighter over the top. The TIE danced before him for a second, prompting Wedge to snap a shot off. The dual burst of lasers clipped one of the TIE's solar panels, but did no serious damage.

This guy is good.

The TIE rolled to port and pulled a tight loop back along its line of flight. Wedge let himself overshoot the TIE, then throttled back as the TIE swung onto his tail. The TIE closed faster than the pilot expected because of Wedge's chopping the throttle back. Wedge tugged back on his stick, nosing the fighter into a climb. He held it for a second, then shoved the stick forward and broke the climb off.

Green laser fire hissed off his shields, but he didn't panic. *And Gate isn't screaming!* The TIE shot past his position, having started to climb to blast Wedge, then trying to follow him as he started flying straight again. Wedge pulled his X-wing's nose back up and triggered two more bursts of laser fire.

Both hit the TIE in the undamaged wing, burning it free of the ship's fuselage. The hexagonal wing went one way while the TIE spun out of control toward Thyferra.

Wedge didn't watch to see if it exploded. He brought his fighter around and found himself staring at the broad expanse of the *Lusankya*'s belly. Nearly an eighth of the ship had been nibbled off at the front, but the guns still fired relentlessly. *It's hurt, but not enough.* "Lead here. Starting my third run."

The fact that no one acknowledged his call sent a chill through him, but he shrugged it off. *Now's not the time to mourn the dead. That waits until the mission is done.* He tossed his fighter into a weave and pointed it at the giant egress hatch in the bottom of the Super Star Destroyer. *We've broken your nose, now it's a shot to the guts.*

Switching over to proton torpedoes, he immediately got a red box and a solid tone from Gate. He waited until his transponder button went red, then pulled the trigger. Two jets of blue fire shot away from his ship and another half dozen joined them. It took four of them to blast a hole in the ventral shields, but that left a quartet of missiles to plow into the *Lusankya's* hangar deck. The explosions spat decking and debris back out into space, then secondary explosions told Wedge that at least a couple of the TIE fuel storage tanks had ruptured.

Out of torpedoes, Wedge shifted over to lasers and started searching for more TIEs. *And if there aren't any more of them, I guess I'll just have to get in close with the* Lusankya *and light it up as much as I can.*

"Yes, Madam Director, I understand." Erisi shivered as the echoes of Isard's voice died in her ears. When she'd spotted the shuttle coming up she had harbored a hope that it was Vorru, but Isard's mocking voice dashed that dream to pieces. Erisi switched her comm unit over to her squadron's tactical frequency. "Elite Leader to squadron. We have a new mission: protect the *Lambda*-class shuttle *Thyfonian*. We are to cover it until it gets clear and can go to lightspeed."

"Six here, Lead. That means we'll be left behind."

"Negative, Six. The *Lusankya* is going to be following *Thyfonian* out and will pick us up."

"I copy, Lead."

"Twelve here, Lead. We have four X-wings coming up fast."

"I copy, Twelve." Erisi shook her head. *Only four? That's a mistake you'll rue, Wedge Antilles.* "Keep your formations tight and help each other out. These pilots will be good, but we can be better. Don't lose your heads and you won't lose your lives."

. . .

Captain Drysso laughed victoriously. As nearly as he could determine his *Lusankya* had been hit by over a hundred and fifty proton torpedoes and concussion missiles, but it had lost scarcely thirty-five percent of its combat ability. Maneuvering was hampered and shield power was falling sharply, but the *Lusankya* still outgunned its opposition. *And the freighters have the survival rate of tauntauns on Tatooine.*

Lieutenant Waroen called out to him. "Captain, the *Freedom* is coming back into the fight."

"Guns, let him have everything!"

"As ordered, Captain."

The *Lusankya* fired its starboard weapons at the Imperial Star Destroyer, mauling it mercilessly. Turbolasers crushed the shields while ion cannon beams skittered over the *Freedom*'s hull. Concussion missiles peppered the smaller ship, opening huge holes in the hull. Explosions wracked the *Freedom,* spraying debris in all directions.

Yet even before the *Lusankya*'s attack left the *Freedom* adrift in space, the Imperial Star Destroyer blasted back at the Super Star Destroyer. Turbolasers drilled through the dorsal shields and stabbed fire deep into the *Lusankya*'s heart. Blue ion lightning capered and danced over the hull, teasing fireballs to life in its wake. The *Lusankya* shook with the violence of those explosions and others.

Drysso shouted at his staff. "Damage reports!"

Waroen was first. "Ventral shields, down; dorsal shields, down; bow shields, down; starboard and port shields, down."

"You mean to tell me I only have aft shields?"

Another explosion shook the ship. "Not anymore, sir."

"Captain," yelled his communications officer, "I have a priority message from Director Isard. She's ordering us out of here. We're to follow the shuttle."

"What?"

"That was the message, sir. She said you should get out of here before you get killed."

"Killed!" Drysso's laugh quieted the bridge. "Killed? We are winning here. The *Freedom* is dead. Freighters are dying.

That War Cruiser is next and we've weathered the worst those X-wings can throw at us. We have won! She can run if she wants, but the *Lusankya* stays here. If she wants to abandon Thyferra, I will take her place and reap what she has sown."

The crew stared at him, gape-mouthed and silent for a moment, then a cheer spread through the bridge, beginning at Lieutenant Waroen's station and building around through the crew. For a handful of heartbeats Drysso thought they were cheering him, but those nearest the viewport stared past him, prompting Drysso to turn.

Out there, hovering off the *Lusankya*'s port bow, was the *Virulence*.

Drysso clapped his hands. "It's the *Virulence* and they have our TIE squadrons. Order *Virulence* to deploy its fighters! Now nothing stands between us and total victory!"

40

Three squadrons of fighters poured from the *Virulence* and entered the fray.

Wedge's heart had sunk when Gate reported the launching of the *Virulence*'s fighters. He brought his X-wing around and resigned himself to one last glorious battle. *That Impstar only carries six TIE squadrons. I always sort of figured Rogue Squadron would go out in a blaze of glory, and this looks like it is it.* "Gate, target me one of *Virulence*'s fighters."

The droid complied with a beep. Wedge glanced down at the image the droid painted on his monitor. "That's an A-wing."

Gate corrected him with a bleat.

"Okay, a Mark II A-wing." Wedge shook his head to clear it. *A-wings? Where did Isard get A-wings?*

A familiar voice crackled through Wedge's comm unit. "Ace Lead to Rogue Leader. Mind if we crash your party, Wedge?"

"Pash Cracken? Where in the Emperor's dark heart did you come from?"

"Booster's flagship. The gravity well pulled my unit out

of hyperspace right on top of *Virulence* during their little standoff. Booster talked the captain into believing it was all part of the trap, so she surrendered the ship to him."

So he finally found a ship that was big enough for him. "The *Lusankya* is all yours, Captain Cracken."

"Obliged, Wedge. We're going in."

Inverting and rolling out, Wedge reoriented his X-wing toward the *Lusankya* as the *Virulence* fired a full broadside into the Super Star Destroyer. The smaller ship's turbolasers and ion cannons wrought havoc upon the *Lusankya*'s port gunnery decks. A ribbon of fire raced along the port gunwale and secondary explosions kept it alive long after the *Virulence*'s weapons stopped firing.

To the *Lusankya*'s aft, the *Valiant* closed to point-blank range and blasted away at the big ship's engines. Sparks cascaded away as turbolasers drilled deep into the Super Star Destroyer. A brilliant flash eclipsed the *Valiant* for a moment. A violent tremor shook the *Lusankya,* snapping free a blackened chunk of the bow.

Fast and nimble, Pash's A-wings slashed in at the *Lusankya*. They flitted over the massive ship's surface, shooting concussion missiles at gunnery towers and sensor domes. Fiery craters stippled the *Lusankya* in their wake. What few weapons did remain on the *Lusankya* fired ineffectively at the A-wings; all of their destructive power proved impotent against a target they could not hit.

"Rogue Lead, this is Three. We're going in for a strafing run."

"I copy, Gavin." Wedge glanced at his monitors, but the only TIEs he saw were the ones escorting the shuttle. *Can't catch them now.* "If you don't mind, Three, I think I'll join you."

Closing with the squints Corran switched his weapon's-control over to lasers and linked them for dual-fire. While a quad burst would be certain to burn a squint down, dual-fire allowed the guns to cycle that much faster. *One shot should still be a kill, but if these guys can put the maneuverability of those squints to good use, I'll need all the shots I can get.* His X-wing still had an advantage because of its shields, but that still didn't make him immune to damage.

"Nine, let's be careful."

"As ordered, Seven. Ten, on me."

"Ooryl copies."

"Whistler, scan comm frequencies and bring up whatever one they're using. Squelch scrambled messages. I don't care what they're saying to each other. I just want to be able to talk to them."

Whistler moaned in a low tone.

"Yes, I do think Erisi is flying with them. I want to let her know who's coming after her."

The droid hooted derisively.

"She can decide to flame me all she wants, doesn't matter." Corran let himself smile. "She already knows I can play hard to get. She's the reason I went down on Coruscant, and I'm bringing her down here."

He picked one of the squints in the middle of the formation as a target, but kept his flight path pointed as if he were preparing to attack one of the closer Interceptors. As the close Interceptors broke, Corran rolled on his starboard stabilizers as if he were going to follow them, but then applied some rudder and spitted his target on his aiming reticle. He tightened up on his trigger.

Two sets of two bolts skewered the squint's ball cockpit. The twin ion engines exploded, launching debris into space from amid a silvery fireball. Pieces of the fighter struck sparks from Corran's shields, but he reinforced them quickly enough. "Scratch one squint."

Whistler keened at him so Corran punched a previously unlit button on his comm unit. "Hope that wasn't you, Erisi. I'd hate to think your flying skill had atrophied so much."

"It's my killing skill that should be concerning you, Corran."

"Eight here. I have a pair on my tail."

"Seven on the way, Eight, hold tight."

Corran rolled and came out in a loop with Ooryl in his aft port quarter. Two TIEs were lining up for a run on

Nawara's X-wing. Tycho pulled a tight turn that brought him around quickly, but he only managed to pick off the trailing TIE. Nawara broke hard to port, then twisted back again to starboard, but the squint stayed with him throughout his maneuvers.

That's got to be Erisi.

The Interceptor fired four times, the first two pairs of green laser bolts burning through Nawara's aft shield. The other two blew out the port engines and hit the fuselage right behind the cockpit. Nawara's astromech exploded, then the cockpit canopy flew apart. When fire filled the cockpit Corran feared for the worst, then he saw the X-wing's command couch jet out from the stricken fighter.

"Eight is extravehicular!" Corran's green eyes narrowed. "Ten, keep them off him. I'm going after Erisi. Whistler, give me her comm frequency again."

The droid complied with the order silently.

"Always did pick off the easy targets, didn't you, Erisi? Couldn't stand to work hard, could you?"

"Is that you on my tail, Corran? All alone?" Her laughter filled his cockpit. "I thought you'd learned from your father that dying alone wasn't something to do."

"That should be your concern, Erisi, because I'm not dying here. Horn out." He punched the comm unit button that cut frequency off. "Come on, Whistler, it's time we collect the debt she owes us."

Corran's X-wing streaked in on Erisi's trail, but the squint juked and danced, making it impossible for him to get a good shot at her. As she broke to port, Corran rolled out into a long starboard loop and began a head-to-head run with her. The squint broke to starboard before they could close, forcing him to turn to port to pursue. *Okay, she knew head to head would be suicide.*

As her ship began to pull away from his, Corran realized killing her wasn't going to be as easy as he expected. While she hadn't been a bad pilot in an X-wing, she wasn't as good as he was. *Her Interceptor, on the other hand, has more speed and maneuverability than my X-wing. That might give her the edge she lacked before. And she knows very well all the performance capabilities of my ship.*

Corran smiled. *You don't fly against a fighter, you fly against the pilot, and her arrogance is one huge flaw I can exploit.* Corran pulled his throttle back to 85 percent of full power, letting her stretch her lead on him. He rolled up on his port stabilizer and started a long loop that would take him back toward the main dogfight. He started in on an attack vector for one of the Interceptors.

While flying along it, he watched his main monitor. The rate of change for the range between his ship and Erisi's Interceptor slowed as the distance stabilized, then the distance started to decrease. The rate of change accelerated, and when the range hit three kilometers, Corran hauled back on his stick. He tightened his loop considerably, then punched his throttle forward and headed straight for her.

Her hastily snapped shots splashed harmlessly over his forward shields. Corran fired back, catching her squint on the port wing. He inverted and dove, then inverted again and cruised out into a long loop that took him past Thyferra's cloudy face. "How badly is she hit, Whistler?"

The droid graphed performance statistics on the main monitor. The Interceptor had suffered a 5 percent reduction in speed, which still left it faster than the X-wing, but not by that much. There also appeared to be a reduction in maneuverability, but not enough to cripple her performance. *This is going to take a while.*

"Nine, are you chasing Erisi?"

"Yes, Seven."

"Finish her fast."

"You need help?"

"Ten is handling things, but the shuttle is running. It can clear to lightspeed if we don't stop it."

"I copy, Seven. I'm on it." He glanced at his monitor. "Whistler, give me range to the freighters who were tied to my torpedo telemetry."

The droid whistled mournfully. "No, it's okay that they're all out of range. I didn't want them wasting any torps."

Just to be on the safe side, he hit the switch that turned the telemetry transponder off, then shifted his weapon's-control over to proton torpedoes. Coming about, he picked Erisi up and started after her again. He nudged his nose up and to port, getting a stuttered beeping from Whistler as the droid tried to get a firing solution for the Interceptor. The tone went constant as the reticle went red.

Corran hit the trigger and launched both torpedoes at Erisi. His last two proton torpedoes streaked out at her and she immediately began maneuvering to avoid them.

I have thirty seconds to kill her. Corran switched back to lasers, then drained energy from his aft shield and fed it into his engines. That kicked his speed up to better than that of an unhurt Interceptor, allowing him to close the gap between their ships fast.

As the missiles approached her Interceptor, Erisi rolled to port and broke hard toward Thyferra's largest moon. The missiles overshot where she had been, then turned and started in pursuit again. She kept her ship pointed straight at the bone white moon and as the torpedoes closed with her again, she rolled to port and pulled her fighter into a glide path that followed the rough terrain of the lunar surface.

One torpedo, unable to fight inertia and lunar gravity both, slammed into the moon and exploded. The second sailed through the gout of lunar dust and started closing with the Interceptor. Erisi bounced her squint up and over a ridge-line and back down again, interposing it between her and the torpedo.

The ridge shielded her from the torpedo's blast.

It also blinded her aft sensors to Corran's presence.

As Erisi pulled her squint up to climb away from the moon's surface, Corran came up over the ridge and pounced. Pairs of scarlet bolts burned into the squint, shredding both solar panels. As the stabilizers disintegrated, the Interceptor's climb became a loop into a dive that brought it in on a collision course with the moon. Both engines thrusting fully, the Interceptor plowed into the lunar surface, gouging out a huge furrow. The Interceptor hit the edge of a small impact crater, skipped up, then battered itself again and again against the moon. Finally, crushed into a shape that was unrecognizable as any part of a fighter, it rolled to a stop as the engines sputtered out.

Corran circled the spot once. "No explosion, nothing spectacular. Erisi would have hated it."

Whistler blatted harshly.

"Right, who cares what she would have wanted." Corran pulled his X-wing away from the moon. "Find me that shuttle, Whistler. I don't care who's on it, we're going to stop it."

Another salvo from the *Virulence* ripped into the *Lusankya* as Wedge swooped low over the Super Star Destroyer and peppered its hull with laser bolts. The *Lusankya* tried to defend itself, but the surface-mounted turbolaser cannons simply made themselves targets for strafing runs by X-wings, A-wings, Twi'leki *Chir'daki,* and the Gands' curious ships. What shots the Super Star Destroyer did get off at the *Virulence* failed to penetrate the smaller ship's shields.

The Lusankya *is fast becoming defenseless. Much more of this hammering and the ship could begin to break up, and that would jeopardize the prisoners we want to rescue from her.* Wedge pulled up and flashed past the bridge. "Gate, get me an open comm channel to the *Lusankya.*"

The droid complied with the order instantly. "This is Commander Wedge Antilles to the Captain of the *Lusankya.* We'll accept your surrender at any time."

An angry, shrill voice arced through the comm unit. "This is Captain Joak Drysso—no, *Admiral* Drysso—of the *Lusankya.* We will never give up."

"Captain . . ."

"How dare you insult me!"

"Admiral, then, even Grand Admiral, if it will make you see sense. Your shields are down. Your engines are hit. You have no fighter cover, you can't hurt your opposition." Wedge let his damage assessment sink in for a moment. "It's hopeless. No one else needs to die. Give up."

"Give up? An Imperial Grand Admiral *never* gives up. If you think one would, you'll rue the day you engaged one!"

"That could be, sir, but *that* day isn't *today*! We'll treat all your people with all due respect." Wedge fought to keep his voice even. "Surrender."

"Never! We are all loyal sons of the Empire. We are not afraid to put death before dishonor. Helm, give me all speed. We're going to ram the planet! There, Antilles, see, a Grand Admiral never . . ." The comm unit popped and abruptly went silent.

"Drysso!"

"Captain Drysso isn't here anymore, sir. Ah, this is acting-Captain Waroen."

"Are you going to crash your ship into the planet, Waroen?"

"Not if I can help it, sir. If you could get the War Cruiser to stop shooting my engines, and if *Virulence* will pull us a bit further out into orbit so we don't crash of our own accord, we'll accept any conditions for surrender you want to offer us."

"I'm happy to be working with you, Captain Waroen. What you're doing is no dishonor."

"I know that, sir, and I think it beats death all hollow."

Corran found the shuttle easily enough and brought his X-wing in on its aft without a problem. He flipped his lasers over to quad fire. "Whistler, see if you can open a comm channel to the shuttle." Corran fired his lasers across the *Thyfonian*'s flight path when Whistler announced he'd found the two frequencies the shuttle was using.

"Just pick one." Corran punched the button on his comm unit. "This is Corran Horn to shuttle *Thyfonian*. Stop now and turn back to Thyferra, or I'll be forced to destroy you."

A moment's delay ended with a voice Corran had never expected to hear again coming through the comm channel. "I should have known it would be you, Horn. Go away. You can't stop me with your lasers."

"Maybe this will warm your heart, Ysanne." Corran dropped his aiming reticle on the shuttle's rear and pulled the trigger. Burst after burst of laser fire splashed against the spacecraft's shields, but did not penetrate them. *What? Shuttle's shields aren't that good.*

"You can thank Fliry Vorru for me, if he's still alive. He ordered heavy-capacity shield generators for his shuttle. Cuts down on the passenger room, but I don't mind. Quite simply, your X-wing lacks the power to burn through them."

Maybe one will. Corran shifted his comm unit over to the squadron's tactical frequency. "Nine could use some help here. It's Isard. I can't get through the shuttle's shields."

"Seven here, Nine. Coming as fast as I can. Keep her from jumping to lightspeed."

"I'll do my best, but I need your lasers to stop her."

"I copy, Nine. I'll hurry."

"Whistler, project how long it will be before she's clear to go to lightspeed."

The droid splashed an image of the solar system up on Corran's secondary monitor. He used overlapping circles of color to indicate the boundaries for gravitational effects of the bodies in the system and showed the shuttle as a pinpoint of light at the edge of Thyferra's hyperspace mass shadow.

Sithspawn, she's almost there. Corran triggered another burst of laser fire, but it only washed a bloody hue over the aft shield. *What if she's bluffing and just has all power going to the aft shield! That's just the sort of thing she'd do.*

He punched power to his throttle and let the X-wing surge forward. He brought it around in a loop that would give him an oblique shot at the shuttle's port side. As he sailed in, the shuttle shifted direction and came about to face him. Corran hit his trigger and pulsed energy into the shuttle's shields.

The shuttle fired back. Green energy darts blew through the X-wing's forward shield and hit the port stabilizer. Corran rolled immediately and dove, then came back up in a weave that took him in behind the shuttle. "Whistler, what just happened?"

Isard's voice crackled over the comm channel. "Did I mention that Vorru also upgraded the lasers on this ship?"

I'll give you an upgrade, Iceheart. Corran snarled as he looked at the diagnostics listing Whistler scrolled up on his main monitor. He winced, then looked to his port S-foil. Where once there had been a pair of laser cannons he had melted metal. *And about a meter less of S-foil.* A glance at the secondary monitor showed Isard had a kilometer before she could begin the run to lightspeed. *Once she gets clear, it's just level flying and she's out of here.*

Corran slowly smiled. *Upgraded that thing, did he, Iceheart?* The Corellian pilot flipped his weapon's-control over to proton torpedoes and dropped it on the shuttle's outline. Whistler began to beep as he tried for a firing solution. Out ahead of the X-wing the shuttle began to juke, broadening Corran's smile. *Yes, he supplied the shuttle with a missile targeting lock warning system. Only good thing you've done in your black life, Vorru.*

"So your shields won't stop a proton torpedo, eh, Iceheart?"

"You'll find out if you ever get a lock on me, Horn."

Corran glanced at his monitor and saw Tycho's X-wing eight kilometers back and closing slowly. *As long as you keep dancing, Iceheart, you can't run up to lightspeed. That means we can burn you down.* "I'll get a lock on you, then you're done."

He painted her with a target lock again, but allowed her to break it. He reacquired it again and shifted his ship around to herd her back toward Thyferra's mass shadow. The shuttle rolled in the other direction, breaking the lock, but Corran came in and got it again fairly easily. "You can't escape me, Iceheart."

Isard's reply came almost languidly voiced. "I've stopped trying, Horn. You're bluffing. If you had torpedoes, you would have used them already." The shuttle leveled out and prepared for the run to lightspeed.

"I was hoping to take you alive, Isard. I'll shoot if I have to."

"Please, Horn, do your worst. Know that when we meet again, to you I shall do *my* worst!"

She can't *get away. I* can't *let her get away!* Corran punched his comm unit with a closed fist. His mind reeled as fury and a fear of failure raged through him. *My lasers can't get through her shields and I don't have any missiles to batter them down. There's nothing I can do . . . nothing . . . wait, maybe there's something . . .*

"Quick, transfer all power to the forward shield!" Corran smiled grimly and reached for the throttle. "Hang on, Whistler, we're going to ram her."

The droid began hooting loudly, but Corran ignored him and focused on the shuttle. "Your logic boards are fried. There's a chance we can survive, but that doesn't matter. If we cripple her ship . . . we have to cripple her ship . . ."

Before Corran could jam the throttle full forward, two blue darts streaked past either side of his cockpit. The first exploded against the shuttle's aft shield and collapsed it. The second drilled through the engine housing, skewing the ship to port. The proton torpedo detonated inside the shuttle's fuselage. Corran saw the angular ship puff up and out before fire lanced out the cockpit viewports, then a golden fireball ripped the ship apart from the inside out.

Corran's X-wing passed straight through the center of the explosion and by the time he brought his ship around the sparks from debris hitting his shields were the only indication that the shuttle had been there at all. *Consumed by fire. Somehow fitting.*

Corran keyed his comm unit. "Who did that?"

"Seven here, Nine. Thanks for giving me the target lock."

"What?" Corran glanced over at the transponder switch and saw it was lit. *When I punched the console, I must have hit it by accident.* The image of Luke Skywalker came to mind. *He'd tell me that wasn't an accident, wasn't luck, just the Force.* Corran slowly nodded. *I prefer to believe it was justice.*

"It was a great shot, Tycho. If I couldn't get her, well, your claim predated mine."

"Corran, *we* got her. That's all that counts."

Tycho's X-wing came into view as Corran headed his X-wing back toward Thyferra. "I don't see any more squints, Tycho. You got a workout."

"I got my share, but Ten vaped the bulk of them. He accounted for six Interceptors all by himself." Tycho chuckled lightly. "And it looks like the *Lusankya* isn't shooting anymore."

Corran smiled. "A tyrant dead; a traitor dead; a Super Star Destroyer dead; and, if Elscol, Iella, and the Ashern have done their jobs, a planet liberated. Not a bad day at all."

41

"Looks different, doesn't it, Corran, when you're walking on the ceiling?"

"Yeah, but not any better." Despite having the lights strung throughout the *Lusankya* prisoners' quarters, the warren's rough-hewn walls still pressed in on Corran. He turned toward Tycho Celchu as he climbed over the low wall into what had been Jan Dodonna's cell. "It's very strange to have mounted this whole operation to try to get Jan and the other prisoners out, just to get in here and find Isard had them shipped out by shuttle to other places months ago. Deep down she must have known we'd win, so she did this to frustrate us."

"You've got it all wrong, my friend." Tycho patted Corran's right shoulder with his left hand. "When you escaped from the *Lusankya*, you ruined it for her. She could no longer view her little prison without thinking about how you beat her. Whereas anyone else would have beefed up security, she decided to scrap the whole facility. And it's just as well, because this section of the ship lost atmosphere—everyone would have died in here. Had Isard really been on her game, she would have let them die that way and would have us blaming ourselves for killing a bunch of the Rebellion's heroes."

Corran nodded slowly. In the week since the battle for Thyferra he'd waited for repair crews to restore atmosphere to the prison area on the ship. To the others that had seen it, the whole area was just part of a ship where the bulkheads had been lined with rock. The fact that the primitive latrines had drained into a zero gravity vacuum, then the waste settled wherever it had drifted when gravity and atmosphere had been brought back, did not help things. Everyone who visited the facility could see very clearly why he hated it.

But the stink and the crudity of its manufacture wasn't why he hated it. Corran frowned. "It feels to me as if despair and failure have permeated these walls. The men who were in here didn't dare try to escape, and yet most of them could have, I'm certain. Jan could have come with me, but he didn't because he felt a responsibility to the others. That made him more a prisoner than these walls."

"But what you saw as a prison for him was not what he saw for himself. Jan knew he was keeping people alive by leading them. He hadn't surrendered, so they couldn't quite do it themselves." Tycho brushed fingers across the rocky surface of the walls. "What he was doing, by staying behind, was as much a part of him as your need to escape was a part of you. I don't remember much of my time here, but I felt certain I was going to die here. It's a terrible thing to come back to your senses after having been out of it, to find yourself in a place where you think you're going to die. Jan told me I wasn't, and I didn't."

"And you escaped from the place where she sent you after you left here."

"Right." Tycho smiled. "We have to hope the others will be able to do that, too."

"It'll be fine if they do, but I'm still on for finding them myself." Corran smiled. "Zraii's already got my X-wing back to normal—well, as normal as it gets after a Verpine messes with it—so I'm ready to hunt. You with me?"

Tycho nodded thoughtfully. "I am, though I think we're going to have some stiff competition. One of the first 'repair' crews in this area was a forensic team from Alliance Intelligence. They are supposed to have swept this place, pulling fingerprints, hair and tissue samples—even samples of some of the solid waste floating around. You know better than I what that sort of evidence can tell them, but I gather they were able to confirm the identities of some of the prisoners from what they got."

Corran smiled slowly. "Which is why General Airen Cracken showed up two days ago. The New Republic is going to hunt for the prisoners, then?"

"That would be my guess. They couldn't do it before because they only had your word to go on—my identifications were spotty and old. Since you chose to resign from Rogue Squadron and started all this, they had to disassociate themselves with our effort. Now they have solid evidence, which changes everything."

"Great, they can race us in finding them."

"Ah, there you are, Corran." Ooryl filled the entryway. "I thought I could find you here."

What? Corran stared at the Gand. "Ooryl?"

"Did Ooryl say that right?" The Gand's mouthparts snapped open and shut excitedly. "Ooryl wanted you to be the first to hear."

Corran looked over at Tycho, but the Alderaanian just shrugged. "Yes, Ooryl, you said that correctly, but I thought Gands didn't use personal pronouns unless . . ."

The Gand's fist clicked off his chest. "I am *janwuine*. The *ruetsavii*, they have declared me *janwuine*. They have returned to Gand to tell Ooryl's, ah, *my* story. What we did here, Ooryl's part in the taking of Coruscant, and the battles against Iceheart, these will become known to all the Gand. If Ooryl says 'I,' they will know to whom I refer."

"That's great, Ooryl." Tycho extended his hand to the Gand. "The Gands have every right to be proud of you."

Ooryl shook Tycho's hand, then Corran's as well. "There is more. Each of you have been declared *hinwuine*. This means that when you come to Gand for Ooryl's *janwuine-jika*, you may speak of yourselves with personal pronouns and will not be thought vulgar or rude."

Corran's eyes narrowed. "You mean to tell me that the whole time you've been here in the squadron you felt the way we talked made us vulgar or rude?"

The Gand shook his head. "Ooryl never assumes vulgarity when ignorance suffices as an explanation."

"Thanks, I think."

Tycho shot him a sly smile. "That should be 'Corran thinks.'"

"But not often," Ooryl added.

"Corran thinks Ooryl should practice using personal pronouns more regularly before he tries comedy." Corran opened his arms wide. "Not much better than the shack we shared on Talasea, is it, Ooryl?"

"The mineral deposits do add some color, but Ooryl, er, I would not like to live here." The Gand held a hand up. "I would explore this place with you more, later, for the story of your time here will be vital to my *janwuine-jika*, but there are other things we must do right now. Captain Celchu, Commander Antilles asked Ooryl to tell you he is waiting for you in the *Lusankya*'s staff officers' mess."

"Last minute things before his party?"

"Ooryl, I mean I, believes this is the case, Captain. And Corran, General Cracken has asked to speak with you."

I wonder what that's about? "Where do I find him?"

"Ooryl will take you there."

The trio of pilots carefully picked their way out of the cavern complex and took the turbolift up. Tycho exited first while the Gand and Corran continued on, climbing higher and higher in the *Lusankya*'s superstructure. When the turbolift stopped, Corran found Airen Cracken waiting for him outside the door to the Captain's ready-room.

He nodded at the Gand as the turbolift's door closed behind him, then turned to the older man. "What can I do for you, sir?"

Cracken raked fingers back through reddish hair tinged with white. "I need you to talk some sense to Booster Terrik."

Corran immediately raised his hands. "Got a Death Star you want killed instead?"

"Close." Cracken shook his head. "Booster wants to keep the *Virulence*."

"And you want him to give it to the New Republic?" Corran laughed aloud. "He won't listen to me."

"Mirax suggested I get you up here."

"Okay, you have me, but I don't know what I can do."

"Back me up, or we're going to have Booster Terrik in command of a fully operational Impstar deuce." Cracken sighed. "Terrik was never as bad as some of the smugglers out there, but now he's hooked up with Talon Karrde and . . ."

"Booster and Karrde are together? Allied? I mean, I knew Karrde had come into the system, but I assumed it was to work a deal with Thyferra's new government about hauling bacta. Are you sure Karrde and Booster are working together?"

"See for yourself." Cracken opened the door to the ready-room and allowed Corran to precede him in. Corran found Booster at the far end of an oval table, with Mirax seated on his right and a handsome man he took to be Karrde seated on his left. Corran went over to Mirax's side of the table and gave her a kiss on the cheek. "Booster, you're looking fit."

"Captaining a starship agrees with me."

Corran extended a hand across the table to the other man. "Talon Karrde, I presume. Pleased to make your acquaintance."

"Better now than when you were with CorSec." Karrde seemed to be watching him very closely. "The resemblance to your father is unmistakable."

"Thanks." Corran sat down, fighting to conceal a shiver. He didn't know why, but he gained the impression that Karrde knew more about him than perhaps even Airen Cracken did, and that disturbed him. *I think I'm happy I didn't meet him when I was with CorSec as well. He would have been to me what Booster was to my father, but I don't think I would have been sending Karrde to Kessel.*

Booster looked up at Cracken, then jerked a thumb at Corran. "Did you think *he* could convince me to give up my ship?"

Great, this is off to a good start. Corran glanced at Cracken and shrugged.

"Booster, I just thought Lieutenant Horn here could supply you with some more perspective on why you're not going to be able to keep the *Virulence.* That ship presents a rather major danger . . ."

"Right, a danger to anyone who tries to take it away from me."

"Let me see if I can rephrase this—the only people with that sort of firepower at their disposal are Warlords and other Imperial renegades. The New Republic has to consider any Star Destroyers that are not under the control of itself or its allies to be an immediate threat to the New Republic's stability."

"Fine, General, fine. I'll just take the *Virulence,* conquer some planet with it, have the planet become one of the New Republic's allies."

Mirax shook her head. "That's pretty much what they're afraid of, Father."

Booster winked at his daughter. "Okay, then try this: I'll make the *Virulence* herself a nation. We'll just move from system to system, trading here and there, and we'll be sovereign and even join the New Republic. Think of all the guns as ground-based defenses."

Cracken's breath hissed in between his teeth. "No, I don't think that will work. That would constitute quite a large threat to peace in the galaxy. Such a threat would have to be dealt with."

Booster's artificial eye's light seemed to flare for a second. "I think there are several different degrees of threat, General, and I'd have to say, right now, you're acting more threatening than I've ever contemplated being. The *Virulence* is *mine.* She was surrendered to me."

"But only after three squadrons of New Republic A-wings appeared in the Yag'Dhul system, giving Captain Varrscha the impression she had been trapped by New Republic forces." Cracken pressed his hands flat against the white tabletop. "She thought she was surrendering the ship to the New Republic, and you know that's true. Your representations to her did not dissuade her of this fact."

Corran looked over at Booster and shook his head. "You let Isard's conviction that we were a covert New Republic operation trick Varrscha into believing we actually *were* part of the New Republic? Not bad, Booster."

Mirax's father smiled proudly. "She was looking for any excuse to get out of trouble, so I just used the one she gave me."

Corran winced. "Unfortunately, that means you've given the New Republic a claim on the *Virulence*."

"What?!"

"Mirax, tell him. It's the same as a partnership for salvaging hulks. Just because one partner is ceded ownership, he doesn't own it—the partnership does."

"Corran's right, Father."

"Nonsense. I've never heard of such a thing."

Mirax laughed. "No? As I recall, that's how you got your share of the *Pulsar Skate*."

Booster frowned heavily. "That's not the same thing at all, not at all. But, for the sake of argument here, let's say Captain Varrscha *was* mistaken about my connection with the New Republic. I still possess the ship, and if they have a share, so do I."

Cracken nodded. "You do. We will justly compensate you for it, of course, and you'll earn our undying gratitude. Even a pardon for any indiscretions you might have committed . . ."

"You can stop there, General. Unless you want to give me back the five years I spent on Kessel, I'm not interested in any judicial rewards, thanks. How much?"

The New Republic's representative hesitated. "The current situation is such that an immediate payment is out of the question, but I think we could compensate you with five million credits."

"Ha! This is an Imperial Star Destroyer Mark II we're talking about. It doesn't have a scratch on it. It is worth billions and billions of credits. I'll settle for a billion credits, payable in two hours, or I'm flying it out of here."

"Ah, Booster, you're dreaming if you think that ship is going anywhere." Cracken smiled confidently. "As you know, Thyferra has voted to join the New Republic. Because of this, all ships in the system are subject to New Republic law. In accord with said laws, your navigation and engineering section crews have been taken planetside for debriefing."

"That's piracy."

"No, it's actually a security concern. As Lieutenant Horn can attest, a number of prisoners who were on this ship are missing. We want to question anyone who might have been used to move them to other locations, and your astronav crews could have been employed in that capacity. Right now, your ship is going nowhere."

Booster frowned. "Okay, I'll come down to five hundred million credits."

The sum seemed to stagger Cracken for a moment, then Karrde spoke. "Booster, be reasonable. Try twenty percent of that."

Booster stared at him. "You're being very generous with my money, Karrde."

"Twenty percent of something, Booster, is better than one hundred percent of nothing."

"True, but if they can't deliver, why not think big?"

Corran raised a hand. "It just struck me that we might be arguing about the wrong thing here. Booster, how serious are you about making the *Virulence* into a hyperspace-capable smuggler's den?"

Booster scratched at the beard stubble on his throat. "Very. I spent my life hauling cargo from one point to another. It would be nice to own a place where the cargo came to me and I just brokered deals for it. The *Virulence* would do nicely in that regard."

Corran smiled. "So would the *Freedom*."

"No!" Booster and Cracken dismissed the idea at the same time. They exchanged surprised glances, then shook their heads.

"I don't want the *Freedom*. Refitting it will take a lifetime. I'd have to get it to Sluis Van, and General Cracken here

would guarantee my work was never scheduled. Stick to flying, Horn, because that idea was really dumb."

Mirax slapped her father on the arm. "Don't speak to my
fiancé like that."

"What?!" Booster's jaw dropped. "No, that's impossible."

Corran raised an eyebrow. "Mirax, I'm not sure this was
the best time to mention that."

Booster pointed at Cracken and then Corran. "*He* wants
to take away my ship, and *he* wants to take away my daughter." He turned to Karrde. "I suppose you want something of
mine, too."

"Perhaps, Booster." Karrde smiled in a very genial manner. "I think I want you to reconsider what Lieutenant Horn
suggested. It strikes me that General Cracken is primarily
concerned with your being in command of a ship with
enough firepower to slag an inhabited world."

"Succinctly put, Karrde."

"Thank you, General." Karrde looked at Booster. "Now
you're concerned that your ship would fall prey to all sorts of
pirates if they take its weaponry away. Even stripped of
weapons a hulk like the *Freedom* would be quite a prize."

Booster nodded slowly. "You're talking sense, Karrde.
This scares me."

"Booster and I agree on something." Corran narrowed
his eyes at Karrde. "Where's this going?"

"You know the law, Lieutenant. A ship the size of the
Virulence, in private ownership, would be allowed to lawfully
carry how much in the way of weaponry?"

Corran sat back. "Nothing that size in private ownership, but it would be something on the order of two tractor
beams, ten ion cannons, and ten heavy turbolaser batteries."

"My calculations exactly, which leaves eight tractor
beams, ten ion cannons, forty heavy turbolaser batteries, and
fifty heavy turbolasers to be pulled off the *Virulence*. General
Cracken, those weapons would pretty much replace what the
Freedom lost here, wouldn't they?"

Cracken frowned. "For having been here less than a

week, Talon Karrde, you know more than I'm comfortable having you know."

Booster shook his head. "Those guns aren't leaving my ship."

Cracken snarled, "The *Virulence* is not your ship."

Karrde held a hand up. "Ah, but it can be. According to the Admiralty regulations governing salvage disputes, Booster has named a fair price for his share of the salvage rights to the *Virulence*. Since you can't meet his price, he can assume control of the vessel by depositing ten percent of that price, in this case ten million credits, with a duly recognized judicial authority—such as the government of Thyferra."

Booster frowned. "I don't have ten million credits, Karrde."

"No, Booster, you don't, but you do have a lot of surplus military-grade hardware that you're going to have to get rid of. I'll buy it for ten million."

Cracken tapped a finger against the table. "I'm no more comfortable with you having that hardware, Karrde, than I was with Terrik having it."

"I expected that, General. I'll sell you the weapons for twenty-five million credits."

Cracken's jaw shot open. "You'll what?"

Booster smiled. "I want fifteen million, Karrde. I have operating expenses."

"I'll make it eighteen if you also sell me four squadrons of TIE fighters." Karrde sat back in his seat. "And the price to you, General, is now thirty-five million, but you'll find I issue credit more easily than my friend. Once the court here on Thyferra has reviewed the *Virulence* case, Booster will pay you whatever additional amount they decide he owes you."

Corran laughed aloud. "The *Virulence*'s appearance here tipped the balance in the Thyferran war of liberation, so I suspect Booster isn't going to owe much."

"I suspect the judges here might be swayed by that fact, but the New Republic will be able to argue its case." Karrde pressed his hands together. "Booster, you get your ship and, General, you get weapons out of his hands and into yours."

Cracken remained silent for a moment, then nodded

slowly. "You bargain very well, Karrde. Perhaps there is other business we can do."

"No, General, I don't think so. I did this for the obscene profit you'll pay me, which, since you don't have liquid capital available, will be rendered in trading concessions for bacta and other things. I don't mind dealing with you, but I'm not of a mind to take sides in this civil war. Isard and Zsinj are two examples of countless Imperial holdouts. I'd like to avoid becoming a victim of future wars."

"You'd rather be caught between us than with us?"

"I'd rather not be caught at all." Karrde's smile carried up into his pale blue eyes. "Have we a deal?"

"The Provisional Council will have a piece of my hide for this, but, yes." Cracken stood and nodded to Booster. "The *Virulence* is yours. Please change the name."

Booster stood at his end of the table. "I already know what I'll call her: the *Errant Venture*."

Corran smiled weakly at General Cracken. "Sorry I couldn't have been of more help."

"It wasn't the solution I wanted, but it *was* a solution." Cracken tossed them a casual salute. "Until later."

Mirax glanced at her chronometer, then stretched languidly. "Two hours until Wedge's party." She smiled at Corran. "Any ideas about how to kill that time?"

Booster settled his right hand over her left. "Yes, my dear. We're going to discuss this engagement of yours. My daughter isn't going to marry anyone from CorSec—they're all of low morals and intellect. Not going to happen. Period."

Corran looked over at Karrde. "You want to help me out here?"

"Do you think you could afford my help, Lieutenant?"

"No, probably not."

Karrde nodded solemnly. "Definitely not. Fortunately for you, however, now Booster has to pay for *my* help. We need to head over to the *Errant Venture* and pull specs on your weapons."

Booster frowned. "Now?"

"Unless you want Cracken to do it first and leave you

with the weapons most likely to break down, we better do it now."

Booster's eyes narrowed. "This discussion is just delayed, not abandoned."

"Yes, Father." Mirax kissed him on the cheek. "See you in two hours at the party."

The two smugglers exited the ready-room, leaving Corran and Mirax alone. He shook his head. "How far away from here can we get in two hours?"

"Not far enough, I'm afraid."

"I'm not looking forward to this discussion of our engagement."

"My father may growl like a rancor, but his claws aren't that sharp."

"Oh, that makes me feel lots better. He'll be insufferable for the period of our engagement, you know."

"Agreed." She took his hands into hers. "However, I think I know a way to deflect him."

"How?"

"You'll see." Mirax stood and pulled him up out of his chair. "Come with me, love, and all shall be made clear to you."

42

Wedge waited until everyone had been seated in the *Lusankya*'s staff officers' mess before he stepped behind the podium Emtrey had found and set up on a table at the far end of the room. He smiled as he faced the motley gathering. Closest sat his pilots; beyond them the Twi'lek *Chir'daki* pilots who had survived, including Tal'dira; Captain Sair Yonka of the *Freedom*; General Cracken and his son, Pash; Booster Terrik and Talon Karrde; Iella Wessiri, Elscol Loro, Sixtus, and a handful of Ashern he didn't know; and several Vratix officials from Thyferra. *The only things we need now for a full-fledged victory celebration are a bonfire and a legion of Ewoks.*

Wedge held his hands up to quiet everyone and aside from the whirring of serving droids passing between the tables, silence reigned. "I want to keep my remarks as brief as possible because, one, I respect you all too much to want to bore you and, two, I know you're all quick enough wits that the heckling will be worse than the fight to take this hulk away from Iceheart.

"I have a couple of pieces of business to transact first, though, with your indulgence." Wedge smiled and nodded over at Asyr Sei'lar. "As you call can tell, Asyr is doing well after spending some time in a bacta tank. The injuries she sustained when her X-wing was hit were fairly minor, but the Onebee droids have already certified her as flight capable."

A polite round of applause greeted that news. "Unfortunately our other casualty did not get away so cleanly. Perhaps you want to explain, Nawara."

The Twi'lek nodded. "While I was out of my X-wing I had the misfortune of having a micrometeorite hit me in the right leg. It severed the limb just above the knee and did so much tissue damage all the bacta on Thyferra couldn't fix it. My suit shut down around the wound, which is why I survived. Actually, the real reason I survived was because of Ooryl vaping all the squints that wanted to finish me off, but the leg was a loss."

Corran turned in his seat. "They can fit you for a mechanical, right?"

"Yes, which is what the Onebees will be doing." Nawara rapped his knuckles against the hollow-sounding lower part of his right leg. "Unfortunately I don't scan as being able to utilize a prosthetic as well as I need to if I want to continue flying. I'll have ninety-five percent use of the mechanical, but that's not enough to keep up with the rest of you—not that I ever could before."

Wedge smiled. "You *were* a bit rough on our equipment, Nawara. That not withstanding, Nawara will remain with the unit as our new Executive Officer. Tal'dira has been invited to join us and has accepted, so we'll have a Twi'lek flying with us still." Wedge led the applause, which started lekku twitching among the Twi'lek pilots.

"Bror Jace has been appointed by his government to head up the formation of the Thyferran Aerospace Defense Force, so we'll lose his services, at least temporarily. The government has also asked us to stay on here for the next couple of months to help train the new unit. This is an assignment I've chosen to accept so we can make sure no one gets too adventurous and tries to repeat what Isard did here."

He looked over toward General Cracken. "After that, well, General Cracken has communicated to me the contents of a resolution voted by the Provisional Council to congratulate us on what we've accomplished here. He also said that, due to a bureaucratic mixup, our resignations were never formally logged to our files. If we want them, our commissions are available to us and General Cracken has assured me that he's looking for an elite unit to be able to follow up on investigative leads concerning the lost *Lusankya* prisoners. Once our work is done here, I intend to rejoin the New Republic and I'd like to bring Rogue Squadron back with me."

Wedge smiled. "I've already spoken with Tycho and Corran, and they've agreed to rejoin. Aril, are you going to keep the *Valiant* or come back with us?"

The Sullustan smiled. "I'm coming back to the Alliance, Wedge. I'll still command the *Valiant*, but I think we can work out a deal with General Cracken to pull missions together."

"Good. Asyr?"

The Bothan looked over at Gavin, got a nod from him, then smiled. "We're both in."

"Rhysati?"

"I'm in."

"Nawara?"

"Can't be an Executive Officer if I don't stay with the unit, can I? I'm in."

"Ooryl?"

"Rogue Squadron made me *janwuine*. I would never say no to the honor of remaining with it."

"Tal'dira?"

The Twi'lek warrior nodded solemnly. "I could not let Rogue Squadron be without a Twi'lek pilot. I am pleased to accept the offer to join the unit."

Wedge smiled at Inyri Forge. "I know serving with Rogue Squadron was your sister's dream, but you've earned your own place with us. We'd be proud to have you if you want to stay with us."

A grin slowly spread across the blue-eyed woman's face. "My sister always wanted the best for everyone else. Joining the squadron meant she got to fight the evil plaguing others, making things better for them. Her example is pretty compelling. I'm in."

With her acceptance, cheers erupted, hands were shaken and backs slapped. Wedge swallowed against the lump rising in his throat. "Two more things, then my remarks. First, we've been invited to Gand for Ooryl's *janwuine-jika*. This is an unbelievably huge honor for one of us who has earned many honors. Second, and equally worthy of celebration, is something I did barely a half an hour ago. As you will recall, the *Lusankya* was surrendered to me, making me its de facto captain. In my capacity as such, with Tycho and Iella present as witnesses, I had the pleasure of marrying Mirax and Corran."

"*What!*" Booster's shout accompanied an immediate reddening of his face.

Wedge held his hands up. "Take it easy, Booster. They plan another, more formal ceremony we all can attend back on Coruscant, but they figured that if you were going to be upset with them for getting engaged, they might as well save themselves that aggravation and just have you mad at them for being married."

"I'm not upset about that, Wedge. I was upset when I thought she was marrying someone from CorSec." Mirax's father smiled. "Now he's part of Rogue Squadron again, so I have no complaints."

"Right." Wedge shook his head. "No complaints you want to voice at this time."

Booster hesitated for a moment, then nodded to an accompaniment of good-natured laughter.

Corran frowned at his father-in-law. "Then the red in your face and the anger in your voice wasn't because of us?"

"You CorSec people always think it's about you." Booster shook his head, then jerked a thumb at Karrde. "He bet me a million credits that you'd go and do exactly what you did, and he even conned me into giving him odds."

Wedge laughed. "Corran, Mirax, I think *that's* going to be a major bone of contention for the future."

"One he's going to worry like a hungry nek." Corran

brought Mirax's left hand to his mouth and kissed it. "Not too steep a price to pay, though."

"Ha," Mirax snickered, "serves him right for betting against us."

Even Booster joined the resulting laughter. To Wedge the sound was a tonic. *In all the time I've been with Rogue Squadron, there has been too little laughter and too many tears.* Again his throat thickened, but he smiled and swallowed to loosen it.

"Again, I want these remarks to be brief. It was about a year and a half ago that I first met most of you. You were bright-eyed and enthusiastic, ready to launch into one grand adventure after another. I had seen that before with other pilots in Rogue Squadron. I remember the days before Yavin when we were all young, armored with the invincibility of youth and fired by the belief that the Emperor's evil Empire could not win. It didn't, but the cost was more horrible than any of us could have imagined. You've all seen the roll of those who died with Rogue Squadron. Had we known at the start of things how few of us would survive, I think many of us would not have answered the call to fight."

Wedge caught his lower lip between his teeth for a second, then continued. "You all came to Rogue Squadron knowing how few of us had survived. Your decision to join us was an informed decision. Yes, the Emperor was dead, Darth Vader was gone, but the Empire's ability to grind up our warriors was not significantly diminished. On both sides of the battle the weak and incompetent had been killed, leaving only the most lethal of each force to stalk each other.

"Nothing we've done—including the conquest of Coruscant—will be compared favorably with the destruction of the Death Stars and Palpatine's death, yet as I look back on what we've done, I feel a greater sense of accomplishment now than I ever have before. Yavin and Endor were battles we had to fight and had to win because if we did not our movement would be exterminated. We fought with the abandon of people who knew, either way, they were dead; and desperation, while not pretty, can often be very potent and deadly."

He glanced down for a second, then looked back up.

"Our missions have been no less critical in the destruction of the Empire than those that went before, but they were different. We took the war to the Empire. We made plans and successfully improvised when those plans fell apart. We did things that no one—not even the seemingly prescient Talon Karrde—could have expected us to do.

"And we did things no one could have ordered us to do. We accepted the burden of responsibility thrust upon us and overcame the obstacles in our way. That has always been the Rogue Squadron tradition, but you've added a new layer to it: You survived those missions. For that I'm most thankful, because I did not join Rogue Squadron to lose friends."

He reached down, accepted a tumbler of Corellian whisky from a serving droid, then raised it on high in his left hand. "I would ask all of you to lift your glasses and join me in a toast. To Rogue Squadron—past, present, and future. Those who oppose freedom and liberty oppose us. Let that fact give them pause to think and encouragement to travel the path of peace."

ABOUT THE AUTHOR

Michael A. Stackpole is an award-winning game and computer game designer who was born in 1957 and hates writing these "About the Author" pieces because they force him to refer to himself in the third person. Being neither a Gand nor a Presidential candidate, he finds this awkward. Perhaps if he had not grown up in a normal family, enjoying an utterly normal life, this third person thing wouldn't bother him, but then he also thinks it's better to be known for what he's written and done than for any vaguely interesting bits of nonsense about his past.

The Bacta War is his nineteenth published novel and the final of four Star Wars X-wing novels. (In answer to a commonly asked question, it takes about 200 hours for him to write a novel—a pace that is disgustingly fast.) In addition to working on the novels he has worked on the X-wing comic series from Dark Horse Comics, building a continuity between the two sets of stories.

Despite having enjoyed growing up in Vermont, he lives in Arizona because he hates shoveling snow. He attends conventions with a frequency that makes airlines rejoice and still somehow manages to get his work done. In the future he plans to write more books and take a trip to Mongolia.

His Web page can be found at http://www. flyingbuffalo.com/stackpol.htm

The World of
STAR WARS Novels

In May 1991, *Star Wars* caused a sensation in the publishing industry with the Bantam release of Timothy Zahn's novel *Heir to the Empire*. For the first time, Lucasfilm Ltd. had authorized new novels that *continued* the famous story told in George Lucas's three block-buster motion pictures: *Star Wars*, *The Empire Strikes Back*, and *Return of the Jedi*. Reader reaction was immediate and tumultuous: *Heir* reached No. 1 on the *New York Times* bestseller list and demonstrated that *Star Wars* lovers were eager for exciting new stories set in this universe, written by leading science fiction authors who shared their passion. Since then, each Bantam *Star Wars* novel has been an instant national bestseller.

Lucasfilm and Bantam decided that future novels in the series would be interconnected: that is, events in one novel would have consequences in the others. You might say that each Bantam *Star Wars* novel, enjoyable on its own, is also part of a much larger tale.

Here is a special look at Bantam's *Star Wars* books, along with excerpts from the more recent novels. Each one is available now wherever Bantam Books are sold.

SHADOWS OF THE EMPIRE
by Steve Perry
Setting: Between *The Empire Strikes Back* and *Return of the Jedi*

Here is a very special STAR WARS story dealing with Black Sun, a galaxy-spanning criminal organization that is masterminded by one of the most interesting villains in the STAR WARS universe: Xizor, dark prince of the Falleen. Xizor's chief rival for the favor of Emperor Palpatine is none other than Darth Vader himself—alive and well, and a major character in this story, since it is set during the events of the STAR WARS film trilogy.

In the opening prologue, we revisit a familiar scene from The Empire Strikes Back, and are introduced to our marvelous new bad guy:

He looks like a walking corpse, Xizor thought. *Like a mummified body dead a thousand years. Amazing he is still alive, much less the*

*most powerful man in the galaxy. He isn't even that old; it is more as
if something is slowly eating him.*

Xizor stood four meters away from the Emperor, watching as the
man who had long ago been Senator Palpatine moved to stand in the
holocam field. He imagined he could smell the decay in the Emperor's
worn body. Likely that was just some trick of the recycled air, run
through dozens of filters to ensure that there was no chance of any
poison gas being introduced into it. Filtered the life out of it, perhaps,
giving it that dead smell.

The viewer on the other end of the holo-link would see a close-up
of the Emperor's head and shoulders, of an age-ravaged face shrouded
in the cowl of his dark zeyd-cloth robe. The man on the other end of
the transmission, light-years away, would not see Xizor, though Xizor
would be able to see him. It was a measure of the Emperor's trust that
Xizor was allowed to be here while the conversation took place.

The man on the other end of the transmission—if he could still be
called that—

The air swirled inside the Imperial chamber in front of the Emperor, coalesced, and blossomed into the image of a figure down on
one knee. A caped humanoid biped dressed in jet black, face hidden
under a full helmet and breathing mask:

Darth Vader.

Vader spoke: "What is thy bidding, my master?"

If Xizor could have hurled a power bolt through time and space to
strike Vader dead, he would have done it without blinking. Wishful
thinking: Vader was too powerful to attack directly.

"There is a great disturbance in the Force," the Emperor said.

"I have felt it," Vader said.

"We have a new enemy. Luke Skywalker."

Skywalker? That had been Vader's name, a long time ago. Who was
this person with the same name, someone so powerful as to be worth a
conversation between the Emperor and his most loathsome creation?
More importantly, why had Xizor's agents not uncovered this before
now? Xizor's ire was instant—but cold. No sign of his surprise or
anger would show on his imperturbable features. The Falleen did not
allow their emotions to burst forth as did many of the inferior species;
no, the Falleen ancestry was not fur but scales, not mammalian but
reptilian. Not wild but coolly calculating. Such was much better.
Much safer.

"Yes, my master," Vader continued.

"He could destroy us," the Emperor said.

Xizor's attention was riveted upon the Emperor and the holographic
image of Vader kneeling on the deck of a ship far away. Here was

interesting news indeed. Something the Emperor perceived as a danger to himself? Something the Emperor feared?

"He's just a boy," Vader said. "Obi-Wan can no longer help him."

Obi-Wan. That name Xizor knew. He was among the last of the Jedi Knights, a general. But he'd been dead for decades, hadn't he?

Apparently Xizor's information was wrong if Obi-Wan had been helping someone who was still a boy. His agents were going to be sorry.

Even as Xizor took in the distant image of Vader and the nearness of the Emperor, even as he was aware of the luxury of the Emperor's private and protected chamber at the core of the giant pyramidal palace, he was also able to make a mental note to himself: Somebody's head would roll for the failure to make him aware of all this. Knowledge was power; lack of knowledge was weakness. This was something he could not permit.

The Emperor continued. "The Force is strong with him. The son of Skywalker must not become a Jedi."

Son of Skywalker?

Vader's son! Amazing!

"If he could be turned he would become a powerful ally," Vader said.

There was something in Vader's voice when he said this, something Xizor could not quite put his finger on. Longing? Worry?

Hope?

"Yes . . . yes. He would be a great asset," the Emperor said. "Can it be done?"

There was the briefest of pauses. "He will join us or die, Master."

Xizor felt the smile, though he did not allow it to show any more than he had allowed his anger play. Ah. Vader wanted Skywalker alive, *that* was what had been in his tone. Yes, he had said that the boy would join them or die, but this latter part was obviously meant only to placate the Emperor. Vader had no intention of killing Skywalker, his own son; that was obvious to one as skilled in reading voices as was Xizor. He had not gotten to be the Dark Prince, Underlord of Black Sun, the largest criminal organization in the galaxy, merely on his formidable good looks. Xizor didn't truly understand the Force that sustained the Emperor and made him and Vader so powerful, save to know that it certainly worked somehow. But he did know that it was something the extinct Jedi had supposedly mastered. And now, apparently, this new player had tapped into it. Vader wanted Skywalker alive, had practically promised the Emperor that he would deliver him alive—and converted.

This was most interesting.

Most interesting indeed.

The Emperor finished his communication and turned back to face him. "Now, where were we, Prince Xizor?"

The Dark Prince smiled. He would attend to the business at hand, but he would not forget the name of Luke Skywalker.

THE TRUCE AT BAKURA by Kathy Tyers
Setting: Immediately after *Return of the Jedi*

The day after his climactic battle with Emperor Palpatine and the sacrifice of his father, Darth Vader, who died saving his life, Luke Skywalker helps recover an Imperial drone ship bearing a startling message intended for the Emperor. It is a distress signal from the far-off Imperial outpost of Bakura, which is under attack by an alien invasion force, the Ssi-ruuk. Leia sees a rescue mission as an opportunity to achieve a diplomatic victory for the Rebel Alliance, even if it means fighting alongside former Imperials. But Luke receives a vision from Obi-Wan Kenobi revealing that the stakes are even higher: the invasion at Bakura threatens everything the Rebels have won at such great cost.

STAR WARS: X-WING
by Michael A. Stackpole
ROGUE SQUADRON
WEDGE'S GAMBLE
THE KRYTOS TRAP
THE BACTA WAR
Setting: Three years after *Return of the Jedi*

Inspired by X-Wing, the bestselling computer game from LucasArts Entertainment Co., this exciting series chronicles the further adventures of the most feared and fearless fighting force in the galaxy. A new generation of X-wing pilots, led by Commander Wedge Antilles, is combating the remnants of the Empire still left after the events of the STAR WARS movies. Here are novels full of explosive space action, nonstop adventure, and the special brand of wonder known as STAR WARS.

In this very early scene, young Corellian pilot Corran Horn faces a tough challenge fast enough to get his heart pounding—and this is only a simulation! [*P.S.: "Whistler" is Corran's R2 astromech droid*]:

The Corellian brought his proton torpedo targeting program up and locked on to the TIE. It tried to break the lock, but turbolaser fire from the *Korolev* boxed it in. Corran's heads-up display went red and he triggered the torpedo. "Scratch one eyeball."

The missile shot straight in at the fighter, but the pilot broke hard to port and away, causing the missile to overshoot the target. *Nice flying!* Corran brought his X-wing over and started down to loop in behind the TIE, but as he did so, the TIE vanished from his forward screen and reappeared in his aft arc. Yanking the stick hard to the right and pulling it back, Corran wrestled the X-wing up and to starboard, then inverted and rolled out to the left.

A laser shot jolted a tremor through the simulator's couch. *Lucky thing I had all shields aft!* Corran reinforced them with energy from his lasers, then evened them out fore and aft. Jinking the fighter right and left, he avoided laser shots coming in from behind, but they all came in far closer than he liked.

He knew Jace had been in the bomber, and Jace was the only pilot in the unit who could have stayed with him. *Except for our leader.* Corran smiled broadly. *Coming to see how good I really am, Commander Antilles? Let me give you a clinic.* "Make sure you're in there solid, Whistler, because we're going for a little ride."

Corran refused to let the R2's moan slow him down. A snap-roll brought the X-wing up on its port wing. Pulling back on the stick yanked the fighter's nose up away from the original line of flight. The TIE stayed with him, then tightened up on the arc to close distance. Corran then rolled another ninety degrees and continued the turn into a dive. Throttling back, Corran hung in the dive for three seconds, then hauled back hard on the stick and cruised up into the TIE fighter's aft.

The X-wing's laser fire missed wide to the right as the TIE cut to the left. Corran kicked his speed up to full and broke with the TIE. He let the X-wing rise above the plane of the break, then put the fighter through a twisting roll that ate up enough time to bring him again into the TIE's rear. The TIE snapped to the right and Corran looped out left.

He watched the tracking display as the distance between them grew to be a kilometer and a half, then slowed. *Fine, you want to go nose to nose? I've got shields and you don't.* If Commander Antilles wanted to commit virtual suicide, Corran was happy to oblige him. He tugged the stick back to his sternum and rolled out in an inversion loop. *Coming at you!*

The two starfighters closed swiftly. Corran centered his foe in the crosshairs and waited for a dead shot. Without shields the TIE fighter would die with one burst, and Corran wanted the kill to be clean. His HUD flicked green as the TIE juked in and out of the center, then locked green as they closed.

The TIE started firing at maximum range and scored hits. At that distance the lasers did no real damage against the shields, prompting Corran to wonder why Wedge was wasting the energy. Then, as the HUD's green color started to flicker, realization dawned. *The bright bursts on the shields are a distraction to my targeting! I better kill him now!*

Corran tightened down on the trigger button, sending red laser needles stabbing out at the closing TIE fighter. He couldn't tell if he had hit anything. Lights flashed in the cockpit and Whistler started screeching furiously. Corran's main monitor went black, his shields were down, and his weapons controls were dead.

The pilot looked left and right. "Where is he, Whistler?"

The monitor in front of him flickered to life and a diagnostic report began to scroll by. Bloodred bordered the damage reports. "Scanners, out; lasers, out; shields, out; engine, out! I'm a wallowing Hutt just hanging here in space."

THE COURTSHIP OF PRINCESS LEIA
by Dave Wolverton
Setting: Four years after *Return of the Jedi*

One of the most interesting developments in Bantam's Star Wars *novels is that in their storyline, Han Solo and Princess Leia start a family. This tale reveals how the couple originally got together. Wishing to strengthen the fledgling New Republic by bringing in powerful allies, Leia opens talks with the Hapes consortium of more than sixty worlds. But the consortium is ruled by the Queen Mother, who, to Han's dismay, wants Leia to marry her son, Prince Isolder. Before this action-packed story is over, Luke will join forces with Isolder against a group of Force-trained "witches" and face a deadly foe.*

HEIR TO THE EMPIRE
DARK FORCE RISING
THE LAST COMMAND
by Timothy Zahn
Setting: Five years after *Return of the Jedi*

This No. 1 bestselling trilogy introduces two legendary forces of evil into the Star Wars literary pantheon. Grand Admiral Thrawn has taken control of the Imperial fleet in the years since the destruction of the Death Star, and the mysterious Joruus C'baoth is a fearsome Jedi Master who has been seduced by the dark side. Han and Leia have now been married for about a year, and as the story begins, she is pregnant with twins. Thrawn's plan is to crush the Rebellion and resurrect the Empire's New Order with C'baoth's help—and in return, the Dark Master will get Han and Leia's Jedi children to mold as he wishes. For as readers of this magnificent trilogy will see, Luke Skywalker is not the last of the old Jedi. He is the first of the new.

The Jedi Academy Trilogy:
JEDI SEARCH
DARK APPRENTICE
CHAMPIONS OF THE FORCE
by Kevin J. Anderson
Setting: Seven years after *Return of the Jedi*

In order to assure the continuation of the Jedi Knights, Luke Skywalker has decided to start a training facility: a Jedi Academy. He will gather Force-sensitive students who show potential as prospective Jedi and serve as their mentor, as Jedi Masters Obi-Wan Kenobi and Yoda did for him. Han and Leia's twins are now toddlers, and there is a third Jedi child: the infant Anakin, named after Luke and Leia's father. In this trilogy, we discover the existence of a powerful Imperial doomsday weapon, the horrifying Sun Crusher—which will soon become the centerpiece of a titanic struggle between Luke Skywalker and his most brilliant Jedi Academy student, who is delving dangerously into the dark side.

CHILDREN OF THE JEDI
by Barbara Hambly
Setting: Eight years after *Return of the Jedi*

The Star Wars *characters face a menace from the glory days of the Empire when a thirty-year-old automated Imperial Dreadnaught comes to life and begins its grim mission: To gather forces and annihilate a long-forgotten stronghold of Jedi children. When Luke is whisked onboard, he begins to communicate with the brave Jedi Knight who paralyzed the ship decades ago, and gave her life in the process. Now she is part of the vessel, existing in its artificial intelligence core, and guiding Luke through one of the most unusual adventures he has ever had.*

In this scene, Luke discovers that an evil presence is gathering, one that will force him to join the battle:

Like See-Threepio, Nichos Marr sat in the outer room of the suite to which Cray had been assigned, in the power-down mode that was the droid equivalent of rest. Like Threepio, at the sound of Luke's almost noiseless tread he turned his head, aware of his presence.

"Luke?" Cray had equipped him with the most sensitive vocal modulators, and the word was calibrated to a whisper no louder than the rustle of the blueleaves massed outside the windows. He rose, and crossed to where Luke stood, the dull silver of his arms and shoulders a phantom gleam in the stray flickers of light. "What is it?"

"I don't know." They retreated to the small dining area where Luke had earlier probed his mind, and Luke stretched up to pin back a corner of the lamp-sheath, letting a slim triangle of butter-colored light fall on the purple of the vulwood tabletop. "A dream. A premonition, maybe." It was on his lips to ask, *Do you dream?* but he remembered the ghastly, imageless darkness in Nichos's mind, and didn't. He wasn't sure if his pupil was aware of the difference from his human perception and knowledge, aware of just exactly what he'd lost when his consciousness, his self, had been transferred.

In the morning Luke excused himself from the expedition Tomla El had organized with Nichos and Cray to the Falls of Dessiar, one of the places on Ithor most renowned for its beauty and peace. When they left he sought out Umwaw Moolis, and the tall herd leader listened gravely to his less than logical request and promised to put matters in train to fulfill it. Then Luke descended to the House of the Healers, where Drub McKumb lay, sedated far beyond pain but with all the perceptions of agony and nightmare still howling in his mind.

"Kill you!" He heaved himself at the restraints, blue eyes glaring furiously as he groped and scrabbled at Luke with his clawed hands. "It's all poison! I see you! I see the dark light all around you! You're him! You're him!" His back bent like a bow; the sound of his shrieking was like something being ground out of him by an infernal mangle.

Luke had been through the darkest places of the universe and of his own mind, had done and experienced greater evil than perhaps any man had known on the road the Force had dragged him . . . Still, it was hard not to turn away.

"We even tried yarrock on him last night," explained the Healer in charge, a slightly built Ithorian beautifully tabby-striped green and yellow under her simple tabard of purple linen. "But apparently the earlier doses that brought him enough lucidity to reach here from his point of origin oversensitized his system. We'll try again in four or five days."

Luke gazed down into the contorted, grimacing face.

"As you can see," the Healer said, "the internal perception of pain and fear is slowly lessening. It's down to ninety-three percent of what it was when he was first brought in. Not much, I know, but something."

"Him! *Him! HIM!*" Foam spattered the old man's stained gray beard.

Who?

"I wouldn't advise attempting any kind of mindlink until it's at least down to fifty percent, Master Skywalker."

"No," said Luke softly.

Kill you all. And, *They are gathering* . . .

"Do you have recordings of everything he's said?"

"Oh, yes." The big coppery eyes blinked assent. "The transcript is available through the monitor cubicle down the hall. We could make nothing of them. Perhaps they will mean something to you."

They didn't. Luke listened to them all, the incoherent groans and screams, the chewed fragments of words that could be only guessed at, and now and again the clear disjointed cries: "Solo! Solo! Can you hear me? Children . . . Evil . . . Gathering here . . . Kill you all!"

DARKSABER by Kevin J. Anderson
Setting: Immediately thereafter

Not long after Children of the Jedi, *Luke and Han learn that evil Hutts are building a reconstruction of the original Death Star—and that the Empire is still alive, in the form of Daala, who has joined forces with Pellaeon, former second in command to the feared Grand Admiral Thrawn. In this early scene, Luke has returned to the home of Obi-Wan Kenobi on Tatooine to try and consult a long-gone mentor:*

He stood anxious and alone, feeling like a prodigal son outside the ramshackle, collapsed hut that had once been the home of Obi-Wan Kenobi.

Luke swallowed and stepped forward, his footsteps crunching in the silence. He had not been here in many years. The door had fallen off its hinges; part of the clay front wall had fallen in. Boulders and crumbled adobe jammed the entrance. A pair of small, screeching desert rodents snapped at him and fled for cover; Luke ignored them.

Gingerly, he ducked low and stepped into the home of his first mentor.

Luke stood in the middle of the room breathing deeply, turning around, trying to sense the presence he desperately needed to see. This was the place where Obi-Wan Kenobi had told Luke of the Force. Here, the old man had first given Luke his lightsaber and hinted at the truth about his father, "from a certain point of view," dispelling the diversionary story that Uncle Owen had told, at the same time planting seeds of his own deceptions.

"Ben," he said and closed his eyes, calling out with his mind as well as his voice. He tried to penetrate the invisible walls of the Force and reach to the luminous being of Obi-Wan Kenobi who had visited him numerous times, before saying he could never speak with Luke again.

"Ben, I need you," Luke said. Circumstances had changed. He could think of no other way past the obstacles he faced. Obi-Wan had to answer. It wouldn't take long, but it could give him the key he needed with all his heart.

Luke paused and listened and sensed—

But felt nothing. If he could not summon Obi-Wan's spirit here in the empty dwelling where the old man had lived in exile for so many years, Luke didn't believe he could find his former teacher ever again.

He echoed the words Leia had used more than a decade earlier, beseeching him, "Help me, Obi-Wan Kenobi," Luke whispered, "you're my only hope."

THE CRYSTAL STAR
by Vonda N. McIntyre
Setting: Ten years after *Return of the Jedi*

Leia's three children have been kidnapped. That horrible fact is made worse by Leia's realization that she can no longer sense her children through the Force! While she, Artoo-Detoo, and Chewbacca trail the kidnappers, Luke and Han discover a planet that is suffering strange quantum effects from a nearby star. Slowly freezing into a perfect crystal and disrupting the Force, the star is blunting Luke's power and crippling the Millennium Falcon. *These strands converge in an apocalyptic threat not only to the fate of the New Republic, but to the universe itself.*

The Black Fleet Crisis
BEFORE THE STORM
SHIELD OF LIES
by Michael P. Kube-McDowell
Setting: Twelve years after *Return of the Jedi*

Long after setting up the hard-won New Republic, yesterday's Rebels have become today's administrators and diplomats. But the peace is not to last for long. A restless Luke must journey to his mother's homeworld in a desperate quest to find her people; Lando seizes a mysterious spacecraft with unimaginable weapons of destruction; and waiting in the wings is an horrific battle fleet under the control of a ruthless leader bent on a genocidal war.

Here is an opening scene from Before the Storm:

In the pristine silence of space, the Fifth Battle Group of the New Republic Defense Fleet blossomed over the planet Bessimir like a beautiful, deadly flower.

The formation of capital ships sprang into view with startling suddenness, trailing fire-white wakes of twisted space and bristling with weapons. Angular Star Destroyers guarded fat-hulled fleet carriers, while the assault cruisers, their mirror finishes gleaming, took the point.

A halo of smaller ships appeared at the same time. The fighters among them quickly deployed in a spherical defensive screen. As the Star Destroyers firmed up their formation, their flight decks quickly spawned scores of additional fighters.

At the same time, the carriers and cruisers began to disgorge the bombers, transports, and gunboats they had ferried to the battle. There was no reason to risk the loss of one fully loaded—a lesson the Republic had learned in pain. At Orinda, the commander of the fleet carrier *Endurance* had kept his pilots waiting in the launch bays, to protect the smaller craft from Imperial fire as long as possible. They were still there when *Endurance* took the brunt of a Super Star Destroyer attack and vanished in a ball of metal fire.

Before long more than two hundred warships, large and small, were bearing down on Bessimir and its twin moons. But the terrible, restless power of the armada could be heard and felt only by the ships' crews. The silence of the approach was broken only on the fleet comm channels, which had crackled to life in the first moments with encoded bursts of noise and cryptic ship-to-ship chatter.

At the center of the formation of great vessels was the flagship of the Fifth Battle Group, the fleet carrier *Intrepid*. She was so new from the yards at Hakassi that her corridors still reeked of sealing compound and cleaning solvent. Her huge realspace thruster engines still sang with the high-pitched squeal that the engine crews called "the baby's cry."

It would take more than a year for the mingled scents of the crew to displace the chemical smells from the first impressions of visitors. But after a hundred more hours under way, her engines' vibrations would drop two octaves, to the reassuring thrum of a seasoned thruster bank.

On *Intrepid*'s bridge, a tall Dornean in general's uniform paced along an arc of command stations equipped with large monitors. His eye-folds were swollen and fanned by an unconscious Dornean defensive reflex, and his leathery face was flushed purple by concern. Before the deployment was even a minute old, Etahn A'baht's first command had been bloodied.

The fleet tender *Ahazi* had overshot its jump, coming out of hyperspace too close to Bessimir and too late for its crew to recover from the error. Etahn A'baht watched the bright flare of light in the upper atmosphere from *Intrepid*'s forward viewstation, knowing that it meant six young men were dead.

THE NEW REBELLION
by Kristine Kathryn Rusch
Setting: Thirteen years after *Return of the Jedi*

*Victorious though the New Republic may be, there is still no end to the
threats to its continuing existence—this novel explores the price of
keeping the peace. First, somewhere in the galaxy, millions suddenly
perish in a blinding instant of pain. Then, as Leia prepares to address
the Senate on Coruscant, a horrifying event changes the governmental
equation in a flash.*

Here is that latter calamity, in an early scene from The New Rebellion*:*

An explosion rocked the Chamber, flinging Leia into the air. She
flew backward and slammed onto a desk, her entire body shuddering
with the power of her hit. Blood and shrapnel rained around her.
Smoke and dust rose, filling the room with a grainy darkness. She
could hear nothing. With a shaking hand, she touched the side of her
face. Warmth stained her cheeks and her earlobes. The ringing would
start soon. The explosion was loud enough to affect her eardrums.

Emergency glow panels seared the gloom. She could feel rather
than hear pieces of the crystal ceiling fall to the ground. A guard had
landed beside her, his head tilted at an unnatural angle. She grabbed
his blaster. She had to get out. She wasn't certain if the attack had
come from within or from without. Wherever it had come from, she
had to make certain no other bombs would go off.

The force of the explosion had affected her balance. She crawled
over bodies, some still moving, as she made her way to the stairs. The
slightest movement made her dizzy and nauseous, but she ignored the
feelings. She had to.

A face loomed before hers. Streaked with dirt and blood, helmet
askew, she recognized him as one of the guards who had been with
her since Alderaan. *Your Highness*, he mouthed, and she couldn't read
the rest. She shook her head at him, gasping at the increased dizziness,
and kept going.

Finally she reached the stairs. She used the remains of a desk to get
to her feet. Her gown was soaked in blood, sticky, and clinging to her
legs. She held the blaster in front of her, wishing that she could hear.
If she could hear, she could defend herself.

A hand reached out of the rubble beside her. She whirled, faced it,
watched as Meido pulled himself out. His slender features were covered with dirt, but he appeared unharmed. He saw her blaster and

cringed. She nodded once to acknowledge him, and kept moving. The guard was flanking her.

More rubble dropped from the ceiling. She crouched, hands over her head to protect herself. Small pebbles pelted her, and the floor shivered as large chunks of tile fell. Dust rose, choking her. She coughed, feeling it, but not able to hear it. Within an instant, the Hall had gone from a place of ceremonial comfort to a place of death.

The image of the death's-head mask rose in front of her again, this time from memory. She had known this was going to happen. Somewhere, from some part of her Force-sensitive brain, she had seen this. Luke said that Jedi were sometimes able to see the future. But she had never completed her training. She wasn't a Jedi.

But she was close enough.

The Corellian Trilogy:
AMBUSH AT CORELLIA
ASSAULT AT SELONIA
SHOWDOWN AT CENTERPOINT
by Roger MacBride Allen
Setting: Fourteen years after *Return of the Jedi*

This trilogy takes us to Corellia, Han Solo's homeworld, which Han has not visited in quite some time. A trade summit brings Han, Leia, and the children—now developing their own clear personalities and instinctively learning more about their innate skills in the Force—into the middle of a situation that most closely resembles a burning fuse. The Corellian system is on the brink of civil war, there are New Republic intelligence agents on a mysterious mission which even Han does not understand, and worst of all, a fanatical rebel leader has his hands on a superweapon of unimaginable power—and just wait until you find out who that leader is!

Here is an early scene from Ambush *that gives you a wonderful look at the growing Solo children (the twins are Jacen and Jaina, and their little brother is Anakin):*

Anakin plugged the board into the innards of the droid and pressed a button. The droid's black, boxy body shuddered awake, it drew in its wheels to stand up a bit taller, its status lights lit, and it made a sort of triple beep. "That's good," he said, and pushed the button again. The droid's status lights went out, and its body slumped down again. Anakin picked up the next piece, a motivation actuator. He frowned at it as he turned it over in his hands. He shook his head. "That's *not* good," he announced.

"What's not good?" Jaina asked.

"This thing," Anakin said, handing her the actuator. "Can't you *tell*? The insides part is all melty."

Jaina and Jacen exchanged a look. "The outside looks okay," Jaina said, giving the part to her brother. "How can he tell what the *inside* of it looks like? It's sealed shut when they make it."

Anakin, still sitting on the floor, took the device from his brother and frowned at it again. He turned it over and over in his hands, and then held it over his head and looked at it as if he were holding it up to the light. "There," he said, pointing a chubby finger at one point on the unmarked surface. "In there is the bad part." He rearranged himself to sit cross-legged, put the actuator in his lap, and put his right index finger over the "bad" part. "Fix," he said. "Fix." The dark brown outer case of the actuator seemed to glow for a second with an odd blue-red light, but then the glow sputtered out and Anakin pulled his finger away quickly and stuck it in his mouth, as if he had burned it on something.

"Better now?" Jaina asked.

"*Some* better," Anakin said, pulling his finger out of his mouth. "Not *all* better." He took the actuator in his hand and stood up. He opened the access panel on the broken droid and plugged in the actuator. He closed the door and looked expectantly at his older brother and sister.

"Done?" Jaina asked.

"Done," Anakin agreed. "But *I'm* not going to push the button." He backed well away from the droid, sat down on the floor, and folded his arms.

Jacen looked at his sister.

"Not me," she said. "This was your idea."

Jacen stepped forward to the droid, reached out to push the power button from as far away as he could, and then stepped hurriedly back.

Once again, the droid shuddered awake, rattling a bit this time as it did so. It pulled its wheels in, lit its panel lights, and made the same triple beep. But then its holocam eye viewlens wobbled back and forth, and its panel lights dimmed and flared. It rolled backward just a bit, and then recovered itself.

"Good morning, young mistress and masters," it said. "How may I surge you?"

Well, one word wrong, but so what? Jacen grinned and clapped his hands and rubbed them together eagerly. "Good day, droid," he said. They had done it! But what to ask for first? "First tidy up this room," he said. A simple task, and one that ought to serve as a good test of what this droid could do.

Suddenly the droid's overhead access door blew off and there was a flash of light from its interior. A thin plume of smoke drifted out of the droid. Its panel lights flared again, and then the work arm sagged downward. The droid's body, softened by heat, sagged in on itself and drooped to the floor. The floor and walls and ceiling of the playroom were supposed to be fireproof, but nonetheless the floor under the droid darkened a bit, and the ceiling turned black. The ventilators kicked on high automatically, and drew the smoke out of the room. After a moment they shut themselves off, and the room was silent.

The three children stood, every bit as frozen to the spot as the droid was, absolutely stunned. It was Anakin who recovered first. He walked cautiously toward the droid and looked at it carefully, being sure not to get too close or touch it. "*Really* melty now," he announced, and then wandered off to the other side of the room to play with his blocks.

The twins looked at the droid, and then at each other.

"We're dead," Jacen announced, surveying the wreckage.

PLANET OF TWILIGHT
by Barbara Hambly

Planet of Twilight is a dark epic of adventure, a visionary tale of courage, betrayal and survival. Packed with action, suspense and adventure, it is a novel that no fan of the bestselling *Star Wars*® series will want to miss.

It all began on a barren backwater world called Renat Chorios – once a dreaded prison colony, now home to the Therans, a fanatic religious cult. To this exiled world has come the ruthless warlord Sati Draconis, who seeks to exploit the vast crystalline deserts that cover the planet's desolate surface.

The first step in his plan is to lure Princess Leia to Renat Chorios for a diplomatic meeting, only to hold her hostage in his isolated fortress. Meanwhile, Luke lands on the planet in search of his lost love Callista, and discovers that any use of the Force has unexpectedly deadly consequences, and, to make matters worse, a plague is decimating the New Republic fleet as it faces attack from overwhelming Imperial Forces. As Han, Chewie and Lando set out on a desperate rescue mission, as Leia seeks to escape the evil Draconis, and as Luke searches through a world torn by plague and riots to find Callista, the planet begins to reveal its unspeakable secret: a long-dormant sentient life form kept in check for centuries is now threatening to gain dominance over the New Republic, the Empire, and the entire galaxy . . .

Coming soon from Bantam Press

0 593 04133 X

STAR WARS: TALES FROM THE MOS EISLEY CANTINA
Edited by Kevin J. Anderson

Droids and mutants rule in sixteen scintillating *Star Wars* tales!

In a far corner of the universe, on the small desert planet of Tatooine, there is a dark, nic-i-tain-filled cantina where you can down your favorite intoxicant while listening to the best jizz riffs in the universe. But beware your fellow denizens of this pangalactic watering hole, for they are cut-throats and cutpurses, assassins and troopers, humans and aliens, gangsters and thieves . . .

A Bantam Paperback

0 553 40971 9

STAR WARS: TALES FROM JABBA'S PALACE
Edited by Kevin J. Anderson

Enter the lair of the galaxy's most notorious criminal in nineteen stories from today's masters of science fiction.

In the dusty heat of twin-sunned Tatooine lives the wealthiest gangster in a hundred worlds, master of a vast crime empire and keeper of a vicious, flesh-eating monster for entertainment (and disposal of his enemies). Bloated and sinister, Jabba the Hutt might have made a good joke – if he weren't so dangerous. A cast of soldiers, spies, assassins, scoundrels, bounty hunters, and pleasure seekers have come to his palace, and every visitor to Jabba's grand abode has a story. Some of them may even live to tell it . . .

A Bantam Paperback

0 553 50413 4

STAR WARS: TALES OF THE BOUNTY HUNTERS
Edited by Kevin J. Anderson

Five stories of the galaxy's most ruthless bounty hunters . . . by some of today's finest writers of science fiction.

In a wild and battle-scarred galaxy, assassins, pirates, smugglers, and cut-throats of every description roam at will, fearing only the professional bounty hunters – amoral adventurers who track down the scum of the universe . . . for a fee. When Darth Vader seeks to strike at the heart of the Rebellion by targeting Han Solo and the Millennium Falcon, he calls upon six of the most successful – and feared – hunters, including the merciless Boba Fett. They all have two things in common: lust for profit and contempt for life . . .

A Bantam Paperback

0 553 50471 1

A SELECTION OF SCIENCE FICTION
AND FANTASY TITLES
AVAILABLE FROM BANTAM BOOKS

THE PRICES SHOWN BELOW WERE CORRECT AT THE TIME OF GOING
TO PRESS. HOWEVER TRANSWORLD PUBLISHERS RESERVE THE RIGHT
TO SHOW NEW RETAIL PRICES ON COVERS WHICH MAY DIFFER FROM
THOSE PREVIOUSLY ADVERTISED IN THE TEXT OR ELSEWHERE.

All Transworld titles are available by post from:

Book Service By Post, P.O. Box 29, Douglas, Isle of Man IM99 1BQ

Credit cards accepted. Please telephone 01624 675137,
fax 01624 670923, Internet http://www.bookpost.co.uk or
e-mail: bookshop@enterprise.net for details.

Free postage and packing in the UK. Overseas customers allow
£1 per book (paperbacks) and £3 per book (hardbacks).